WAR IN HAGWOOD

THE HAGWOOD TRILOGY

Thorn Ogres of Hagwood
Dark Waters of Hagwood
War in Hagwood

WAR IN HAGWOOD

THE HAGWOOD TRILOGY

BOOK THREE

ROBIN JARVIS

OPEN ROAD

INTEGRATED MEDIA

NEW YORK

Cover design by Andrea Worthington

978-1-4532-9922-7

Published in 2016 by Open Road Integrated Media, Inc.
180 Maiden Lane
New York, NY 10038
www.openroadmedia.com

· CONTENTS ·

· CHARACTERS ·

GAMALIEL TUMPIN
*A young, clumsy werling, once stung by the monstrous
Frighty Aggie; the lingering traces of her poison affect
his wergling in peculiar ways*

KERNELLA TUMPIN
Gamaliel's bossy older sister, who has a crush on Finnen Lufkin

FIGGLE AND TIDUBELLE TUMPIN
Gamaliel and Kernella's loving parents

BUFUS DOOLAN
*The twin brother of Mufus, who was recently
killed by the High Lady's thorn ogres*

FINNEN LUFKIN
*Disgraced young werling, who was once the best
wergle student; Finnen feels he has a lot to make up for*

TOLLYCHOOK UMBELNAPPER
Timid young werling, more interested in food than adventure

LIFFIDIA NEFYN
*A gentle classmate of Gamaliel; loves all animals
but is afraid of birds*

DIFFI MAFFIN
An elderly member of the werling council

TERSER GIBBLE
*The once proud and haughty Great Grand Wergle Master of the wer-
lings who betrayed their secrets to the High Lady*

RHIANNON RIGANTONA
The High Lady, merciless Queen of the Hollow Hill

CAPTAIN GRITTLE, WUMPIT, AND BOGRINKLE
*Three spriggans from the Hollow Hill who are part
of the High Lady's bodyguard*

LORD BRIFFOLD FANDERYN
*A highly respected elfin noble of the Hollow Hill who
is determined to overthrow the High Lady*

LORD LIMMERSENT
*A noble of the court who longs for the end of the High Lady's
reign but is horribly afraid and trusts no one*

WAGGARINZIL
*The pig-faced goblin commander of the door guards
within the Hollow Hill who is treacherously ambitious*

GABBITY
The goblin nursemaid who cares for Rhiannon's captive human infant

GRIMDITCH
*A slightly crazy barn bogle who has lived alone on
Moonfire Farm for many long years, with only rats
and his memories for company*

PEG-TOOTH MEG
*The strange ruler of the damp caves beneath Hagwood.
Her true identity is Princess Clarisant, the High Lady's
young sister, who disappeared many years ago.*

THE TOWER LUBBER
*The inhabitant of the ruined tower at the western edge of
Hagwood who has wooden pegs instead of eyes. He is really Prince
Tammedor, who ran away with the Princess Clarisant.*

NEST
Mysterious ancient being who dwells deep beneath Hagwood

GWYDDION
*One of the legendary human wizards who are remembered
in werling tales as Dooits*

BLACK HOWLA
*Leader of the dreaded troll witches. She plunged to her death
from the Witch's Leap many years ago, but her angry spirit still
haunts that lonely crag.*

WAR IN HAGWOOD

RHIANNON RIGANTONA, THE HIGH LADY OF HOLLOW HILL and pitiless tyrant of the Unseelie Court, clung tightly to her midnight horse as it thundered through the forest of Hagwood. In the clear blue sky above, a barn owl flew low over the treetops, its golden gaze cast downward.

With her raven hair streaming about her, Rhiannon commanded the beast to halt, but her mount had endured too much that morning to pay her fierce words any heed. It had never known such terror.

Its great, dark eyes were rolling in their sockets and it galloped heedlessly between the tangled trees, plunging deeper and deeper into that ancient, wooded realm.

The clearing in which it had been attacked was now far behind, but the horror of the slimy creatures that had assailed it there was still fresh and terrible.

Loathsome, jellylike imps with wide gibbering mouths and bulging toad eyes had leaped upon it—clinging with cold wet fingers and clambering up its neck.

The horse's hooves pounded ever faster. The High Lady wrenched at the reins to no avail. She was not afraid of being thrown. Her life was enchanted and there was only one way of harming her. She was merely enraged that every moment bore her further away from the enemies she thirsted to strike down.

Foremost among those was her sister, Clarisant, who had fled from the Hollow Hill many years ago with Prince Tammedor, a suitor from a distant elfin kingdom.

Disguised and hidden, they had evaded the High Lady's searches for many long years and the mere thought of them alive and reunited twisted Rhiannon's beautiful face with hatred and she screamed at the horse to stop once more.

White foam flew from the beast's mouth, splashing its sleek muscular flanks like milky clouds curdling across a blackened sky.

"Be still!" the High Lady raged. "I order it!"

But the horse's pace did not slacken and the more she threatened, the wilder the charger became. Casting the reins aside, Rhiannon Rigantona seized a great hank of its luxuriant mane and tore it up by the roots.

The horse neighed shrilly, but still it raced onward.

Branches and brambles raked and scored its sides and the frothing sweat blushed pink with blood.

Rhiannon glared at the handful of black hair clutched in her pale fist and flung it aside contemptuously. No power in this world could interrupt her charger's terror-filled flight. It would career on until its legs buckled with exhaustion. By then it would be too late; too many vital hours would have been wasted.

The High Lady ground her teeth and a wintry glint shone in her eyes. There was only one thing to do.

She drew a long knife from her belt. Grasping it tightly, she raised it over her head. The cruel blade flashed and dazzled in the dappling sunlight.

When the horse screamed, it was so loud and piercing, the clamor caused the owl above to falter and its snowy wings thrashed the morning breeze as the forest beneath resounded with whinnying death.

The thundering gallop faltered. There was a violent crash as the steed smashed into an oak and the tree shivered from root to bud.

Mighty hooves smote the trunk and shards of bark flew like hail. A silver horseshoe was ripped clear and spun through the air, hitting another tree with a clanging din.

The forest floor ran crimson, and old, ragged leaves were borne away on steaming rivers. The horse's powerful limbs ceased their flailing and grew still. The calm and silence of the March spring morning returned.

With a fluster and a shake of its wings, the owl alighted upon the oak's lowest branch and surveyed the gruesome sight below. From the moment the great steed had bolted from the clearing, the bird had followed. In the whole of Hagwood, the Tyrant of the Hollow Hill had no truer servant than that of her provost, the owl. It knew her deepest secrets and guarded them jealously.

It clicked its beak with satisfaction and gave a flourish with one wing. "Was there ever so plainly deceased a beast?" it announced with macabre glee. "How the gore doth pump and fount, enough to flood the Hagburn and run it red."

There was a snarl and the horse's headless body shifted as Rhiannon hauled herself from beneath its lifeless weight.

She rose like a specter from a ruin. Her gown was torn and the knife she still clutched in her hand rained a scarlet drizzle into the grass. Cuts and grazes disfigured her face and arms, but already they were closing and fading until the only marks upon her were the splashes of the dead steed's blood. The horse already forgotten, her pitiless mind was aflame with the scorching fires of vengeance.

"Only one child of Ragallach, the High King, will live this day out," she swore to herself. "My sister and her blind, vagabonding prince will die before the moon rises."

"So endeth all who dare defy thee, My Lady," the owl chimed enthusiastically. "Let us return thither with due dispatch and let thy blade guzzle some more!"

Rhiannon shook her head.

"Not alone," she said with a growl. "This time I shall lead the entire host of Redcaps against that brace of beggars and their frogspawn rabble."

"To the Hill, then!" the owl cried, leaping from the branch and taking to the air.

"Yes," she answered softly. "To the Hollow Hill, to call out the most vicious of my subjects."

Climbing into the sky, the bird glanced across the green forest roof to where, in the distance, a great grassy hill jutted high into the morning blue.

"'Tis many miles northward, My Lady!" the owl cried down. "In its madness, thy steed did bear thee far beyond the southern bounds. Noon shalt be but a memory by the time thy dainty feet tread within thine own halls this day."

The High Lady narrowed her eyes and grunted with impatience. Then, in a hissing voice, she pronounced a curse upon the dead horse.

"Never shall you find rest," she breathed, calling upon the arts taught to her by the troll witches long ago. "By oak and by blood I bind and tether you and with the twin serpents' might I charge you. 'Round and 'round you will gallop, in terror unending, headless and sightless, upon this spot forever."

The sunlight dimmed and the branches overhead stirred as a cold wind blew through them and ever afterward that place was haunted by the sound of thunderous hooves and no living creature dared to venture there.

Rhiannon looked up at the owl circling above.

"Lead the way!" she commanded. "I shall run as fleetly as your wings ride the air."

Taking hold of the silver talisman at her throat, she muttered softly. At once, the torn, blood-stained gown dripped from her shoulders and the cloud of her dark hair wrapped tightly about her. She stooped over the ground as her arms transformed into delicate forelegs, her neck lengthened and her brow stretched. In an instant, her elegant form was gone and in its place there stood a deer—a beautiful hind with a sleek sable coat and black, sparkling eyes.

"My Lady!" the owl hooted and it sailed over the trees, flying northward.

With a graceful bound, the deer leaped after it, darting through the forest, as swift as her evil thoughts.

CHAPTER 1

WITHIN THE HOLLOW HILL

SINCE EARLIEST TIMES, when the world was raw and savage, the Unseelie Court had dwelled within the Hollow Hill, and the burdening years had swollen its numbers.

The subjects of Rhiannon Rigantona were strange, fierce folk. Hidden for uncounted ages from the eyes and minds of Man, they had become the half-forgotten creatures of fireside tales told on winter nights, when the wind moaned under the eaves and twigs scratched at the shutters. But they were still spoken of in fearful voices and country people were wise to respect them.

The world of faerie was a dangerous, treacherous place and few people trod the old cinder road that ran between the Lonely Mere and the western shoulder of Hagwood in easy spirits. The threat of the hill-men was a constant dread and nervous travelers would glance at the green summit of the Hollow Hill in the distance with quailing courage and hurry on their way as fast as they were able.

If they had known the truth, that those creatures of legend were not only real, but on the brink of a bitter and bloody war, they would never have dared journey along that path at all.

BENEATH THE LOFTY, GRASSY SLOPES, under the soil and stone, silver lamps illuminated the winding halls and pillared chambers of the Unseelie Court. When the sun reared over the surrounding treetops, the denizens of the Hollow Hill retired to their mossy beds and stone couches to sleep away the dazzling day and await the dusk.

In the subterranean stables, blue-faced bogle esquires slept alongside snorting steeds while, in the straw strewn byres nearby, a yawning goblin milkmaid lifted her last full pail and waddled dozily between the sleeping faerie cattle. Thin green milk slopped onto the floor and splashed over her gnarled toes, but Squinting Wheyleen was too tired to notice or care. Smacking her lips, she poured the contents of her bucket into one of the many silver churns lined against the wall like a regiment of gleaming sentries, then pattered off to seek her space among the other milkmaids. Fat Jansis, Cheesy Maudlynne, Dugmilla, and Auld Gronk with the Hairy Dairy Hands were already snoring on their cots. It was not long before Wheyleen's whistling breaths joined that slumbering chorus. Contentment and warm, stale air filled the rock-roofed place.

From down the passageway came the sound of purposeful footsteps. A long shadow swept over the dozing cattle and a tall figure headed for the stables.

Lord Fanderyn peered into the gloomy stalls. The horses were asleep. Some were standing with drooped heads; others lay on the rushes with the noses of their attendant bogles nuzzled into their shoulders.

The stalls were arranged in order of rank; the brutish steeds belonging to the goblin knights were housed in the roughest quarters while the delicate-hoofed gray stallions of the nobles were lodged with greater comfort. Fresh, midnight-gathered flowers festooned their walls and their elfin names were carved on wooden plaques above each door. The grandest stall, however, was set apart from the rest.

Glimmering over that door were large, curling letters wrought of pure gold. "Dewfrost," they declared. The dark-green velvet saddle that hung nearby was trimmed with jeweled tassels and embroidered with even more gold.

Lord Fanderyn glanced inside and sure enough, the High Lady's silver-white mare was asleep within.

"For once, my suspicions were unfounded," the noble murmured with surprise. "The rumor that She ventured out into the forest was false. She must, in truth, have been in the little lordling's cradle chamber a day and more."

With an air of disappointment and a furrowed brow, he turned to leave, but something caught his attention. He took a dark lantern from its hook and uncovered it.

The green light of its flame fell upon his features and glittered in the silver circlet he wore on his brow.

Lord Briffold Fanderyn was one of the most august and powerful of the High Lady's courtiers and the quality of his proud lineage was graven on his stern features. He had a long, lean, solemn face, with piercing eyes the color of summer twilight and a firm, serious mouth that was neither kind nor cruel. His dark chestnut hair was braided in one long plait that hung in a thick rope down his back, and his robes were of shadowy silk, swirling with a pattern of forest ferns.

Holding the lantern aloft, he strode to the far end of the stable. The saddle that should have been hanging outside the furthest stall was missing.

Thrusting the light inside, he stared within.

The stall was empty, except for an astonished-looking bogle esquire, who was sitting cross-legged on the floor, blinking up at him.

"Who be there?" the creature squawked, unable to see past the glare of the lantern.

Lord Fanderyn brought his grim face into the light and the bogle fell forward in a respectful bow.

"M'lord!" he cried. "Hogmidden craves your deepest pardonings, he did not spy it was Your Lordlyship peeping in on him. What may Hogmidden do to serve Your Mightiness?"

"Tell me," Lord Fanderyn commanded. "Why are you here alone? Where is the beast in your charge?"

The bogle esquire blinked some more and wrung his large hands as he struggled for a satisfactory answer.

"Ain't here," was all he managed to say.

"I can see that, you leaden-witted fool. Who took it and why, and how long have they been gone?"

Hogmidden shook his head in defiance. "Doesn't knowed that neither!" he replied.

Lord Fanderyn ground his teeth impatiently but he could see that a terror greater than any he could provoke was upon the esquire and nothing would induce him to surrender that information.

"Then tell me of the steed in your care," he relented. "How long have you tended and groomed it?"

At once the bogle brightened and his eyes shone with pride. "Since it was foaled in this here stall!" he declared. "Back in the days of Good King Ragallach. . . ." He paused and checked himself. It wasn't prudent to speak of the old times in such fond terms; folk had been flogged and had their eyes torn out for less, and there was always some spiteful tongue eager to inform on you.

"Mind you," he continued in a louder voice, "there's no finer ruler than our own dear High Lady. May She ever grace us and keep us."

Lord Fanderyn waved his worries aside.

"You were telling of your steed," he said. "I am keen to know more."

"Why, His Majesty the Old King even put His royal blessing upon my sprightly lad. The best of the chargers he's proved to be: fastest of them all, stronger than three harnessed together and six times more braver. There's none to match my Nightflame—he's a full sack smarter than even his own rider knows."

"Nightflame," Lord Fanderyn repeated. "Of course—why, he is the pride of the Hollow Hill. That preening goblin knight, Sir Ogbin Moldweed, the oafish braggart—he won the beast in a crooked wager did he not? A prize far too grand for that rogue."

Hogmidden drew a scandalized breath then gurgled with laughter.

"That's him right enough," he said, disarmed by the noble's scorn. "I never did think he was fit to shovel out my gorgeous lovely's stall, let alone mount him."

"He's a foul, lowborn swaggering bow leg," Lord Fanderyn continued candidly. "Nothing more than a common spear waver, risen far above his base station through toadying, informing, and betrayal. He's unworthy of such a magnificent beast. It must please your heart when She comes to borrow your precious Nightflame from time to time."

"That it does!" the bogle agreed with fervent nods. "And my grand lad, he knows he's in for a rare good gallop when he sees Her at his door. His hooves are a-stampin' an' his tail's a-swishin' an' it's all I can do to put the bridle on. . . ."

Hogmidden gave a choking gasp and clapped his hands to his mouth. He had said too much and he sprang back into the shadows, afraid.

Lord Fanderyn's eyes sparkled. "So the Lady Rhiannon has gone riding," he said thoughtfully. "I find myself wondering why. What could have lured Her outside? What new tempest is She brewing?"

"Beggin' Your Loftly Lordship's pardon!" the bogle pleaded. "Don't tell Her I squeaked, it weren't my fault. You're too brain bright by far, Your Nobleyness—you tricked it out of me. Please don't tell Her. She made me swear not to. I doesn't want that spying owl to chew on my poor old eyes and the rest of me fed to the Redcaps."

But Lord Fanderyn was already walking away, returning along the passage that led to the lower halls. Hogmidden shrank into the corner of the stall, shivering with fright at what would become of him.

THERE WERE NINE OFFICIAL ENTRANCES to the Hollow Hill but there were many more secret ways in and out of the hidden kingdom, created down the centuries by the noblest families for their own private and furtive use. But Rhiannon Rigantona had spies in every noble family. Treachery was easy to buy in a realm ruled by fear. There was not even a stoat-sized gateway she was unaware of. She of course had many exits unknown to all, save herself.

Deep in thought, Lord Fanderyn had left the stables far behind and was on his way to visit the first of the three official southern entrances.

He had decided to question the door wardens and glean what he could from them. There was no doubt in his mind that the High Lady was up to something. His own spies had brought word of the thorny fiends seen marauding through the forest recently and those monsters could not have entered the wood without her leave.

He would have to take care in questioning the doorkeepers, however, for his interest would undoubtedly be reported. He was just phrasing what he would say in his mind when a large, broad shape stepped out in front of him and barred the passage.

"You're going the wrong way M'lord," growled a thick, gutteral voice. "Your fine chambers are above and westward."

Lord Fanderyn glared at the creature before him.

It was a fat, sallow-faced and scaly goblin, with a porcine snout and enormous flapping ears that dangled before his sly green eyes. A chain mail coif covered his head and he wore a long leather tunic, belted beneath his belly with a great silver buckle.

"Waggarinzil," Lord Fanderyn greeted coldly when he recognized the commander of the door guards. "Are my movements now to be watched and directed?"

"When were they ever not?" the goblin replied with a grin that showed his gray teeth. "Are not all our to-ings and fro-ings keeked on and made note of by some rat-hawk or other? But on this uncommon morning t'would be best for you to seek out your own dear bed and not tarry in the hallways."

Lord Fanderyn eyed him curiously. "Why is this morning more uncommon than the rest?" he asked, wondering if Waggarinzil knew about the High Lady's absence.

The goblin rubbed his gauntleted hands together. "For one thing, *you're* still up and tramping about, M'lord," he began with a drawl and a wink. "That's worth someone's jotting it down by itself, but 'tweren't that I meant."

He glanced around warily then leaned a little closer and whispered, "Didn't you hear about the call out?"

"Call out?" Lord Fanderyn repeated. "What tidings are these?"

Waggarinzil chuckled and the mail of his coif jingled and rattled. "Ho!" he snorted, flicking his ears from his face. "By the Great Wyrms' breath, I thunk as not, it was all hushed and cloaky. Well listen to me, my lordship, summat's occurring—summat big."

Again he looked about him and his voice sank into an even lower whisper.

"'Twas nigh two hour since, when that . . . fine feathery fellow—may his beak never be blunted—our most blessed Lady's owl, comes calling outside the third south door. In a real fluster he was and fit to exploding with the urgence of his errand. Soon as my lads let him in, he swoops off—and where does he swoop to, eh?"

"Tell me."

"Straight to the spriggan quarters, that's where!"

The goblin gave a grunt, then lifted the corner of a nearby tapestry to make sure nothing was lurking and listening there.

Lord Fanderyn narrowed his eyes. "To what purpose?" he asked. "What did the owl do there?"

"Only stirs up the captains," Waggarinzil hissed. "Gets them to rouse their soldiers, all stealthy quiet like."

"And then?"

The goblin cupped a gauntleted hand around his mouth. "The entire garrison sneaked off," he breathed. "That bird done led them through a secret way from the Hill and off into the forest they marched—every last hobnail-booted one. Not a word nor a sign has been heard from them since. Now that's what I call an uncommon morning."

Wiping his piggy snout with the back of his hand, he stared into Lord Fanderyn's dark-blue eyes.

"What make you of that then, M'lord?"

The noble's mind was racing. What was the High Lady doing? Had she been waylaid in the forest and sent the owl to summon her soldiers to save her? No, who would dare attack the Tyrant of the Hollow Hill? Besides, she, with her enchantments, was unassailable. But then why summon the spriggans? Whatever the reason, he did not have the answer—yet.

"I make nothing of it," he answered slowly. "We must not question the designs and policies of our deathless Queen."

"But the whole garrison," Waggarinzil persisted, "and all so silent and armed to the lugs—what lies out there in yonder forest to make

Her so sudden fearful? What enemies are out there to cause such alarm? A baffler, that's what it is—but I'd dearly like to know the root of it, by the Big Wolf's ears I would."

Lord Fanderyn stepped back from the goblin. Was he trying to make him say something indiscreet, as he himself had tricked the bogle esquire?

"Spriggans love their knives and spears more than they do their whiskery mothers," he finally answered with a dismissive shrug. "They eat and sleep with their weapons and, if they weren't so terrified of water, would bathe with them too. If the Lady Rhiannon wishes to drill them in the forest, it is Her right to do so, and a very sound decision it is. Their slovenliness has become a byword among the nobles at court; they need a sharp reminder of discipline—as do a good many more in this realm."

Waggarinzil let out an injured-sounding sigh.

"Now, now," he said in a conciliatory tone. "There's no need to huff and be overwatchful on my account. By Howla's broken bones, I'm not out to sell tattling stories to no one. I remembers when this was a sweet kingdom, yes—even during the wars with the troll witches. Never was a finer king than old Ragallach—may His glorious memory never dim. Strange how so hale a tree bore such a sour and poisonous apple."

Lord Fanderyn backed away in alarm. The goblin was openly speaking treason. Was he mad? They could both lose their heads for this.

"Be silent!" he commanded. "I'll hear no more of your sedition. It is I who should report you."

The goblin smiled. "I don't believe you'll do that, M'lord," he said. "Not if what my little whisperers tell me is true. Seems you've no liking for wormy apples any more than us, even if they is golden—if you understand my meaning. Time we tasted the fruit of a different tree is what we say. Plenty of high-born varieties in this here orchard, though there's few with such quality as one not so far away from me right now."

Lord Fanderyn was too astonished to speak, so Waggarinzil continued quickly.

"Should the chance present itself," he said, "there's many who'll fight under your colors, goblins and kluries and a great number of the lesser folk. All us needs is for the golden apple to be found lacking."

"That will never happen," the noble uttered flatly. He didn't trust this goblin for a moment. He had seen too many betray themselves with misplaced trust.

Waggarinzil scratched one of his great ears. "Then by the Great Boar's bristles, what is it out there that's made Her so fearful?" he asked. "For the first time ever, She, who never has before, has got more flutters than a cave full of bats. So I says to you, be watchful and be ready."

Lord Fanderyn was about to answer when a sudden pounding din rang down the hallway.

"Who's banging on my doors?" the goblin cried, wheeling about and hurrying away.

The noble followed him and they hastened to a small courtyard where two goblin guards with pikestaffs were braced against the large boulder that served as one of the Hollow Hill's doorways.

"Open in the name of the Lady!" bawled an angry voice from the other side.

Waggarinzil signaled for the guards to stand aside, then planted himself squarely before the tall rock and folded his powerful arms.

"Who's that a-yellin' out there?" he shouted.

"Don't you go askin' such slack-wit questions!" came the stern reply. "Shift yerselfs and open this 'ere door."

"What's the watchword for the day?"

"How should I know? We've been out this past night. Now open up or there'll be skulls to crack when I does get in and you'll have to answer to Her Dark Ladyship, for 'tis Her bidding we're doin'."

Waggarinzil stood aside and cast a quizzical look at Lord Fanderyn. "Open the way," the goblin grunted.

The guards heaved at the two iron chains on either side of the boulder. There was a grinding of stone, the rock swung inward and the courtyard was flooded with brilliant sunshine. They shielded their eyes and uttered dismal groans and their commander shuddered, for all goblins shun the sunlight.

Lord Fanderyn stared at the squat, mail-clad figures already lumbering over the threshold. They were spriggans—three of them. The bloodthirsty Captain Grittle, who was forever sniffing for assassins and conspiracies in every corner, led the way, and two of his idiot lackies, Wumpit and Bogrinkle, brought up the rear. But what were those two carrying between them, Fanderyn wondered.

"Took you long enough!" Grittle scowled as he barged inside. "I'll be sure She gets to hear of that."

"Not so fast," Waggarinzil instructed. "By Ragallach's sword, you can't just stroll in here without answering the usual questions; I got me my orders as well—and what's that your lads are lugging? You been out hunting? Is that some skinny breed of otter? Who dressed it in them rags? What new sport is this?"

Captain Grittle had no liking for Waggarinzil at the best of times, but that morning, he would have liked to hack off his ugly great head.

"This 'ere's a barn bogle," he growled. "An' we got to deliver it to Old Gabbity to see what she can do fer it."

Lord Fanderyn stepped forward and looked down at the sorry creature they were carrying. It was covered in hair and a dagger was buried in its back. In the words of the old saying, the bogle was as limp as a boned badger.

"But this beast is dead, surely?" he declared.

Captain Grittle noticed the noble for the first time and regarded him suspiciously. He didn't like him much either. Lord Fanderyn smelled like a plotter more than most.

"There's a snatch of life left still," he said gruffly.

Wumpit, who was carrying the barn bogle by the shoulders, piped up, "Leastways there was when we set off from the Crone's Maw. I isn't so sure now."

"If him's a goner, we're done fer!" Bogrinkle sniveled wretchedly.

With a twitch of his head, their captain motioned for them to continue on their way.

"If I was you, sir," the spriggan told Sir Fanderyn, "I wouldn't try detainin' us. She'll not like that, She won't."

The noble nodded. "Of course," he agreed. "You must hurry on to Gabbity."

"But my orders!" Waggarinzil objected.

"The responsibility shall be on my shoulders alone," Lord Fanderyn assured him. "We must not hinder any of our Queen's commands. In fact, I shall accompany our stout and stalwart spriggans to the Lady Rhiannon's private chamber, where Gabbity watches over the human child."

Captain Grittle shook his head and stomped across the courtyard. "No need fer that, sir," he said. "Me an' my lads have managed all this way; we doesn't need no escort now."

"I insist," Lord Fanderyn replied firmly. "I would hear of your adventures, for it is plain you have had them. Your faces, arms, and legs are bitten and bloody as if a thousand tiny swords have slashed at you."

"Blood moths!" Bogrinkle explained with a shiver. "Almost made lacy doilies of our hides, they did."

"Tell me more!" Lord Fanderyn implored. "Such a tantalizing hint of a bold, heroic excursion. How did you come to be out in the forest, and what news of your fellow soldiers?"

He set out to follow them, but Captain Grittle turned on his heel and, with a hand gripping the hilt of one of his many knives, said threateningly, "We're on Our Lady's commission, sir. Stand back—I'll not warn you again."

Stung by this insolence, the noble clenched his teeth and bowed. He made no further attempt to follow them. The spriggans clumped off down a passageway and Lord Fanderyn turned to Waggarinzil.

"An uncommon morning indeed," he observed. "Discover what you can and bring word to me—I shall be waiting."

The goblin tugged one of his ears in salute.

"Maybe the golden apple really is about to fall," Lord Fanderyn said softly.

WITHIN THE PRIVATE CHAMBER OF THE HIGH LADY, Gabbity, the goblin nursemaid, examined the shawl she was knitting and sucked her one tooth. The shawl was turning out very well, one of her rare successes. Mingling nettles and thistles in with the dirty wool had been an inspiration and she held her handiwork at arm's length, letting out admiring gasps.

"An entwined border of cowbane or monkshood?" she asked herself. "Or maybe just good old strangling ivy? Yes, very dainty, and with a few laburnum flowers to match my eyes and a sprinkling of nightshade blooms to accent my nose."

She cackled with delight and squirmed on her stool, causing the steeple of her white wiry hair to wobble on her head. What a ravishing spectacle she would be at the next court revel. So many envious eyes would be on her and she tapped her large feet at the happy prospect.

Setting her needles clacking once more, she glanced into the cradle next to her. A pale pink radiance emanated from the human infant sleeping peacefully within. Cooing croakily, the goblin pushed her bulbous nose through the webbed canopy and basked in the soft, rosy glow.

"Yes, little lordling," she crooned. "Lie still as death, be silent as the stones and never grow a day older."

Sneaking a quick, savoring sip of the child's life force, she gave a gummy grin and was about to return her attention to her knitting when a fierce thumping battered upon the door.

Gabbity fell backward off her stool in fright and her dirty skirts flew over her head.

"Elves' bells!" she squealed indignantly, her legs wriggling in the air.

The hammering persisted.

"If it's them young kluries up to their annoyances, I'll jab an' slap some sense into 'em!"

Struggling to her feet, she pulled one of the spare knitting needles from her hair then shuffled over to the stout door and gave it a kick.

"Be off with you!" she called through the keyhole. "M'Lady'll put an end to your foolery when She gets back."

Gabbity bit her bottom lip in self-reproach. "Ooh, I shouldn't have said that!" she muttered. "M'Lady's s'posed to be in here with me, that's what She told me to tell anyone who dared come a-knockin'. Ooh, you're in the stew now, Gabbity Malatrot."

"It were Her what sent us!" Captain Grittle's voice barked back through the door. "We've a bundle 'ere what needs your nursin'—desperate quick."

The goblin rubbed her warty chin. "You doesn't worm your way in here that easy!" she shouted back. Those spriggans were always trying to catch a glimpse of the mortal child.

"On my life I swears!" Grittle yelled back. "There's a three-quarter dead barn bogle with us that's like as not gasped its last, but if there's a sliver of hope for it then you've to do what you can to aid the thing. 'Tis a strict order from the High Lady Herself."

Gabbity picked her nose and pondered. The quarrelsome lout would never make such an audacious claim if it were not true.

Cautiously she turned the great silver key in the lock, opened the door a chink, and pressed a swiveling eye to the gap.

In the hallway outside, Captain Grittle stood back and gestured to the motionless figure carried by his subordinates.

The goblin nursemaid ogled the bogle but did not open the door any further.

"Looks long dead," she said sniffily. "Best you can do is smoke it over oak chips—easiest way to hide the bitter, bogley taste, barrin' pickling."

Captain Grittle clenched his teeth and tried to control his temper. "You doesn't know its proper dead till you inspect it," he told her.

"Me waste my good nursin' on a common barn bogle?" she cried. "What do M'Lady want it for? She's got better pets than that hairy skelly bones."

"There's questions it must answer," the spriggan explained. "Vital questions, so you see, you have to keep it livin' long enough for that."

Gabbity grumbled to herself then pushed the door wide.

"Get you over there at a safe distance," she told Captain Grittle as she came out, waving her knitting needle at him. "Now, you two dim daisies lay the beast down and back away."

"Doesn't you want us to carry it in there?" Wumpit volunteered.

"And have you gawp and slobber over my little lordling?" she shrieked in outrage. "I'll pop all three of your heads like balloons first."

Lunging forward, she thrust her needle at them. Wumpit and Bogrinkle put their burden down smartly and sprang away.

Gabbity pursed her lips and crouched by the barn bogle.

Grimditch—the poor, bedraggled, impish creature who had guided Gamaliel Tumpin through the deadly forest—was deathly still. Lying on his stomach, his face against the floor, the bogle looked stone dead. The rags that covered his back were dark with blood and Gabbity stared at the dagger hilt that jutted from his shoulders with a sorry shake of her head. Gingerly, she placed a bony finger to his neck and groped for any sign of life.

Long moments passed. The three spriggans looked on with anxious faces.

"Well?" Captain Grittle asked at length.

Her knees clicking, the goblin rose.

"There's a gnat's cough of a chance," she said, rolling up her sleeves and gently lifting the bogle in her sinewy arms. "I'll sees what can be done, but the mangy beast's got both feet in Death's own country and only a toenail in ours."

With that, she carried the creature into the chamber and shut the door behind her.

Left outside, Captain Grittle exchanged gloomy looks with the others. Then he cursed and spat on the floor.

"I didn't get me knife back!" he fumed.

GABBITY PLACED HER NEW PATIENT ON A STONE TABLE and lit several candles.

"Now," she said, begrudgingly. "Let's see what the High Lady's old nurse can do for you. You was lucky them brutes didn't dip their blades in Redcap poison before spearing you. They do that sometimes. Of course, you'd have been luckier still if they'd have missed."

Humming to herself, she tore the tattered fragments of cloth from Grimditch's back and then hunted in her knitting bags, fishing out bundles of dried herbs and two jars of foul-smelling ointment. Adding a pinch of mud-colored powder from a small wooden box in her pocket, she mixed the ingredients vigorously in a bowl and smeared the noxious concoction around the wound before attempting to draw the dagger out.

Very gently, she placed a hand upon the hilt and pulled. The weapon slid clear while, with her other hand, Gabbity clapped even more of the reeking mixture over the wound to seal it, calling on the ancient forest gods to imbue her paste with healing virtue.

The barn bogle uttered a feeble cry of pain and shuddered.

Gabbity gurgled with satisfaction, but her delight was soon replaced by frowning concern and she gave the bogle a cautious prod.

"Don't you die now!" she warned. "Not after I've gone to all this trouble!"

Hurriedly wiping her hands on her skirts, she felt for the creature's pulse again and moaned dismally.

"On its last croak," she lamented. "Won't be long now. M'Lady won't be pleased with you, stupid bogle—or with Her Gabbity."

Unnerved by the prospect of her mistress's wrath, the goblin nurse-maid grimaced and crept miserably back to her stool, but was too nervous to resume her knitting. The spriggans should have brought the beast to her sooner. Yes, they must take the blame.

Within the cradle, the infant stirred and kicked his chubby legs in enchanted slumber. The pale radiance welled up for a moment and danced in Gabbity's eyes.

"Be still, my Podgy Pup," she whispered. Then, suddenly, an idea gripped her and she leaped to her feet once more.

"Just a meager scrounging!" she cried out. "Nothing that would be missed. Why, less than a cap's worth would do it, I reckon."

Excited, she drew the gossamer canopy aside, and the spiders that crouched there scuttled to safety.

Reaching down, the goblin dipped her fingers into the cradle. The soft light of the child's life force flickered and trembled and Gabbity held her breath. Carefully, she scooped out a shimmering handful. It shone upon her palm like the first frail beams of daylight and she hurried back to the table before it could fade.

"Here now," she addressed the dying barn bogle. "Gulp this down and be healed."

She pushed her hands under Grimditch's nose and, as he gasped and sighed his final breaths, the pulsing glow was drawn into his mouth and nostrils.

When it was done, Gabbity clasped her hands under her chin and waited in anticipation.

She did not have to wait long.

In an instant, every hair on the barn bogle's scalp bristled and his beard crackled and writhed. A shiver ran through him and his toes jiggled.

Groggily, he raised his head, opened one bleary eye, stared at the goblin nursemaid, and yelped, "Urgh—you be powerful ugly!"

Then his head fell forward again and he began to snore.

Gabbity scowled and regretted saving the ungrateful wretch.

"You'll not be so full of chaff when M'Lady's back," she scolded.

She was about to return to her seat when her glance fell upon a small leather purse strung about the waist of the barn bogle's torn breeches.

It was a moment's work to open it, delve inside and fish out the contents.

"Rat bones!" she snorted in disgust, sorting through a well-gnawed selection. "I've always said barn bogles are nowt but . . ."

The insult died on her crabbed lips as she lifted up something that was certainly no rat bone. Between her thumb and forefinger gleamed a dainty, golden key.

• CHAPTER 2 •

THE DRUM OF WAR

GAMALIEL TUMPIN STARED MISERABLY at the rat bone in his
hand. "Grimditch swapped it!" he repeated to the others around him.

His friends Finnen Lufkin, Tollychook Umbelnapper, and Liffidia
Nefyn; his sister, Kernella; and the two large, strange-looking people—
Peg-tooth Meg and the Tower Lubber—said nothing. Bufus Doolan,
however, had plenty to say.

"Oh, well done, Gammy!" he jeered. "Our one chance to get rid of
the High Lady and you've gone and messed it up—typical, that is. You
stupid, great lump of . . . of stupidness! Have you been taking lessons
on being extra thick and gormless? You must be top of the class in
idiot school. How can anyone be so hopeless and dim? I've trodden
in things with more sense than you and sneezed out more brains than
you'll ever have."

While the Doolan boy ranted, Finnen Lufkin tore his eyes from the rat bone in his friend's hand. Even he was furious with Gamaliel. After everything they had endured, the perils they had survived, to have lost, here at the end, through sheer carelessness, was a bitterness beyond anything he had ever known and he didn't trust himself to speak.

The sunlight beat upon his neck and he looked around the clearing as if searching for an answer to their plight.

Bodies of spriggans, birds, and sluglungs littered the surrounding grass. The battle had been brief but bloody and Finnen knew a greater, deadlier confrontation was yet to come. The High Lady's wrath would soon crash down on them.

The two score surviving sluglungs crowded around the wellhead where he and the others were gathered. Their toadlike eyes were fixed upon their mistress, Peg-tooth Meg: a hunched figure with lank green hair and pallid gray skin who had hidden in the caves beneath Hagwood for many, many years.

Finnen stared at her. It was almost impossible to believe that, in truth, she was Princess Clarisant, Rhiannon's sister who had fled from the Hollow Hill with her lover, Prince Tammedor. In order to escape the tyrant's vengeance, they had assumed grotesque new forms and hidden from her, waiting for some new hope or chance to present itself while the years rolled by. But even that had been in vain.

Finnen looked down at the stone ring of the wellhead. A golden casket glittered in the sunlight next to him, containing the High Lady's one weakness: Rhiannon's own heart, still beating due to dark magic. Without the key there was no way of reaching it.

Frustration boiled up inside him and he almost threw the casket down the well. Instead, he let out a cry and kicked the empty air.

"Kick Gammy down," Bufus suggested, shrewdly guessing what was running through his mind. "He's not good for anything else, and it'd save me the bother of throttling him."

Ashamed and disgusted with himself, Gamaliel hung his head. He had failed everyone.

"I'm sorry," he said in a voice choked with emotion. "I didn't know Grimditch had swapped it. . . . If I had . . ."

"Oh, stop sniveling," his sister, Kernella, scolded, looking more vexed than ever before. "You'll get no sympathy from me, nor no one else."

The Tower Lubber's eyes had been plucked out long ago by the High Lady and replaced with wooden pegs. Now he turned his blind face to the miserable boy and asked gently, "Who is this Grimditch? What manner of creature is he?"

Gamaliel was grateful for the softness of his tone, but he had to clear his throat to steady his voice and struggle not to burst into tears when he answered.

"A barn bogle," he replied. "A bit barmy and impish, but he saved my life more than once. He won't give the key to the High Lady—I'm sure of it."

The Tower Lubber laughed bleakly. "She'll rip it from him quick enough," he said. "And that's before She throws him upon the mercy of the torturers for their sport."

Peg-tooth Meg lifted the golden casket in her large, clammy hands. A mournful weeping could be heard coming from the enchanted heart within.

"We were so close," she murmured. "So close to putting an end to her reign once and for all."

"Are you sure there ain't no way of opening that thing?" Bufus asked. "How about whacking it with a great big stone? It's sure to smash—or even a dent would do. We only need a little crack or chink, just big enough to push a knife in and turn the heart to mincemeat."

"There is no way," Peg-tooth Meg said flatly. "The Puccas crafted this, and their skill with metal had no rival. The casket is woven about with spells and only the key will unlock it. My sister is safer now than she has been in all the long years she has sat upon our father's throne."

A grumbling rumble interrupted her and Tollychook blushed. The mention of mincemeat reminded him that he was famished and his stomach growled loudly.

"'Scuse me," he mumbled shyly.

"So what are we going to do?" Kernella demanded, ignoring him.

"Rhiannon will return," the Tower Lubber answered grimly. "She will bring her most bloodthirsty servants: the Redcaps. We will not survive the onslaught."

"So we're supposed to just stand here and wait for that?" she cried. "I don't think so!"

"Me either!" cried Bufus.

"There is no escaping them," Peg-tooth Meg said. "They are little more than wild beasts and they revel in carnage."

"Well, I'm not stopping to meet them!" Kernella declared and she took hold of the rope that trailed down into the well.

"There is no refuge down there," Meg told her. "My sister will drive them into every cavern."

"You would be devoured in the darkness," the Tower Lubber added. "It is better to die here, beneath the sun."

The jellylike creatures around the well muttered to themselves. The sluglungs blinked their great round eyes in the bright daylight. They preferred the damp and dark places underground, but if Meg, their mistress, chose to remain here, then they too would stay.

Liffidia stroked the neck of Fly, her fox cub, and hugged him tightly. "I don't care what happens," she whispered to him. "So long as we're together."

Bufus scrunched up his freckled face in disdain.

"So that's it then?" he shouted. "We just give up? We might as well march to the Hill and deliver ourselves to save Her Ladyship the bother."

"There is nothing we can do," the Tower Lubber said gently.

Bufus rounded on him. "There's always something we can do!" the boy yelled vehemently. "If Her Redcaps want to breakfast on werling, I'm not going to make it easy for them. I'll fight back with every bite they take out of me! I'll rub poisonous leaves on my skin and stuff more in my pockets. I'll be one unhappy meal they won't enjoy the taste of."

"That's just like you," Kernella said sniffily. "You've always made everyone sick."

"Wait!" Finnen cried, his despair changing to excitement. "Bufus is right. So what if we don't have the key? I'm not simply going to bow down before Her—I'm going to fight till the end."

A smile spread over the Tower Lubber's wind-burned face. The werlings' defiance was infectious.

"In my old kingdom, there were few knights as stout of heart as you small folk!" he exclaimed. "Great courage blazes in the littlest breast. We shall make one last stand against Rhiannon Rigantona and Her bloodthirsty horde. One final battle before the eternal dark takes us."

The sluglungs gripped their rusty swords and shook them excitedly.

"Megboo!" they called, brandishing the blades before Peg-tooth Meg.

The woman clasped the Lubber's large leathery hand and squeezed it. "I would have gladly died with you those many years ago," she said. "Now I know that not even death shall divide us."

"No more talk of death," her blind lover answered. "This open ground is no place to meet the Redcaps; we must hasten to my tower and there speak of war—quickly."

Urgently, the Tower Lubber led the way from the well and through the trees. He had walked that path every day for hundreds of years and knew every stone upon the soil and every root that lifted it.

Hunched beside him, the golden casket clutched in her hand, Peg-tooth Meg hurried as fast as her cave-warped bones permitted. She sent one of her sluglungs back down the well to fetch her macabre harp and the rest of the slimy creatures swarmed thickly about her. Some formed a guard around the werlings who, now under her protection, were treated with the highest honor and respect.

And so they hurried to the broken watchtower. Climbing a flight of stone steps, they crowded inside the infirmary where the Tower Lubber tended to sick and wounded birds. It was busier than when they had last seen it, for the survivors of the battle had swelled the numbers of the patients and the Lubber's helpers were scurrying to and fro, giving what aid they could. A chorus of agonized squawks and frightened twittering filled the great circular room and the featherless chicken matron was clucking and fussing around those in the greatest need.

Gazing at the scene, Liffidia was filled with pity and compassion. She wanted to go and help, but Fly needed her too, and she would not be parted from him. Liffidia drew the cub to one side and he laid his head upon her lap. He needed rest more than anything, for he had run a long distance to be with her and, almost at once, fell into a deep healing sleep.

The Tower Lubber took Meg, Finnen, Gamaliel, Kernella, and Bufus up the winding stone stairs to the roof.

Tollychook chose to remain with Liffidia. If there was any food available, it would be in the infirmary. He hoped his last meal before the battle would prove to be something better than breadcrumbs and worms.

Meg instructed the sluglungs to stay behind, and told them to care for the stricken birds and await their orders. The creatures bowed obediently but they did not like to be parted from their queen and stared at the empty steps once she had departed, croaking miserably.

THE RUINED WATCHTOWER CLIMBED into the bright blue March sky. It was the highest point for miles around and the great forest of Hagwood spread into the west beneath it.

When Kernella ventured out onto the roof, she recoiled from the dizzying height and clung automatically to Finnen. She caught her breath at the thrill of this hasty embrace and silently reproved herself for never having thought of this ploy before. She would have to contrive to be a lot more frightened in the future.

The girl shivered as the stark truth struck her. There would be no future. They might have only hours—maybe just minutes—left before the attack. Chilled by the thought, she moved toward the small fire that the Lubber kept constantly burning on the roof, but it did not warm her.

With the breeze streaming through her long lank hair, Peg-tooth Meg leaned against the weather-worn stones of the broken battlements that ringed the bare roof. In the distance, across the undulating treetops, the vast shape of the Hollow Hill rose in majesty. It was the first time she had seen it since she had taken refuge in the caves.

"The kingdom of my father, the High King," she murmured. "I spent my childhood in that great green mountain. During the wars with the troll witches, it was the one safe place in all the land. Now I can hardly bear to gaze on it, knowing the evil that has sat enthroned there these many years."

"It is against that evil we must fight," the Tower Lubber told her. "What chances have we against that? You know better than most the strength of Her forces—how can we defend ourselves?"

Meg tore her eyes away from the hill and slowly shook her large head.

"This is a strong place with thick, high walls," she said. "But Redcaps will scale them or delve beneath them or hurl fire at us and, when the sun sinks behind the trees, the goblin knights will follow—if we are still alive."

Bufus gave a bad-tempered snort. "I should've legged it and left you lot to face this music while I had the chance," he said.

"We'll defend this tower as long as we can!" Finnen declared. "And I reckon we can do a pretty good job! The sluglungs can be stationed at the windows with spears and some can even cling to the wall outside to prevent anything from climbing up. We could do with a lot more weapons, but we can bring a load of stones up here to fling down at the army—and why wait for them to throw fire at us when we can drop burning torches on top of them?"

"Yes," agreed Kernella. "And we can pour scalding water on their heads!"

Bufus sniggered. "If any try to dig their way in," he added, "we'll be ready with big hammers. Ten points for every Redcap smashed back into its hole."

The Tower Lubber laughed.

"That's right!" he cried. "We shall not be conquered as easily as the High Lady might think. A fine stand we shall make of it."

The werlings cheered but Meg held up her hand and called for quiet.

"War is not a game," she reproached them. "Remember, we cannot hope to win this fight. Their numbers are too great and we have no chance of surviving. My sluglungs are faithful and I love them. They have shared in my exile beneath the ground and though they are willing to die for me, I wish I had not led them to this. Let us be mindful that what we decide now will not bring us victory but merely decree the manner of our deaths. Show respect when you choose how to spend a life, or you are no better than my accursed sister."

Her sobering words silenced everyone.

"And those of Her forces that we may kill," she continued, "they are also my subjects. Many of them served under my father. Rhiannon rules them now through fear and they do not know the truth of how She gained the throne. She murdered our father, the High King; therefore I am the rightful heir. So every death this day, on either side, will be a grievous loss."

"I'll feel guilty when it's over," Bufus mumbled under his breath. "If I've still got breath in me."

The Tower Lubber tilted his head then raised his face to the sky. Above the wooden pegs that were in place of his eyes, his brows drew into a knot.

"News flies to us on hasty wings," he said.

Everyone stared into the cloudless blue. A tiny speck was rushing toward the tower. Soon it was clear to everyone that it was a blackbird, flying straight and swift.

The Tower Lubber held out his hand and, moments later, the bird landed upon his forefinger.

"Welcome, little friend," he said, stroking its breast and listening to its frantic chirping. "No, you need not be ashamed; you were instructed to remain behind and keep watch. I know you would have fought bravely in the battle. What tidings do you bring?"

The blackbird chattered urgently to him and the Lubber's face became grave.

"Thank you, friend," he said. "Now go below and search for your loved ones—if they survived. There is no more you can do for us out there."

The blackbird flew off, swooping down the stairs to the infirmary, calling a mournful song.

The Tower Lubber turned to the others.

"The High Lady is darting through the forest in the form of a black hind," he told them. "Even now she will be at the Hollow Hill. We have hardly any time to prepare."

"Then what are we piddling about here for?" Bufus cried as he ran to the stairs.

The Tower Lubber followed him. "We must give orders, and quickly," he said.

"I'll get some of the sluglungs to collect stones," Finnen called. "Others must climb the walls and be ready. I wish I still had the Smith's magic knife."

"I'll need lots of water!" Kernella called as she trotted after them. "And as many pots and pans as you've got."

Their voices disappeared below and Peg-tooth Meg wiped her eyes. "The drum of war is beating," she said, "but the rhythm is of my sister's making and every spirit that hearkens will dance to its grave."

Gamaliel was standing close by and heard her despondent words. He stared forlornly out across the forest. The quiet corner of Hagwood, where the werlings lived, was far away by the western fringe and he wished he were there now.

Everything had happened so fast. Only a few days ago, the High Lady had been a remote and unseen figure and they had never had any dealings with the hillmen. Werlings never ventured beyond the boundaries of their pleasant realm, or ever went seeking danger. They were a secretive people who hid from the world. With the aid of a token of any small animal's fur, werlings used their powers to transform into that animal. This "wergling" was their chief delight. Why, Gamaliel's own father, much to Kernella's embarrassment, sported a squirrel tail most of the time.

A chance meeting with the Wandering Smith had put an end to those carefree days, however, and embroiled them in the schemes and hopes of the proud and mighty. It was he who had cured Gamaliel's shoulder, after young Master Tumpin had been stung by Frighty Aggie, the terror of the werlings. Gamaliel recalled that fateful night ruefully. That was when the Smith had hidden the golden key inside his wergling pouch and now everything the boy knew was about to end. Gamaliel was terribly afraid, but worst of all, he felt completely useless.

Unfolding his arms, he put his hands to his sides, closing his fingers about the magical silver talisman, shaped like a fire devil, tucked into his belt. He reflected wryly that the Wandering Smith had made that object, too, and with its power, Peg-tooth Meg had created her sluglung followers.

Suddenly Gamaliel lurched backward as though an invisible hand had struck him. Then he whirled around and a fierce gleam shone in his eyes.

"I've got an idea!" he yelled.

Meg stared at him but, before she could speak, the boy was already leaping down the stairs.

"Just how hungry are those Redcaps?" he shouted.

• CHAPTER 3 •

IN THE DARK BEYOND

ON THE LOWER SLOPES OF THE HOLLOW HILL, a black hind came running from the forest. The owl that had been waiting flew down from a branch and alighted on its shoulder.

The deer stamped the ground with its forelegs and reared its head. The air trembled and Rhiannon Rigantona cast off her animal shape.

Striding forward, she approached an outcrop of rock, held out her hand and called her name, announcing her presence.

At once the grass in front of it began to writhe like tiny tongues of green flame, then the turf split apart and peeled back, revealing a narrow staircase, leading deep into the hillside.

It was one of the High Lady's secret doorways. Without hesitation, she descended and the sod closed silently back into place behind her.

The steps were lit dimly by slender, silver lamps and had been cut into the eternal stone. Rhinannon almost flew down them. At their foot a long passage curved off to the right and she ran the length of it.

At her shoulder, the owl remained silent. It could sense the malice burning fiercely in its mistress's mind and dared not utter a word in case she vented some of that intense fury upon it. The force of her malevolence was a constant revelation to the owl, but it had never known her to be as thoroughly consumed with hatred as she was that morning. Like everyone else in her realm, it feared her, yet that fear was matched in equal measure by love and adoration.

An ancient tapestry hung across the passage. The High Lady snatched it aside contemptuously and passed into the deserted hallway beyond. The owl knew she was heading for her bedchamber, no doubt to bathe her face in the life glow of the human infant—to refresh the unnatural, pitiless beauty of the High Queen of Faerie.

Through hall and courtyard she hurried until, at last, the door to her chamber stood before her.

Reaching out, she put her palm to the lock. There was a click and the door swung open.

Inside that shadow-filled place, Gabbity, the goblin nursemaid, was sitting upon her low stool by the cradle. She seemed to be examining something closely in her dirty fingers and jumped with a start when the door opened.

"M'Lady!" she cried, fumbling with her hands and catching up her knitting.

Rhiannon sailed past her and glared at the unconscious barn bogle lying on the table.

"Does it live?" she demanded.

"Why . . . why yes," Gabbity stammered. "But 'tweren't easy, it was touch and go for a fair while, your poor old nurse thought it were a goner and they spriggans, why it's a marvel there was a twitch left in the beast—them's not the gentlest handlers. I said to them—"

Her words were smacked into silence as the High Lady struck the goblin across her warty mouth. The force of the blow knocked the last remaining tooth from her black gums and it went skittering over the floor.

"If I want to hear your endless chatter," the High Lady snapped, "I'll cut out your tongue and keep it in a jar so it can wag when requested." The owl bobbed its head up and down, glad that it had remained silent and that the nursemaid had borne the brunt of his mistress's rage. It turned its face to stare at the stupefied goblin.

Gabbity was on her knees, rubbing her stinging mouth and shivering with shock. Tears had sprung to her yellow eyes but there was something else in her glance that the owl had not observed there before—mutinous embers were smoldering. The bird shifted its weight from foot to foot and committed the look to memory. Here was another of its mistress's subjects it would have to watch closely.

Gabbity crept back onto the stool and fearfully stuffed her hands into her pockets.

The owl wondered if tongue would make a pleasant alternative to eyeballs as a beaksome delicacy. It shook its feathers in revulsion—no, not hers. It would be too tough and stringy, and probably extremely bitter.

Rhiannon's glacial countenance gazed down at the barn bogle. Grimditch's breaths were steady and slumbering, but just to make sure he wasn't feigning sleep, she yanked his head back by his shaggy, matted hair and wrenched one of his eyelids open.

The enlarged pupil was black and insensible and rolled slowly in its socket.

"Has it spoken?" the High Lady demanded.

Gabbity shook her head. "No, M'Lady!" she answered timidly.

The High Lady released her grip and Grimditch's head fell forward, his nose banging heavily against the table.

"If this creature so much as coughs," she growled, "I must know of it immediately. Let no other speak to it before I return—do you understand?"

The goblin nurse nodded at once. "As you command," she said, anxious to appease.

"Did you search it?" Rhiannon asked severely. "Was there aught in its possession?"

Gabbity clenched her fist tightly in her pocket until the tiny key bit into her palm. She had been toying with the daring idea of holding on to the golden treasure for a little while before "discovering" it and handing it over, but now she had a mind to keep it herself. She had suffered the injustices of her mistress's temper more than most. But this last slap stung her more than any she could remember. The tip of her tongue dabbed at the hole where her tooth had been and her wizened face clouded.

"No, M'Lady," she lied. "Old Gabbity only used her healing arts on it. That barn bogle's bouncing with fleas, an' a darn sight worse. Made me retch just touching the nasty louse magnet. I've been itching ever since."

Rhiannon stepped away from the table and wiped her hands on her gown.

"Yes," she agreed. "It is a filthy, verminous runt. But I want it watched closely."

She turned her attention to the cradle and drifted across to it. The delicate pink light flickered through the webbed canopy and moved over her lovely features. Reaching in, she lifted the sleeping infant in her pale arms and held him close, stroking his golden hair. There was no affection in her actions, not the merest bruise of love for the child who had been stolen from his crib many years ago. He was important to her only as a means of sustaining and feeding her ethereal beauty. His life force refreshed and nourished her.

She inhaled deeply and the glimmering light wound around her, painting color on her frozen cheeks and rippling through her raven hair. Soon she seemed to be wrapped in a column of reviving pink and golden flame that cut through the chamber's gloom and cast stark shadows around her. She appeared to grow, her cold beauty filling the room. It was breathtaking and horrible, like a distorted vision of a monstrous marble statue illuminated by a lightning strike.

"I could eat him," she said, and Gabbity knew that was no pretty sentiment; she really meant it. Would the other lords and ladies permit that, though? Surely not even Rhiannon Rigantona would go so far as to eat a baby?

Gabbity cast her eyes to the floor. She could not look on that sight for long. The immortal splendor of the Tyrant of the Hollow Hill, wrapped in the nourishing flame of human innocence, was an injury to the eyes and made her feel faint. Never had the world seen anything so monumentally worshipful yet so wincingly cruel and repellent.

By the time Gabbity next looked up, the child was being returned to the velvet cushions in the cradle. Rhiannon Rigantona was more ravishing and looked more powerful than ever. Cloaked in a mantle of white and gold, her midnight hair entwined with fine golden wire threaded with white jewels, she appeared nothing less than a living goddess.

"Now, to war," she said coldly, her delicate fingers stroking the infant's soft, smooth brow. "This day will end in blood; death is my gift to those who defy me."

A cruel smile crept over Rhiannon's face as she lifted her gaze to where Grimditch lay sleeping.

"When that wakes," she instructed, "I want you to search it, strip it, scrub it clean—to the very marrow if necessary—and then . . . shave it."

"Shave, M'Lady?"

"Until it is as smooth as my little lordling—no, smoother. Let us discover what lies beneath that crawling tangle. I don't want to see a single strand of hair remaining, not one bristle of an eyebrow. Pluck those nests from its ears and tear the clumps from its nose. Let it be as bald as an adder."

"As you order it."

The High Lady laughed quietly to herself. It was an icy, empty sound. Gabbity sucked her gums uncomfortably and watched as her mistress left the chamber. The heavy door closed, but she waited until she heard the lock click into place before letting out a shivering sigh of relief. Gingerly touching her mouth where the force of Rhiannon's slap still throbbed, she took the key from her pocket and cooed over the winking gold.

"She'll not get so much as a glimpse of you, my glisty dainty," she vowed.

WITH THE FOLDS OF HER SNOW-WHITE MANTLE BILLOWING about her and the owl fluttering ahead, Rhiannon moved quickly through the galleries and mansions of Her kingdom: past trickling fountains and down spiraling stairs where the walls were inscribed with images of past kings. A carving of twin dragons snaked the length of the steps. Tattered banners of faded silk stirred gently overhead, hanging from spears black with age: the captured heraldry of forgotten fiefdoms conquered so long ago that not even the dustiest books in her library recorded them.

She was nearing the iron-gated dens where the Redcaps were kenneled. Thirteen large bogles kept them in order with whip and rod and the daily ration of milk from the faerie cattle. But it was the taste of flesh for which the Redcaps ached, and the High Lady occasionally furnished them with what they craved. Her father, the late King, had not been so generous, and, in spite of their love for him, they had twice attempted to revolt in his time.

The keepers slept on cots by the scrolling ironwork of the entrance to those rough dens with whips and pointed sticks clutched in their hands.

"M'Lady," the owl whispered into her ear as she stepped up to rouse them, "thou cannot keep a spurring of the Redcaps secret, the whole court shall hear of it."

"We are beyond concealment now," she answered. "The lovers must be slain before evening falls. I will not permit them to live through another night. They have eluded me long enough."

She glanced around the shadowy passage and in a low voice breathed, "My sister had many friends among the nobles. There have always been malcontents and treasonous whisperings, but if they were to learn Clarisant still lived, her name would be a rallying cry for open rebellion. Even those who held no regard for her would exult her name, merely because they hate me."

"Ingrates and wretches, each one!" the owl hooted severely. "Yet, they would not dare to rise up against thee."

"Would they not? Would that I could be so certain; then I could be rid of them. To reign without doubt or dread, with no need of the court."

"Just thou and I?"

"No, my provost," she answered with a secretive smile. "There are *others* who have long desired to dwell within the Hollow Hill. We would not be alone, you and I. And then my rule would truly commence."

The owl looked at her questioningly, but Rhiannon had turned her attention to the nearest cot. The head keeper, Dedwinter Powfry, was sleeping deeply, his wheezing snores rustling his brindled whiskers. The bogles of the Hollow Hill were a breed apart from solitary barn bogles. These creatures were larger, with grayish-blue skin and sharp features, and less impish and capricious in nature.

The remains of the head keeper's supper were on a shelf gouged into the rocky wall nearby. The High Lady took up a half-filled tankard and threw the contents over his face.

"Aiyeee!" he cried, jolted from sleep and spluttering as he wiped turnip beer from his eyes. "Who done that? I'll put some stripes on your back you won't forget too quick!"

"On thy knees!" the owl commanded. "How dare thee raise thy voice to thy Queen!"

The bogle let out a strangled squeal of horror when he realized who was standing before him and he tumbled from the cot to grovel on the ground.

"Forgive me!" he beseeched her. "I thought . . . I didn't . . . oh, most forgiving Majesty . . ."

Ignoring his anguished pleading, she stepped past him and looked through the iron gate that penned in the Redcaps. Amid the darkness, slivers of reflected light stared at her keenly.

"I have need of them," she told the bogle. "Wake them."

Dedwinter shifted on his knees as his fear subsided. By now the other wardens were standing by their cots and bowing respectfully. He threw them a hasty glance and knew what they were thinking. Each of them hoped to step into his boots and wear the head keeper's feathered hat. Well, those ambitious bogles would have to wait a little longer for that day.

He rose to his feet and pulled the whip through his hands. "They will be alert and aware already," he said. "When they do sleep, my love-lies keep one eye open and roving. They miss nothing."

"They had better not," she said sourly. "Drive them to the main south gate. I shall meet you there. I have a task for them that cannot be delayed."

"What of the milk ration?" he reminded her. "They always gets it first thing. Blunts their appetite; without it they'll be ravenous and a torment to control."

The High Lady was already striding away down the passage.

"No milk today," her stern voice came echoing.

Dedwinter looked at the other twelve keepers. They were fidgeting nervously.

"You heard Her!" he barked. "Get in there with your sticks and herd them out. And don't be too gentle neither."

Gulping and shuffling uneasily, the wardens drew back the bolts. From the darkness there came the sound of hissing and grinding fangs, rustling straw and countless claws scratching over the stony floor.

The Redcaps were hungry.

· CHAPTER 4 ·

GLUTTONS AND WEAPONS

WHEN THE OTHERS HAD GONE to the roof of the broken watchtower, the sluglungs had attempted to follow Meg's orders and help the sick and injured birds in the infirmary.

Their good intentions, however, were not a great success. They had spent far too long underground. Not only had they forgotten their former lives before becoming creatures of slime and jelly, they had also forgotten what birds were.

Many of them were amazed at these strange patients with such musical voices. The wildly differing sizes and varieties were a marvel to them and they poked and prodded the peculiar things to make them sing and see how they worked.

Liffidia saw what was happening and slipped away from her exhausted fox cub to help.

"Stop that!" she told two sluglungs who were holding one of the magpie attendants by the feet and were trying to shake a song out of it. "Put her down! Meg will be cross with you."

Tollychook did not know what to do. He edged hesitantly toward a group of sluglungs, mumbling, "Shoo, shoo!" but they paid him no heed.

The bald chicken matron was running between the clumsy creatures, clucking and scolding and flapping her naked wings in outrage.

When the sluglungs saw her, they gabbled with laughter. Even to their goggling eyes she was a bizarre sight: pink and devoid of feathers and wearing a woolen smock to keep out the chills.

Incensed, she lunged at the nearest fat leg to peck it hard. But her beak plunged through the sluglung skin with a splattery "gloop" and, to her horror, her head was encased in its thigh.

The chicken gargled a shriek, then wrenched herself free with such force that she went reeling backward, straight into another of the creatures who was thrown off balance and promptly sat on her—heavily.

Liffidia covered her eyes, aghast, but opened them almost immediately when the sluglung started laughing, loud and hysterical.

The poor hen had been completely engulfed by the creature and was flapping wildly in its belly. Through the translucent, gluey flesh, Liffidia could see her jiggling about in terror, but her frenzied movements were merely tickling the sluglung who roared and roared with laughter.

"Let her go!" the girl commanded.

"*Big ha ha!*" the sluglung guffawed in reply.

"She'll drown in you!" she cried in desperation. "Don't you see? You're hurting her—you're hurting all of them."

The sluglung stopped laughing and his toadlike face looked crestfallen. Sorrowfully, he reached inside his stomach to pull the chicken out.

The matron stumbled into Liffidia's arms. Then she fainted.

"*Ussum no mean harm or badness,*" the sluglung gibbered unhappily.

The sluglungs were so dejected and sorry that Liffidia could not remain furious with them. They simply knew no better.

"Why don't you go search for something to eat?" she suggested. "The Tower Lubber must keep a store of provisions here somewhere."

"I'll come!" Tollychook volunteered brightly.

Meg's followers filed from the great round room and every bird that was able sang a chorus of good riddance.

Barging past them to lead the way, and claim the best pickings for himself and his friends, Tollychook leaped down the steep stone steps that wound to the lower level. He had not had a chance to explore earlier and was keen to see what sort of a larder the Lubber kept. Surely he didn't eat eggs all the time?

"There must be a bun or two, or maybe even seed cake—that'd make sense."

Excited at the prospect, he hastened under a large archway and into the room beyond. Catching his mood, the sluglungs bounded after him.

Tollychook stumbled to a halt and rubbed his eyes.

In the center of that spacious room, a small fire was crackling within a ring of square stones, sending a thread of sweet-smelling smoke spiraling to the high ceiling. By its cheery light, the hungry werling saw that the rest of the room was crammed with supplies.

Surrounding the fire, arranged in ordered piles, were stacks and stacks and row upon row of his most favorite fruits. Beautiful russet apples glowed in the dancing light, each one carefully placed in an old nest to keep from bruising. There were mountains of chestnuts, shining like nuggets of bronze; three hills of hazelnuts; a pyramid of pears; stone jars brimming with berry juices; a large iron pot filled with dried mushrooms and basket after basket overflowing with grain and seeds and dried plums.

There was enough food to satisfy a besieged army for many days. The Tower Lubber and his feathered helpers had harvested it from the surrounding woods and the boy almost wept to see such a delicious feast.

"If I be dreamin', then it be the bestest dream ever," he murmured, enraptured.

The only problem was deciding what to eat first. His mouth was watering so much he didn't know what to do or where to begin.

The sluglungs did.

"*Ragabaah!*" they yelled and at once all forty of them rushed forward, leaping and diving into the baskets, slithering into the apples, sending them rolling over the floor and avalanches of hazelnuts clattering in all directions.

"Hoy!" Tollychook wailed. "You're making a mess!"

The sluglungs ignored him. They threw apples into the air and caught them in their gaping mouths, swallowing them whole. The werling boy saw the fruit go bouncing down their gullets and spin into their bellies, immediately followed by hails of chestnuts.

One of the creatures stuck his head into a jar of blackberry juice and slurped and slurped, kicking his legs up into the air, falling into the jar and disappearing inside. His guzzling continued to echo from within until every drop was drained and he hauled himself out, his stomach heavy and sloshing. From head to toe, his translucent skin was now flushed and stained a dark purple color.

They were eating everything. Having existed on a diet of black mold and raw eels for many long years, these new delicacies were a revelation and they had no intention of stopping. They tipped up the baskets to their lips, poured the grain down their throats, and gulped down entire mouthfuls of nuts.

Tollychook was thunderstruck. Their gluttony was frightening. They shoveled so much into their wobbling bodies that their shapes became distorted; pears bulged out of knees, shoulders became lumpy with apples and chestnuts that were popping up all over like monstrous boils. To satisfy their voracious appetites, they even cast their rusted armor aside and unbuckled their sword belts in order to cram more in.

"You're guzzling the lot!" he shouted. "There won't be none left fer the rest of us!"

"*Ullug Bukbah,*" one of them gurgled. "*Thissum yum yum.*"

Nodding in wholehearted agreement, nine of the others let out fruity belches.

The boy could only watch as they continued to gobble down everything they found. One sluglung got so carried away that he not only ate a basket full of seeds, but he ate the basket as well. He had already eaten so much that there wasn't any room inside his body; it lodged in his neck and the wicker handle pushed his forehead up so high that he couldn't blink and looked extremely startled.

"Stop!" Tollychook protested, but his cries were in vain.

Close by were some lidded pots and he hurried to the nearest before it could be snatched away. Anxiously, he tore the lid free and delved inside.

"What's this tastiness then?" he asked, groping an unfamiliar, squirming mass.

"Oww!"

He toppled backward, kicking the pot over. A large black beetle was clinging to his finger and biting it. Tollychook shrieked and brushed it off, then saw that scores of other beetles were streaming from the overturned pot.

The sluglungs warbled with pleasure and fell upon the insects with relish, licking them up with their horrid wet tongues, then emptying the other pots into their mouths. They were filled with worms and grubs, moths, millipedes, and green caterpillars, and all went flooding down the sluglungs' necks. The creatures burbled and gargled as the insects wriggled and writhed inside them. It was a nauseating sight.

Tollychook felt sick and wondered if he'd ever be hungry again.

Within minutes, everything was gone: every last grain, every morsel of fruit, every single hazelnut, every crawling insect. Only one jar of elderberry juice remained, and three of the sluglungs were quarreling over who should drink it.

Tollychook stared around the ransacked storeroom at the upturned bowls, broken pots and empty nests and baskets and shook his head desolately.

"You dirty girt gluttons," he groaned. "You barrel-bellied gutsies."

The engorged creatures grinned at him, patting their distended tummies with pride and contentment.

It was then that the Tower Lubber came rushing down the stairs and into the room, followed by Finnen and Bufus.

"Hurry!" he shouted. "The High Lady is on her way. We must be ready to defend this place and fight. Half of you run outside and gather as many large stones as you can find; the rest take up your arms and climb the walls."

Tollychook scratched his head and looked at the sluglungs. "I doesn't reckon them'll be running nowhere," he said. "And I'm certain sure they won't be able to do no climbin'. Them's way too fat now."

"What has happened?" the Tower Lubber demanded.

"They done found your larder and gobbled the lot," the boy told him sheepishly.

"Everything?"

"Apart from one last jar of berry juice, and that won't be fer much longer."

Bufus scrunched up his face and jabbed an accusing finger at Tollychook.

"Why didn't you stop them?" he demanded. "How're they supposed to fight now? They can't hardly walk! I bet you was stuffing your own greedy gob—always thinking of grub, you are."

"I never had so much as a nibble!" the boy protested. "Don't blame me—'tain't fair."

While they argued, Kernella came huffing up behind them and gaped at the obese, misshapen sluglungs. Most of them were on their backs, too heavy to move and tittering at the action of the insects inside them. The argument over the jar was still in progress, and in one corner, two others had discovered an iron ring on the floor and were sniffing it experimentally.

"I thought they were ugly before!" she exclaimed. "Who knew it could get worse?"

"It's Chookface's fault," Bufus told her.

"Stop squabbling!" Finnen told them. "We're wasting time."

"Oh, are we?" Bufus cried, rounding on him. "Do tell us, what does know-it-all Lufkin have up his sleeve to get us out of this one? We didn't stand an earthly chance before, but now . . ."

"I can still boil some water," Kernella suggested feebly.

The Tower Lubber covered his face with his large hands and his humped back bowed even more. "We are beaten before we begin," he said.

"Nuts and pips!" a defiant voice rang out behind them. "Don't give up—the battle hasn't started yet."

Everyone turned and there was Gamaliel, his round face beaming. In his hand, he brandished the silver talisman.

"The fire devil!" Tollychook gasped. "How'd you get hold of that? 'Twas round the High Lady's neck."

"Not this one," Gamaliel declared. "We brought this up from the caves. Peg-tooth Meg had it in a huge pot of dark water that poor Finnen had to drink."

"That's right," Kernella said. "And it made him turn into a sluglung too for a while." She was going to say more but she suddenly remembered that she had kissed Finnen while he was one of those slimy creatures and the repulsive memory made her gag and feel queasy.

The Tower Lubber reached out and Gamaliel passed him the talisman.

"Harkul," he whispered, running his fingertips over the silver. "Crafted in the forge of the Puccas, so many years ago. . . ."

He paused and touched it to his lips, remembering that rain-lashed night when he had fled the Hollow Hill with the Princess Clarisant.

"It was this," he said softly. "The Wandering Smith used this dainty talisman to change Clarisant and me into the distorted grotesques you see today."

"Then use it to turn yourselves back!" Kernella urged. "Be a handsome prince again."

"Not yet," he answered. "The time is not right—we will know when, if by some miracle we make it through."

"You're barmy," Bufus snorted. "Or lubbing's a lot better than you crack on."

Finnen brought them back to their present predicament.

"How do you think the talisman can help?" he asked Gamaliel. "We'll never be able to touch each Redcap with it when they come marauding. There'll be too many."

His friend smiled and looked across the room.

"Tell them sluglungs to get away from that jar," he said. "I've got a better use for it."

Finnen thought he understood. "You mean put it in there? But even if we could get the Redcaps to drink the juice, would it work the same as the dark waters?"

"Excuse me, Mister Redcap," Bufus began in an arch, mocking tone. "Would you please be so kind as to halt your rampaging a moment and try our magic drink? Thank you muchly."

"Don't seem likely they'll do that fer us," Tollychook put in with a shake of his head.

"I do not believe that is what our young friend is suggesting," the Tower Lubber said. "Continue, Master Tumpin."

Gamaliel took a deep breath.

"We can't force the Redcaps to drink," he began. "But they're always hungry; if we dunk something they can't resist in juice that the fire devil has charged with the power of change and scatter it between the edge of the forest and the tower, then we might have a chance."

"Some chance!" Bufus cried. "Why didn't you tell us before the ten bellied sluglungs stuffed their froggy faces? Haven't you noticed? The cupboard is most definitely bare! Unless you've got a secret stash of pies stuffed down your jerkin."

"It's flesh that Redcaps crave most of all," Finnen said slowly. "Gamaliel, what are you thinking?"

The boy looked up at the Tower Lubber. "This is a desperate hour," he said in a steady and entreating voice. "It's not just us, here in this place, that are in danger—there's our folks back home and no doubt others in the Hill, and maybe more I don't know about and can't even guess at. Sacrifices have to be made. Some already have been made. . . ."

A look of pain passed over the Lubber's face.

"My fallen children?" he breathed.

"They died fighting bravely, and now they can help us again."

Bufus looked at Gamaliel in astonishment. "The birds!" he said as realization dawned on him. "All them dead birds out there, what the spriggans killed!"

"Perfect Redcap breakfast," Finnen murmured.

"And our only chance," Gamaliel said.

Tollychook grimaced and wiped his large nose. "That be downright 'orrible," he said.

Finnen gripped Gamaliel's shoulders. "You're a marvel!" he cried. "That's brilliant."

"Well I'm not touching any dead birds," Kernella announced with an emphatic toss of her head.

Before the Tower Lubber could speak, there came the sound of grinding stone and grunts of exertion. Two sluglungs in the corner were heaving on the iron ring they had found set into one of the flagstones.

The flagstone moved; lifting from its place in the floor, and, straining their bendy, bloated backs, the sluglungs dragged it aside.

The Tower Lubber had never realized the true purpose of the iron ring he encountered in the first sightless mapping of his ruined home. He had assumed it was for shackling prisoners.

A draught of cold, stale air drifted up from the uncovered darkness and the werlings wrinkled their noses and shivered as they peered down into the pitch black.

"Is it a dungeon?" Bufus wondered aloud.

"A bottomless pit to throw folk down!" Tollychook whimpered. "With poisonous snakes at the bottom—if it has a bottom."

"Or an escape tunnel," Gamaliel suggested.

"With vipers that bite and make you drop down dead!" Tollychook felt compelled to add.

"We don't have time to find out," Finnen said firmly. "Let's put Gamaliel's plan into action." He hurried over to where the three sluglungs were quarreling over the juice and, with a fierce shout, ordered them to leave it alone.

"Any idea what's down there?" Gamaliel asked the Tower Lubber.

"None."

"Only one way to see!" Bufus declared and he ran to the fire, pulled out a burning stick and cast it into the hole.

The flames flickered in the draughty drop as the stick twirled and tumbled. It did not have far to fall—in a moment it hit the ground with a burst of sparks and the fire was extinguished. But the brief flare of light had been enough to illuminate part of what was down in that chamber.

Bufus whistled through his teeth and Kernella let out a cry of astonishment.

"Ooer," said Tollychook.

"What is it?" the Tower Lubber demanded. "What can you see?"

Gamaliel was almost laughing. "What was this place built for originally?" he asked.

"It was a watchtower and fortress," the Lubber answered, a little tetchily. "Built by Man to spy on the eastern moor, fearing invaders. But no mortal men can dwell nigh Hagwood for long, and so this was abandoned. Old tales tell that the soldiers went mad and slew one another."

"I'd like to hear that story!" Bufus said, ghoulishly.

"Well, whatever happened," Gamaliel declared, "they must've been expecting a huge invasion—they left their weapons behind."

In the fleeting flurry of light, an arsenal of ancient weapons had been revealed: spears and swords, shields and axes, sheaves upon sheaves of arrows, forests of longbows and large timber constructions for hurling missiles great distances.

"If those sluglungs hadn't stuffed themselves stupid," Bufus grumbled, "I bet we could've won the war with that lot."

"No amount of arms can give us victory," the Lubber reminded them.

Kernella put her hands on her hips and snorted. "I'll settle for just making it through the next few hours," she said.

"Fetch more torches!" Gamaliel urged. "Let's bring it all up."

Frowning, Finnen joined them and swept the hair from his eyes as he peered into the gloomy pit.

"I've put the fire devil in the jar," he announced. "That's our best hope—not blunt old knives. We should dash outside while we can and start collecting."

"This won't take long!" Gamaliel promised. "Don't you see? We need every little scrap of hope we can find. What about the Redcaps who don't eat the birds? What if the talisman doesn't work? We'll need to fight with something."

Folding her arms, Kernella tutted. "We also need a rope to climb down there," she remarked.

Her brother shook his head and beckoned a sluglung over. "Oh no we don't!" he said. "Not when we've got these fellows with us."

Grasping a burning stick, he explained to the sluglung what he wanted. The creature nodded, then grasped him around the waist, leaned over the hole and started to lower him down, its arm extending and stretching into the darkness.

Finnen muttered under his breath. This was madness. Every moment was vital. He strode away to see which of the sluglungs were able to walk and follow him outside. Kernella would have gone with him, but the thought of those slaughtered birds was too great a deterrent. She could always praise his courage when he returned—provided he wasn't covered in blood and feathers.

"Be careful," she told him. "And hurry back!"

Finnen was too busy assessing the sluglungs to hear her. Out of their number, there were only fifteen who could still stand, and only nine of those were able to waddle or walk.

"This way," he commanded. "Bring as many baskets and pots as you can. One of you bring that jar of juice out to the entrance."

Burping and squelching, the bloated creatures obeyed. There was a squeal of rusted hinges as the great door was pulled open and they lumbered into the bright sunshine.

Gamaliel's descent into the hole was smooth and steady. Holding the torch above his head, he saw the flame glinting in hundreds of tarnished blades around him. But the light did not penetrate far into the darkness and he wondered how vast this secret hoard could be.

His knees bent gently when his feet met the floor and he tapped the clammy fingers that held him.

"I'm here," he called up to the hole in the ceiling. "You can let go now!"

The hand retracted and began rising upward. Gamaliel heard Bufus's impatient voice demanding to be next. Then he turned about to examine this hidden chamber.

"Aarghh!" he howled.

He had pushed the torch right into the empty nose cavity of a great, grinning skull.

The flames bounced up into the hollow eye sockets and the shadows whirled around, making the skull seem alive and ferocious.

Gamaliel wailed again, then tottered backward and thrashed the fire before his face. "Get away—get away!" he squealed.

He was so afraid that he did not notice the sluglung's hand sliding down beside him or the Doolan boy hopping onto the ground.

"Ha!" Bufus snorted when he saw the skull. "This your new girl-friend, Gammy?"

He knocked on the dome of its forehead with his knuckles, sending up a cloud of ancient dust that made him cough and splutter. Then he pulled a succession of rude faces at it before placing his hand into the open jaw and feigning panic.

"It's got me, it's got me!" he joked.

Conquering his fear, Gamaliel leaped forward and pulled him away.

"Don't do that!" he shouted. "It isn't funny!"

"Oh, get your head out of your breeches," Bufus jeered. "It's only a musty old skully. I really don't think it minds."

Gamaliel walked away in disgust. He ventured further into the dark chamber. Mighty posts of oak that gave extra support to the beams of the ceiling emerged from the gloom as he pressed onward. Most were sound and solid but one or two had rotted or were chewed through by worms and crumbled into brown powder under his fingertips. The ground was uneven and sloped downward, with large holes here and there. He stumbled several times and, if it wasn't for the torchlight, he would have fallen in or broken an ankle.

Picking his way around these hazards, he marveled at the scores of weapons stowed in that forgotten place. They were too massive for a werling to wield—even the arrows were too long to use as spears.

"The sluglungs have got to be able to fight," he muttered in desperation. "They must."

Behind him, another burning torch came gliding down from the room above. With some reluctance, Kernella had allowed herself to be gripped about her middle and was descending with a regal and non-chalant air as if she traveled this way all the time.

"What's taking you two so long?" she demanded before she even touched the floor. "Those slimy monsters are too fat to squeeze down that hole so we've got to guide their hands to the swords and such and then they'll hoist them up."

She reached the ground and the fingers released her. Another hand was already stretching down and she glanced quickly around while she waited.

The first thing she saw was the skull. Its jaw opened slowly and, in a sepulchral voice, it let out a long desolate moan. Then it said, "Have you seen my hat?"

Kernella tapped her foot and pursed her lips, unimpressed. "You always did have a big head," she told the figure squatting behind the teeth.

Bufus crawled out, sniggering.

"You Tumpins have no sense of humor," he laughed. "If we get through this, I'm going to take skully back home in triumph. I wonder who it belonged to originally? Probably one of them soldiers who went loopy. Do you think he cut his own head off, or someone else obliged?"

The girl ignored him and planted her torch firmly in the earthen floor. The sluglung's other hand was already dangling at her side like a cluster of wobbly stalactites and, taking the forefinger of both, she led them to a great pile of swords and yelled upward.

"Get a move on; don't take all day."

The glistening, clammy hands scrambled over the blades like two jelly crabs. Then each fumbling finger coiled around a sword and, with a scrape of metal, lifted them into the air. Kernella watched the deadly array rise upward with satisfaction. A few more hauls like that would do very nicely. Then she cast around for her brother.

Gamaliel had discovered other skulls. They were impaled on spears and the leaping shadows painted accusing or piteous expressions across their bony faces. He did not like to look at them. The men who built this tower must have indeed been driven mad. It was a chilling reminder—not that he needed one—of just how dangerous a place Hagwood was.

"Anything different over there?" Kernella called to him.

"More swords and lots and lots of shields!" he shouted back. "It goes on a bit farther; I'll just take a look."

Placing the sluglung hands on a bundle of arrows, his sister took up her torch, determined to go explore as well.

"You supervise the next haul," she told Bufus. "Get some of those spears up and then try tackling one of these big wooden contraptions."

Bufus sneered at her. "Stuff that, Bossydrawers," he refused. "I'm not missing out." Tilting his head back, he yelled up to Tollychook to come down next and take over.

"Down there?" came the woeful response. "Me in that girt dark hole?"

"Yes, you fat, dithering lump!"

So Bufus and Kernella hastened after Gamaliel.

Bufus was thrilled to see the other skulls but the girl was more interested in the weapons. There were so many. She wished she had a little sword and shield of her very own, perhaps even a helm. She was sure she would be an impressive, striking figure, but she had to admit she would be of little use against marauding Redcaps.

Some way ahead and down the slope they could see the bobbing flames of Gamaliel's torch, nipping left and right behind heaps of rusting breastplates and regimented rows of shaft and blade. Kernella and Bufus hurried on, taking care to avoid the treacherous holes in the ground.

With a wretched look on his face, Tollychook descended. He yelped when he beheld the skull but, in a jittery panic, guided the hands that brought him to a rank of spears.

They were quickly drawn upward through the hatch and Master Umbelnapper suddenly felt horribly alone. The skull unnerved him and he turned his back to it to look searchingly across the densely filled darkness toward the glimmering torches of his friends.

"Don't 'ee be too long!" he shouted.

One of his friends called something in reply but he couldn't make out what was said, or even who said it. He shivered nervously and the hairs on his neck began to prickle.

"That evil old skull be staring clean at you!" he whispered to himself.

Summoning his tiny courage, he turned, shakily. He had been expecting the skull to have moved—to have somehow crept a fraction closer—but it was in the same place.

"You're daft, lad," he chided, feeling foolish but immensely relieved.

Tollychook let out a sigh and leaned against the rusted blade of a sword propped against one of the huge wooden catapults. The weapon shifted, then slid away, falling against another sword, which knocked into another, until a whole row of them went clattering to the ground—but not before the last three swung into the poles of a dozen spears. They went clonking against a stack of round, metal shields that toppled over with a resounding crash and went rolling down the slope, bowling and spinning recklessly. They smashed into the heap of breastplates with a tremendous, clanking racket, then bounced and rebounded wildly. Other unseen things came thundering down and the darkness was fogged with teeming dust.

"Lumme," Tollychook breathed, aghast. "What've I done?"

Everything in that armory was in motion, falling and toppling, rolling down the slope right toward the three small flaming torches.

Gamaliel had gone as far as he was able. At the end of the chamber the floor had fallen away completely and a deep chasm lay before him. He stooped to pick up a pebble and tossed it in. It rattled down the immense, slanting shaft to an unimaginable depth, echoing in the foundations of the earth—further down even than the caverns of Pegtooth Meg.

"Tollychook was right," he muttered. "There was a bottomless pit after all."

With a shivery shrug, he turned to go back and rejoin the others. His sister and Bufus were still picking their way toward him.

"There's nothing more down this way," he told them. "Just a huge deep hole."

"I've had enough of those!" Kernella declared, disappointed.

"No more bones?" Bufus asked.

Before Gamaliel could answer, they heard the first thudding rumble caused by Tollychook's blundering.

"What's that?" Kernella cried.

"Bad news!" Bufus predicted.

The uproar grew louder and closer, and clouds of dust came billowing from the gloom. A wooden support post was struck by the full toppling force of a mountainous stack of heavy bronze shields. There was an explosion of sound and a sickening *CRUMP* that shook the soil beneath the werlings' feet.

Suddenly, a shield came whooshing over their heads. It glanced off the far wall and came zinging back.

Yelling with fright, they sprang out of the way and the shield drove into a pile of helmets, scattering them like skittles.

"That nearly cut our bonces off!" Bufus shouted, clamping one hand on top of his curly hair. "I might like skulls, but I want to keep my own attached to the rest of me."

Kernella was too busy fleeing a bouncing helmet to heed him. A sword flew past her, somersaulting in the air, and she veered sharply left, colliding with her brother. Both fell to the ground—just as the blade of a spear sliced through the air above. Kernella dropped her torch and the flames fizzled and died.

Pandemonium reigned. An avalanche of arrows swept toward them and they hopped about in a mad dance to avoid it. Nearby, another support post shattered, firing splintered shards into the swirling dust.

The Tumpins became separated from Bufus, each dodging perils of their own. Gamaliel was the next to lose his torch. It was smacked from his hand by a flying post fragment and the cavern grew even darker.

"We're sitting ducks!" Bufus cried, breathlessly. "We're going to get hacked or stabbed or squashed—or all three together."

A drizzle of dirt and debris was now raining from the ceiling and Gamaliel ran to one of the helmets that had rolled to a halt and dove beneath it for protection.

"Hide and be safe, hide and be safe," he repeated to himself. That was the werling creed and had been drummed into him for as long as he could remember.

"In here!" he yelled to the others.

Kernella darted in after him, but Bufus was farther away. Anxiously, they watched him hurrying toward them. A hail of stones drummed onto the helmet and Kernella covered her ears.

"Faster!" Gamaliel hollered to Bufus.

The Doolan boy jumped over another surging tide of arrows, then stumbled to a stop as all expression drained from his face. He stared over at the helmet in which Gamaliel and Kernella were sheltered and then raised his eyes to the ceiling.

"What's he doing?" Kernella demanded. "He'll get killed out there."

Gamaliel could not understand. He saw him lift his torch as high as he could, then heard him call in a strangled, panic-filled voice, "Get out—get out of there!"

"What did he say?" Kernella asked.

"GET OUT!" Bufus bawled at them.

The Tumpins looked at one another, dumbfounded.

There was a deafening, splintering roar overhead. The ceiling was collapsing.

At once they charged from their shelter and pelted toward Bufus. Above them, the oak beams were sagging and bowing. A moment later one came slamming down and the helmet they had taken refuge under was pulverized.

Another beam buckled ominously.

"When that goes, we're done for," Bufus told them. "That's the only thing keeping the flagstones up on the next level. If they come down on top of us . . ."

Gamaliel hunted around wildly. There was no chance of escape, no way out. He knew they were completely trapped—except perhaps . . . no. That was sheer madness.

A *creak* ripped through the choking atmosphere. The beam directly above the werlings split into kindling, and the flagstones it had supported began to quake alarmingly.

His mind racing, Gamaliel seized hold of the upturned shield and started pushing it toward the far wall, raging at the others to help him.

They were too astonished and terrified to argue. They grasped the rim of the great bronze dish and together they heaved it down the slope. The heavy shield gained momentum and skimmed even more swiftly over the lines of fallen arrows.

"Jump on!" Gamaliel yelled.

Bufus and his sister obeyed. Gamaliel gave it one final, running shove, then leaped in beside them.

The ground shuddered as the flagstones came thundering down in their wake. The shield was jolted into the air and Kernella finally saw her brother's plan. Clamping her eyes shut, she screamed.

They were speeding directly for the huge hole in the earth.

"Hold tight!" Gamaliel cried.

Bufus looked behind them. Grinding destruction was chasing

them with cataclysmic force. He saw the small fire in the room above come pouring into the rubble storm as the floor collapsed. Then four massive stones smashed into view, pounding straight after them.

Bufus wailed.

The shield tilted and tipped. Clinging on for their very lives, the werlings went shooting down into the vast, gaping pit.

· CHAPTER 5 ·

DEFENDING THE TOWER

IN THE CHAMBER ABOVE THE ARMORY, the Tower Lubber had heard the tumult below and felt the floor quiver under his feet. He called into the hatchway to summon the werlings, but only Tollychook's fretful cries answered him.

"The others!" the boy howled. "They're stuck at the far end . . . they're—"

At that moment the beams collapsed. There was an ear-splitting crash as the flagstones in the center of the chamber caved in and went smashing down. The fire disappeared, swallowed in the sudden gulf and a storm of choking debris was hurled upward. Gargled shrieks of dismay erupted from the engorged sluglungs as they tumbled in helplessly. Standing closer to the wall, the Tower Lubber felt the floor shudder beneath him. He lost his balance and fell to his knees.

"What has happened?" he shouted, his blind face turning left and right.

In the infirmary, Liffidia heard the din as a violent tremor gripped the tower. Every bird fell silent and the fox cub awoke with a start. Fearing they were under attack, bombarded by some infernal witchery of the High Lady, she leaped down the stairs with Fly at her heels.

When she reached the lower level, she ran under the archway and looked at the wreckage beyond in alarm.

Dust and grime was still whirled in the air and she peered through it to discover that the floor in the center of the storeroom was gone, fallen into the cellars beneath. Only the flagstones around the edges and in the corners remained in place.

Fearfully, she looked for her friends but could see only the flailing, bendy limbs of gibbering sluglungs crawling and hoisting themselves up from the rubble. Across the room, on the broadest section that remained intact, the Tower Lubber was staggering to his feet and groping about blindly. He took a shuffling step backward—one more and he would topple over the brink and into the devastation below.

"Stay where you are and don't move!" Liffidia called out to him. "The floor is gone. I'm coming to get you."

She ran her hand through Fly's fur and told him to stay put, then hared nimbly along the edge of the chamber, pausing only to navigate around frightened sluglungs that had dragged themselves free and lay gasping in her way.

All the while, Liffidia searched for any sign of the other werlings. Where were her friends? They were nowhere to be seen.

"Are you hurt?" she asked as she approached the Tower Lubber.

He shook his head. "I am unharmed," he answered, but she could see he was severely shaken. "We are blighted this accursed day."

"Where are they?" the girl cried. "Finnen and Kernella, and the rest?"

The Lubber took a moment to collect his jangled wits. "The boy Finnen went outside," he said. "But the others . . ."

He waved vaguely at the hatch, and to where the cellars were buried beneath tons of stone.

"They were down there."

Liffidia uttered a cry of despair and clutched at her throat. "No," she uttered in a shocked and broken voice. "They can't possibly . . ."

"This is my doing," the Tower Lubber reproached himself. "I should have sent you all from this place, as far from Rhiannon's vengeful spite as possible. She is too great a foe for such small folk as you. The Wandering Smith erred when he enmeshed you in our hopes and designs and I compounded that folly."

The girl stretched out her hand and squeezed his large thumb. The tears rolled down her cheeks and she lowered her eyes. At their side, a sluglung made soft, sad burbling noises and wiped its snotty nose.

"Help!" a despondent voice called from below. "Get me out of 'ere!"

Liffidia leaped forward and stared down. There was Tollychook, looking forlorn and frightened and covered in grime.

"You're alive!" the girl exclaimed joyously. "Oh, I'm so glad! Where are the others?"

Tollychook fidgeted uncomfortably. "They're goners," he told her. "They went exploring down that far end and . . . and . . ." He stammered into silence when he realized his clumsiness had set everything in motion.

Grasping that dreadful fact for the first time, he burst into tears. "The ceiling came down on top of them!" he howled. "'Twas my clumsy fault; I killed them!"

Liffidia was too distraught to respond or offer comfort. She ran her gaze over the demolished floor and called out, "Gamaliel—Kernella—Bufus! Can you hear me? Please answer!"

There was only silence broken by the glutinous grunting of the sluglungs.

"They're dead," the Tower Lubber said gently.

"No," Liffidia replied firmly. "I refuse to believe that. They have survived somehow; I know it. Cowering in the smallest of gaps between the stones and the floor—the narrowest hole would be enough. They're just trapped in there, that's all. They need rescuing."

Inspired by this idea, she ran back around the room and called to Fly. The fox cub hurried to her and she led him down into the wreckage, stepping carefully over the fallen rubble.

"Help me," she begged Fly. "Help me find my friends. Your nose is so keen and clever, it can smell the faintest trace. Go seek them for me, please."

The fox nuzzled her and such was the love between them, he understood and was eager to obey and ease her anxiety. Immediately, he put his nose to the stones and began questing for a scent.

Liffidia held her breath and waited. She clasped her hands around her wergle pouch. As soon as there was a sign, she would transform into a mouse and go crawling between the cracks and crevices to find her friends.

While the fox searched, the Tower Lubber bade the sluglung to lift Tollychook clear. The unhappy boy was soon standing beside him and staring over at Liffidia and her cub. They were still desperately hunting for the slightest trace, the slightest hope. As much as he wished it to be possible, Tollychook knew nothing could have lived through that devastation.

"Flat as pancakes they'll be," he lamented between sobs. In the whole of his short life, he had never felt so wretched and bleak.

It was into this mournful scene that Peg-tooth Meg came shambling. Even at the top of the tower she had felt the collapse and hurried down as fast as she was able. She did not need to be told what had happened—the expression on both werlings' faces was enough.

"My poor shobblers," she murmured in sorrow.

Liffidia was growing more and more anxious. Fly had not picked up anything. Though the cub darted back and forth, left and right, he could find no hint of anyone buried below.

"Then we must dig," the girl said. "It's the only way to reach them."

The Tower Lubber stood up as straight as his humped back permitted and stiffened. He inclined his head and his large ears twitched.

"We are out of time," he declared grimly. "*They* are here."

Everyone froze. Outside, the spring day was filled with a wild yammering and blood-curdling shrieks. The most savage creatures in the Hollow Hill were streaming through the forest: the Redcaps had arrived.

"But," Tollychook whimpered. "Master Finnen's still out there!"

FOLLOWED BY THE GROUP OF NINE SLUGLUNGS, Finnen had hurried the length of the grassy ridge to where the conflict between the Tower Lubber's birds and the spriggans had originally commenced.

He could not understand why Gamaliel had not joined him. This was his idea after all. Arms would be useless against the High Lady's forces. They had to fight her with her own weapons: cunning and enchantment.

"I don't suppose we'll last long either way," he told himself somberly.

The boy waited for Meg's creatures to catch up with him. They were groaning and puffing with their extra weight, but swinging about their baskets and pots as if on the way to a jolly picnic, delighted to be of service.

"And what about them?" Finnan wondered. "Shouldn't Meg change them back to their previous selves? But if she does, whose side will they be on?"

He had come to the edge of the forest. Within those crowded trees, forbidding shadows lay thick and deep; but out there, on the ridge, the noon sunshine was warm and delicious and laced with the fragrance of early flowering gorse. It really was too lovely a day to fight a war.

"But then, every day is," he murmured.

He waved to the sluglungs to hurry. They were gabbling merrily to each other and began singing the Song of Meg:

Three young chicks left chirping in the nest.
One went swimming and only two were left.
Another flew away though the hunter did her best.
One chick left that can never ever rest.

On the word *rest* they stomped to attention in front of Finnen and saluted. In spite of everything, the boy could not stop himself laughing. They looked so ridiculously bloated and funny as they grinned at him. To laugh at that dire, fearful time was such a marvelous, carefree feeling, he never wanted it to end. The sluglungs chuckled back at him and for some precious, beautiful moments their predicament was forgotten.

Then Finnen's laughter ceased and the familiar dread clutched at his heart once more. His face became grim.

"Now," he addressed them. "You understand what we have to do?"

They waggled their heads at him uncertainly.

"One more time, then. We're collecting the dead birds. Put as many in your baskets and pots as you can and take them back into the tower. Then come back for more. Is that clear?"

"*Ussum find um,*" they promised.

And so they began to search. It was not difficult. The first casualties they found were the bodies of warning geese. They would be far too large to dip in the berry juice but Finnen knew he could not leave them here. If the Redcaps came upon them they would ignore the smaller birds. He instructed two sluglungs to take them to the watchtower and hurry straight back.

It was farther down the ridge's slope that Finnen discovered the first of the other birds. Sparrows and thrushes, hawks and finches: every feathered species in Hagwood had fought bravely that morning. A trail of death led down toward the glade where the wellhead stood, the number of feathered bodies steadily increasing with every footstep.

"Treat them with honor," Finnen ordered. "Every one died a hero. Remember that. We're not picking strawberries or daisies here."

In a solemn procession, the sluglungs gathered the birds from the ground, filling their baskets and crooning a dirge over each tiny corpse. They were almost done when they heard a commotion in the distance.

Finnen's heart sank. "So soon," he breathed. "We're not ready."

The terrible sound was the yammering of the Redcaps. They had been released from the Hollow Hill and the whips of their bogle keepers drove them forward. Their ghastly shrieks and frenzied whooping rang through the forest and every creature who heard them darted for cover or went to ground.

The sluglungs gibbered in consternation and looked back to the tower.

"*Megboo!*" they jabbered. "*Ussum go defend Big She.*"

All thoughts of their other task were abandoned and at once they began laboring back up the sloping ground. They would have cast their feathery burdens aside had Finnen not been there to order them otherwise.

The hideous shrieking grew louder. The Redcaps were swarming swiftly through the trees. Finnen knew they would soon come tearing across the ridge. High overhead, the High Lady's owl was circling, guiding them straight to the tower. The werling boy looked up at the ruined fortress. Could he and the sluglungs reach it?

"Hurry!" he yelled, running alongside them. "As fast as you can!"

The creatures huffed and waddled more briskly, but their swollen stomachs were brushing along the grass and haste was impossible. One of them tripped over its own drooping belly and rolled, squelching, back down the slope.

Finnen stared after it, then turned away and spurred the others on. There was no chance of rescue—the sluglung was doomed.

"Keep going!" he shouted. "Almost at the top now—we can do this."

Even as he said the words, the Redcaps came charging from the forest. At the sight of them, Finnen's courage failed.

There were over a hundred of them: hunched, stunted beings with bony, unwieldy heads and long snouts crammed with sharp teeth. Their legs were short and their arms long, and they loped over the ground like demonic apes. Apart from kilts made of animal skins and the scarlet headgear that gave them their name, they were naked. Their clawed feet were bare and they wore no armor, yet each carried a bow across his bare, piebald back, along with a quiver of poisoned arrows.

The forerunners spied Finnen and the sluglungs immediately and loosed ghastly shrieks before tearing toward them.

"Run!" the werling yelled.

The sluglungs howled fearfully. They had left their swords behind in the tower with their discarded belts and were completely defenseless.

Jabbering in panic, they lumbered onto the level ground. The tower was not much farther, but the Redcaps would be upon them in moments.

Below them, the sluglung that had slipped was toiling back up the ridge. A group of Redcaps saw it and went charging down. Screaming vile oaths, they leaped on it. The slimy creature tried to fend them off but was hopelessly outnumbered. The vicious beasts merely whooped the louder and tore it into small, quivering globs with their teeth and claws.

Running faster than he ever had in his life, Finnen pelted into the tower. The Lubber, Meg, Tollychook, and Liffidia were already there to meet him, but there was no time to speak. He spun around. The remaining eight sluglungs were still out there and running too slowly. They would be caught before they reached the entrance.

The Redcaps were bounding after them, their teeth already snapping at the air in anticipation. Behind them, Finnen saw the bogle keepers hurrying to stay close to their fiendish charges. Their whips were useless now. Nothing could control those nightmares—the kill was sighted, the hunt almost over, and the heady scent of fear filled their snouts. They were inflamed by it and gaped their jaws wide in readiness.

At the rear of that terrible spectacle, Dewfrost, the silver-white, elfin mare, cantered from the forest and her rider reined her to a trot.

Rhiannon Rigantona surveyed the scene with a rancorous glitter in her lovely eyes. Watching her savage servants swarm toward the ruined tower gave her immense pleasure. Soon they would be stripping the clammy flesh from the bones of her sister and her deformed prince. The High Lady smiled, wider than she had done for countless years, then licked her teeth as if she too were hungry for the Redcaps' imminent banquet.

In the tower entrance, Meg was calling to her sluglungs, urging them on.

"We must close the door," the Lubber told her, "while we still can."

"Not while my people are out there!" she protested.

Just then, the sluglung who was bringing up the rear was seized by many claws and thrown to the ground. His baskets went rolling into the mob and they fell upon the contents that tumbled out of them. He was torn asunder and the dead birds were snatched up and ripped apart.

Peg-tooth Meg called out in horror and Liffidia buried her face in Fly's fur. Tollychook covered his eyes.

"Wait!" Finnen cried. "That's given the others a chance!"

The slaughter of their comrade and the fights over the dead birds had been enough of a distraction to let the pursued sluglungs make a last dash. They piled over the threshold, running heedlessly into the sluglungs that had remained in the tower and for an instant they were squished together in a great wriggling mass.

"Slam the door and bar it!" Finnen shouted as soon as the seventh and last was safely inside.

The Tower Lubber heaved his strength against the heavy door. The hinges screeched and Finnen saw the horde of Redcaps surge toward them. They were so close he could see the trails of dried blood that stained their faces and smell the unclean, hot breath that gusted from their filthy throats. The foremost leaped at the threshold; arms outstretched, its evil squinting eyes fixed on Liffidia. With a resounding *BANG!*, the door swung shut in its repugnant face. There was a thud of bone against oak and a shriek of pain. Then a ferocious battering of many fists assailed the thick door.

"Now it begins!" the Tower Lubber said, dragging the iron bolts across. "This won't keep them out for long."

"Long enough," Finnen declared. "Help me with those baskets. We must put Gamaliel's plan into action first. Where is he? Up on the roof? Is Kernella boiling pots of water? We're going to need everything we have to fight these monsters!"

The others looked at him uncomfortably.

"What is it?" he asked. "Where are they? And where's Bufus?"

Liffidia opened her mouth to speak but it was Tollychook who blurted it out.

"Them's dead!" he cried. "Crushed under girt stones—an' it were my fault!"

Finnen could only stare at him, unable to take in the dreadful news. "Can't be," he murmured. "It can't be."

"Now is not the time to grieve," Meg told the werlings gently. "May we all be granted that later, if we are spared."

Before anything more could be said, there came a frantic noise of splintering wood and they turned back to the door.

"They're chewing their way in," the Tower Lubber muttered. "Redcaps can do that faster than rats, especially when there's something tasty on the other side."

Not wasting another second, Peg-tooth Meg took two baskets from her sluglungs and began dipping the birds' bodies into the jar of elderberry juice.

"Hear my voice, Harkul," she chanted to the silver talisman lying at the bottom of the jar. "'Tis I, Clarisant. In the dim long ago, Gofannon the Smith made you to do my bidding. Hearken to my command. Let your power enter this dead flesh and change any who consume it."

One by one she quickly dipped each feathered body into the juice and piled the baskets high.

"Take these to the roof, my subjects," she told the sluglungs.

Still bulging from their feast, some of them went grunting up the steps, while the rest went in search of their discarded armor and the weapons from the cellar.

The furious biting and gnawing grew louder, but Finnen hardly heard the horrible sound or even noticed the feverish movement of the shadows beneath the door.

"Gamaliel can't be dead," he repeated in disbelief.

"We will be if those things get in!" Liffidia told him harshly. "I don't want to think of our friends lying under that rubble either, but just standing here fretting is a sure way to get us killed."

Finnen stared at her as if lost in a dream, then passed a hand over his brow and forced himself to push his grief and shock into the furthest corner of his mind.

"Let's start defending this place," he said gruffly. "Those horrors outside won't just be attacking this door, they'll be scaling the walls. We have to station someone at every window to keep them out. Put whatever dead birds are left at the bottom of the stairs. It may delay them when they burst in and buy us a few more seconds."

They hurried up the steps and had almost reached the infirmary when they heard a terrible commotion below.

"They're inside!" the Tower Lubber shouted.

The Redcaps had indeed climbed the tower walls. They needed no rope or ladder—their clawed hands and toes were more than capable. Clinging to the weathered stonework like lizards, they clambered effortlessly around the curved walls, seeking a way in.

From the moment the hideous yammering had started out in the forest, the injured birds had been twittering in fear. They recognized the cries of the Redcaps.

The plucked hen saw a sinister shadow move across the window. Startled, she glanced up and saw a long sinewy arm come reaching in, followed by a horrific face.

Flapping her naked wings, she clucked in alarm and then every bird began to screech.

A Redcap squeezed inside, grinning foully from ear to ear. His leering eyes flicked about the room and a long black tongue darted out to lick his pointed chin. He let out a gloating laugh at the panicked spread before him. His deathless mistress had promised him and his vile crew any of the fresh, frightened morsels they could find in this draughty old tower.

He dropped to the floor and reached for the nearest tidbit: a nice plump pigeon, squawking in a nest.

Suddenly, a crowd of strange creatures came bursting into the room: a bow-legged cur with pegs for eyes; the ugliest woman he'd ever seen; three small, frightened-looking runts; and a fox cub. They were followed by over a dozen repulsive toadlike things brandishing swords and spears.

The Redcap hissed in annoyance. He reached for the bow slung across his shoulders but, before he could draw back a black-tipped arrow, a spear came flying through the air and caught him in the throat. The force of it hurled the Redcap to the floor, kicking and gargling. A moment later, he was dead.

Peg-tooth Meg lowered her eyes in dismay and stared at her trembling hand.

"Amazing shot!" Finnen exclaimed.

"I was aiming for its shoulder," she said bitterly. "Killing does not come as easy to me as it does my sister."

"Then you'd better learn fast," the werling told her.

"There's more comin' in!" Tollychook wailed.

Ravenous faces had appeared in both windows. This time the sluglungs were ready: They barged across the room, thrusting their rusted swords between the invaders' eyes and cutting off their heads.

The dead Redcaps dropped from the wall but more appeared in

their place, jabbing with their arrows and trying to scratch the defenders with the poisonous tips.

"Three to each window!" Meg ordered. "The rest remain behind to defend these stairs. Little shobblers, come with me to the roof."

The Tower Lubber and the werlings hurried after her. Finnen hesitated. He leaped over to where the first Redcap had dropped his arrows and cautiously picked them up, taking great care to avoid the darkly stained points. They were the perfect size for a werling to use as spears. Taking the lot, he ran after the others.

On the roof the sluglungs with the baskets were awaiting Meg's orders.

"Why have you not cast them over the side?" she asked when she saw that they were still heaped with dead birds.

"*Megboo not say,*" they gibbered unhappily.

With Fly at her side, Liffidia ran to the edge and looked over the wall. What she saw made her gasp in terror and she staggered back, just as an arrow came glancing off the stone where her face had just been.

The tower was swarming with Redcaps. They were crawling up the walls like wasps. Many were almost within reach of the roof. She could already hear their barbarous cackling.

A clawed hand came grappling over the battlement and the tip of a scarlet hat reared into view. Fly's hackles rose and he stood before his beloved werling, ready to jump at the brutal face when it showed itself.

"Get back!" Finnen yelled and he bolted forward, skewering his arrow deep into the scrabbling hand.

There was a yowl and the Redcap fell from the tower. A defiant roar issued from the forces below.

"I'll kill as many of them as I can," Finnen promised and he swiftly passed an arrow to Tollychook and Liffidia. "Make good use of these!" he said.

"The bait!" Meg shouted. "Throw it, now!"

The sluglungs hurried to obey. They lifted the baskets and started flinging the dead birds over the walls.

Finnen positioned himself by a cleft in the stones and peered down warily. The Redcaps hooted with glee when they saw the delicacies hurled from above. Some of the fiends clinging to the tower tried to catch them while the ones still baying on the ground beneath reached up their long arms expectantly.

Several fights erupted when the bodies landed among them and not one Redcap managed to claim a whole bird for himself.

They champed and crunched and swallowed and stared upward for more.

On the roof, the werlings held their breaths.

"Is it working?" the Tower Lubber asked.

Finnen shook his head. "Nothing!" he cried. "They're not changing!"

Peg-tooth Meg fingered the silver talisman and closed her eyes.

"Then the plan has failed," the Lubber announced.

Three more pairs of claws came groping over the wall. The obese sluglungs lunged with their swords, thrashing and slashing, and three Redcaps fell from the tower in pieces. Another swung himself up and over the battlement, landing right in front of Tollychook.

"*Sssssnnaaar!*" the horror hissed at him.

The werling shook and immediately dropped his arrow. The Redcap went for him but toppled over, his legs hewn from under him by a sluglung's axe.

Tollychook stammered his thanks and plucked up the arrow again.

Suddenly, a tremendous commotion broke out on the ground below. The Redcaps who had eaten the birds were retching and choking. They fell to their knees and thrashed their limbs wildly. Those around them leaped back and watched as they screamed and kicked and flailed in the grass.

Hoarse cries of astonishment rippled through the onlookers. They could not understand what was happening and wary circles formed. The others were changing. As they writhed and twisted in pain, dark needles were spiking from their skin and unfurling into plumage. Soon they were covered in feathers: some speckled, some raven black, others pale yellow, and one even had elderflowers sprouting from his head.

A stunned quiet descended.

Fifty-eight new feathery creatures were blinking and looking about them with sharp, jerky movements. When they tried to speak, only a dry croaking came from their now-rigid lips and they scurried around the encircling crowd, bewildered.

The bogle keepers watched incredulously and wondered just what powerful entity dwelled in that tower.

The Redcaps scratched their bony heads and sniffed the bizarre, feathery creatures uncertainly. There was a deathly pause. Their transformed pack members uttered pitiful chirps and looked helplessly at one another. The unchanged Redcaps' lips quivered in a rippling wave around them. With a single hate-filled shout, they pounced and butchered each of these new changelings.

Seated upon her horse, the High Lady regarded the scene with contempt and gazed up at the broken tower.

"Nursery tricks," she muttered. "Is that the best you can do, sister?"

At her shoulder, the owl fluffed out its feathers. "Soon she will perish," it hooted wickedly.

"Take wing, my provost," the High Lady said. "Observe what is happening atop that ruin. Tell me when Clarisant dies."

Watching from the battlements, Finnen allowed himself the ghost of a smile. "Bless you, Gamaliel Tumpin," he whispered. "It worked."

"A large number are destroyed," Meg declared. "Now we must fight the rest. Though we are still outnumbered, we have the high ground. Do not abandon hope."

"I ain't had none of that fer days," Tollychook grumbled to himself.

"Are all the baskets empty?" the Tower Lubber asked quickly.

"There are no birds left," Meg answered. "And I do not think the Redcaps could be tricked that way again."

The Tower Lubber laughed. "It is the baskets I'm after," he said. "I have another use for them!" Leading two sluglungs, he disappeared down to the infirmary.

There was no time for Meg to guess what he was doing. The enemy was crowding up the walls now and many evil faces appeared suddenly over the battlements. The sluglungs gathered around their mistress and swung their swords in readiness, but they were far too stuffed and ungainly to challenge the ferocious Redcaps. Overlooked for the moment, the small werlings and the fox cub had to duck under the sluglungs' jellylike legs to avoid being trampled or struck with arrows.

One sluglung's axe was wrested from his hand and at once, three Redcaps leaped upon him. Snarling, they pinned his arms against the wall while another took up a bow.

The sluglung's great round eyes glared at them. Then he clamped them shut and strained with such force that his entire body rumbled and quivered. The slimy creature's froggy eyes and wide mouth snapped open, and everything it had eaten exploded forth in a devastating belch. A violent torrent of chestnuts and apples bombarded the Redcaps in front of him and, shrieking, they fell back, lost their footing and tumbled over the edge. The Redcaps holding the sluglung's arms were next. A barrage of hazelnuts fired directly in their faces and they let go to shield themselves.

Guffawing, the sluglung grabbed them while they were still squinting and cringing and hurled them from the roof.

When the rest of Meg's followers saw what had happened they took huge gulping breaths and, within moments, the summit of the tower boomed with cloud-ripping burps. Everything inside their engorged bellies shot out, hammering the Redcaps backward. Jets of juice swept them, slithering and struggling, from the battlements and a blizzard of pears punched them mercilessly in the eyes and on their snouts. They had never encountered anything like this before and some jumped rather than face this terrible foe. The others were killed with sword and spear and soon the roof was clear of them again.

Meg looked around at her peculiar, glistening subjects, now returned to their normal girth, with only the occasional caterpillar or beetle wriggling under their translucent skin, and her pride in them made her heart swell.

"A thousand blessings upon you, my clever, slimy sweets," she cried.

The sluglungs gave a burbling cheer and brandished their weapons, hopping from foot to foot in an invigorated dance. Now they were fit and ready for proper combat.

Liffidia was staring at them, almost doubting her eyes. Even Bufus would have found the vomiting disgusting, but at the same time she admired them enormously. Tollychook decided there and then that he never wanted to see another apple or pear as long as he lived, and as for chestnuts, he would never touch another pasty that contained them.

"Now we have something to throw down at them," Finnen exclaimed, paddling through the jetsam and rolling the fruit to the wall. "They're as good as stones!"

Already more Redcaps were clambering over the battlements but the refreshed, sprightly sluglungs bounded up to them with swords and axes ready, and the fierce fighting resumed.

In the heat of that battle, the Tower Lubber returned with the baskets. They were now heaped with old nests from the infirmary, and the sluglungs he had taken with him were carrying more. Swiftly he lit one in the fire and threw it, flaming, over the side.

"Now the rest," he told the sluglungs.

Soon the ruined tower was cascading with fireballs. They fell into the besieging Redcaps and onto the upturned faces of those climbing up the walls.

"When you run out of nests," the Lubber shouted, "burn the baskets!"

Liffidia marveled at his ingenuity. She wished she too could be of some use when an idea flashed into her mind. She hurried to an abandoned Redcap bow and pulled a suitable stick from the edge of the fire.

But even as she set to work, wrenching the string from the bow, the sound they had all been dreading reverberated within the tower. The entrance had finally been breached—the Redcaps were rampaging up the lower stairs.

· CHAPTER 6 ·

THAT WHICH SHE MOST LOVED

GIVE ME AN AXE AND A SWORD!" the tower lubber demanded. "My place is with the sick and injured in the infirmary. I have not tended them these many years to abandon them now."

Two sluglungs gave him their weapons and he ran down the steps to the infirmary, where a furious battle was already raging.

"Fight well, my love in the sky," Meg said softly.

There was no time to think. They were surrounded on the roof. The battlements were crawling with Redcaps. Dozens of snarling fiends leaped forward. Sword and spear cut through snout and shoulder, but there was always another ferocious Redcap behind it.

Peg-tooth Meg fought alongside her subjects, a rusty blade in her hand and an ancient shield on her arm. She took no delight in dispatching the invaders, but she cut down just as many as her gelatinous warriors.

Finnen was lobbing apples with deadly marksmanship. He had already struck six Redcaps from the wall. A seventh fell, and he reached for another missile and lifted it over his head as he took aim at his next target.

He was so engrossed he did not see the Redcap that was creeping up behind him. The savage creature bared its teeth and prepared to spring. Finnen let the apple fall and whisked about. Suddenly, it gasped and collapsed on the ground. Standing by the dead Redcap, looking shocked and afraid, was Tollychook, his arrow buried deep in the Redcap's back.

"Dab crack, Master Umbelnapper!" Finnen greeted him gratefully.

Tollychook blushed, then scurried off to find himself another arrow.

In the infirmary, the sluglungs who defended the entrance stairs were dismayed at the multitude of Redcaps who came gushing through the chewed-up door. The stairway was narrow, however, and no enemy could pass the sluglungs' fence of ancient swords without being hacked to bits. The Redcaps growled and took up their bows. Soon arrows were shooting through the air. The sluglungs held up their shields, which juddered under the striking blows. Then one dart found its mark.

It pierced the quivering frogspawn-like flesh and passed straight through the other side. It was natural for the sluglungs to withstand any such injury. Wounds normally healed in a moment. But this time the poisoned arrow left behind a blackened hole that did not close up and venomous threads were already flowing from it. The sluglung groaned as the dark veins branched inside his bloated body. He wavered and sagged, dropping his weapons with a clatter. Then, with a frothing wail, he toppled forward and fell among the Redcaps—dead.

A hellish, triumphant crowing erupted and the Redcaps trampled him under their stomping feet as they waved their arrows. The remaining sluglungs gibbered dolefully. Another torrent of Redcap arrows sang toward them, thudding into their shields.

"All shall die!" the Redcaps hissed. They could hear the terrified chirping of the birds in the infirmary and ached to devour them. "Our pretty darts will prick the toadlings like so many hedgepigs and then we shall eat lark and thrush, sparrow and crow."

But the sluglungs stood their ground and the bravest of them slashed with his sword and cut off a Redcap's pointed ear.

Incensed, the enemy surged forward, trying to push the obese obstacles up the stairs, but the sluglungs planted their feet squarely on the steps and drove them back with their shields. There was a scuffle and a tangle of long limbs and snouts. One of the Redcaps managed to barge through the first rank, but was swiftly chopped in two.

Then the savage creatures saw how they could win through and began crawling up the walls to scurry upside down along the stair-well's ceiling, high over the sluglungs' heads.

And still the blizzard of arrows rained down. Another of Meg's subjects caught one in his neck and was dead a moment later.

The first of the Redcaps that had dashed along the ceiling leaped clear when he reached the infirmary. He somersaulted in the air and landed on the floor with a *slap* of his great flat feet.

A shrill chorus rang out when the injured birds saw him. Snatching up a starling, he chewed its head off and his dark eyes roved covetously over the rest. A freakish chicken was raging toward him and he craved to bite its throat out.

A shadow fell across the Redcap's knobbly shoulder, and he glanced around sharply. He was amused to see a stunted figure standing behind him, with crudely carved wooden pegs instead of eyes, bearing an axe and a sword.

The Redcap laughed creakily. "Blind fool!" he taunted. "Strike out in your darkness and cut me if you can. One jab of my little points will see you gone."

Before he could reach for his arrows, he was cloven in two by the Lubber's axe.

"I may be blind," the Tower Lubber said. "But did you really think these great ears of mine are without use?"

He spun around. Another soft *slap* announced a second Redcap had dropped from the ceiling. The Redcap snarled. There was a crunch of steel against bone and it was no more.

One of the sluglungs guarding the windows was struck by an arrow and collapsed. Then another was shot on the stairs and died gasping and croaking as the poison did its work.

More and more of the enemy came jumping from the ceiling and the Tower Lubber slew them all. One of them was still somersaulting down when the Lubber's axe sliced it in two and the severed halves went spinning in opposite directions. When five leaped down at once, he lashed out and killed four, but the fifth ducked out of the way and sprang farther into the chamber.

The Redcap put an arrow to his bow as he ran. The Lubber jerked his head around, trying to locate him. The bowstring was pulled back and the Redcap took special aim to hit the blind guardian right between those wooden pegs.

Suddenly, from nowhere, a hazelnut hit the Redcap's snout with stinging force. The brute squealed and the arrow fired wide. The Tower Lubber's sword drove into the foul archer's chest.

Fly had come bounding down the stairs, Liffidia riding on his back. The girl had fashioned a small catapult for herself, and had removed her snookulhood and stuffed it and her satchel with hazelnuts. She was already loading up another round.

"Behind you!" she called as two more Redcaps dropped to the floor.

The Tower Lubber laughed and swung his mighty arms with deadly effect. Liffidia proved to be an excellent shot and knocked three Redcaps from the ceiling. They dropped, yelping, on top of others and vicious arguments broke out among them.

A heap of hacked Redcap bodies and an ever-widening pool of their black blood littered the infirmary. No one encountered the Tower Lubber's fury and survived. Abruptly, his enraged sword thrusts and wild axe swings slowed and he stumbled backward, falling onto the corpses of his enemies. A single arrow had punctured the shabby leather of his coat and was embedded deep in his shoulder.

Dismayed, Liffidia watched him collapse. She saw the evil shaft standing proud and cried out in despair. Fearfully, she slid from Fly's back and rushed over to where the Lubber lay gasping.

"Don't move!" she urged him. "I'm going to pull out the arrow. If I can cut the poison out . . ."

The Tower Lubber forced a weak smile onto his ugly face. "Too late," he whispered. "'Tis done. Tell Meg, my bonnie bonnie Clarisant, tell her . . . tell her Tammedor died with her name on his lips. Ask her to forgive him, there can be no . . . no more flowers from above. . . ."

His barrel chest heaved one last time and the Tower Lubber's final breath sighed out of him.

"No!" Liffidia cried. "It isn't fair, it isn't fair."

The girl threw her arms around his neck and hot tears streamed down her face. "After everything you've done!" she wept. "Everything you suffered!"

Riotous whoops and screeches issued from the Redcaps as the fearsome axe wielder fell and they danced a foul jig of victory.

Liffidia rose and wiped her red-rimmed eyes angrily. Around her the injured birds were lamenting and crying sad, keening songs. Those who could walk crept toward their guardian and laid their heads upon him. The hen matron stepped forward in silence and rested her beak upon his nose. He had been more than a protector to them. He had been their truest friend. He had loved them as dearly as if they were his own children.

"Fly," Liffidia said in a cracked voice to her fox cub. "Go find Meg. She must be told."

The animal licked her hand then ran to the stairs and up to the roof.

Liffidia gazed at the grieving flock and her loving heart bled for them. If by some miracle they survived this day, who would carry on the Lubber's work? Who would tend to them?

"I will," she promised. "If I am spared."

Fly's sharp barking cut through the noise of battle and, in moments, Peg-tooth Meg appeared at the top of the steps. The Redcaps ceased dancing and prowled forward once more.

OUTSIDE IN THE WARMING SUNSHINE, the Lady Rhiannon heard her sister's bellowing howl of grief. It was a soul-wrenching sound that seemed to fill the entire sky. Dewfrost, her silver-white horse, jerked her head and shuffled backward. Even the Redcaps halted and looked about them, amazed and confused.

The only noise was Meg's voice. Across the forest, every animal grew silent as Meg's anguish screamed across the trees. Even the door wardens of the Hollow Hill heard it echoing through the stones and shuddered. Eardrums quailing, some of the Redcaps were scuttling down the tower to escape it—they had never heard such a sound before.

Gritting their teeth against that profound, raw torment, the bogle keepers cracked their whips to drive their craven charges back.

A supreme, gratified smile stole onto the High Lady's face and she held up her hand to summon the owl.

The bird spiraled down from above and alighted on her wrist.

"Tell me!" she demanded. "What glad circumstance has wrung such misery from my sister?"

"The faithless suitor, Prince Tammedor, is slain, M'Lady."

Rhiannon drew a marveling breath and cast her cold, sparkling eyes to the battlements. "He is dead?" she asked. "You are certain?"

"Mine eyes are not as his were," the owl chuckled. "I have glimpsed her through yon slit windows, cradling his oafish head in her lap, her grooly face contorted with woe."

A cold, prickling laugh left his mistress's lips. "Then I have taken from her that which she most loved," she drawled with genuine pleasure. "I could not have wished to wound her more deeply. Oh, may she savor that delicious bitterness and plumb the depths of her grief awhile. I would not deny her such treasured moments."

"How mean you, M'Lady?" her owl ventured.

"Do you think I would rob my sister of this, her blackest hour? Oh no, the Redcaps must not end her sorrow too soon. I want her to drain that cup to its dregs before she joins her prince."

Spurring her horse, she galloped along the ridge to where Dedwinter Powfry, the head warden, was herding the few unwilling Redcaps back up the tower walls, beating them brutally with his stick. They glared at him murderously before starting the climb once more.

"Master Dedwinter," the High Lady called to him. "I want the attack to cease. Sound the retreat. Call the beasts back—every one."

The bogle stared at her, bewildered. "But, Majesty!" he exclaimed. "It cannot be done. Save for the tender eared, the rest are still consumed with famine and lust for butchery. No power can draw them down."

"No power?" she asked archly. "You dare contradict me? You think you know better than I?"

"Of—of course not, Highness!" he stammered. "Yet I know these creatures well. They have been promised great pickings and no whip nor force will lure or compel them till they are sated."

The High Lady laughed lightly. "And you do whip and beat them with such passionate dedication," she declared with approval. "But do not underestimate your Queen. Come here, Master Dedwinter. I will show you the very thing to entice every single Redcap from the heat of battle."

Curious, the bogle approached her and she reached beneath her white mantle. Her long dagger glinted in the sunlight and she laughed coldly as she killed him.

"There," she said as he hit the ground. "What better inducement could there be?"

Throwing her head back, she called to the swarming Redcaps. "Hear me, my savage pets!" she commanded. "Leave this fight and come feast on your keepers. Yes, come—massacre them all!"

When the other bogles heard this, they could not believe their ears—but when they saw Dedwinter, lying in the grass with his throat cut, they knew they were finished.

Every Redcap crowed with vengeful glee and came scuttling back from the battlements and surged, yammering, out of the tower.

The keepers tried to run, tearing down the slope or back into the forest. But the Redcaps were too fast for them. Amid vengeful shrieks, they overtook the bogles and leaped upon them. Every punishing blow and lash was repaid in full. Their screams did not last long.

Rhiannon watched indulgently, then returned her attention to the ruined watchtower. Meg's cries had diminished—they were softer now, but that pain would never be quenched.

"What use are hearts when they break so very easily?" Rhiannon murmured. "Now, my sister, sup long from the chalice of your despair. Stew in that salty sorrow. When dusk falls, I shall deliver you from it. Was there ever such a generous sister as I?"

She turned her horse and walked it between the feasting Redcaps. Most of them had already steeped their headgear in the bogles' dark-red blood and it streaked down their loathsome faces. The small fiends groveled before her and kissed the hem of her mantle, staining it with gore.

"Remain here," she ordered. "Set up camp and ensure nothing, not even a mouse, leaves that tower. Do not presume to make a second assault, or you will yearn for the days of the whip once more. Do you understand? Look for me at sunset. Obey your Queen and she will feed you on flesh more tender than this."

The Redcaps bowed and worshipped her, croaking her name and falling on their ugly faces.

With a final, smiling glance at the battlements, the High Lady cantered into the forest as her owl flew after.

"Whither now, M'Lady?" it cried.

"This day many accounts shall be settled," she told him. "Whilst Clarisant suffers, there are others who have not yet paid the price."

"Who M'Lady, who?"

"The list is long, My Provost," she declared. "My realm must be cleansed of the vermin that infests it. The time has come to avenge my thorn ogres."

And with her mantle flapping around her, she galloped through the trees.

• CHAPTER 7 •

CONSPIRACY

GRIMDITCH UTTERED A GROAN and opened a bleary eye.

"There!" Gabbity announced, swilling the shears and razor-sharp knife in a bowl of hot, now-filthy water. "Scoured and scraped and done."

The barn bogle watched her swim in and out of focus as his eye drifted left and right. His dazed thoughts did the same, flitting in and out of his head, waiting to be sorted into an order. He had no idea who he was or what this shadowy place might be, or the identity of the astonishingly ugly female. Wherever he was, he only knew he was thirsty and cold.

"You're awake then," the goblin nursemaid observed dryly. "You've me to thank for saving your scraggy skin, you nasty barn bogle."

"Mother!" he burbled.

"You lowly cur!" she scolded. "Don't you slander me so! The very idea! Why, I've been nursemaid to the royal house since before even King Ragallach was born. Then I tended to his children, all three. And now I bide by the little lordling and see to his wants. Me, mother to such as you? Oh, the scandal of it!"

Grimditch's wits, such as they were, slotted back into place and fear seized control of him. He raised himself on his elbows. The sharp pain in his back instantly changed his anxious expression to a grimace and he slumped down one more.

"Me was at the waterfall," he murmured, thinking back to what had happened at the Crone's Maw. "With the nice skin swapper and then . . . then She came!"

"Spriggans carted you here," Gabbity said with a sniff. "Now don't you go jiggling about, you'll open that wound again and I've bound it right well with good thick webs and a staunching bandage steeped in the juice of periwinkles culled 'neath a hedge at midnight."

The barn bogle peered down at the strip of cloth wrapped tightly about his chest.

"Aaaaaiiyyee!" he shrieked. "Me's been plucked!"

He stared at his arms, polished, shiny and totally devoid of hair. Then he clapped his hands to his chin and scrabbled frantically for the tangled, bushy beard that was no longer growing there. His fingers reached up to his head and patted his egg-smooth pate and he let out an anguished howl.

"Like a baby squeaker!" he bawled. "As pink and nekkid as a nibbler's newborn runt. Poor Grimditch! Oh, cursed sack of bones he is. Stripped of all his cuddlesome thickets, what kept him tickling snug in the straw through the long winter nip."

Gabbity had followed her mistress's instructions to the letter. Not one hair remained on the barn bogle's body. Even his eyebrows and eyelashes were gone. He looked like a very scrawny, big-nosed, red-lipped, bald goblin whelp.

"And me be stripped!" he cried, suddenly aware that his rags had been removed and his bare, bony bottom was jutting into the air. That too had been shaved.

The goblin laughed at him. "You've naught I haven't seen before," she scoffed.

"But you filched Grimditch's vestyments! The farmer's missus needled them with her own clean plumpsy fingers."

"Them tatters?" the nursemaid scorned. "If they was clothes, then a frayed kerchief and a bootlace make a bride gown."

"No, no, no, no, no! Grimditch liked the missus. Now he don't have nowt left to remember her by. Where did you steal them off to, you warty old baggage?"

Gabbity threw him her sourest look. "They've gone to be burned!" she declared. "Along with the mattress worth of hair and whiskers, and who knows what else I sheared off you. Stink the whole hill out, that will, when it sizzles in the fire. You're a mangy flea-bitten beast, no mistake."

Wincing, Grimditch tried to get up a second time. He swung his long-toed feet off the table and sat upright.

"There was keepsakes too," he began, watching her intently. "In a little skin purse. Where did that go, me asks?"

The nursemaid nodded toward the end of the table. "That paltry bag of grotty bones?" she cried in disgust. "'Tis yonder. I would have sent that to the flame as well, 'cept I know my mistress would want to inspect it Herself first."

Grimditch snatched up his purse and rifled through it, kissing each favorite rat bone that he found inside. Then he raised his large eyes and stared at her accusingly.

"Not all here," he said. "There's things gone—one special thing."

Gabbity was an expert liar and she brushed the accusation aside with a careless shrug.

"That's all you was brought in with," she told him. "Weren't never no more. Maybe them spriggans took it? Or most like you lost it as they carried you here."

"Give it over!" the barn bogle demanded, swinging his legs impatiently. "'Twasn't Grimditch's. Me was only borrowin'. Me would've sneaked it back. Grimditch weren't for keeping it! Little skin swapper would've never knowed."

"So whatever it was weren't yours in the first place!" she said with a disapproving shake of her head that set her spire of white hair swaying. "Don't you get no ideas of thieving in here."

"Give it back!" he implored her.

"I don't have your smelly old rat bone!" she retorted crossly.

Grimditch glared and ground his teeth together. "Weren't none of that," he said mutinously. "Were handsomer and more delicates than a jooly crown. Me only wanted to look at it and keep it for a titchy while. Them said it were important."

"Them?" the nursemaid repeated, curious. "Who's them and what was it? How come something so small could be so important?"

The barn bogle's eyes glittered back at her. "Somethin' small?" he said.

"Must be small to fit in that purse of yours," she answered. "I could only squeeze three fingers inside."

Grimditch regarded her a moment then pawed gently at the purse in his hand.

"Overheard them, me did," he murmured. "The two changing folk with the furtley bags. Oh yes, Grimditch heard what they was a-sayin' as we tramped through the forest. Keen ears he has."

"What did you hear?" she asked sharply.

Grimditch returned her steady stare. "Bad doings for your cruel Lady," he told her. "That's what they said it was. Do Her no good, it wouldn't. An' been a-hunting long time for it, She had. In old grave mounds, She'd gone delvin'—out there in the haunted woods."

Gabbity snorted. "There's naught in Hagwood, nor beyond, to give a moment's worry to M'Lady," she boasted. "Deathless and mighty She is. What could give Her cause to fret?"

The barn bogle jiggled the place where his eyebrows had once sprouted so unkempt and bushy. "Then why She go guising through the forest, huntin' for my skin swappers?" he said. "And why me brought here and not left gurgling in the stream?"

The goblin nursemaid's wizened face crinkled even more. Her mistress had been acting strangely recently. She had overheard some very curious exchanges between Her and that owl. Did the answer really lie in the treasure she had hidden in her pocket? Could there be enough power in that tiny golden key to frighten the High Lady of the Hollow Hill? A dangerous thrill tingled through each one of Gabbity's warts and a slow smile creased her crabbed lips. Then she saw Grimditch watching her closely.

"Barmy bogle talk!" she snapped hastily. "Just you keep your daft fancies to yourself. I'll hear no more of them, and when M'Lady gets back, you'd better have a more pleasing song to sing to Her. Not gentle is She and you'd best answer Her with proper courtesy or it's straight to the torturers you'll go. Could do with a bit of stretching, you could— and more besides."

She bustled away, but instead of returning to her stool by the cradle, she headed for the door. She needed to set her devious goblin mind to thinking, away from his suspicious stares and questions.

"Gabbity will fetch you something fitting to wear," she declared. "'Tisn't decent for you to meet M'Lady nekkid, wretched raw spectacle that you are. Just you stay sat on that table and don't be moving or get up to no mischief while I'm gone. If you're a good beast, I'll bring you some milk back from the faerie cattle. Best glug you've ever tasted, no doubt."

With a last, piercing glance at him, she closed the door behind her and locked it.

Grimditch's eyes remained transfixed on that firmly sealed entrance. He was mortally afraid. The impending encounter with the High Lady in all her dark majesty was a harrowing prospect. He was sure he would expire from the fear of being tortured long before a hot pincer came snipping at him.

"Or the thumb twiddlers," he sniveled, licking every finger in morose abstraction.

Finally, he tore his eyes away from the door and tried to dispel the horrors that were crowding in. For the first time he began to look about him. The chamber was large and gloomy. Swathes of dark gray-green silk smothered the walls. Stone pillars, carved to look like strangling weeds, rose to the lofty, shadow-draped ceiling. Behind him was a high, wide bed, framed on each side by curtains of olive-colored velvet, fringed with silver tassels. The pillows were whiter than a dove's wing and the coverlet was embroidered with the High Lady's emblem, the badge of the black owl.

Grimditch marched his gaze across large wooden chests at the foot of the bed, but was too fraught to even wonder what they might contain. He turned his head toward the only source of light within that shadow-thronged place and marveled that he had not recognized it sooner.

The soft pink glow that emanated from the cradle was pulsing slowly. It licked along the interwoven strands of the webbed canopy where large spiders spun in industrious silhouettes, mending their work tirelessly.

At once, the barn bogle forgot about his plight and slipped gingerly from the table to patter across and take a closer look.

Grasping the edge of the cradle, he stood on tiptoe to see inside and his large eyes swam with pity and compassion. The human infant was still sleeping soundly, the pale rosy glow lapping over him.

"Farmer's littl'un," Grimditch breathed in a melancholy whisper, remembering that terrible evening, so long ago, when the hillmen raided Moonfire Farm and carried the baby away. "O' gentle, swainly tot, there you is."

Cautiously breaking the web, he reached in and stroked the child's golden head. "Too fair a fly," he said mournfully. "Kept here so long, with never no chance of scaddling. Trapped bad and proper you be. She binds you close and snares you forever in Her bewitchery."

And in that moment, the barn bogle's fears left him. Nothing could compare to the ageless imprisonment of this infant. The sweet bundle that the farmer's wife had sung over, rocked in her loving arms, and nourished at her breast could never leave this place. Away from the High Lady's magical restraint, the mortal world would burn away those stolen years as swiftly as Grimditch's hair was shriveling in the fire.

Sighing sadly, the barn bogle could not imagine any fate worse and he hoped that whatever dreams visited humankind, only the sunniest called upon this tiny one. The farmer and his wife had been the closest Grimditch had ever come to having a family. In his own peculiar boglish way, he had loved them dearly and they had, in their turn, permitted his trespass with kindness and affection. The farmer had even thought him important enough to warrant coming to the entrance of the barn and announcing the birth of his son.

"Ol' boggart!" his joyous voice had rang. "There be a new member of this household born here this day! A fine an' perfect son, no less. First of a long line, if the Lord allows us to flourish. So a health to you and a blessing on us all."

Grimditch sniffed as he gazed down. "Grimditch would give his neck to save you," he murmured. "If I could."

Then in a low, unpracticed voice, the barn bogle began to sing. It was one of the lullabies he recalled hearing in those long ago dusks when he would creep out into the yard, to hear the farmer's wife comforting her child. Sometimes he pretended it was meant only for him, and he had memorized every cherished word.

A peaceful smile spread over the child's face. Grimditch no longer cared what would happen to him. He had caused the precious baby to be happy. That was the only thing that mattered now.

FAR FROM THAT CHAMBER, in one of the deepest regions of the Hollow Hill, in the remote sepulchre of the royal house, Lord Fanderyn waited. It was a grim and lonely place, forbidden to all save Rhiannon Rigantona, and he was risking everything by calling a meeting here. But where else was safe from spying eyes and straining ears? By the feeble light of a partially covered lantern, set upon the magnificent tomb of High King Ragallach, Lord Fanderyn nodded courteously as those he had summoned entered. Solemnly, he welcomed each one to this most secret and treasonous gathering.

The twelve figures who had stealthily made their way to that secluded spot were now standing before the imposing stone tomb and regarding one another warily. Five tall elfin nobles, from the highest-ranking families, were present: Lord Limmersent, descended from a house of princes in a lesser kingdom long fallen into ruin; Marquess Gurvynn of the lost land that bordered the Cold Hills; Earls Brennant and Tobevere of the Flowering Woods, long since burned; and the Lady Mauvette. She had been lady-in-waiting to the late Queen Winnifer, whose dust now lay in that very tomb alongside the bones of her beloved husband, the High King. Also gathered in that cool mausoleum were four kluries: Ambert Bilwind, Dolofleur Spony, Hengot Vintril, and Trimple Munnion. The remaining three were goblins: the knights, Sir Begwort and Sir Hobflax, and the commander of the door guards, Waggarinzil.

Lord Fanderyn held up his hand to quell their anxieties and draw their attention to him alone. If anyone else had summoned them here, they would not have come, but Lord Fanderyn commanded much respect and trust among the nobles and better creatures of the Hollow Hill.

"Put your doubts aside," he reassured them, his calm voice echoing somberly around the walls. "There are no spies here, no hidden ears nor clacking tongues to report your attendance."

He paused and Earl Tobevere, aged and venerable with a sunken face and a wispy beard that cascaded in silver curls from his chin, said what the majority was thinking.

"How now, my lord," he began in cautious tones. "Why are we sent for? 'Tis not long since the passing of noon in the world above. Why bid us hither from our beds and why such unseemly haste?"

He gestured to his attire. He was still dressed in his robe and slippers.

"And why do the galleries reek of burned hair?" asked Earl Brennant, flicking at his drooping nose disagreeably. "I cannot chase the foul fume from my nostrils."

The goblin knights both nodded grumpily and Sir Hobflax rubbed the drowse from his yellow eyes. They had not even had time to put on their hauberks and felt ill at ease without the weight of cold mail hanging from their shoulders and clinking when they moved.

"It is certain death for us to even approach this vault!" Hengot Vintril uttered in a scared whisper. "I should know, I scribed it in the law book myself whilst M'Lady stood over me. I doesn't like it. I doesn't like it."

Lord Fanderyn smiled gravely. "What better spot to speak of that which we crave most?" he said. "Here we may speak freely, and he who would betray our trespass would betray his own. Each of you knows that, and I judge that each of you desires the same as I."

"And what is that?" demanded Lord Limmersent, proud and raven haired and determined not to trust anybody.

"Liberty!" Lord Fanderyn answered. "To rid ourselves of Her tyrannical yoke once and forever more."

He had spoken so loudly that his voice bounced off the other tombs and the echoes took many moments to die. There was a stunned silence. Never had his audience heard such audacious words, voiced so openly and with so little regard for secrecy and discretion. They had expected a furtive meeting of whispered malcontent and an airing of grievances and displeasure. This was too much.

The kluries, who were smaller in stature and lineage than the rest, spluttered and shushed and threw their hands up in horror. The noblemen stiffened and turned pale, while the Lady Mauvette stared desolately at the tomb of her dead mistress.

The stone was ornately carved in the image of a beautiful faerie woman sleeping next to the likeness of her royal husband.

"Every twilight I came here," Lady Mauvette said, her hazel and amber eyes bereft and brimming. "To lay flowers and keep the candles burning—until the High Lady forbade it. To what purpose was my life then? I, who had served my queen with my every breath. Yes, I would be done with Her bans and Her vicious reign."

"And you others," Lord Fanderyn continued. "Each of you has, at one time, murmured discontent to me—of the slights, the humiliations, the cruelties, the false charges brought against those closest to you, the banishments, the murders done for spite and sport. I know what stirs in your private minds. You would be rid of this loathly Lady and bring an end to Her tyranny."

"Do not presume to speak for me!" Lord Limmersent decried, his haughty face scanning the surrounding darkness suspiciously. "I want no part of this conspiracy. Long may the daughter of Ragallach remain upon the throne and longer still shall I, and all in my household, pay homage and swear fealty unto Her."

With a scared expression, he turned on his heel. Were they all mad, speaking so brazenly of rebellion? She would find out; She would learn who was there and what was said. Her agents lurked in every shadow, even here in this forbidden place that Fanderyn the fool deemed so safe. There was no sanctuary in the Hollow Hill. The whole reckless plot would be exposed before dusk. Perhaps if he fled directly to Her chamber and confessed everything, She would be lenient with him.

He was about to leave when a heavy, gauntleted fist closed around his shoulder.

"Stay a moment, my lord," Waggarinzil said gruffly. "Hearken a whiles longer."

Lord Limmersent pulled himself free of the goblin's tight grasp. "Do not dare lay your claw on my person!" he commanded.

Waggarinzil brought his piggish snout close to the aquiline nose of the frightened noble and snorted threateningly. "By my old nanna's lung spots," he said with a growl, "you doesn't think you'd be let out of here with your head still wed to your shoulders, does you?"

Lord Limmersent pushed him away and, with a superior sneer on his face, strode toward Lord Fanderyn.

"Her fair, ageless Majesty shall hear of this!" he threatened. "And all of you shall pay with your lives. Aye, and the lives of your families and servants also! Now, command that swinish brute to let me pass. Hail to our deathless Queen!"

"Deathless?" Lord Fanderyn shouted back. "Do not be so sure of that!"

"What riddles do you speak?" Lord Limmersent cried. "How can you question the immortality of Rhiannon?"

"Yes," said Earl Tobevere, eyeing Lord Fanderyn shrewdly, with his wrinkled hands clasped over his beard. "What flows beneath those words? You are not given to idle talk. Our very presence here is a testament to that. There is no other with repute enough to fetch us from our beds to this forsaken place."

The others murmured in agreement and stared at Lord Fanderyn expectantly.

"Waggarinzil," he began. "Tell them where our most supreme Lady is this very hour."

The goblin stood to attention, which caused his ears to flap and bounce in front of his scaly face.

"Riding," he reported. "In the wild forest—with the Redcaps."

"How many?"

"All of them, my lord."

Eleven pairs of curious eyes regarded him keenly.

"Out there?" exclaimed Sir Hobflax, blustering with indignation. "Without an escort of knights?"

"With those untameable savages?" gasped Lady Mauvette. "They can turn in an instant."

"Oh, the keepers are with them," Waggarinzil added. "They was ushered out by whip and by rod, not two hours since."

"'Twas only a few nights ago the court trooped through the forest," one of the kluries blurted in confusion. "Why should She ride again so soon? The bounds have been beaten and honor given unto to the ancient serpentine forces as tradition insists."

Lord Fanderyn observed the astonished and puzzled faces of his audience.

"That is not the only intrigue this morning," he continued. "Before that, the spriggans were called out. Only three of them have returned and She came back unhorsed."

His listeners shook their heads in disbelief. What was happening? This was unheard of.

"Hagwood is throttled with secrets," he resumed. "Yet this is one that even She is afraid of. Yes, even She. Out there, under oak and beech, something has happened, a thing that has never occurred before. Rhiannon Rigantona is in fear."

Lord Limmersent stroked his sharp chin thoughtfully. "How can the Deathless One be afraid?" he wondered. "'Tis only the promise of death that disquiets the spirit."

"Yet even now she is abroad," Waggarinzil stated. "Attacking a foe that has already scattered one army and caused Her to flee for reinforcements."

The kluries glanced at one another nervously. The goblin knights glowered as they clenched their fists and the nobles frowned as they considered this disturbing revelation.

"If She is afraid," Marquess Gurvynn said slowly, "then surely the Unseelie Court also has reason to fear. We should be battling alongside Her. This unknown enemy is like to destroy us all."

Lord Fanderyn laughed. "If this menace was a threat to the Unseelie Court," he assured him, "She would not ride out to meet it with the lowest ranks and keep we nobles unaware. No, She has encountered a thing that imperils She alone, and we are to remain ignorant of it, lest we also use it against Her."

"What can it be?" Lady Mauvette asked. "An enchanter, mightier than She?"

"Some monster crawled from the bogs on the moor?" added Trimple Munnion.

"A magical device with power enough to blast Her to dust?" Dolofleur Spony suggested, with a hopeful grin on his wide face.

Lord Fanderyn smiled at them. "I too have pondered hard on this," he said. "But now, I believe, the answer is found."

They stared at him and waited.

His keen eyes gleamed at them. "Long ago," he said, his clear voice resonating in that dismal place, "when the Puccas still labored in the forge, making artful toys for the royal prince and princesses, there was rumor of one special trinket, most cunning and splendid."

"Rumors do not overturn thrones," Sir Begwort interrupted with blunt impatience.

Earl Tobevere stroked his silver beard and half closed his eyes as he thought far, far back.

"There was whisper of something at the time," he remembered. "But the nine Puccas were ever secretive at their labors. Was it not some great gift for the King?"

"Surely," Lord Limmersent interjected, "that was just before the murder of Ragallach—by Alisander, his own son and heir?"

Lord Fanderyn nodded. "So it was," he said. "And thus was it forgotten. When the heinous murder was discovered, the Redcaps slew the Puccas, for they had made the crystal-handled knife that had killed the King. Then, with the spriggans, they hunted Alisander through the forest and shot him with poisoned arrows as he was crossing the Lonely Mere."

"A black time in our history," Earl Tobevere commented grievously. "We had dared to hope the evil years were over. The troll witches had been defeated and, for a brief while, the forest was fair and wholesome. Dunrake it was called in those faraway days. Then a curse fell upon Ragallach's house. Clarisant, the High King,

Alisander, all gone. . . . The forest grew dark and hostile and Dunrake became Hagwood."

"And shadows lengthened beneath the Hill," Lady Mauvette agreed.

"And this trinket?" the Marquess asked. "Do we know what it was?"

Ambert Bilwind, the klurie, had not yet spoken, but now he cleared his throat with a stuttering cough and peered up at them through one of the three pairs of spectacles that were balanced on his beaky nose.

"My elder brother, Yimwintle," he began in a sorrowful voice, "was librarian to the High Lady. Two days ago, she killed him. Why, I do not know, though does She ever give a reason? Whim and fancy are enough."

No one said anything. They knew the lethal caprices of Rhiannon Rigantona and the countless she had put to death without cause.

"There, among his books, she murdered him," Ambert murmured softly. "His lifeblood spilled across his beloved scrolls and tomes, flooding through and spoiling the pages, blotting out the words he so adored. I cannot forgive Her for that, and so I tell you now what I have told my Lord Fanderyn and what Yimwintle once whispered unto me. My brother knew what the Puccas forged for the King. It was at Rhiannon's bidding. She said it was to be a present for her royal father and stood by them in the forge to oversee its making. The Puccas put all their skill and cunning into this gift for their beloved King, but they had been lied to—Rhiannon wanted it for herself alone."

He paused to take a much-needed breath, while his listeners held theirs.

"The thing they made," he continued, "was a box—an enchanted, golden casket. Not large, yet stronger than the hardest diamond, and, once locked, impossible to open without the one magical key. As soon as it was complete, Rhiannon, or Morthanna as she was called then, snatched it away."

"Whence and for what purpose?" demanded Lord Limmersent.

Ambert shook his head, and the spectacles on his nose clattered together. "I know not," he said. "Nor what She placed within."

"No one does," said Lord Fanderyn. "But I, too, have my spies and this I know: Amid the confusion and shock that followed the King's murder, Gofannon, the Smith, stole that box. He was not slain with his eight brethren, but fled out into the forest carrying that thing with him—and the High Lady has been searching for it ever since."

"When She ordered us to plunder the ancient mounds," Sir Hobflax declared, "it was that box She was seeking? Not gold coin and treasure?"

"What need does the High Lady have for moldering jewels torn from brittle bones?" asked Lord Fanderyn. "No—She was anxious to find that casket, to discover the place where the Smith had hidden it."

Waggarinzil scratched his large, bristled ears and nodded. "Many's the time She stole out at night, alone," he said. "From the gates, I watched Her slink into the gloom, sometimes in guise, sometimes not. By my gristly joints, how many holes and dens did She pry into?"

"But She never found it," remarked Earl Tobevere. "Else I am sure we would know. Have we not observed the doubt which dances in Her eyes in unguarded moments? Do you recall when Lady Visset boasted of a treasure box given her by her husband? Remember the fear and the fury on Rhiannon's face? She had the entire household arrested and put to torture. The Lady's face was peeled like a pear and when Rhiannon found the box to be naught but a small wooden chest containing baubles and trinkets, did you mark Her relief and hear Her shrill laughter?"

"Aye," said Lord Fanderyn. "And then a dread seemed to clutch at Her and She flung the box away."

Marquess Gurvynn held up his hand. "I was nigh Her that very moment and I heard Her words when She stormed by. I did not understand them at the time. Now I begin to have the sense of it."

"What did She say?" Lord Fanderyn asked urgently.

"'Not the one, it was not the one—and so my fear remains. When will I be free of that final fetter?'"

"By my wormy liver," Waggarinzil snorted. "Why is She so scared of a box?"

"Not the box itself," Lord Fanderyn corrected him. "But whatever it contains."

He stared at those gathered around him, but none of them could begin to guess what that mystery may be. It was incredible to think that Rhiannon was afraid of anything.

Presently, the Lady Mauvette broke the thoughtful silence.

"A final fetter," she repeated in a horrified breath. "How much more of a tyrant would She be if She was freed from whatever that may be and naught was left to brook Her cruel ambitions? What further cruelties would She commit?"

Lord Limmersent's eyes narrowed. "And it is your belief this golden box, containing Her only fear, has been found at last?" he asked Lord Fanderyn. "Out there, in the forest, and She is battling to win it back?"

"I do not believe it has been found," came the noble's confident reply. "I know it."

The others looked at him in amazement.

"How do you know this?" the Marquess snorted. "Tell us at once!"

"I shall do more than tell you," Lord Fanderyn answered. "I shall show you."

Reaching for the lantern, he uncovered it fully. Then he stepped around the large tomb and gestured to something hidden behind it.

"Now is the time," he said. "Come, show yourself."

The others started in surprise.

"You lied!" Lord Limmersent cried. "There is a spying presence here, maybe more than one!"

"Peace," Lord Fanderyn told him. "Have no fear of this, the newest recruit to we conspirators. She is risking her life just as much as the rest of us."

"She?" the goblin knights asked in unison.

The noble nodded and held out his hand. "Come," he instructed. "Show them."

There was a brief hesitation. Then they heard a shuffling noise and something stirred behind the tomb. A squat shape moved in the darkness and finally shambled shyly into the lantern's light, her dirty skirts brushing along the dusty floor and the steeple of white hair teetering from side to side.

It was Gabbity.

"The nursemaid!" Lord Limmersent exclaimed in astonishment. "What crooked jest is this?"

Lord Fanderyn stepped aside and Gabbity ambled forward with a timid, gummy grin on her warty face.

"Well met, m'lords," she addressed them shyly.

"This is your proof?" Lord Limmersent cried. "This filthy drab is as close to the High Lady as Her accursed owl!"

The goblin nursemaid jabbed a finger at him. "Not no more I ain't!" she retorted. "Gabbity's done with Her. If it weren't for my little lordling, I'd have mixed up my strongest poison and quaffed it clean down long ago. Hate Her I does. No one knows how much. She were always a bad, broody child. I had no liking for Her then—proper sour I reckoned when I first glimpsed Her and I was proved right. No, m'lords—I want Her gone more than most. That's why I done found Lord Fanderyn as soon as I could this day."

"And why I summoned all of you here," Lord Fanderyn told them. "A most extraordinary fortune has brought to us our deliverance."

He bowed slightly and signaled that the time had come.

Gabbity reached into her pocket and slowly drew out the golden key. It flashed and shone under the lantern light and sparkled in every staring eye.

"Soon as I peeped it I knewed it were important," she boasted, twirling it in her thumb and forefinger, casting glittering reflections up into their wondering faces.

Lord Limmersent was the first to master his surprise.

"It is the very key?" he asked.

"How can you doubt it?" Lord Fanderyn said. "Have you ever seen work more delicate, more proclaiming of its makers?"

"Never," he murmured almost reverently. "But . . . what use is it without the box? Where is that? How do we know it has even been found? The key alone will avail us naught."

"Beggin' your lordship's posh pardon," Gabbity interrupted. "My waxy lug holes can't help but flap at times and they do catch the rarest talks twixt M'Lady and Her owl. I know as how that very Smith was in the forest just a few days back and not a moment's peace has M'Lady had since. Now you tell me, if he hadn't brought back some great thing She's in high terror of, why has She been like a cat on the fire?"

"The Smith?" Lord Limmersent cried. "The Last of the Puccas has returned to Hagwood? We must seek him out!"

Gabbity smacked her empty gums. "Oh, you can't be doing that," she said. "M'Lady made sure he can't help no one no more."

"The Smith is dead? Then tell us, crabbed crone, how did you chance upon this key?"

Gabbity gave a gummy grin. "Was brought in by a dirty barn bogle," she said. "Dirtiest, stinkiest, hairiest, scratchingest spit of vermin you ever did see."

"How came such a lowly creature by this treasure?"

"He filched it. Stole it from some mighty personages out there in the forest, from what I gathered by his bogly chatter. You know what thieves barn bogles are. Fingers like glue they've got."

"Personages?"

"Two skin swappers, he said, but what that may mean, the serpents alone know. Great magicians or warriors I'll be bound. Who else would the Smith have given the box to?"

"Warriors . . . aye. That must be the truth of it if Redcaps and spriggans were required to deal with them." Sir Begwort grunted. "Surely doughty heroes from a far-off kingdom that the Smith met upon his travels."

Lord Limmersent stroked his chin as he considered all he had heard. "That would make sense. The Smith would not have entrusted so mighty a thing to anyone less."

"And whatever that box contains," Lord Fanderyn said, "it has the power to destroy our deathless Queen. That is why She is out in the forest now, endeavoring to win it back."

Excitement and hope thrilled the air and they stared at Lord Fanderyn with scared yet exhilarated faces.

"We must acquire that box before She does!" he urged them. "Therein lies our only hope. Go rouse the trusted of your folk, take your horses from the stables, ride into the forest, and if we cannot bargain with whoever possesses it, we must wrest it from them. We cannot fail in this—we cannot!"

Jubilant beyond measure, buoyed with the dream that the impossible was now almost attainable, they hurried out to return to their halls and commence this bold scheme.

Lord Limmersent took Lord Fanderyn by the shoulders and clasped him close. "By nightfall we may be regicides!" he laughed deliriously. "Was there ever such a happy prospect?"

With a wave of his hand, he saluted then hastened from the sepulchre. Only Gabbity and Waggarinzil remained behind.

"Long may your name be sang evermore in the ballads, Gabbity Malatrot," Lord Fanderyn praised her.

The goblin nursemaid performed a clumsy curtsy then handed him the golden key. "Use it well, m'lord," she said, furling his fingers around it and patting his closed fist. "Now I must be back; I've a barn bogle to clothe and the little lordling will be missing his faithful Gabbity."

With a cackle and a waggle of her warty jaw, she scurried off, humming to herself and wondering what might rhyme best with *Malatrot*.

The enchanted key safe in his possession, Lord Fanderyn leaned against the tomb of the late king and let out a long sigh of relief and gladness.

"So it begins," he said with an exhale, bowing his head. "Triumph is nearly ours. Ha—I can almost taste it."

"That's burnt hair, m'lord," Waggarinzil reminded him.

The noble laughed and threw back his head. It had been a long time since genuine laughter had been heard in the Hollow Hill.

Waggarinzil blinked at him. The silver lantern light shone starkly against that aristocratic profile, delineating each strong, proud feature. He almost looked like he too was carved from stone and the goblin commander could easily imagine a golden crown resting upon that dignified brow.

The goblin wondered what manner of king Briffold Fanderyn would make. Would he be fair and just? Would he heal the divisions at court? Would there be no more fear thronging the hallways, no more murders, no more spies tattling malicious tales? Perhaps his reign would be as glorious as Ragallach's had been and the Hollow Hill would ring with music and song once more.

Waggarinzil scratched his piglike snout and sucked his fangs thoughtfully. Even if Lord Fanderyn was a rotten king, he wouldn't ever be as tyrannical as Rhiannon.

"There is much to be done!" Lord Fanderyn declared, clapping him on the back. "Let us make this day one to remember!"

"A moment, m'lord!" the goblin called.

"What is it?" Lord Fanderyn asked, his eyes bright and eager to be gone.

"Just this," Waggarinzil said, with an apologetic tilt of his great ugly head that rattled the mail of his coif as he rammed his sword home.

The noble gaped at him, his eyes round and startled. He snatched several breaths, then crumpled and his body slid off the blade to the floor.

"Why . . .?" he asked, gasping, as his life leaked out.

Waggarinzil shrugged diffidently and stooped to prize the golden key from the lord's hand.

"There's no advancement for a lowly door warden in such a world as you might rule," he uttered in a matter-of-fact tone. "Besides, you ought not to have trusted me with your grand plots. You said as how the High Lady had eyes and ears everywhere. You was right. Very rash of you—thought you was smarter than that. Just goes to show, don't it." He held the key aloft and smiled broadly. "Imagine the reward She'll bestow on me for giving Her this, and informing on the lot of you? By my horny toenails, I might even move into your grand hall, Fanders old chap, and take your fair daughter to wife. Shame you won't be around to dandle your grandchildren on your knee. I wonders what they'll look like?" And he let loose a filthy laugh.

Lord Fanderyn made no answer. His eyes were already dim and the hope of the Unseelie Court and the whole of Hagwood expired with him.

The goblin commander stepped over his body and rubbed his gauntleted fists together.

"A most memorable day indeed," he chuckled.

• CHAPTER 8 •

MYTH AND SACRIFICE

THE UPTURNED SHIELD HAD RACED through the darkness at terrifying speed. Bufus Doolan's torch was extinguished by the rushing air almost immediately and so the three young werlings were blind as they juddered and bounced down the perilously steep chute-like chasm.

Kernella had not stopped screaming since the first moment they had plunged down the hole at the start of this wild journey, but she had long since grown hoarse and her terrified yell had dwindled to a perpetual croak.

It was a horrible, jarring plunge. The shield slid and skimmed and spun around as it flew ever downward. Sometimes it banked against the sides of the sheer tunnel wall; sometimes it threatened to flip right over and they had to lean as far back the other way as they dared in order to try and keep from capsizing.

The shield's leather strap was the only thing they could grasp hold of, but it was ancient and crumbling in their hands and would not last much longer.

A violent pounding pursued them. Stones from the collapsed ceiling had tumbled down the hole and were thumping close behind, hurtling in a wild, rumbling chase. At one point, a hot coal from the Tower Lubber's fire glowed ruddily as it rattled along until a boulder crushed it in a burst of fizzing ruby cinders.

Gamaliel wondered when their luck would run out. If they did not overturn, then one of those enormous stones would smash into them—sooner rather than later. Even if they managed to survive this breakneck plunge, what would they find at the bottom? Freezing cold water in the pitch dark of the deep? A maze of passages where they would blunder around till they perished? Or maybe just an abrupt, bone-smashing end, before being buried beneath stones.

Bufus felt as though every bone in his body had been shaken loose. His joints were aching, his teeth were clattering in his head, and he had bitten his tongue twice. And yet, in spite of the danger and the terror and the sore tongue, he found the ride exhilarating and breathtaking. So what if they were careening to their deaths? Death held little fear for him now. It was the most fantastic, intoxicating thrill he had ever known. If Mufus, his twin, had been there, he would have relished it too. Thinking of his dead brother, Bufus giggled at the thought that he might be joining him soon and began laughing uncontrollably.

Sitting beside him, bumping and thudding along, Kernella heard him laugh and stopped screaming.

"He's gone crackers!" she cried croakily. "Let me off—let me off!"

Gamaliel wished he could close his ears. The situation was dreadful enough without listening to them shouting and laughing as the stones thundered closer behind.

The shield shot deeper into the earth, rocketing around twisting bends, going faster and faster until suddenly the tunnel fell away and it went soaring through empty air. With a tremendous, walloping smack, it hit the ground and whizzed ferociously around like a spinning top. The leather strap finally disintegrated and the werlings were flung clear—just as the pursuing rocks and boulders came storming behind.

There was a crunch of metal. The shield was flattened and crushed, mangled into misshapen fragments as the avalanche surged down.

The noise was unbearable. Gamaliel shouted for his sister but his voice was drowned in the tumult.

The larger stones toppled on their sides and silence descended.

Gamaliel spluttered, his face covered in dirt. He lay scrunched in a corner against a rocky wall, where he had rolled when the shield had thrown him clear. Cautiously, he wiggled his fingers and toes. Nothing seemed to be broken. He could feel a few cuts and grazes on his hands and knew his back was smothered with bruises, but he was otherwise unharmed.

Unable to see anything in that impenetrable darkness, he sat up and listened. Where were the others?

"Kernella?" he called. "Where are you?"

A strange muffled noise answered him. His sister had landed on her head and was wedged in the gap between two boulders. Although she was not injured, she did not like being upside down and it took several undignified grunting efforts to pull herself free.

"You and your barmy ideas!" she scolded in the direction of her brother, unable to see him in the inky black.

Still tittering, Bufus Doolan was clutching his aching sides and in a great happy voice, shouted, "Let's do that again!"

"You're both loopy," Kernella rasped. "How are we supposed to find our way out of this? We dropped for ages and ages. This is a lot deeper than Meg's caves. I can't see the hand in front of my face. It's blacker than a mole's armpit down here. We're trapped!"

Gamaliel groaned. Compared to listening to his sister's vexed carping, being crushed to death suddenly didn't seem so bad after all.

"I can't see a thing!" she repeated. "We're done for and it's all your fault!"

"If you'd studied harder at wergling and mastered bats," Gamaliel countered, "we wouldn't be blind down here and you could lead us out."

"You know I don't like bats!" she retorted. "I did sparrows instead."

"And what a mess you made of that!" joined in Bufus. "Lumpiest bird I ever saw. 'That'll never fly,' Mufus said to me."

"Birds are difficult!" she countered defensively. "Why, only Master Gibble and Finnen could do them properly."

"Oh, here we go," Bufus muttered. "Finnen this, Finnen that."

"He was the best wergler of us all!" she cried.

"Till they caught him cheating!" the Doolan boy snapped back.

Kernella huffed and folded her arms. "I'd feel a lot better if he was with us," she grumbled. "He'd find a way out somehow, wergled or not."

Bufus blew a raspberry. "Just 'cos you think the sun beams out of his backside, doesn't mean it does!" he jeered. "He'd be doomed along with the rest of us down here."

"I think he's got enough problems of his own," Gamaliel said softly. "The battle may have started by now. I wonder what's happening up there?"

"We'll never know," Bufus replied in a matter-of-fact tone. "No one will ever find us. We're as good as dead."

"You're as cheerful as Tollychook," Gamaliel told him.

"Just being practical, Gammy. Unlike you and Goofy Nelly over there, I'm not scared. If I gasp my last in this horrible hole that's fine by me; I'll be with Mufus all the quicker. I was hopin' to do a bit more in the war and maybe get called a hero or summat, but this will have to do."

He frowned and looked over to where Kernella was shaking with silent laughter.

"What's so funny?" he demanded.

"You!" the girl blurted. "A hero? As if!"

They began squabbling and Gamaliel covered his eyes so he didn't have to see them. Then he bolted upright.

"Shush!" he hissed.

His sister put her hands on her hips and glared at him. "Don't you tell me to—"

She stifled her words and gazed about her. Without them even realizing, a pale light had been growing steadily. It was a gentle, ruddy glow that poured through a low passageway into the farthest corner of the cave.

The werlings drew together and stared around them. High over their heads, the opening to the pit they had tumbled from was now blocked by tons of fallen stone. They could never return to the upper world that way. The only escape from that cave was through the dimly glimmering passage.

"But what's beyond there?" Gamaliel whispered. "What's making the light?"

Memories of the fearsome candle spright made Kernella shudder. "I don't like it," she said. "Could be anything through there."

"Can't be worse than what's in here," Bufus sniggered with a sideways look at them both.

Suddenly, a voice cut through their fear and apprehension. It was a kindly lilting sound and there was a definite chortle when it said, "Are you going to dawdle out there long? Shall I go back to sleep till you make up your minds? What a racket you make. I'm afraid you disturbed such a pretty dream I was having, such bonny vivid colors . . . I wonder if I can retrieve it?"

The werlings stared at one another. The voice had come from beyond the passage.

"Doesn't sound frightening," Kernella admitted.

"But who can it be all the way down here?" her brother asked.

Bufus snorted and was already marching away toward the light. "One way to find out," he told them.

Gamaliel and Kernella hurried after him. Crouching under the low roof, they walked the length of the passage, then shuffled to a stop when they emerged into the space beyond.

Bufus let out a long, admiring whistle.

It was a huge, pear-shaped cavern that tapered high beyond the reach of their eyes. Rising in the center was a cone of steps climbing in an ever-diminishing circle and carved with two enormous serpents. They coiled about the stone and each other until their tremendous heads met at the bottom; their large eyes stared fixedly into the opposite face.

One serpent was black and hideous, mottled with livid moss and lichen, and with a starved and cadaverous appearance. A long row of bones protruded through the sculpted scales. Its monstrous, pocked face had terrible bulbous eyes and a fearsome jaw filled with jagged teeth. Two misshapen horns twisted from its spiky brows.

Not even Bufus liked the look of that horrible face.

The other, however, was beautiful. It seemed to have been carved from some glimmering, honey-colored mineral. The scales were like facets of a long, winding jewel and its form was lithe and elegant, looping around the steps in shapely, stately rings.

Kernella marveled under her breath. The sculpture's head was ravishing. It was wrought of gold and amber, with sparkling amethyst eyes that shone beneath gem-encrusted brows. Wisdom and benevolence were written on that peerless, opulent countenance. Whatever hand had fashioned that head had created a wondrous thing to be admired and adored and spoken of in hushed, venerating tones.

Gamaliel could hardly believe it. What was this place? He took a step closer. The unexpected spectacle of the serpents had so dazzled him that he had not yet examined the source of the light.

Between those incredible faces, hanging from a slender chain suspended from a silver bracket, was an egg-shaped, bronze lantern. The joyous light within spilled out through differently sized round holes and spread over the surrounding stone in a rich, golden mist, flooding the cavern floor with deep buttery hues.

Gamaliel and the others came a little closer. Then the voice they had heard outside spoke once more.

"How disagreeable," it said. "I do enjoy a really good dream. That really is irritsome."

"Hello?" Kernella piped up, looking searchingly around them. "Who's there?"

"Dear me, no," came the voice. "You'll have to come a lot nearer than that, and don't drag your feet. A body would think you had all the time in the world. Well you don't, not a bit of it. Hardly any time left for you to do what has to be done. You trudge so slowly. I'm shocked, I really am."

Bufus pulled a face. "Show yourself!" he called crossly.

"Bother," the voice said; "I so dislike sitting in a draught."

Approaching cautiously, the werlings peered up at the steps for any sign of movement. Gamaliel expected a concealed doorway to swing open and he watched the stonework closely. Kernella was convinced the voice was coming from one of the serpents' heads and was sure one of those jaws would hinge open. She hoped it wasn't the ugly head. It was Bufus who saw it first and he elbowed them both. "There!" he cried.

He pointed at the copper lantern. It was the same size and shape as a duck egg and it was jiggling on its chain. As they watched, a section at the front of it opened with a tiny squeak and there, within, was the strangest sight any of them had ever seen.

Sitting inside was a small, shining creature. It looked like a wizened old man, half the size of the werlings, wrapped in gossamer strands of fine golden hair from his head and his beard. It cocooned him completely and only his wrinkly little face was visible. But his lustrous skin glowed like a summer's afternoon and his eyes were brilliant and penetrating.

The cavern was suddenly swamped in a richer, warmer light and the shadows went flying up to the unseen ceiling. Kernella gave a yelp and hopped back but Bufus and Gamaliel were too amazed to move.

"There," said the strange creature. "Is that better? Now do be quick, I don't want to catch a cold, you know."

Bufus was the first to recover. "What are you then?" he asked impertinently.

The creature twitched his little nose and nibbled a strand of beard. "I don't think you would understand, Master Doolan," he answered at length.

Bufus started. "Here!" he cried. "How do you know my name?"

"I know all your names," came the smiling reply. "You were in my dream. I may even be dreaming still—sometimes I don't know if I'm awake or sleeping."

"I'll pinch you if you like," Bufus suggested dryly.

The stranger chuckled then looked at the others.

"And to you, Gamaliel and Kernella Tumpin," he said, "welcome."

The werlings stared at him in astonishment. They had never heard of any being like this before. Finally, Gamaliel overcame his stupefaction and took a pace closer.

"You know our names," he began, shyly. "Might we know yours?"

The creature leaned back and the lantern bobbed up and down. "There were so many," he said with a slow shake of his golden head. "You can't expect me to recall them all. Most of them were quite ridiculous and undignified, absurd in fact. I told them so but they would insist and as for the propitiatory offerings . . ."

He frowned gently as he considered. Then he brightened and the radiance swelled. "You may call me . . . Nest," he said. "Yes, that will do for now; I like that—nice and cozy and sleepy. An ideal place for the beginning of things, from which new life will one day hatch. No need to confuse you with any of the other silly titles, now is there?"

"Suppose not," Gamaliel answered, still bewildered.

"He's a nutcase," said Bufus.

The creature called Nest laughed and nodded back at him. "Oh, I've certainly been inside many of those," he agreed.

Kernella disliked nonsense of any sort and felt this had gone on quite long enough.

"Listen," she said, "I don't care who you are or what you call yourself. You could be Danny the Dangly Dewdrop for all I care. The only thing I want to know is how to get out of here."

Nest beamed at her. "She's so right," he said. "That's what you should be searching for, the way out and back to your little world up there. I dreamed it; I know."

"If you know there is one then tell us!" said Bufus.

"Oh, it isn't that easy," Nest answered with a tut. "I can't give you advice; it isn't allowed. I can't help you or influence you one way or the other. I'm just supposed to be dreaming here, until—well, until the proper time. You shouldn't really be here at all and you must never tell anyone about me. I can't have sightseers mobbing the shrine, throwing litter about and chipping bits off the Wyrms for souvenirs."

"Worms?" repeated Gamaliel incredulously and he gazed up at the gigantic serpents. "They're the biggest worms I ever saw."

"Imagine the fish you'd catch with them," Bufus sniggered.

Nest shifted in the lantern, causing it to swing from side to side.

"Have memories up there faded so much?" he asked despondently. "Does no one recall the twin Wyrms of Dunwrach? How very ungracious and thoughtless of you all."

"We've never heard anything about them," Gamaliel said. "But then, we're only werlings; no one takes any notice of us. Or at least, they never used to."

Nest stared into a space above their heads. "That really is no excuse," he said petulantly. "It is their might and vigor that courses through the forest and makes it what it is. It is to appease and honor them that the hillfolk troop forth every quarter of the year and process along the ancient serpentine track. Do they not remember that? I really do call it most ungrateful and wretched."

"I'm sorry," said Gamaliel. "It isn't our fault."

"Without the Wyrms, there would be no forces to draw on, no ancient channels to tap. There would be no High Lady and the troll witches could sit on their teetering heaps of stone till every one of their bottoms turned purple and still be just as powerless as before. As for you shape changers . . . well, at least you surrender yourselves back into the cycle when your time is over. Your Silent Grove shows some respect and is more powerful than you realize."

Kernella grunted in exasperation. "Will you stop wittering on and tell us the way out?" she demanded.

Nest's bright eyes fixed on her, and the keenness of his radiant glance inflamed the red in her hair and made her freckles stand out even more than usual.

"I told you," he said. "I'm not permitted to help. Your world is no longer mine. What I can do, though, is grant you a choice. Actually, *Choice* was another one of my old names and may be again one day. If you choose wisely—oh, let's be reckless and bend the rules a tiny bit. If you make the right choice, you may ask three questions of me and I will do my best to answer."

"You mean like three wishes?" asked Bufus.

Nest looked at him in surprise. "If you refuse to listen properly, Master Doolan, then you really should keep silent. You only make yourself appear more foolish than you are and that is a feat indeed."

Bufus made a face and looked away, but his curiosity soon overcame his indignation.

"What is this choice?" Gamaliel asked.

Nest grinned and his soft, shining beard parted as two small hands emerged and gestured to the serpents upon either side.

"The glorious Wyrm," he began, indicating the golden head on his left, "is called Myth. The other, unlovely Wyrm is named Sacrifice."

"Morning, Myth!" Bufus tittered.

Kernella thumped him.

"So what do we have to choose?" she asked.

"Oh, not you," Nest answered. "Didn't I make myself clear? How remiss of me. No, it is Gamaliel who must decide. He alone has the responsibility—for all of you."

"Gammy?" cried Bufus. "It's because of him we're in this mess. I wouldn't trust him to pick his own nose. Why him?"

Kernella wanted to thump her brother too. "Yes," she chimed in. "Why him? He's hopeless."

"Because," the creature told them, "he himself has already been chosen, and not by me—by another."

"Me?" Gamaliel asked in surprise. "Who's chose me, and what for?"

"You will realize that when the time comes," Nest said with a gentle smile.

Gamaliel chewed his lip. He was certain he would bungle it and get it wrong, whatever it was.

"So what do I have to choose here and now?" he murmured.

"This trial is simple," Nest said. "Hold out your hands."

The young werling obeyed and the stranger raised his arms. The radiance flashed and shimmered and the werlings blinked. Gammaliel felt a sudden weight in his grasp and when the light subsided, he discovered that he was now holding a large, golden crown.

"It's way too big for his daft head," sniffed Kernella jealously.

"The diadem is not for your brother," Nest chortled. "It is for one of the Wyrms. You, Gamaliel, must choose which of their heads it should grace and place the crown upon it."

Gamaliel looked at the serpents' heads again. The beautiful golden one, called Myth, truly was ravishing and spectacular. The crown would sit so perfectly upon that stately brow. It seemed made for it and he could feel his sister willing him to place it there.

Swallowing nervously, he looked across at the other and remembered, with a shudder, that its name was Sacrifice. That head was repulsive and frightening. The bulging eyes looked ferocious and savage and the two tortured horns that grew above them left no room for any crown.

Instinctively, he edged away from it.

"Hang on," Bufus interrupted. "What happens if cloth head Gammy here gets this wrong?"

The creature in the lantern grinned back at him. "Oh, forgive me," he said. "I thought I'd told you. Most forgetful—I'm still a little drowsy, I expect. If Gamaliel makes the wrong choice, then nothing will happen."

"Nothing?"

"Absolutely nothing. Fancy me forgetting that; what a silly old bright seed. You three will remain down here until you die from thirst and starvation, while your friends and the world you know up above will perish."

The three werlings stared at him, aghast.

"W-What sort of choice is that?" Gamaliel stuttered. "That isn't fair."

"I don't believe I mentioned anything about it being fair," Nest said with a laugh. "Whatever gave you that idea? Nothing is fair in any world, neither mine nor yours. Surely you have learned that much already. What you must do is choose the best course, use your insight and experience. Inform your choice by using everything you have learned. That is the best anyone can do. And if young Gamaliel Tumpin cannot choose, then I'm quite sure no one else in Dunwrach can. You are the key to this whole sorry business; remember that."

Gamaliel looked helplessly at Bufus and his sister.

"Don't foul this up!" the Doolan boy warned him.

"Put the crown on the pretty one!" Kernella prompted. "Even you can't get that wrong."

Gamaliel took a faltering step toward the great, golden serpent head. It really was stunningly beautiful. The amethyst eyes were scattering Nest's wondrous light in a thousand violet splinters and the amber depths of its being seemed to throb with a secret, inner life.

Myth was the most ravishing and exquisite thing his rustic eyes had seen, except perhaps for . . . the High Lady.

Gamaliel choked back a cry and stepped away. He thought of the Tyrant of the Hollow Hill and how her beauty was but a mask to conceal the evil corruption within. Then he thought of Peg-tooth Meg, her sister. She was deformed and grotesque, and yet she was loved. The Tower Lubber had devotedly waited an age for her and she was adored by the sluglungs.

Turning a determined but fearful face to the others, he said, "If I'm wrong, I'm sorry!" And he rushed toward the ugly serpent and drove the crown between the horns, wedging it in and bending it out of shape.

"No!" Kernella yelled. "What are you doing?"

"You mad freak!" Bufus shrieked, lunging forward to pull the boy and the now-buckled crown away, but it was stuck firmly in place.

"The choice has been made," Nest announced solemnly.

"That wasn't my choice!" Bufus protested, shoving Gamaliel to the ground.

"Nor mine!" fumed Kernella.

But it was too late. There was an ominous cracking of stone and the immense, horrendous serpent began to break away from the steps as supernatural life coursed through it. The famished-looking body lifted itself clear and the bony coils unraveled from the shrine with a *crick* and a *clack* along its entire length. The monstrous head shook itself and the bulging eyes blinked and roved around. It reared up above the terrified werlings, the massive horns ripping into the darkness overhead as the horrifying jaws snapped open and from that great throat came a rumbling bellow. It was so bass a sound, it was like the cataclysmic movement of mountainous rocks in the stomach of the world. The werlings felt it travel through their bones rather than heard it with their ears. It shook the cavern and set the loose stones on the floor dancing.

"You idiot!" Kernella wailed, slapping her brother. "Look what you've done!"

The Wyrm writhed and twisted and glowered down at them. Both Kernella and Bufus threw their hands in front of their faces.

Sprawled on the quaking ground, Gamaliel stared up at the night-marish vision and waited for it to strike. But the stone serpent did not attack. The forbidding face descended slowly, the jaws closed and the impossibly deep roar ceased. With a crunching of scales the repulsive body unwound and spread itself around the cavern until the forked tip of its tail was switching in front of its eyes and it encircled the shrine completely.

"What a song and dance," Nest said mildly. "Still, it does him good to have a stretch now and again." He looked at the werlings' petrified faces and chuckled.

"Why so dismayed?" he asked. "Gamaliel Tumpin has done well. He has chosen Sacrifice and that blessed choice will prove to be the saving of you all. It would behoove you to thank him, while there is time."

Bufus and Kernella gawped in astonishment. They could not believe Gamaliel had got it right when they had been so mistaken.

"But it's a monster!" Kernella squawked.

"He has such a sweet nature," Nest assured her. "A trifle clumsy, but he can't help his size any more than you can help being so covered with freckles. He does love to have his chin scratched, so bear that in mind. Dear me, child, have you not yet learned to look below the surface? How many more lessons must you endure? If Myth here had been chosen, well . . . he exhales poison—nasty filthy habit."

Gamaliel lumbered to his feet, feeling awkward and apprehensive. He eyed the great Wyrm warily then mumbled, "Can we ask the three questions now?"

"You may indeed," Nest replied, with a slight bow. "I will do my best to answer, although I feel the tiredness stealing over me again, so make it swift."

"How do we get out of this crazy place?" Bufus snapped.

"There are many ways out," the creature laughed. "It depends whither you wish to go."

"Back up there of course!" Kernella told him.

Nest looked at Gamaliel. "There are many places you could go," he said. "But here is yet another choice. Only one is the right spot for you to be in this desperate hour. Which shall it be?"

"I don't know," Gamaliel answered. "I thought back to the tower, but are you saying we should go somewhere else?"

"Is that your second question?"

"No," cried Kernella. "We must go back to Finnen. Is he all right?" The creature in the lantern turned to her. "Hear me now, mistress," he told her gravely. "The watchtower is under siege and Prince Tammedor is slain. If you return thither, Finnen Lufkin will not be there to meet you. He has a grimmer task ahead of him. The last battle for Dunwrach is fast approaching. Blood will be shed on many sides, for the pulpy fruits of treachery are now being harvested, and they are the most bitter."

"The Lubber is dead?" Bufus uttered dismally. "That stinks!" He kicked the lower step angrily. He had liked the Tower Lubber and regretted the harsh things he had said to him.

"Such is the price of war," Nest said. "And many more will die before a new day dawns. Enemies unlooked for will ride under bough and branch tonight."

Gamaliel felt numb. The news of the Tower Lubber's death stunned him. He thought of the years Prince Tammedor had waited to be reunited with his true love and how painfully brief that eventual meeting had been. He hoped Liffidia and Tollychook were safe—but what was going to happen to Finnen?"

Kernella was wringing her hands in alarm. "Are we going to die?" she cried, unable to keep the question bottled in any longer.

"That is a very poor third and final question," Nest answered.

Gamaliel whisked around. "That wasn't it!" he denied, clapping his hand over his sister's mouth. Kernella pulled his fingers away frantically. She was already regretting asking the stupid question.

"No, don't tell us!" she gabbled hastily. "I was scared and upset; I don't want to know. It just popped out without me thinking."

Nest gave a little sigh. "Yet it has been given voice," he said solemnly. "And I must answer."

"My big fat mouth," Kernella warbled reproachfully.

"You great hefty lump!" Bufus snarled at her. "Gone and wasted our last question. You Tumpins are rubbish."

Nest gazed at each of them in turn and took a long breath. "Of you three who stand here, before the Shrine of the Wyrms of Dunwrach," he began, "only two will see the rising of the dawn."

"One of us is going to die?" Gamaliel murmured, appalled.

Bufus jerked his head back and grinned. "That's fine by me!" he said darkly. "I've been ready since Mufus was killed."

"But it might not be you!" Kernella hissed, afraid and panicky. "It could be me! Oh, why did I have to ask?"

Gamaliel looked at them sorrowfully. The Doolan boy was miserable without his brother and Kernella was beside herself with dread. But grief and worry would have to wait. He stirred himself and moved closer to the lantern.

"Please," he began. "You still haven't answered the first question. "Where are we to go? If not the tower, then where? What should we do? Can anything even be done?"

The shining creature smiled sadly at him. "I have said too much," he tutted. "Advice is a danger at the best of times. But this small crumb I will spare you. Evil must always be fought. It must never be allowed to flourish unchallenged. Resist it always. Every precious life is worth the losing if it keeps evil at bay but a moment longer. It is who and how you fight that defines you."

"Oh, blah blah!" Bufus groaned impatiently. "Just tell us where we've got to go!"

Nest's eyes sparkled at him. "Though fire burns the homely sky and knights march upon your friends," he said, "and though fearsome riders storm the forest, your best road leads elsewhere. Seek the dolmen, the ancient stones known as the Devil's Table. When the first shades of dusk creep through the grasses, you will find someone close by who can aid you more than I."

"The Devil's Table?" Gamaliel asked. "Where is that?"

Nest rubbed his eyes sleepily and the radiance began to flicker and dim.

"The Wyrm will take you," he said with a yawn. "If you ask Sacrifice politely, he will bear you thither, for those old stones are but markers along the ancient serpentine trackways and he knows the route well. He is the answer to your question and will see you safe through the darkness."

The werlings turned to where the enormous head of the Wyrm watched them. The bent crown on his head looked extremely foolish but he was still a frightening sight. His great jaws opened slightly and rows of jagged teeth sawed the air.

"You're kidding me!" Kernella exclaimed, shaking her head resolutely. "I'm not going anywhere near that!"

Bufus laughed at her, then strode fearlessly up to the terrible stone face and crouched in front of those cruel-looking fangs. Stretching out his hand, he reached under its chin and gave it a vigorous scratch.

The bulging eyes rolled back and a peculiar, hollow purring vibrated through the serpent's body.

"He likes it!" Bufus declared.

"You're a braver wergler than me," Kernella told him.

"Always did like that," Nest murmured drowsily. "From the beginning of days, before the ice, before the ways were lost. Now climb up and hold tight to those horns of his."

The Wyrm twisted his vast head to make it easier for them to clamber on and Bufus ran around to be the first on board. Kernella and Gamaliel hung back. The girl was anxious, but her brother wanted to continue speaking to Nest.

"Who are we going to find at the Devil's Table?" he asked. "What sort of creature is it?"

Nest curled up snugly and closed one eye. The cavern fell further into gloom.

"He is one whom you have forgotten," came the mysterious answer. "But it is his wisdom you need more than mine, young Master Tumpin. Now let Sacrifice take you from this place and do not try to find the shrine again, for you shall not. I must return to the dream, I'm so very, very . . ."

He pulled the front of the lantern closed and the glazed holes in the copper glimmered dimly.

"It's going to get pitch black in here again!" Bufus warned them. "Get on while you can still see."

Gamaliel took one last look at the egg-shaped lantern and scrambled onto the serpent's head.

"Come on," he told Kernella.

His sister pulled a reluctant face. "I'll wait for the next one," she joked nervously.

The light was growing ever more feeble and darkness was pouring down from above.

"Hurry!" Gamaliel shouted at her.

Taking a deep breath, Kernella took his hand and hauled herself up.

"Grab hold!" Bufus advised them.

They wrapped their arms around the horns and the Doolan boy yelled, "All right, you giant bird's breakfast—take us to the Devil's Table!"

Sacrifice lashed his tail then swung it in a high sweeping arc around the cavern walls as his snaking body began to move forward. Around and around the massive Wyrm went, picking up speed with every revolution. Kernella clamped her eyes shut and held on grimly. Bufus yodeled with relish and Gamaliel saw the shrine whirl by. The lantern light was almost gone now. He could just make out the glazed holes but nothing more. The strange luminous creature within was dreaming and Gamaliel knew they would never meet again. But what Nest had told Gamaliel had placed a cold shadow over the young boy's spirit, and his thoughts were troubled.

The darkness rushed by. The serpent was tearing around ever faster, roaring and growling. Then, suddenly, with a thrash of his enormous body, he left the ground completely. He flew over the curving wall, spiraling higher and higher. The conical steps of the shrine were left far below and the monstrous Wyrm raced into the absolute night at the top of the cavern.

"We're going to smash into the ceiling!" Gamaliel yelled.

Without opening her eyes, his sister screamed. Bufus was whooping hysterically, and Gamaliel's own terrified shrieks joined them.

· CHAPTER 9 ·

APOTHEOSIS

THE SUN HAD JOURNEYED FAR into the western sky when Rhiannon
Rigantona rode her horse up the slopes of the Hollow Hill. She did not
pause until she reached the summit. Only then did she allow the poor
beast to rest. The silver-white mare snorted and stamped, its sweat-
smeared flanks shivering.

The hilltop was bare, save for solitary clumps of heather and gorse
and one nub of stone that resembled a worn-down tooth. It commanded the best view of her wild land.

The gilding glory of the late afternoon blazed over the High Lady's
white mantle, and if any spied her from a distance, they would have
thought the hill was tipped with flame.

Sitting erect in the saddle, her dark eyes surveyed the country
spread beneath her.

Hagwood stretched far in every direction. The leafy ocean of the vast forest rippled and shimmered. Far away, three wooded humps broke the undulating surface and, to the south, the pine-crowned crag known as the Witch's Leap thrust into the sky.

The High Lady glanced to the east, where the watchtower was only a hazy finger of stone jutting above the horizon. Knowing her sister was grieving inside that broken fortress drew a smile upon Rhiannon's face.

"Mourn long and keen, sister," she hissed. "At last I have hurt you deep."

Her eyes lingered on the remote tower a moment more, then she turned the horse and gazed on the bare cold hills to the north.

"Soon," she murmured. "Soon."

"My Lady?" asked the owl on her shoulder.

Rhiannon only smiled in answer and looked westward. The full gold of the lowering sun flamed over her symmetrical features.

Beyond the edge of the forest, the sheet of water called the Lonely Mere looked like a fiery lake under the apricot sky. Farther still, the country became wild, rolling, scrubland.

"Yonder my realm ends," she said. "And many leagues hence stands the nearest inhabited farm. So many isolated dwellings of man surround us. And then there are small hamlets and villages, market towns and the germ of cities."

"Man is a creeping pestilence," the owl commented. "He breeds too swiftly and often and his whelps gobble up the land. Thy kingdom alone is safe from the rash of his accursed huts. Never again shall he dare to live so close to Hagwood."

A single crease furrowed the High Lady's smooth brow. "Hagwood was always too small for me," she breathed. "If I could be free of fear, then my rule would extend farther than the wind blows."

The owl fluttered its eyelids in surprise. "That would be a kingdom indeed!"

"What else is fitting for a goddess?" she answered. "My name should be feared and lauded in temples across the land and over the seas. Mortal men should make sacrifices unto me and abase themselves before my shadow. Is that so very much to ask for?"

"Not for thee, oh matchless Queen!" the owl fawned.

"But I can never attain divinity while the chance of death dogs my every thought," she spat bitterly. "Oh, my provost, if I could only be free of that threat. Such a ruler as this world has never imagined would arise and I would set torch to this petty, squalid realm."

The owl sank its head into its shoulders and feared to say any more. There were always new layers to its mistress's malice and ambition.

Her merciless eyes returned to the western border of the forest and the ghost of a sneer marred her loveliness.

The owl could not begin to guess what new evil that expression portended.

Rhiannon jerked the reins and the mare began to descend the hill once more.

"Some corners are too green," she observed.

CAPTAIN GRITTLE REMOVED HIS HOBNAIL BOOTS and thick woolen socks, then rubbed his calloused feet. A blissful expression passed across his knobby face and he grunted with pleasure.

After delivering Grimditch to the goblin nursemaid, he and Bogrinkle and Wumpit had returned to the spriggan quarters and were confounded to find them deserted. Every hard wooden bed was empty. Wumpit even searched beneath them, but no other soldier could be found.

Commanding his two subordinates to remain there, Captain Grittle had stomped off in search of answers—but none of the door guards would tell him anything, and Waggarinzil had laughed at him as a reward for his earlier insults.

Now, sitting on his bunk, he squeezed his toes and contemplated the rows of empty beds.

The spriggan quarters were sparsely furnished and had few comforts. Combat was their main passion and everything they owned pertained to that. Each spartan, regimented bed was separated by a rack of weapons and zealously maintained armor hung above the mean headboards. Special stout posts known as kill tallies stood at the feet of the beds and every notch represented a slaying. Many of the beds were decorated with trophies: garlands made from teeth, the occasional skull, inherited or stolen medals, carvings of warlike faces, the captured helms of fallen foes, a blanket made from hides stitched roughly together, jars of ears, and charms to bring glory in battle. At the far end of the dormitory was a large snarling wolf's head made of brass. It was a depiction of Batar, the spriggan god of war. Offerings were made to it before every battle, but the call out that morning had been so sudden there had been no time, and that disturbed Captain Grittle even more.

"Summat's up," he said for the thirtieth time. "The whole garrison emptied out. . . . That's not happened since the dead King's day."

"And we missed it," Bogrinkle groused, lying on his own bunk with his shield as a pillow, as was their custom. "You and yer notions of plots and assassins and having a secret scout 'round. All we did last night was fall foul of the High Lady, and if She didn't need us to ferry that barn bogle here, She'd have sent us for the chop."

"Might still do that," Wumpit added. "And don't forget that pong of singed hair earlier. That weren't normal."

Captain Grittle glowered at his subordinates then began picking his scabbed legs where the blood moths had chewed him. He thought about rubbing filth into the tiny wounds and infecting them to encourage scarring, but trying to brag a victory over moths sounded piteously feeble.

To make himself feel better, he reached for the family medals hanging above his bed and pinned them to his breastplate.

"Then the Redcaps were droved out," Bogrinkle put in. "There's a big fight happenin' someplace."

"Our lot oughtn't've gone into battle without making offerings to Batar," Wumpit said gloomily. "The Big Bad won't like that, mark me. Summat sore will happen."

"How many of our lads bought it, I wonder?" mused Bogrinkle.

"If old Ruffnap's finally curled up his ears," the captain said quickly, "I bags his silver knives."

They began arguing about spoils and only stopped when a slovenly milkmaid came sloping in with two large wooden buckets yoked about her fat neck and one grubby finger lodged up her nose. It was

Squinting Wheyleen, a shiftless goblin girl with a lazy eye and two long plaits of seldom-washed hair that trailed in her buckets.

"'Tis true then," she said, slopping green milk over the floor as she planted her bare feet apart and regarded the almost-empty barracks. "I'd heard your lot had run off. How come you stayed behind? Scared, was yer?"

The enraged spriggans sprang to their feet and snatched up their daggers.

"We ain't scared of nowt!" Captain Grittle roared, puffing out his chest so that the family medals clattered together. "An' they did not run off, orders from Her Majesty most like."

"We was out the whole night on special commission, catchin' barn bogles!" Wumpit boasted. "If we'd have been here for the order, we'd have marched out with the rest! Hearts and stomachs of iron we have."

"Don't you be leavin' that nasty wet mess on our floor!" Bogrinkle warned her.

The goblin scoffed and slopped a bit more milk on purpose. "Such brave warriors," she laughed. "'Fraid of naught, 'less it's wet an' drippy. Then you hitch up yer skirts and pelt, squealin' like so many urchins bobbin' in a pot."

"Get you gone!" the captain threatened.

"'Least we ain't affrighted of the sunshine!" Wumpit barked.

"Where's Fat Jansis with our ration of worms and cheese?" Bogrinkle demanded.

The milkmaid chortled and spilled even more of her burden. "Jansis thought it weren't needed," she told them. "The Redcaps weren't there fer my milk dole, an' seein' as how some of your crew have only just started dribblin' and drabblin' back, all shamed an'—"

"They're back?" Grittle cried. "Where? How many? And when?"

She shrugged and again the buckets tipped.

"About a dozen or less," she said. "'Least there was when I went to gander at the south gate. The door guards are holdin' them there till they knows what to do with 'em. Ooh you should see the bruisy glares your lads are flinging 'em. But them's proper scared all the same and look like kicked dogs. The guards are havin' good sport chafin' 'em."

Captain Grittle pulled his boots back on, too angry to even bother with his socks. "Oh, is they?" he growled. "I'll not stand by and allow that!"

He leaped over the widening pool of green milk and stormed off down the hallway, heading for the main south gate. Ordering the milkmaid to mop the floor and fetch their rations, Wumpit and Bogrinkle hurried after him.

Squinting Wheyleen dredged the finger from her nose and flicked the harvest into one of the buckets. Then she shambled her way to the dairy.

At the south gate, fourteen spriggans were lined against the wall and Waggarinzil was taunting them. They were the first to have returned after the humiliating fiasco that morning at the Battle of Watch Well. Peg-tooth Meg had sent them fleeing into the forest when she summoned the well waters to burst forth and rain down. Once their blind panic had ebbed and they found themselves wandering in the trees, they immediately realized the horrendous trouble they were in. They were deserters.

The bravest of them decided the only honorable course was to return to the Hollow Hill and face their punishment. Others slew themselves rather than confront the High Lady's wrath and many more were still lost in the wild woods.

Those brave fourteen now stood, sheepish and cowed, in front of Waggarinzil. He was having a very satisfying day and could scarcely wait for the Queen to return, but whiling away the time tormenting this sorry lot was the most fun he had enjoyed in ages. The spriggans had always bragged about their courage and how being infantry was so much more honorable than sitting atop a horse in battle. They had often derided the door wardens, calling them nothing more than ignoble butlers.

Waggarinzil licked his lips. He had years of conceited insults to repay.

Each one had been disarmed as soon as he had come staggering through the gates and the confiscated weapons were ranged in a gleaming row on the ground before them.

"By the old wolf's blood!" he bawled. "If you had tails they'd be clamped tight twixt your legs! I never saw a more hobbled clump of craven daisies. Where's your vaunted dandy-cock swaggering now, eh?"

Parading up and down, his gauntleted thumbs tucked into his belt, his ugly, piglike smirking face mocked them.

"Look at you," he scorned. "The famous standard bearing foot soldiers, sniveling and trembling like the frightened sheep you really are. So, what happened out there? What scattered you and forced the High Lady to come back and whip the Redcaps to finish what you'd started?"

The spriggans shook their heads miserably. They were too ashamed to repeat it and they bitterly regretted returning to the hill.

It was then that Captain Grittle came blustering in.

"What's this slouching?" he shouted. "There's no room for slacking in my garrison. Straighten up there, Jibbler, and you, Chumpwattle— wipe that snotty nose!"

The old training seized control of them immediately and they stamped to attention.

"Don't you barge in here and spout your orders," Waggarinzil told him crossly. "This is out of your jurisdiction."

Grittle grabbed the hilt of one of his knives. "Step aside, gate slave!" he snapped. "This is infantry business and I'll have your head as a basket to keep our old socks in if you don't move out of my way."

"By my leathery liver," the goblin breathed, narrowing his fierce green eyes. "You'll pay for that before this day is done."

"What's a servile chain puller goin' to do to me?" sneered Captain Grittle. "Set hoity-toity Fanderyn on me if you want. He don't scare me neither. I'm the High Lady's bodyguard, remember."

Waggarinzil chuckled foully. "You won't get no bother from m'lord Fanderyn," he said with a sly, inscrutable smile. "But this matter comes under gate regulations so these straggly pigeons are mine. Cast your slanties on that wibbly lot; they're half jelly with fear and I mean to find out why."

Hearing the word *jelly* the spriggans grimaced and shuddered at the memory of the sluglungs they had fought.

"They was 'orrible!" one of them burbled.

"Who was 'orrible?" Captain Grittle demanded.

"Nasty frogspawn vilies," answered another. "But we was battlin' like heroes and would've won through if . . . if the wet hadn't come gushing up and pouring down."

The captain slapped his own face. "And you ran!" he seethed. "One spit of drizzle and you scream like popped mice."

Waggarinzil let out a belly-shaking laugh. "So that's all it was!" he cried. "The mighty garrison went scampering in case their bloomers got drenched. Hoo hoo—She won't have liked that."

He nodded at the other door wardens and winked at one of them to run and tell the torturers to stoke their braziers and get the tongs ready.

"I shouldn't like to be in your skins once they gets to work on you," he sniggered. "But then, in a day or two, you might not be wearing your skins anyway."

Captain Grittle knew he was right. The garrison had fled in the midst of battle. There was no crime worse than that for a spriggan. The traditional, deserved punishment was to be strangled by their own mothers in order to preserve the honor of the family name. Yet he understood too well that morbid, unreasoning terror of water. He would have done the same.

"Is this all there is of you?" he asked in a leaden voice. "Where are the other captains?"

The shame-faced soldiers shook their heads and stared at the floor.

"Still racing like hares 'neath the trees, I'll wager!" Waggarinzil cackled. "What a day this is!"

While he guffawed, Bogrinkle and Wumpit came running up behind their captain—but before they could ask what was happening, they all heard a steady thudding rhythm overhead. Out on the hillside, a horse was descending.

"It's Her!" the spriggans wailed as one.

Waggarinzil rubbed his gauntleted hands together. After he watched the High Lady vent her fury upon those cowards, he would give her the enchanted key and inform against the conspirators. It really was the best of days.

Suddenly, the great doors yawned open. The first pale shadows of evening were gathering outside and Dewfrost, the silver-white mare, came cantering into the Hollow Hill bearing Rhiannon Rigantona on her back.

Waggarinzil was the first to greet the Queen with a flourishing bow. The High Lady ignored him and turned her lovely face to the petrified spriggans.

"So," she said, in an icy voice that chilled them even more. "Is this all who have slunk back?"

"Aye, Your Supremeness," Waggarinzil informed her, still locked in his scraping bow.

The owl on her shoulder opened its golden eyes wide as he stared at the commander of the door guards. The untrustworthy goblin had never groveled quite so much before, and the bird's well-honed suspicious mind pondered on it. What treasonous wheels were in motion under that mail coif? But its mistress was speaking and the owl had to spin its head about to pay attention. He would cogitate on the goblin's unprecedented smarm later.

"You have debased the repute of the Hollow Hill," she condemned the spriggans. "Never in the long history of this realm was there ever such a faithless dereliction of duty. I should not suffer you to live an instant longer, unless it be wracked by the worst torments my dungeons can devise, for throttling is too lenient a sentence for you rabbit-hearted lice. Your names will be bywords for cowardice and dishonor for as long as the standing stones endure."

Her soldiers fell on their knees and wept. They could not bear the pitiless glint stabbing from those cold eyes.

Captain Grittle and his two lackeys set their jaws against the inexhaustible malevolence that flowed from her. The others were doomed to agonizing and lingering deaths. Grittle stared at the floor. His only consolation was the bright thought that he could have the pick of the booty in their quarters now.

Then, to the amazement of everyone present, spriggans, goblins, and even the owl, the High Lady said, "You have disgraced your once-proud legion, yet there is still a chance for your redemption."

Waggarinzil started and stood upright, his surprise displayed fully on his porcine face.

"My Lady?" blurted Captain Grittle.

She bestowed a smile upon them, perhaps more terrible than any sign of anger because it was so wholly unexpected.

"I have a task for you," she announced. "Succeed in this and your dereliction of duty will be atoned for and forgiven."

The spriggans could hardly believe their ears. Surely this was some trick?

"Wha-what would you bid us do, M'Lady?" one of them stammered.

Rhiannon ran her fingers through her horse's silver mane. "There is a strip of woodland," she began, "in the western corner of my realm. It lies between the old cinder track to the west and the Hagburn. I want you to march there at once, without delay."

The spriggans nodded briskly, unable to understand why they had been pardoned, when none had ever been before. But they weren't about to argue or question it.

"That woodland is overrun with vermin," she continued. "Disease-ridden wer-rats have infested the trees. They must be destroyed and the wood purified with fire. Do you understand? Let none of those creatures escape. I want them killed, every last one. Leave nothing but charcoal and smoking bones behind."

"W-wer-rats?" the spriggans murmured ignorantly.

The High Lady's eyes flashed at them with impatience.

"Some of them were present at the well this morning," she said. "But the redoubtable Captain Grittle knows them also. He encountered one by the Crone's Maw."

"The spying soapy weasel!" Grittle declared.

Wumpit pulled a face. "Is there more of them lickle things?" he asked. "Eewww!"

"Just so," Rhiannon said. "Now be gone, Captain. Lead your foot soldiers and be sure the task is accomplished."

The reprieved spriggans hastily grubbed up their weapons and praised the High Lady for her clemency, and they were out of the door before she could change her mind.

Last to leave, Captain Grittle and his two subordinates saluted her. "For the honor of the legion," he announced.

"No Captain," she corrected. "For obeying your Queen and the extermination of Her enemies. See that you do not fail in this."

"Not one of those pink rats will escape my knives," he promised. And with a final nod, he, Wumpit, and Bogrinkle hurried out into the evening.

While they had departed from view, the owl held on tightly to its mistress's shoulder as she dismounted and gave the reins to Waggarinzil.

"Keep Dewfrost here," she commanded. "There is not time to summon the esquire from the stables; I shall return swiftly and ride out once more."

The goblin bowed again, but by the time he raised his head, she was already striding through the courtyard, headed for the hallway beyond.

Waggarinzil pushed the reins into another guard's hand and went lumbering after her.

"Gracious Majesty!" he called urgently. "I would have words with you."

The High Lady showed no sign she had heard him and continued on her way. Only the owl turned its head around to see the goblin come running after them.

"If it please you, Your Ladyship?" Waggarinzil implored. "I have information of the highest import to relay, and . . ."

"Do not dare hound thy Queen in this fashion!" the owl hooted back at him. "Return to thy gate duties."

"But I have this day unmasked a most treasonous plot," Waggarinzil insisted. "They are conspiring to usurp our most fair and noble ruler!"

Rhiannon wheeled about and the full power of her wintry glance fell on him.

The goblin halted and cast his eyes down.

"Tell me," she demanded. "Yet I warn you, if this is some minor, prattling species of testimony intended to paint your own petty enemies in unfavorable colors, you have chosen the wrong day. I shall cut off those flapping ears of yours and feed them to you, then nail your tongue to the very door you are supposed to be guarding."

Waggarinzil shook his head so hard that his whiskery jowls joggled and one of his ears hit him in the eye.

"Never, My Queen!" he vowed. "By my scales, I swear it. This is most vital, the biggest hazard to your throne there ever was."

Her eyes burned at him.

"Explain," she commanded. "And quickly!"

The goblin took a breath as he marshaled his thoughts and sorted them in order. He would save the revelation of the key till last.

"It was Lord Fanderyn," he began. "This very day he called a secret meeting by the tomb of your dead father, the High King."

The High Lady and her owl regarded him afresh.

"'Tis death to enter there!" the owl cried. "What miscreants attended this heinous assembly?"

With the exception of Gabbity, Waggarinzil recounted everyone who was there. The nursemaid's presence was bound up with the key and therefore part of his main disclosure.

"Suspected brewers of dissent, each one," the owl remarked. "Such vain folly. What doth they hope to achieve? They are but paltry spiders, spinning trifling webs to catch the lightning."

The unrelenting glare that beat from Rhiannon's eyes pricked and stung the door guard. He could feel her seeking out his innermost hidden thoughts, trying to peel away his guile and uncover the truth.

"Why was this meeting so different?" she demanded. "Why risk so much to repeat the same tired bleating?"

"Ah," Waggarinzil said. "You put your royal finger straight on it, Majesty. Fanderyn told them there was summat out there in the forest, summat new found, that you was frighted of—"

"He dared say that?" the owl screeched in outrage. "Noble or no, his head is forfeit!"

Rhiannon's face became even more frozen. "Did he say what manner of thing this was?" she asked in a glacial voice that made the goblin catch his breath and set his scales crawling.

"Said it were a gold box," he answered.

There was ghastly pause. The owl was so shocked to hear those words that its talons bit into its mistress's shoulder and blood welled through the cloth of her mantle. No trace of pain showed on her face.

"A gold box?" she repeated in a calm yet deadly voice. "Why should I fear such a thing? Did Fanderyn say what it contained?"

"N-No, Your Mightiness," the goblin stuttered, wishing he was far away from her baneful glance. "If he knew, then he weren't telling. But he sent the others into the forest to hunt for it. The nobles and their followers left some while ago by their own hidden ways, but the goblin knights are still here, waiting for the sun to set. They'll be creeping out soon, I'll wager. And the kluries have been sneaking here and there with poisoned words all the day."

"But the others have gone in search of this box?" the owl screeched. "With the sole intent of doing their Queen harm. Death is too generous a gift to bestow upon them!"

Rhiannon held the goblin with her penetrating stare. "There is more to tell," she said. "Continue."

Waggarinzil felt as though a thousand scorching knives were slashing at him and sweat was pouring from under his coif.

"One other was there!" he confessed in a rush. "One close by you, Your Sovereign Majesty."

The High Lady's head reared slightly and for an awful instant the owl thought the goblin was accusing him. His creamy feathers were already fluffed in righteous indignation when his mistress whispered, "Gabbity."

"Yes, Highness," Waggarinzil declared. "She was there; she betrayed you."

Rhiannon Rigantona's eyes left the commander of the door guards and at once the horrendous, piercing tension collapsed. His knees buckled under him and he mopped his face, breathing hard.

"The lordling will need a new nursemaid," the High Lady said malevolently.

"What will you do to her?" the owl hooted with vicious enthusiasm. He had never held any regard for the nursemaid. She was far too vulgar and overly familiar toward his mistress.

"Something new must be devised for Gabbity," Rhiannon said. "I will attend to that personally. The torturers will be too busy with the others—I do not wish to overwork them. Theirs is a careful, precise, and considered art. Yet what did the crone think she was doing? What use could she be in any plot against me?"

"Her head is addled by years of cradle coddling and knitting," the owl muttered with disdain. "She is lack witted, that much hath always been plain."

"And yet Briffold Fanderyn is nobody's fool," the High Lady stated. "He must have seen some merit in her presence. He has never courted her lowborn company before. Why now?"

Her eyes gleamed suddenly. "The barn bogle!" she declared. "Gabbity learned something from the beast when it awoke and went scuttling straight to Fanderyn. Oh how his lordship must have relished that."

"May his death be a prolonged symphony of agonies," the owl cried, scandalized. "With every fresh instrument playing a new chord of pain."

"It will," she promised.

Waggarinzil made a strange wheezing noise, which he hastily tried to cover up with a cough.

Rhiannon turned her eyes upon him once more.

"I fear," he began in a flustered, mumbling voice. "I fear there won't be no dungeons for Lord Fanderyn."

The High Lady's eyes burned with her imperishable anger once more. She took a predatory step closer to him.

"And why not?" she hissed.

Waggarinzil was shaking. "Be-because," he stammered with gulping breaths. "Because . . . I run him through with my sword."

There was a heavy silence, which not even the owl dared break. The immeasurably dark centers of Rhiannon's eyes grew larger than ever and the goblin felt as though they were devouring him.

"You ran him through?" her voiced stabbed. "You, a base door guard, presumed to murder one of the highest ranking nobles of my court? It is not for you to decree such a death."

"I-It was the only way!" he cried. "The only way to save you from his plot."

"What have you omitted?" she commanded. "Do not think you can conceal any intelligence from your Queen."

The goblin fell against the wall and held up his gauntleted hands. "Spare me!" he wailed, trying to ward off that unbearable stare. "I was not trying to hide it from you, Majesty, by my miserable bones, I was not! I was merely saving the best till the end. To show how loyal I am, to prove my worth to you and praise your glory."

"Show me?" she asked. "Show me how?"

Breathing hard, Waggarinzil tore off his right gauntlet and shook it over his bare palm. For an instant something bright glittered on it. Then he plucked it up and held it out to her.

For the first time in many hundreds of years, Rhiannon Rigantona's frozen composure was completely overthrown. A gasping cry left her lips and the tiny enchanted key reflected its golden, dancing light in her midnight eyes.

"My Lady!" the owl exclaimed in wonder.

With a tremulous hand, she took the key from the goblin's grasp, then clenched it fiercely to her empty breast.

"After so many years!" she breathed through her teeth. "So many uncertain years. Now this returns to me."

If she had been capable of any tender emotion, her eyes would have bled with tears—but all she felt was colossal relief and the aching sweetness of victory. Finally, beyond her wildest and most impossible hope, her only fear was over.

Opening her slender hand, she looked again at the small, intricately worked key, inset with the ruby that so resembled a prick of blood.

"It is mine," she whispered to herself. "I, Morthanna, have won—at last."

The owl blinked its tawny eyes and felt an exultant tremor travel through its mistress's elegant frame.

"Thy glory and success were never in doubt, Majesty," it truckled to her. "Now let thine enemies tremble and know the full measure of thy vengeance."

Waggarinzil watched in fearful silence.

Lady Rhiannon clasped both hands together, with the key sandwiched between them as if she feared it would fly up like a moth and escape her again.

"My enemies must wait," she announced. "There is something of higher import to attend to—come!"

With her hands knotted before her, she set off, almost at a run, down the hallway. Waggarinzil was not sure whether that last command was intended for him or the owl, but he followed her anyway.

Through the Hollow Hill Rhiannon hastened: past carved entrances to the mansions of the highest nobles and across the mosaic floors of the courtyards. Dusk was approaching, and her subjects were already stirring from their halls. Bogle pages were running errands. The lesser folk of spindle limbs and ashen faces, covered with pale gray veils, were drifting through the galleries, singing their haunting songs to welcome the new nightfall. Dumpy goblin maidservants were filling silver pails at the fountains and taking them to the great houses where their masters were rising and their mistresses were taking up colored threads to busy themselves in weaving and setting expert needles to tapestries. The eerie world of the Unseelie Court was shaking the drowse of the day from itself once more.

Shy, crawling creatures slid from ancient holes and scuttled up the walls to graze on the moss that grew around the silver lamps, only to flee from sight as Rhiannon stormed by. A group of oakmen, a race who had dwindled and declined in stature over the many years till they resembled bundles of autumn leaves when crouching, scampered out of her way, and their panicking flight looked as if a sudden gale had torn across a forest floor. The mournful shadow widows—gaunt, spectral figures, their sunken cheeks forever flowing with tears, their skeletal frames wrapped in cheerless dun raiment—bowed their heads even lower as Rhiannon passed and wailed more wretchedly than ever when she had gone.

The High Lady swept through her domain like a tempest, hurrying along the passageways and up the winding stairs. Toiling along behind, Waggarinzil's ungainly bulk somehow managed to keep up with her. His face dripped with perspiration and his bowed legs were aching. He had no idea where she was headed. They were now close to the old Pucca lodge, empty since the Redcaps had slaughtered them for crafting the crystal-handled dagger that had murdered King Ragallach.

The lamps were dim in this region of the Hollow Hill and huge shadows swept over the walls like vast midnight wings as Rhiannon pressed on. When the forlorn, blank windows of the Pucca dwellings were behind them, finally, Rhiannon halted.

They had arrived at the forge where the Puccas had once crafted beautiful metal objects. In their strong hands and by their unmatched skill, metal was more malleable than clay and took any form they wished. They could spread it across an anvil like butter and twist it and curl it and stretch it and temper it and mutter spells of burnished permanence over it.

The Puccas had broiled tirelessly before the coals of their forge, wearing their long leather aprons, with their sleeves rolled high and their beards smoking in the furnace heats. In the glorious reign of the late King, a constant thread of black smoke had climbed from the Hollow Hill—such was their unflagging industry.

Breathing hard, Waggarinzil caught up with the High Lady and looked around him.

The smithy was now a sad, neglected place. Nothing here had been touched since the Pucca killings so long ago. No one ever came here; it was another forbidden place in Rhiannon's realm. Dusty webs smothered the overturned benches, and the tools still lay scattered over the floor where they had fallen during the Redcaps' frenzied attack. Unfinished armor and half-completed instruments hung from the beams under the arched ceiling. In the corner, dominating that desolate gloom, was the forge.

The coals were cold and the great bellows woven about with webs. All metalwork was now the province of the kluries in their modest smithy near the stables, where they also shod the faerie horses.

Rhiannon took up a lump of coal and crushed it in her fist. Turning to Waggarinzil, she said, "Awake the fire; make this forge scorch and bake once more."

Astonished and slightly flustered, the commander of the door guards searched for his tinderbox, then smashed up a stool for kindling.

The owl on the High Lady's shoulder paid close attention to Waggarinzil as he nurtured a spark into a flame and set it among the splinters. The fire was soon leaping high and the coals began to glow a dark red, like a heap of smoldering plums.

Rhiannon, however, was not watching. Her mind had slipped back to that delicious day when Gofannon the Pucca had proudly presented her with the golden casket —the pinnacle of his life's work. If he had but known the true purpose for which it was intended, he would have sooner cut off his own hands at the wrists.

"By the sun's stove!" Waggarinzil panted, sweltering in the shimmering heats as the coals blazed more fiercely. "I've never been so poached in all my life. What a blistering day this has turned out to be."

His gruff voice recalled the High Lady to the present. She stepped across the dusty floor to stand at the goblin's side and gazed into the blazing center of the forge. Unable to tolerate being so close to such an inferno, the owl left her shoulder and roosted upon a beam as far away as possible. Fluffing out its slightly singed feathers, it preened itself and waited.

Rhiannon was twirling the tiny golden key in her fingers. The entire smithy was jumping with orange and cherry light, which sparked and flared over the yellow metal and caused the tiny ruby to burn like a bloody star.

The enduring spells that the Puccas had bound about the key could only be undone here. The High Lady knew that well and so, with a contemptuous snarl, she threw the glittering thing into the forge's scorching heart. Bathed in that infernal glare, she held her breath.

A spout of emerald fire flew up, spitting with sapphire sparkles.

Working the bellows, Waggarinzil felt faint. He did not understand what the High Lady was doing, but he wished she would hurry up so he could leave this stifling place. The sweat was running down his ears in steaming, salty streams that dried up before they could drip from the ends. He was sure the top of his head was melting under the mail coif. His eyes were stinging and he could almost feel them shriveling in their sockets. He longed to find a chill damp shadow to rest in and thought yearningly of the cold sepulchre where he had killed Lord Fanderyn.

"Time enough," Rhiannon said suddenly and, to the goblin's wonderment and fear, she thrust her naked hand deep into the searing coals.

"Majesty!" he yelled. "The fires!"

She did not hear him. Her fingers searched in the intense heats and at once a flame leaped along her bare arm and wrapped around her head and shoulders.

Waggarinzil shrieked and leaped up. Was she so completely mad? He gasped and hesitated, not knowing what to do, for a figure wreathed in fire now stood before him. He could do nothing to save her.

And yet, as his green eyes bulged and gaped, he realized that she was unharmed—the fire was not burning her. The greedy tongues licked up through her hair but those raven tresses remained unwithered and her skin did not blacken or char.

She became a pillar of flame: an immortal statue, wound about with streaks of crackling light, wearing a crown of fire. It was a horrendous vision and the goblin drove his knuckles into his eyes to blot it out. Then he fell to his knees and worshipped her.

He had never guessed the full extent of her power. Rhiannon Rigantona was greater than his goblin mind had ever dared to imagine.

Rhiannon had forgotten he was even there. She had taken a small, glimmering shape from the forge and was staring down at the key that now shone with a light all its own. It was so hot that it bubbled the skin of her palm but the blistering wounds healed even as they were made.

Quickly, she strode to the anvil, took up a mighty hammer and dealt blow after blow upon the soft gold morsel. Under the relentless violence of her hate, the key flattened and the ruby cracked.

The smithy trembled and the beams shook. The owl struggled to retain its balance as thick dust spilled down. Throughout the Hollow Hill, the key's destruction caused a quaking disturbance. Lords and ladies rose in fear while goblins gripped their swords and kluries muttered in dismal whispers. Out across the land, the echoing blows went ringing. The trees of Hagwood shook and a rumble of thunder growled through the darkening sky. At the edge of the forest, the Redcaps surrounding the broken watchtower gibbered and covered their ears.

Within those circling walls, Tollychook and Liffidia drew close to one another while Fly whined. Standing upon the battlements, his hair streaming in the sudden cold breeze, Finnen Lufkin stared across the forest roof, flinching with every thunderous crash. Behind him, the sluglungs quivered and pressed close together, their gelatinous flesh oozing into one another for comfort.

Down in the infirmary, the injured birds hid their faces beneath their wings and Peg-tooth Meg lifted her gaze from the face of her dead lover.

The sound was like the tolling of a great bell—and somewhere close by, there came an answering chime.

Meg took out the golden casket and held it up. A piercing, vibrating note was singing out from it, so shrill and high that the surrounding stones began to resonate and crack.

The casket in her hand shivered. "Our hopes are ended!" she cried. "The key has been discovered. Naught can threaten my sister now—she is invincible."

Even in the caves beneath the Cold Hills of the north, the demise of the key could be felt and, in those remote shadows, croaking voices began to mutter.

And then it was over. In the smithy, there was only a thin, shapeless wafer of yellow metal upon the anvil.

The High Lady lowered the hammer and a terrible laugh left her lips, a laugh that seemed to roll through the heavens. Now there was nothing for her to fear. No power could ever harm her. The casket that contained her beating heart would be sealed forever. Only that tiny key could have opened it.

"I am free!" she cried. "The chains of dread and fear are finally unlocked. My true reign can begin!"

Waggarinzil dared to look up from the floor where he was groveling. He could not comprehend what he had just witnessed or what had happened but he could already feel the unparalleled strength that flowed from the High Lady. He was in the presence of a goddess and the realization terrified and awed him. A new order was dawning.

"May I be the first to revere you!" he declared, scuffing around on his knees to kiss the hem of her mantle. "I must worship my mighty Queen, Most Divine Goddess of the Night."

Rhiannon Rigantona lowered her lovely face to look on him and a cruel smile lifted the corner of her mouth.

"Most blessed are you," she said. "To have been here at the moment of my ascendance. You shall be the first of my subjects to venerate me."

"By my worthless scaly skin, I am most privileged, dearest High

Queen of Heaven and Earth. Let me sacrifice a beast to you—or perhaps make an offering of one of my fellow guards. I could go fetch one and spill his undeserving giblets at your feet. Let this humble place be sacred unto your undying name, it shall be your first temple and I . . . I, Waggarinzil, could I . . . ? I mean . . . I could, I could be your high priest."

The High Lady regarded him coldly then stared into the distance, looking beyond the smithy's confining walls. "There will be many temples," she agreed. "Across the land and over the seas and the tributes paid unto me shall be of the richest. Yes, there will be sacrifices, many sacrifices, but I do not think a common door warden is fit to be a high priest."

Waggarinzil caught his breath. He had overreached himself and tried to catch too grand a position.

"Forgive me, Your Holy Goddessship!" he implored. "It is enough to be here at the beginning of your new reign. And, if your lowly servant here played some small—nay, no greater than a gnat's nudging—part in your ascendance then that is reward enough for him."

"You?" she asked.

"The key, Your Most Hallowed Celestialness—'twas me what rescued it from Fanderyn for you, remember?"

Rhiannon's eyes glittered. "Of course," she declared. "The nobles and their squalid meeting, where only you were loyal to your Queen. Uncover your head, most faithful of subjects."

The goblin obeyed at once, dragging the mail coif from his brutish, perspiring head, breathlessly anticipating the honor she was about to confer on him.

"I am grateful to you, beyond the measure of your mind, most trustworthy commander of the door guards," she purred. "You have given me that which I have craved for so many years, the final piece of the riddle that is Rhiannon. Now, at last, I am fully whole, precisely because I can never ever be 'whole' again. It is that special, enchanted emptiness that completes me."

Waggarinzil blinked in confusion, unable to comprehend her words. He had no way of knowing she was referring to the empty space in her chest where her heart should have been.

Perched above, the owl turned its flat face to stare down at them. It recognized the tone in its mistress's voice and waited expectantly.

"Henceforth," the High Lady continued, "you shall be raised to the rank of Knight of the Grand Order of the Hammer, to commemorate this glorious moment when the key was destroyed."

"You honor me, Supremeness!" the goblin declared, while wondering what this change in status would mean for him. "I hope you will permit me to assist you in punishing the other conspirators in Lord Fanderyn's plot."

"Ah yes," she said with a thin smile. "That trespass into the tomb of my late father. . . . Those present must certainly be killed. That shall be done; but what of you, Sir Waggarinzil?"

"Me, Your Highliness?"

"You too were present at that treasonous gathering, and to merely set foot there is, as you know, punishable by death. What is to be done?"

The goblin stared up at her, afraid. "B-B-But, Majesty!" he pleaded. "How else could I have taken the key and foiled Fanderyn's plan had I not been there?"

"I owe you so much," she admitted. "But it is not fitting for a goddess to be indebted to anyone."

Waggarinzil fell on his face, but he knew he was doomed.

"Spare me!" he cried.

The High Lady lifted the heavy hammer once more and raised it above her head.

"My laws must not be broken," she said with terrifying calm as she brought it smashing down. "There can be no exceptions."

A moment later, the goblin's lifeless body slumped to the floor and a look of callous amusement passed over Rhiannon's face.

"By your shattered skull," she laughed, mocking his manner of speech. "What an unlucky day it turned out to be for you after all."

Discarding the hammer, she stepped over him and left the forge behind her. Silently, the owl came fluttering down to her shoulder.

"Now, my provost," she said in a voice charged with malice. "Before I destroy those insolent nobles and my true reign can commence, I must pay a call on Gabbity."

• CHAPTER 10 •

GWYDDION

GAMALIEL TUMPIN CLUNG DESPERATELY to one of the Wyrm's great horns. Bufus was still yahooing, while Kernella's screams had finally dried up and her voice was more hoarse than ever.

They could not believe what had happened. The stone serpent had rushed straight for the vaulted stone ceiling of the shrine chamber at a shattering speed, and they had been certain they were going to die. And then, an instant before they were going to hit, the ceiling opened up before them, peeling back magically, revealing a round tunnel boring high into the rock above.

Through this, the ancient Wyrm called Sacrifice had sped, rushing and tearing through the darkness. It was an exhilarating ride. At first they had soared furiously upward, then there was a jerk sideways and a dip, followed by a complete revolution that made their stomachs flip over and now they were traveling almost horizontally through the earth. They could not tell how long the mad journey lasted. The suffocating blackness of the subterranean world obliterated all sense of time and their thoughts were consumed with trying to keep from falling off. Sometimes the serpent twisted recklessly along the tunnel, and Bufus's shrieks of enjoyment warbled and juddered, the echoes spiraling after them. Finally, there was another violent jerk and they raced straight up once more.

Immediately, the blind darkness was snatched away and dazzling light blasted into their eyes. There was a tremendous jolt as Sacrifice came to an abrupt halt and they were hurled from his monstrous head. The three young werlings were flung clear.

For a moment, they somersaulted through the air. Then they bumped onto soft, springy turf and lay there grunting and gasping for breath, shielding their eyes from the amber rays of the sinking sun.

Gamaliel was the first to recover. He sat up and glanced around, squinting under the open sky. They were above ground once more, in a remote part of Hagwood he did not recognize.

Magnificent oak trees grew in every direction, but he and the others were lying on a grassy, daisy-sprinkled mound within a small clearing. Gamaliel turned to look behind him and what he saw brought an exclamation of surprise to his lips.

Upon the brow of that hillock reared four great stones and, resting on top of them was an even larger slab of lichen-spotted granite.

"The Devil's Table!" he said. "It must be."

Then, with a shock, he realized that one of those huge support stones was actually the head of Sacrifice, jutting from the grass. Even as he stared at it, the Wyrm's features became indistinct. The eyes closed and the horns retracted. The golden crown slipped free to go rolling down the mound, crumbling as it went, the gleaming fragments falling into the grass where they transformed into dandelions and buttercups. The serpent's jaws fused together. Gamaliel blinked. Every trace of the fearsome head was gone and in its place stood a huge boulder, worn smooth by time and scoured by the weather.

"Thank you," he murmured.

"That was the best thing, ever!" Bufus burbled as he picked himself up. "One more time! Hey, where did old Snake Eyes go?"

Gamaliel smiled faintly. "I think he's gone back to journeying through the earth," he replied. "Following the ancient invisible courses underground to renew them with his ancient power before he returns to the cavern."

"How do you know so much?" the Doolan boy asked sarcastically.

"Just a feeling," Gamaliel said.

"Stop showing off and pretending you know more than you do," rasped his sister in a cracked whisper as she plodded over to join them. "I'm the eldest here, so listen to me, the pair of you. We've got to get back to Finnen and help him. If the sun's setting over there, then that's west and we need to go the opposite direction—follow me."

She began walking down the side of the mound.

"What are you doing?" Gamaliel called after her. "You heard what Nest said. We have to wait here and meet someone who's going to help us. Finnen won't even be at the tower anymore. Weren't you listening to anything?"

Kernella gave one of her annoying sniffs. "I don't believe a word of it!" she answered. "How would he know anything, stuck down there in his silly lantern? He was barmy and we're barmy, too, for believing he was real in the first place. I reckon we bashed our heads and dreamed the whole thing."

"But the serpent!" her brother shouted. "He was real, you know he was. How did we get here otherwise?"

Kernella shook her head. "I don't want to talk about that!" she said stubbornly. "Don't mention it again."

She had made up her mind to dismiss everything that had happened as a delirious figment. Her practical, skeptical nature did not want to believe in such things and so she was determined not to. She had encountered far too many outlandish creatures recently and a long tramp through the forest would do her jangled wits and snappy temper the world of good.

"Come on you two!" she ordered. "There's a long way to go to the Lubber's tower."

Gamaliel glanced at Bufus.

"Your sister's mental," the Doolan boy commented.

"Hurry up!" she croaked.

"We're not budging!" Gamaliel yelled. "You go get lost in the forest by yourself if you're mad enough, but we know what we have to do."

Kernella had reached level ground but halted and looked back at them still standing resolutely up there. Her brother sounded different. He had changed so much in the past few days. She had always been able to boss him about and tell him what to do.

She returned her gaze to the forest. The violet shadows of evening were deepening beneath the trees. Did she really want to journey through there alone? It would be night very soon and Hagwood was a perilous place even without the threat of the High Lady's soldiers lurking in the shadows. Other unnamed beings dwelled out there in the wild.

She recalled the chilling answer that Nest had given to her foolish question. One of them would not live to see another dawn. In spite of her assertion that they had imagined that mysterious creature, she had to admit it was a very convincing hallucination and she did not want to tempt that grim prediction by risking the forest on her own.

With a peevish expression on her face, she began stomping back up the mound. Her brother might be impossible to control, but she could still thump him, and Bufus too.

As she puffed her way up the slope, however, she forgot about hitting them. Something new had caught her attention and her eyes grew wide.

"When are these silly delusions going to stop?" she cried, folding her arms and scowling.

Puzzled, the boys followed her gaze and turned slowly.

A gray mist was creeping from the grass beneath the Devil's Table. It rose up, swelling under the capstone and soon that space was filled with dense, spectral fog that swirled and rolled like a trapped cloud.

The werlings gasped in wonder. Then, within that impenetrable mist, they heard a gruff cough and, to their surprise, a large human hand emerged from it, followed by another.

The figure of an old man crawled out of the fog. With a glad grunt, he straightened and stretched himself and waggled his fingers in front of his face as if to make sure they were still in working order. Then he stamped his feet and rubbed his back.

He was dressed in long white robes. A broad collar of gold adorned his shoulders and the last flickering rays of the dying sun gleamed and flashed over it, glinting in his gray hair and stiff, grizzled beard. Beneath the Devil's Table the fog was thinning and, although the air was still and calm, it blew out across the mound and vanished into the night.

To the werlings' relief, the stranger did not turn to look at them; in fact, he did not seem to be even aware of their presence. Rubbing his hands together as if wiping the last traces of the mist, he lifted his hawk-like eyes and fixed them on the horizon, out across the forest to where the lofty, pine-crowned crag of the Witch's Leap reared up against the sky. His brows slid together and he became lost in concentration.

The more Gamaliel studied him, the more he decided the human did not appear particularly fierce or alarming. The old man wore a chaplet of oak leaves upon his head and a leather bag overstuffed with herbs that was buckled to the wide belt about his waist. His face was criss-crossed with many lines and wrinkles and he carried no weapon, except for a small curved knife used for cutting plants.

When Kernella reached Bufus and her brother, she jabbed a finger toward the trees, signaling for the boys to run to them and hide.

To her annoyance Gamaliel shook his head. "But he's the one!" he whispered. "The one we were sent to meet."

Before she could argue, Bufus marched forward and, with his hands in his pockets, called out in a breezy voice, "Oi, granddad! It's dangerous to smoke in your nightie, you know. What you gawking at then?"

The man started and cast his eyes around the surrounding forest.

"Down here!" Bufus shouted impatiently.

The stranger lowered his gaze and noticed the three werlings for the first time. A delighted smile parted his brindled beard.

"Thus spoke the prophecy," he murmured, sticking a little finger into his ear and grinning to himself. "The savior and his companions are come, here at the weeping end of days. Though they are more meager of limb than I did guess."

"Fabulous," Bufus groaned. "Another loony!"

Kernella stepped up with a scowl. "I might be small," she cried, reaching for her wergle pouch, "but I can change into a ferret and bite you on the shin easy enough!"

The man bowed low. "Peace, Carrion Hag," he declared in a reverent tone. "I seek no quarrel with you. Indeed, I would fear such a thing."

"Ha!" Bufus laughed at her outraged face. "Even the big barmies have heard of you, Carrion Hag."

Kernella pinched him.

"I am but a mortal man," the stranger continued. "Guardian of the Groves, Priest of the thundering Sky Father, oak seer, augur, and teacher of the old ways. I am only a servant to mighty spirits such as you."

"Mighty spirits?" Bufus repeated with a snicker. "That sounds about right. You should water it down a bit, mister."

"Your words are veiled in mystery," the man said, enthralled. "The meaning escapes me but I rejoice to hear them from the Trickster's own lips. Far have I journeyed to be here at this ending, to hearken to the dying music of the world."

"He's not going to sing, is he?" Kernella grumbled, her heart sinking.

"In that frock, anything's possible," Bufus answered. He rolled his eyes at Gamaliel and said, "Hey Gammy, you speak fluent nutter. Try and squeeze some sense out of Beardy here."

Gamaliel sighed. His sister and Bufus Doolan really were aggravating. Placing his hands behind his back, he smiled shyly up at the old man, then cleared his throat.

"Good evening, sir," he began in his most polite manner.

"You are so lame!" Bufus mocked behind his hand.

Gamaliel ignored him. "Good evening, sir," he continued. "We were sent here to meet you. I am Gamaliel Tumpin; this is my sister, Kernella; and that is Bufus Doolan . . . a friend."

"Don't exaggerate, Gammy," Bufus blurted.

"We were told you would help us," Gamaliel carried on. "Our

friends and families are in danger and a terrible battle is being fought on the eastern edge of the forest. We need to know what to do."

The stranger listened keenly then raised his eyebrows in bewilderment. "How can I counsel such as you?" he asked. "You who are chosen to open the way to victory. You need no aid from me. I am but mortal—dust and clay."

"I think that fog went in through his ears and melted his brain," Bufus muttered.

"Ask him who he is," Kernella prompted. "What he's doing here and whose side he's on."

The man heard her and placed his left hand upon his chest in greeting. "I am named Gwyddion," he announced.

"Fancy!" said Bufus archly.

"I am come to witness the final stroke, as sung in the prophecy poem of the great bard."

To Bufus's amusement, the man replaced his little finger in his ear and continued. "For long years that poem has burned in my dreams. It is sung that when the great hill cleaves in two and the hidden peoples ride to war, when armies clash and the battle's roar shakes the stars, then shall the terror come. Horrors conjured from the great burning shall storm 'neath leaf and shadow, scattering foe and kin before them. Then shall the world be still and dawn or darkness everlasting will be decided. In that dreadful hour, the Blessed One will point the way."

He stared over at the forest, his eyes sparkling. "That is why I called on the Thunderer, the sky god," he said in a whisper. "To rip apart the curtaining years that I may step beyond and voyage through time. To gaze on that awful moment, to learn at last whether light or dark is the victor, for the verses do not tell. Nine nights I fasted whilst nine fires blazed and I sat vigil within these stones, calling for the way to open so I might pass—and thus it was granted. Behold, I stand upon tomorrow's soil. The sons of the sons of the oaks are heavy of years. The greenwood is greater and wilder and the stones we placed here are grown weary with time."

"Do you think it's just us who get the crazies?" Bufus hissed at Kernella. "Or do other folk get lumbered as well?"

"Wasps to honey," she replied with a resigned shrug.

Gamaliel turned an impatient face on them. "Shut up, the pair of you!" he ordered. "Why can't you keep quiet, just for once? You know how serious this is!"

He returned his attention to the stranger, with bright, eager eyes. "Now I know what you are," he announced, jumping up and down and punching the air. "You're a Dooit!"

"Then we are not wholly forgotten," the old man said, smiling faintly. "Though our own word is Deruwydd, Blessed One."

"The wizards who raised the standing stones," the boy continued. "Even the Hag's Finger we have back home."

"They are our markers along the backs of the earth serpents," Gwyddion told him. "Their strength flows mightily through this great forest."

"Dooit, blew it, chew it," Bufus scoffed. "Why do you keep shoving your finger in your ear? Growing turnips in there or something?"

Gwyddion regarded him with kindly patience and held up his little finger. "This is my instrument of divination," he explained, "and I must attend to it."

Both Bufus and Kernella burst out laughing.

An exasperated Gamaliel shook his head. He couldn't remain next to them and speak to the old man if they were going to keep interrupting and being scornful. So, with a final warning glare that told them to stay put and caused them to pull faces back at him, he scrambled up the nearest support stone and swung himself onto the top of the Devil's Table.

"That's better!" he declared, standing on the weathered capstone, almost level with the stranger's chest. "I don't have to crick my neck talking to you now. Take no notice of Bufus and my sister, they've had a rough time—we all have."

Gwyddion bowed again. "You honor me, Little Master," he said. "It is sung that the Blessed One shall journey with his protectors, the Trickster and the Grim-Faced Carrion Hag. Their aspect is not so loathly as I did fear and worse times are yet to come."

"Then tell me," Gamaliel asked. "What are we to do? How can we help our friends?"

"Friends?" the man said. "What matter your friends at this time? It is the Deathless One you must contest with."

"Me?" the boy cried.

"It is sung that when the black feather spills the blood of the white, the Blessed One shall make the challenge. The power lies in his hands alone."

"Me?" Gamaliel repeated. "Fight the High Lady? That's madness! How does the poem say I manage that? It's impossible!"

Gwyddion heaved a solemn sigh. "That is where the poem ends," he said and, half closing his eyes, he began to recite:

> *Then high upon the haunted crag,*
> *whence swine and witches fly.*
> *The Blessed One shalt use His power,*
> *'gainst She who cannot die.*
>
> *Thus when the world is failing,*
> *and doom is at the door.*
> *Shalt all the days be darkened,*
> *or golden evermore?*

He took a deep breath and stroked his beard thoughtfully. "There are no more verses and not even the greatest among us could foretell what will pass. That is why I have come, to see with my own eyes whether eternal darkness will cover the land or golden day will prevail."

"But I'm not this Blessed One," Gamaliel protested. "I don't have any power—even my wergling is useless and messy. The poem must mean someone else—I'm a nobody."

Gwyddion put his finger in his ear again and gazed at the boy for a moment. "My insight tells me you are indeed he," he said eventually. "You have been chosen. Within you lies the whole hope of the sunlit world."

"If I could do anything to stop the High Lady, I would!" the boy cried. "But I can't!"

He would have said more but at that moment there came a terrible sound that boomed beneath the heavens. Far off, within the Hollow Hill, Rhiannon Rigantona was hammering the key on the anvil of the Puccas.

The terrible, unnatural noise quaked in the evening sky. On the mound, Bufus and Kernella covered their ears while, above them on the Devil's Table, Gamaliel shivered and his face drained of color. Gwyddion held up his palms to the trembling clouds and called upon the Thunderer to cease.

"The sky god is tolling the end of days!" he declared.

Gamaliel shook his head. "That isn't your sky god!" he shouted above the din. "It's Her! That can only mean one thing: She's taken the enchanted key from Grimditch. She's destroying it!"

"You can't know that!" Kernella yelled.

"The Blessed One shalt know many things," Gwyddion cried out.

And then the hammering stopped. One sour, lingering note vibrated in the air, ringing dully in their ears and setting their teeth on edge. Then silence returned.

"There's not one shred of hope left now," Gamaliel murmured. "Without the key, the box can never be opened. The High Lady has won."

He wiped his hand across his forehead and tried not to think about the terrible things that must have happened to Grimditch inside the Hollow Hill.

The old man frowned and let his eyes wander to the pitted, lichen-spotted surface of the capstone. "Before we journey to the haunted crag," he said, "I must find me a wood beast. How I wish there was an ox to be found, but a lesser offering must suffice."

"What's an ox and why do you want one?" Gamaliel asked.

Gwyddion looked at him in surprise. "An ox is a most suitable beast for sacrifice," he said. "I must examine entrails and learn what I may from them."

Gamaliel caught his breath.

"That's horrible," he said.

"It is the only way!" came the stern answer. "I must read the signs before we set forth. The auspices must be observed."

Gamaliel looked down at the capstone. "Then this isn't really a table," he murmured, feeling sick. "It's an altar. You killed things on it." A wild light gleamed in Gwyddion's eyes. "The gods demand blood!" he cried. "And how else am I to unravel the mysteries unless I unwind the internals of the dead and dying and interpret them?"

"The poor animals . . ." Gamaliel whispered in a faint voice.

The old man gave a callous laugh. "Animals?" he said. "Yes, for the most part. But the important rituals and festivals require perfect victims. Why, to please the Thunderer so he might send me hence, we built nine wicker giants in a ring about this place and set one to burning every night. Within each of them was a flaxen-haired maiden arrayed in fine white linen—bride offerings unto Him. It was a glorious sight. Their screams must have pleased Him most highly for the way was opened into the distant tomorrow and here I am."

Gamaliel could not speak. He stared at the man in revulsion and horror and stumbled away from him.

"You're as bad as the High Lady," he managed to utter at last. "Or maybe . . . maybe you're worse than Her. She knows she's wicked and heartless—but you . . . you put the blame on your gods. And yet, you actually enjoy the evil things you do."

Gwyddion looked at him in confused surprise. "It is our way," he said as if that was enough justification. "It has always been the same."

"Go away!" the boy shouted angrily. "You're disgusting. I always thought the Dooits were amazing, wise wizards, but you're just foul killers."

The old man reached out to him, but Gamaliel dodged aside.

"I will not hurt you," Gwyddion promised. "I am here to watch and discover whether dark or light will triumph."

"You wouldn't know the difference!" Gamaliel snapped back. "You burned nine maidens alive just to satisfy your curiosity. You revolt me. Go back into the past where you belong. There's enough murder and madness here already."

Unable to bear being on that foul altar any longer, he climbed over the side and began hurrying down one of the support stones. In a moment, he was leaping onto the grass and running back to his sister and Bufus.

"I must accompany you," Gwyddion objected. "I must know."

Kernella and Bufus had heard everything and they stared at the man with the same contempt as Gamaliel.

"Come on," Gamaliel told them. "We're leaving—just the three of us."

"I can help you, Blessed One!" the old man cried.

Gamaliel glared up at him. "You really believe we'd accept help from something like you? I'd sooner fight the High Lady on my own. I can't even look at you. Go on—call up your fog and crawl back to the past."

"Yes, get lost and inspect your own guts!" Bufus bawled. "Or the Carrion Hag here will do something nasty to you."

Gwyddion looked alarmed and stepped back in fear. The werlings' faces were fierce and full of hatred. He did not understand why they were making such a fuss over something so fundamental as sacrifice.

"But the poem of prophecy," he said. "I must know what follows."

"Try shoving your finger somewhere new," Bufus suggested.

The werlings turned their backs and began walking down the mound. Gamaliel was too enraged and shaken to say another word. He was desperate to leave that awful place. In his eagerness to find help, he had been too quick to trust Gwyddion. Why did Nest send them there? It made no sense to Gamaliel.

Behind them, the old man was calling, begging to be allowed to join them, but the children ignored him. Kernella quietly slipped her hand into her brother's and the three of them marched into the surrounding trees.

Gwyddion stared after them, bewildered and broken. Then, miserably, he crouched down and sat beneath the Devil's Table, waiting for the mist to return and claim him.

"I told you he was a nutter," Bufus muttered as they walked through the deep evening shadows under the oaks.

"I'm not even sure he was the one Nest meant us to meet," Gamaliel said, frowning. "Nest told us it'd be close to the Devil's Table, not crawling out from under it."

"So is it back to the tower or not?" Kernella asked.

Before Gamaliel could answer, a riotous commotion erupted in the branches overhead. Leaves ripped and twigs snapped and frenzied cries squealed in the treetops.

The werlings halted and looked up.

"Squirrel fight!" Bufus chuckled.

"One of those voices doesn't sound like a squirrel," Kernella declared, critically. She was an expert on those particular animals.

Gamaliel pulled her away. "We can't hang around to find out," he said. "We've got our own fight, remember."

Just as he finished speaking, there was a crash and a shriek and a bundle of rags and twigs came falling from the leaves above. Five squirrels came racing down the trunk in pursuit, chattering and snapping and bristling with fury.

The rags landed with a *crump* on the ground. To the werlings' astonishment, they groaned loudly. At once the squirrels came charging after. They leaped upon the bundle and began tearing at the tattered black cloth and tugging on the twigs inside.

"Hey!" Kernella shouted. "Get off that. Shoo!"

The squirrels froze and noticed the children for the first time. Kernella folded her arms and made a threatening, growling noise in her throat.

With terrified chittering, the squirrels tore back up the oak tree, their tails disappearing into the leaves.

"Nice squirrel snarl!" Bufus congratulated her.

The girl grinned proudly. "They're my favorite shape," she confided. "I was best in my year at them."

Gamaliel had wandered over to the ragged bundle and was crouching next to it, about to lift a strip of cloth to see what lay beneath, when a strident but muffled voice exclaimed from within.

"No you were not, Kernella Tumpin! Stookie Maffin was twice the squirrel you ever were. Your tail looked like a startled hairy caterpillar and your ears were in the wrong place."

The werlings gasped and Gamaliel fell backward in shock. As they gawped, the rags rose up on two spindly legs. There was a flurry of dust and a shaking of cloth as a pair of twiglike hands emerged and a gaunt face with shining beady eyes reared on a long thin neck.

"Deary me—the Doolan nuisance as well," the creature declared without enthusiasm as those gleaming eyes fell upon Bufus. "Can this day get any worse?"

Gamaliel could not believe it.

"Master Gibble!" he breathed.

"Oh," observed the former Great Grand Wergle Master. "It just has."

· CHAPTER 11 ·

THE SQUIRREL RAIDER

TERSER GIBBLE, THE ONCE HIGHLY RESPECTED INSTRUCTOR in the art of wergling, surveyed his former pupils with a disagreeable and superior sneer—at odds with the rest of his appearance. In the days since his infamous betrayal and surrendering of the secret wergling passwords to the High Lady, drastic changes had come over him.

The most striking was the loss of his long, tapering nose that used to whistle when he became agitated. The High Lady had commanded it to be cut off. Now a bandage, torn from his black tutor's gown, was bound about his head, covering the wound and making him look like a masked highway robber. His once-dignified and proud appearance was gone, replaced by a disheveled, beggarly aspect, and he had developed a nervous twitch of the head.

For several long moments, the children gaped at him as he dusted

155

himself down and methodically checked to see that none of his gangly bones were broken after the fall. Then their mute surprise gave way to resentment and anger.

Bufus was the first to vent it. "Well well," he began. "It's Old Gibble. Gibble the Coward, Gibble the Traitor. Why haven't you dropped dead from shame yet?"

"You left us at the mercy of those thorn monsters!" Kernella joined in. "And you told them to hunt for Finnen! I hate you; everyone back home hates you!"

Master Gibble remained calm and aloof but at the mention of Finnen's name, he squeezed his eyes shut and his head gave a nervous jerk to the side. Finnen Lufkin had been his most magnificent pupil and showed every sign of becoming a greater wergler than even he. Master Gibble had become rabidly jealous of the boy's talent and had grown to despise him. It was he who had urged the werling council to banish the boy when he had exposed Finnen's cheating.

"Does Lufkin still live?" he asked bitterly.

"No thanks to you," the girl replied. "At least he did when we left him this morning."

"And those pernicious brutes of thorn and briar?"

"We beat them!" Bufus crowed. "Every single one. Yeah, that's surprised you, hasn't it, Bluntface. I bet you thought we was done for."

The tutor's eyes glittered. "So, has the council dispatched everyone, even children, to seek me out and bring me to justice?" he drawled slowly. "I shall not be apprehended easily. I am still the Great Grand Wergle Master and you are nothing. What unseasoned folly is this? I credited Yoori Mattock with more sense. I see I was mistaken—the fatuous old oaf."

"Mister Mattock is dead," Gamaliel said sharply. "And you've got it wrong. We haven't come looking for you. No one cares about you anymore. You're the last thing on our minds."

"Typical of our stinking luck to bump into you," Bufus added.

Master Gibble would have snorted with derision if he'd still possessed a nose.

"You cannot deceive me!" he exclaimed. "I'm far too wily and sagacious. How easily I see through your clumsy, juvenile perjuries. I am the remarkable Terser Gibble. It will be a peculiar day indeed when I—and my arch treachery—are not uppermost in our people's thoughts. Am I not already an audacious, legendary figure in werling history? Of course I shall be remembered! So I warn you: Beware, and let me pass. Do not try to hinder me or you will suffer."

As he boasted, he thrust his arms out wide in a flamboyant, dramatic gesture and at once several objects dropped from his tattered gown and fell at his feet.

"Hazelnuts!" Kernella cried.

Bufus let out a shriek of laughter. "That's why those squirrels were chasing you!" he guffawed. "You'd pinched their hoard. Is that what the legendary Terser Gibble has sunk to, robbing squirrel's larders? What a sad joke!"

Master Gibble flinched and jerked his head again. He lowered his arms and his narrow shoulders drooped sadly.

"Vainglorious vagabond," he muttered in a hollow, defeated voice. "Behold my ruin and degradation. Was there ever such a consummate humiliation as mine? Dishonor and ignominious exile I could bear, but this is too harsh a punishment—to be reduced to a nut burglar."

"I dunno," Bufus interrupted. "I can think of a few really nasty punishments for you."

"You do not understand the full extent of my downfall," the tutor lamented. "My wergling powers are gone, yes—all of them. I am unable to transform into even the simplest of shapes. They are denied me and so here you see the once–Great Grand Wergle Master, locked in his own sorry skin. I am compelled to scavenge like a scabious rat, living off whatever I can plunder or the moldering scraps that other creatures refuse to touch."

"It's better than you deserve," Gamaliel told him.

"You won't get any sympathy from us," Kernella put in.

"I do not ask for it," the tutor said wretchedly. "I was tested and proved unworthy of the trust invested in me. Everyone should spit upon my memory. Yet, in these past few days I have suffered much."

"Join the club!" Bufus snapped. "You haven't got a clue what we've been through!"

"I am not excusing myself," Master Gibble said. "What I did was indefensible, yet never in my life had I been so afraid as when I looked into the eyes of that owl. I would have confessed anything. The power of the Hill was in them."

"It's that power we've been fighting ever since," Gamaliel told him. "Yes, the High Lady. And we've got to keep on fighting. You just run off and annoy some more squirrels. We have to be somewhere."

Master Gibble regarded him with wonder. "Can this be the same tomfool child who fainted the first time he tried to change into a mouse?" he murmured. "The boy with the untidiest wergle pouch I ever saw? Was that only mere days ago?"

"Wergling happens on the inside as well," Gamaliel said softly.

With a curt nod of goodbye, he began walking deeper into the forest. Kernella and Bufus followed.

"See you, No-nose," the Doolan boy jeered.

"Don't talk to him," Kernella scolded.

In mournful silence, Terser Gibble watched them venture farther into the darkening shadows. His eyes blinked and he jerked his head in consternation. He despised his new life. It was desperate and lonely and terrifying. Seeing those children again reminded him how much better it had been before and he longed to remain in their company. He knew he could never redeem himself but if they would only let him tag along, he would be incredibly grateful.

"Wait!" he called out suddenly.

Only Bufus paused and turned around.

"What?" he shouted back.

Master Gibble reached out his long knobbly hands to them but even then his old pride caught in his throat and he couldn't bring himself to beg. Instead, he cast around and his eyes lighted upon his stolen hoard.

"Won't you stop to eat?" he asked, snatching a hazelnut from the ground. "Surely there is time for that?"

Gamaliel and Kernella halted. Bufus didn't wait to be asked twice; he was already haring back.

"I'm as hungry as an Umbelnapper!" he exclaimed, sinking his teeth into one of the proffered nuts. "But don't think this makes us pals or anything. You're a still a filthy traitor."

"The hazel is the ancient tree of wisdom," Master Gibble said, with a hint of his former lecturing manner as he passed the nuts around. "May we all be granted that. I confess mine has suffered lapses of late."

The children ate quickly. The nuts were stale but, to their famished appetites, tasted delicious. There was not enough to satisfy them completely, but the gnawing emptiness in their stomachs was placated for the time being.

"Thank you," Gamaliel told Master Gibble when the last mouthful had disappeared. "Now we really have to be on our way."

"Where are you going?" the tutor asked anxiously.

"That's our business!" Kernella answered, although she had no idea herself.

"Could . . . May I accompany you?"

Gamaliel shook his head. "We don't need you," he said, remembering Gwyddion had asked the same.

"Quite so. . . ." Master Gibble began in a sorrowful whimper and he finally choked back his pride. "Yet . . . yet I need you. Please don't leave me behind—please."

He began to cry. It was a desolate blubbering and, once it had started, it all came flooding out. The former Great Grand Wergle Master slumped to the forest floor, wailing uncontrollably. Bufus was glad the long nose with all its tiny nostrils had been cut off. There would have been snot everywhere otherwise.

The children looked at one another awkwardly.

"You can't take him," Kernella hissed at her brother when she saw his stern expression soften. "He'll betray us the first chance he gets. Remember what he did before!"

"But look at him," Gamaliel said. "Could you really abandon him?"

Kernella stated that she could, very easily, and so did Bufus.

"Please!" Master Gibble implored through his sobs. "Just for a little way. I'm not made for abject solitude; I have been so very, very lonely—I cannot endure it another moment longer."

"You've only been out here a few days!" Bufus reminded him scornfully.

"And they have been the worst of my life!" he answered. "You cannot know how interminably long each hour becomes when you are utterly alone, how the desolate moments crawl by. Let me walk with you; I can raid other squirrel hoards and fetch more food for the journey. I will do anything you ask, only do not forsake me."

Bufus folded his arms. "We can do that ourselves, Flatbonce," he said. "And we can still wergle, so we'd be better at it than you."

"Leave him," Kernella agreed.

Gamaliel rubbed his chin thoughtfully. "That isn't what Finnen would do," he said at last. "He'd bring him along, even though he knows Master Gibble hates him."

"That's 'cos Lufkin is stooopid!" Bufus said, rapping his knuckles against his temple.

Kernella wavered. Her brother was right. Her beloved Finnen wouldn't leave the old tutor out here on his own.

Master Gibble pawed at Gamaliel's arm. "Take me to Finnen Lufkin," he cried. "Let me beg his forgiveness. I'm changed—I'm not the vain, selfish creature I was. I swear it, by the mighty beech of the Gibbles in the Silent Grove I swear it."

"Oh, come on then!" Gamaliel said, shaking him off. "But no lagging behind, and if you run off, we'll not come looking. Just do exactly what we tell you."

"I am undeserving of your kindness and favor," the tutor sniveled, rising to his feet once more.

Bufus groaned. He thought the Tumpins were too soft and he found Gibble's lightning changes of mood irritating.

"Too right you're undeserving," he told him. "You may have conned this daft pair, but I'm keeping my eye on you, Dribble. I don't trust you and never will."

Master Gibble clapped his hands together in delight. "Even your scathing mistrust is a music to my empty ears!" he laughed, performing a spindly sort of dance. "Now let us be off, together—intrepid werlings of Hagwood! Where are we bound?"

Bufus and Kernella looked questioningly at Gamaliel.

"'*High upon the haunted crag*,'" he said, repeating the line from Gwyddion's poem.

Master Gibble's elation collapsed. He jerked his head nervously. "How very inviting," he mumbled in a voice of lead.

"Where's that then?" Bufus asked.

"I'm sure it's the Witch's Leap," Gamaliel answered. "When I was standing on that . . . the Devil's Table, I saw it in the distance."

"And that's where Finnen will be?" his sister asked hopefully.

"I don't know, but I think that's where the final great battle will be fought. According to the prophecy, that's where the end is going to take place."

"End?" Master Gibble inquired with caution. "What end would that be?"

"The end of the High Lady's reign, or the end of everything else," came the stark reply.

The wergle master smiled weakly. "How you're spoiling me," he simpered without enthusiasm.

They pressed on through the mounting darkness. Bufus tried to keep them cheerful by regaling them with tales of the worst pranks he and his late brother had played on people. Only Kernella giggled. Many of those practical jokes had centered on Master Gibble. He pretended to be insulted, but it was good to think of happier times and even his long face was lifted by occasional smiles. Gamaliel, however, had grown very quiet, and his forehead slowly creased with worry about what lay ahead.

Bufus reached the end of a story in which he and his brother, Mufus, had lain in wait for the elderly Diffi Maffin and emptied a sack of slugs onto her white hair, and then gave a heavy sigh.

"I miss him," he breathed. "Every moment of the day. We were going to do so many things together: put hedgehog poo in Mrs. Umbelnapper's pasties and see if Chookface noticed the difference, nail up the door of old Granny Lufkin's place with her still inside . . ." His voice trailed off sadly.

"The Silent Grove will keep Mufus safe till your time comes to join him," Master Gibble said in as gentle a voice as he could manage.

Bufus thought of the previous night by the Pool of the Dead, where he had spoken with the ghost of his twin, but he kept it to himself and hastily wiped his eyes.

It was Kernella who broke the ensuing silence.

"I miss home," she said. "I wonder what everyone is doing right now? Mum and Dad must be worried sick, what with me and Gamaliel going off without a word."

"I don't reckon we'll ever see our folks again," Bufus said flatly. "According to Nest, one of us definitely won't, and there's no chance we'll even make it to the Silent Grove after the other two snuff it."

Kernella pulled an unhappy face. She knew he was probably right. She would have given anything to be back in the Tumpin Oak with her parents, but they were far away and she felt the pain of that keenly. She turned to their old tutor and asked, "You know lots about the history of us werlings, don't you?"

"Indeed I do," Master Gibble answered. "There are few who are as learned as I."

"Don't set him off," Bufus grumbled.

"I just wanted to hear something about home, something to make it feel closer," Kernella explained. "There must be lots of stories we've never heard."

"Are you requesting a lesson?" Master Gibble asked in astonishment.

"Not a lesson, you noseless twit!" Bufus said crossly. "Did you land on your head when you fell out of that tree?"

"Just a story," Kernella repeated. "Make yourself useful and tell us something comforting about our kind, something to take my mind off this horrible tangled part of the forest. Every shadow might have a monster lurking in it."

"There probably is," Bufus muttered.

Master Gibble considered for a moment. "A tidbit of history, perhaps?" he ventured. "How the first werlings came to settle in our humble corner?"

"That would be okay," she said.

Bufus groaned. "I can't believe you just asked Yawnface to drone on at us," he said to Kernella. "You want him to bore us to death?"

The tutor pursed his lips and steepled his fingers beneath them.

"It was a time of darkness and danger," he began.

"That's not very cheery," Kernella rebuked him. "*This* is a time of darkness and danger—right now!"

"It was when the wars with the troll witches were at their height," he continued. "None could withstand them. They sought to destroy every faerie realm, stealing their secret magics to add to their own. They were savage and without mercy; their powers were mighty and they grew stronger with each conquest. One by one the lesser kingdoms fell. Hills and fortresses, woodland hamlets, and cave towns were blasted by their fearsome arts. Countless were slain, but the survivors fled to the Hollow Hill to seek refuge with the High King. There were many different tribes and races—some had once been enemies, but all quarrels were forgotten when they united against the one true foe, Black Howla and her haggish host."

He paused and saw with satisfaction that he had her complete attention and she was eager for him to continue.

"The fathers of our fathers' fathers' fathers, and quite a few more fathers beyond that, came from a green land near to one small kingdom. The marauding troll witches drove them from that place, so what remained of our people joined the straggling troop of the dispossessed in the Hill."

Kernella gasped. "We once lived in the Hollow Hill? We were lordly folk?"

Master Gibble tutted at her. "Not everyone who dwells in there is of noble blood," he said. "Remember, there are servants and cooks and grooms and drudges and many strange creatures without title or lineage. We too were on the lowest step of that society, and in those far-off days, we had not yet discovered the art of wergling. We were just a small race of no importance."

"So we was goblet washers and muck shovelers," Bufus butted in. "No better than slaves, then."

"But we were slaves in the middle of a war," the tutor said. "The Hill became an island besieged by Black Howla's terrifying hag army. It was a fearful time to live through."

"So what happened?" Kernella demanded. "How did we get from there to our little wood?"

Terser Gibble gave a jerk of the head. "It was actually an ancestor of Finnen Lufkin, Channin Luffud, who saved us. He volunteered to act as a spy out in the forest and discovered many of Black Howla's secrets. His daring and courage was so great and he performed such heroic deeds that, when the War was finally over, the High King told him to name his reward. Channin asked for a grant of land at the western edge of the forest and for his people to be released from servitude and for them to be left quite alone and forgotten. Hide and be safe, that was always our motto."

"And Finnen is descended from him?" the girl cried. "I might have guessed."

Bufus grimaced. "I'm going to throw up," he muttered.

"And so the High King generously instructed all record of our people to be erased and we were not to be spoken of again, so that we might pass out of memory. Then, in his far-sighted wisdom, he gave Channin Luffud one last gift, which he said would aid us in our desire to remain out of sight and out of mind."

"What was it?" Kernella asked.

"A velvet pouch containing a score of enchanted beechnuts. Channin did not know how they would help keep our race secret, but he planted them in the new land beyond the Hagburn and thus the Silent Grove came into being."

"What a steaming dollop of bullfinch doings," Bufus said.

Master Gibble looked affronted. "I have read the parchments and scrolls kept in the council chamber!" he declared. "They are older than the towering elm in which your family dwells!"

"Don't prove nothing," the boy argued. "Just a load of old lies and . . . well, faerie stories."

"What about the wergling?" Gamaliel asked abruptly. "When did we learn to do that?"

Master Gibble smiled, greatly pleased. He had managed to engage each of them. He was still capable of commanding an audience's attention, in spite of his heinous crime and disheveled appearance. For the first time in days, he began to feel good about himself.

"The very first spring, the beech saplings put forth their flowers," he answered. "That was when the first true wergle occurred, without warning. Hamjin Fepple had been hunting mice all morning and, as he rested beneath the beech's catkins, he drifted off to sleep and dreamed he was running with them. When he awoke, he had sprouted whiskers and a tail. Of course, it was a very crude and rudimentary transformation by our standards, but it was the beginning. Over the years, we learned how to master that skill and hide from the world most successfully, until—"

"Until those thorn ogres killed my brother," Bufus interrupted grimly.

"But the wergling," Gamaliel pressed. "How did we learn? How did we know what we could and couldn't change into?"

"Mostly trial and error and common sense," Master Gibble replied in his old, familiar lecturing tone. "Those early werglers found they could only change into animals that were roughly the same size as themselves. And they learned, to their cost, that some shapes cannot be undone, such as insects, for the few werling masters who dared to do so forgot their true selves and could not change back. Only the greatest wergler of them all, Agnilla Hellekin, succeeded. Several times she wergled into diverse crawling shapes. Then, at last she was trapped, caught in a nightmarish mongrel form of wasp and spider, from which there was no escape, and her mind was broken. Since that day, Frighty Aggie has been a grave warning to anyone who might be thinking of doing such a thing."

"Frighty Aggie, sting not me," Kernella whispered with a shudder as she recalled the old nursery song.

"What about wergling other things?" Gamaliel asked. "Not insects or animals, but . . . oh, I don't know . . . flowers or stones, things like that."

Bufus snorted with laughter. "Only Gammy would ask such a daft question!" he cried.

Kernella shook her head at the absurdity of her brother.

"We must never disrespect our great gift," Gibble concluded with a tut. "We must adhere to the rules—or pay the price. We must never flout them, like Finnen Lufkin did when he cheated."

There was a silence. Kernella scrunched up her face. She wished Finnen had not done that horrible thing. Bufus fell back to brooding about his brother and Terser Gibble was doing his best to look impressive and knowledgeable but, with the strip of cloth bound about his face, he looked simply ludicrous. As for Gamaliel, he was thinking about wergling into something far more dangerous than anything anyone else had ever attempted and the dread of it made him shiver.

"Wait!" the tutor hissed suddenly. "What was that?"

Everyone listened.

"I can't hear anything," Kernella said, after a few moments had elapsed. "What did you think you—"

She gasped and jumped into the air. The ground was trembling.

Bufus and Gamaliel spun around and saw that the trees were quivering. A deep rumble of grinding stone was echoing through the earth.

"Beeches spare me!" Master Gibble shrieked as he staggered from side to side.

"What's happening?" Kernella cried.

Overhead the leaves shone brightly with a silvery green light that came flooding over the forest.

"It's the end of everything!" Master Gibble howled.

"Bring it on!" Bufus yelled above the din.

"It can't be the end," Gamaliel told himself hopelessly. "I know what I have to do now. It can't end before then—I just need a bit more time!"

CHAPTER 12

GABBITY AND GRIMDITCH

WHEN THE GOBLIN NURSEMAID LEFT Lord Fanderyn that afternoon with a skip in her step and a wonky tune on her warty lips, she had visited the abandoned royal nursery. There, she spent a good while searching through large wooden trunks and reminiscing over the things she found. The old toys of King Ragallach's three children filled her mind with swarming memories. Holding them close, she could almost hear the happy voices of the past surround her.

Eventually, she tore herself away and, laden with a bundle of clothing and a pail of green milk from the dairy, returned to the High Lady's private chamber where she discovered Grimditch leaning into the cradle.

"Get away from there, you nasty bogle!" she cried, laying her burdens down. "Caught you trying to steal my dumpy dainty's life glow—ha! Keep your scavenging paws off him!"

"Me weren't pilfering nowt!" Grimditch protested. "Me was keepin' his grooly dreams at bay."

"A graspy starveling like you?" she cried in disbelief. "I'll give you grooly dreams what need keeping at bay!"

Flapping her hands in front of her, she slapped Grimditch's clean-shaven face and, with an onslaught of blows, drove him back to the table.

Grimditch yelped and leaped away. The goblin's big hands delivered painful smacks on his bare skin and he jumped clean over the table to escape them, running along the wooden chests and then bouncing onto the High Lady's bed.

Gabbity screeched in outrage. "How dare you be on there!" she yelled. "Come here so I can thump your ears!"

The barn bogle responded by hurling a pillow at her, followed by another and another. Then he scrambled up the bed curtains and swung from the rail like a monkey—which infuriated her even more.

"Come down this very moment!" she fumed. "M'Lady will hear of this. She'll deal with you!"

It was then the hammering began. The terrible smiting clamor as the key was destroyed reverberated through the Hollow Hill and the barn bogle loosed his grip and dropped back onto the bed.

Gabbity stared fearfully around her. The quarrel was at once forgotten and the dread of that forbidding sound united them.

"What be that racket then, missus?" Grimditch asked. "An' why do it bite through old Grimditch's bones so?"

"I don't know what that be," the goblin nursemaid answered in a wavering voice. "But my prickling thumbs tell me it's spelling the end of summat—summat big and grand and glorious. Just hark at it clanging and clashing."

Frozen by the awful sound, they wondered what was happening and then a new noise began that caused both of them to spring forward. In the cradle, the human infant was crying.

The pair of them rushed over and Gabbity lifted the child in her arms.

"Hush now," she soothed. "'Tis only a tuneless old bell that some fool is bashing. Don't you let it scare you none, my pudgy duck."

The child wept and struggled in her embrace. Grimditch leaned over and stroked the infant's golden head then started to sing to him once more. The sobs subsided and the little lordling returned to his deep sleep.

Gabbity looked at the barn bogle in surprise. As she regarded him, the fierce hammering ceased as abruptly as it had begun. The silence seemed to throb in their ears.

"You've a rare calming way with my precious pudding," she muttered eventually, with grudging respect.

"Me heard his mam crooning them words over him," Grimditch explained. "Long ago, before the hillmen come."

The nursemaid stared at him, then returned her charge to the cradle.

"There's clothes and milk there," she said over her shoulder. "Gabbity keeps her promises."

The barn bogle eyed the bundle she had brought in, but first busied himself with the pail of milk. Taking it in his hands he put it to his lips and drank the green contents down. The guzzling, slurping noises he made would have revolted the nobility but Gabbity's table manners were not much better so she paid them no heed.

Creamier, cleaner, and much richer than that of ordinary herds, the milk of a faerie cattle was a feast in itself, nourishing and invigorating. If Grimditch's hair had not been shorn, it would have started to curl and grow thicker than ever.

Grimditch let out an enormous belch. "That's better than nibblers," he grunted, lying on his back with contentment.

Gabbity cackled. "You've never had better than that," she declared. "Even the nobles have a noggin of it most nights. Now put some cloth on your back. I'm tired of seeing your naked, bony carcass. You barn bogles would gad about as stripped as the day you was borned if left to your own ways. We'll have none of that here; you can't be meeting the High Lady in naught but a bandage."

Grimditch sat up and turned his attention to the bundle. Unfastening the belt that bound it, he unrolled a suit of clothes that made him gasp with glee. There was a clean linen shirt with lacy cuffs and a pair of dark-burgundy velvet britches with gold buttons. Then there was a matching waistcoat with even more gleaming buttons and a beautiful frock coat of the same sumptuous stuff, richly embroidered around the pockets and lapels. Finally, there was a long pair of warm woolen socks and shoes of soft leather that were polished to a shine as glossy as a beetle's wing.

"Oh missus!" he sang, jumping into the britches and clambering into the shirt. "'Tis fancy fiddle faddle trappings for sure!"

The nursemaid watched him stumble around the chamber as he hopped on one leg, pulling on the long socks that stretched up past his knobbly knees.

A faint smile lit her wizened face. "Them belonged to Prince Alisander," she said, "when he was but a boy. He got into more mischief than even you're capable of. A bonnie little elfin princeling he looked in it—such a painful long age ago. Everyone adored him. That's what made his crime all the more 'orrible."

"Me, wearing royal clobber?" Grimditch marveled as he buttoned the waistcoat up wrongly. "Me always knowed me was refined and a nob."

Gabbity shrugged. "I couldn't think what else would fit," she said. "It's much too grand for such a beast as you—may as well stud a cow pat with diamonds. I pray M'Lady won't mind."

The barn bogle tried to pull on the shoes but they were too narrow for his large feet so he cast them aside. He was more than happy with everything else. He pulled on the velvet frock coat and whimpered with pride and pleasure, stroking his cheek against the soft sleeves.

He looked extremely ridiculous in this new finery. The clothes were not a perfect fit—they were slightly too baggy, for he was very scrawny—but he loved them passionately. Capering in giddy circles, he whirled around and the tails of his coat flapped wildly.

"Prince Grimditch!" he shouted. "King of barns and ruler of all things that scratch in the hay!"

He jigged about until he was out of breath then let out a long and blissful sigh and danced across to the nursemaid. To her astonishment, he puckered his lips and gave her a big wet kiss on the cheek.

"Thank you, missus," he said. "Like as not me'll be stone dead after I meet your foul Lady. But Grimditch is grateful for the pretty clobber, even if 'tis only for a short while."

Gabbity was too stunned to slap him for being so audacious. She touched her cheek tenderly. It was the same place that Rhiannon had struck so violently earlier that day. She could not remember the last time anyone had shown her the slightest dab of gentleness and affection.

"What dust there is in here!" she exclaimed, rubbing her eyes quickly and turning away.

Grimditch glanced over at the locked door and his spirits sank. "When She gets back," he began in a solemn voice, "that'll be the end for Grimditch. If She don't finish him, he'll be given to the hot pincers and spine stretchers."

The goblin nursemaid nodded. "M'Lady's never spared no one," she said. "Some of the deeds She's done . . ." Her words trailed off; many of the things she had seen her mistress do were too horrible to repeat.

Normally, Grimditch would have wailed and howled with self pity and despair, but ever since the werlings had found him in his barn he had become a different bogle. Instead of feeling sorry for himself, his thoughts turned to the small but brave Gamaliel. He wondered how Master Tumpin was faring in the caves beneath the Crone's Maw and if he had found the friends he had gone searching for down in that frightening darkness. Then he felt horribly guilty for having stolen the pretty little key from the wergle pouch and wished he could undo that crime.

Gabbity saw his face fall—as well it might. Only pain awaited him, poor beast. Death would be a welcome release when it was eventually granted.

"Missus," the barn bogle began, "them lully words what the littl'un likes so much—while there's time and still a tongue in this head, me'll learn 'em to you. Puts the shiniest smile on the mite's face, them do."

The nursemaid blinked at him. She had forgotten what it was to be selfless, to put others beyond her own desperate need. Here was a lowly barn bogle, a creature she had always detested as nothing more than a leeching straw dweller, about to meet an undoubtedly grue-some and drawn-out end, yet his only thought was to teach her a lul-laby to soothe and calm her beloved little lordling. A stab of shame made Gabbity wince and she chewed her gums uncomfortably as her long-neglected conscience began to smolder.

"Don't stop here waitin' for M'Lady!" she blurted suddenly. "I'll unlock the door and you run out—as fast as them skinny legs of yours can whisk you. Fly from this blasted hill! Gabbity can tell you the quickest path, one that dodges the guards and other curious eyes. Don't you stop running till you're clean on the far side of the forest and even then don't stop."

Grimditch gaped at her. Had she gone mad? Or was it some cruel trick to confuse him and raise his hopes?

"Stop standing there like a stuffed gnome on a stick!" she urged. "Get going and save your scabby skin. This ain't no trap—'tis your only chance."

"Why you doing this, missus?" the barn bogle asked skeptically. "If Grimditch escapes, then your witchy Queen will have your head. Be you more stupid than you be ugly?"

A smug expression appeared on the nursemaid's warty face and she ran a preening hand as far up the spire of her white hair as she could reach. "When M'Lady returns," she told him in a boastful, con-spiring whisper, "She'll find the wind is changing and might blow Her clean away ere long—and it's Her own Gabbity what set the weather cock to spinning."

"You been sat in this dark room too long, missus," Grimditch answered with a roll of his eyes.

She cackled and bustled him toward the door. "Just you do as Gabbity tells you and run out of here as though your heels was on fire," she ordered. "I'll tell Her you darted off hours ago so She'll reckon you've gone a good distance by now. It's a good hope you've got of getting clear."

The barn bogle looked into her yellow eyes and saw that she meant it. She really was setting him free. He gasped and clapped his hands and hopped from foot to foot. He would have capered around her if she had not pulled him closer to the door and jabbed a knobbly finger at it.

"When you're through that," she instructed, "turn left first, then straight to the big tapestry with the two serpents woven all over it, then . . ."

Gabbity paused and pressed an ear against the wood. Her wizened brows knotted together and she drew back sharply. A familiar tread was striding down the passageway beyond.

"'Tis Her!" she exclaimed in a hiss. "M'Lady is returned!"

Grimditch leaped backward and hugged himself. "No, no, no, no, no . . ." he warbled. But Gabbity was not to be beaten so easily.

"Quick!" she commanded, half dragging him back across the chamber. "Climb into that big chest and keep quieter than a dried-up corpse till M'Lady has gone."

Fizzing with fear, the barn bogle wrenched up the heavy lid of the chest and leaped inside without bothering to see what he was jumping onto. The lid closed on top of him with a thud and he crouched in the cramped darkness and waited.

Meanwhile, Gabbity hitched up her dirty skirts, pelted to her stool, snatched up her knitting, and tried to look as calm and composed as possible.

Behind her, the lock clicked and the door swung open.

Rhiannon Rigantona entered her private chamber. A dangerous light was glinting in her eyes as they fell upon her old nursemaid. At her shoulder, the owl's small tongue licked the corners of his beak.

The High Lady moved silently through the shadows, all the while keeping her gaze trained on the goblin, like a cat circling a petrified bird.

"Gabbity," she said at length, "I am returned."

The nursemaid gave a little start as if she had been unaware of her sovereign's entrance.

"M'Lady!" she greeted as warmly and as convincingly as she could manage. "The little lordling has been such a prize this day, but then he's never no trouble, the priceless jewel. Only woke the once, there was an ear-blistering racket a short whiles afore—did you hear it? Summat frightful it were. Enough to wake the stones, it was."

"I heard it," her mistress answered with silken menace. "Indeed, I was the cause."

Gabbity's glance flicked back to her knitting. The hostility in that voice was unmistakable and it set her hands trembling.

"You know best, M'Lady," was all she could find to mutter in reply. Rhiannon moved a step closer. "How absorbed you are with that knitting," she observed. "Always so busy at it."

"'Tis my only amusement, M'Lady—eats up the long hours, it does."

"It is selfish of me to consign you to this room. Keeping vigil here, you see so little of the court."

"Why . . . I've seen enough of it in my time to last me a good whiles yet, M'Lady."

"Nevertheless, I believe the time weighs heavily upon you in here. You must crave companionship."

"Bless you, M'Lady. But my rosy dumpling here is the best company I could wish for."

"You cheer me. I am pleased you are not so weary of your post that you are forced to seek the society of others."

"Why, M'Lady! There's none in this whole hill I'd rather sit with."

"Are you sure you would not like to mingle with the noblest blood of the court? The great houses are not completely without interest. What of Lord Limmersent, or even Lord Fanderyn? Why, Gabbity— you have dropped several stitches."

The knitting needles fell from the nursemaid's shaking hands and she lifted her terrified gaze. The expression on the High Lady's face cut into her like a sword of ice.

"M-M-M'Lady!" she began.

"Did you truly believe your commonplace plot could ensnare me?" Rhiannon spat. "It unraveled before it could even be spun. The traitor Fanderyn is dead and the key you gave him is destroyed. The rest of your pathetic band will be captured and turned on the wheels of my vengeance very soon. But I have selected a special fate for you, Gabbity."

The nursemaid could only stare at her and shake. The owl clicked his beak with satisfaction.

"How long have you fussed and fetched for the royal line?" Rhiannon asked, but she continued without waiting for an answer. "You were my mother's nurse when she was a child, were you not?"

The High Lady paused and cast her eyes around the shadowy chamber.

"They were dark years, when the troll witches rampaged through the forest. Yet Winnifer, my mother, thrived in these deep mansions and grew to marry the High King, my father. Unto you, they entrusted the care of their firstborn, Alisander, my brother—and then myself."

Rhiannon's eyes grew dark and her nostrils flared at the memory. As a young elfin child, when her name was still Morthanna, she and her brother would creep from the hill at night to gaze down at the dangerous forest. The terror of the marauding witches thrilled and excited the royal children. They were desperate to catch a glimpse of them charging through the trees upon the backs of their huge wild boars as the tales described. Yet they saw nothing but the rustling treetops and heard only foxes barking in the distance.

One night, Morthanna stole out alone and ventured down the hillside. But she explored too far into the crowded trees; the troll witches quickly captured her and she was taken to Black Howla.

The headstrong child's haughty arrogance and dark, accusing eyes amused the leader of the powerful sisterhood and a strange, secret alliance formed between them. Falling under Black Howla's corrupting spell, she became furtive and solitary and sneaked into the forest as often as she could to learn the hidden and sinister arts.

No one in the Unseelie Court suspected the young princess's terrible secret. Their attention was trained elsewhere. The troll witches were growing stronger and more deadly. It was as if Black Howla knew where the defenses of the Hollow Hill were weakest and was informed precisely when and where to strike. Distrust and anger filled the subterranean halls but King Ragallach refused to believe any of his subjects would betray him. Nobody surmised the traitor in their midst was the brooding princess who lurked in the corner of their war councils, watching and listening so she could trade war secrets for evil lessons from the troll witches.

And then Queen Winnifer was taken abed with a third child, but her confinement was different from before—she sickened and wilted daily.

A sneer formed on Rhiannon's face as she remembered and when she next spoke it was in a hissing, hate-filled voice.

"Let there be truth between us," she said. "Here at the end of your . . . devoted service, it seems appropriate you should finally know one or two of my secrets. Do you recall when my mother was heavy with my sister? Of course you do. You and the Lady Mauvette were always at her side, fretting and worrying and administering physic and your foul reeking herbs."

Gabbity's face was a picture of bewilderment. "Your mother the Queen was unwell," she spluttered. "We did all we could to save her from that malady. At first 'twas only a chill, but she sank deeper into that fever, that terrible, sweating consumption what drained her lovely life away. Her saving was beyond us; it were a marvel your sister survived her birthing. Your poor dear father was so distraught."

"As was I," Rhiannon countered. "But something had to be done. I already had a brother. I had no wish for a second, and a sister would have been worse—as indeed she so proved."

Gabbity shook her head in confusion. "What are you saying?"

"There was no fever!" came the monstrous, boastful confession. "Black Howla supplied me with what was needed and I set to work. It was so easy, just five drops a day into the stinking gruel you gave my mother."

The goblin nursemaid choked and clutched at the knitting on her lap. "You poisoned her?" she cried.

"It was meant for the unborn thing within," Rhiannon said scornfully. "Yet my foolish mother poured what was left of her strength into her belly so that my sister should live. She chose to sacrifice her life for Clarisant—I never understood that decision. How could she be so weak? I despised both her and the child all the more for it. As for my father . . . there was only one sun and one moon for him after that—his devotion to Clarisant eclipsed all else. I was no longer his favorite."

"Curse you," Gabbity breathed, crooking her little finger and drawing a snake shape in the air.

The High Lady laughed. "Save your crude oaths," she taunted, "till you hear how I eventually plunged Alisander's dagger into my father's back."

The nursemaid let out a cry of horror. "Then your princely brother was innocent!" she uttered with shock. "You let the Redcaps and the spriggans slay him for that crime!"

"Two birds for one throne," Rhiannon explained with a smile. "And now I have further news for you. My misplaced sister and the suitor she absconded with have returned to Hagwood. Don't excite yourself. She is now even more hideous than you, and I have already had him killed. Very soon she shall follow in his dead footsteps. The whole court shall witness her final moments: I am going to empty the Hollow Hill, and none shall miss that long-awaited and long-postponed spectacle."

Gabbity could scarcely believe the list of depravity and madness she was hearing. Rhiannon had always been a cruel and vicious ruler, but no one in the court had ever imagined she was guilty of being in league with the troll witches, or that she had murdered her own parents and brother.

The goblin's stricken look of horror amused the High Lady greatly. She watched every dreadful admission register on that wizened face, savoring the expressions of shock and pain. Then she moved close to the cradle and reached inside.

"As for this little lordling," Rhiannon began, with an even more bitter edge in her voice. "He has served his purpose well, but I tired of him long ago. I want a new one. Mortals breed so swiftly and so carelessly. There will be plenty more."

As she caressed the plump, sleeping face she dug her nails into his cheek till he squirmed and began to cry out despite his deep slumber.

"Leave him be!" Gabbity wailed. "Have you no heart?"

Her words prompted a peal of hellish laughter and the High Lady's form shimmered. Her white mantle became a glittering black robe, trimmed with sable fur and a crown of silver thorns, entwined with golden ivy leaves, encircled her brow.

"Can you not see?" she demanded. "Are you as blind as my sister's lifeless lover? Your Queen has ascended among the gods. At last, I am truly unassailable. My heart, you ridiculous harridan, can never be reached—I am finally free."

But Gabbity was only aware of the infant's distress and she begged the High Lady to stop hurting him.

Rhiannon gave a scornful laugh. "You are soft as curd," she said. "He can so easily be replaced. When the human world grovels before me and fears my very name, among their tributes will be countless pink morsels such as this—and even younger. Every new day, I shall select a fresh bite of innocence."

Her gloating anticipation was horrible to watch and she stared into the cradle in a way that made Gabbity's warty flesh creep.

Then, for the first time, the owl spoke. "Majesty . . . Divinity," he said directly into her ear. "Hath thou marked? Yon table is empty. The barn bogle is absent."

The owl's mistress pulled away from the cradle and the goblin threw down her knitting to rush over and appease the child's cries.

"Where is the beast?" Rhiannon demanded. "Did you set it loose as a reward for the key you found upon it?"

Gabbity held the infant tightly in her arms. Perhaps she drew courage from the aura that flickered around him, or perhaps it was her own innate goblin nerve that surfaced. Now that she knew all hope was lost, she no longer felt afraid. With a defiant gleam in her aged eyes, she stuck out her jaw and said, "Aye, the skinny fellow's gone! I sent him skedaddling from this place hours ago. He'll be deep in the forest by now if he's any sense. You'll not catch him easily."

The High Lady raised her eyebrows. "The toothless cannot bite, Gabbity," she told her. "Do not attempt to snap at me."

"'Twere an evil night that delivered you," the nursemaid answered hotly. "The forest was filled with screeching and lightning zagged about the hill. I knowed it were a bad omen. The cattle went dry for nine days. Born bad you was, and badder you became."

"Curb thine insolence!" the owl shrieked.

Gabbity threw him an angry glare.

"And the egg that hatched you should have been stamped underfoot!" she yelled. "I sorely wish my heel had done it. But this much I'll do, Master Beak, eater of stolen eyes and feathered toady. I'll lay a goblin curse upon your head. By the serpents' breath, may you be ripped from the sky and your snowy plumes shout red with your own heart's blood."

"Enough," Rhiannon interjected. "I have one last use for Gabbity.

But I promise you, my provost, you will watch her die an amusing death."

Concealed within the wooden chest, Grimditch had heard everything and a cold sweat had broken out over his bald brows. The High Lady's crimes had stunned and sickened him. Curled up in that cramped space, his legs had grown numb but he was too afraid to shift his position, in case the movement was overheard.

Suddenly, he heard Gabbity let out a pitiful shriek and the sounds of a brief and desperate scuffle broke out. He heard the stool kicked over and the owl cackling contemptuously. Then the nursemaid's voice was muffled and Rhiannon's strident tones were mocking her.

"That will keep you here till you're needed to play your part," she said. "Now, the Under Magic of the Hollow Hill must be awakened and the stones shall rise. I will rouse the Unseelie Court. We have an appointment with my sister; she has been kept waiting too long. Then, when I return . . ."

Her words turned to callous laughter and the infant cried out in pain once more.

"A feast fit for a goddess will be waiting," Rhiannon declared.

Grimditch heard Gabbity's stifled screams. He was anxious to lift the lid of the chest and peer out to see what was happening, but even his impish wits knew that would be a fatal mistake. So he remained in that squashed darkness, breathing as silently as possible. Presently, he heard the door of the chamber open and close. A few moments more and Gabbity's frenetic struggles began again; this time he was sure they were meant for him to hear and were the signal for him to emerge.

Cautiously, he raised the lid and looked out.

The goblin nursemaid was half lying, half sitting on the floor at the foot of the cradle. Grimditch thought it seemed a very peculiar and most uncomfortable position and he tilted his head curiously. Only then did he realize she had been tied to one of the cradle's legs by her own hair, which had also been bound tightly around her mouth as a gag. Her hands had been fastened behind her back by her knitting and she could do nothing to free herself.

She was staring, wild eyed, over at the barn bogle and making frantic jerks of her head to summon him to her aid. A number of the large spiders that spun the cradle's canopy had scurried down and had begun throwing their silk across her face.

Grimditch clambered hurriedly out of his hiding place but instantly tumbled head over heels and went slithering across the floor. His legs had been so cramped within the wooden chest they were now completely numb and felt heavy and clumsy. Gibbering with frustration, he rubbed and slapped them vigorously to get the blood pumping around again.

Then his scatty wits remembered Gabbity and he hurried over to her.

"Grimditch save you, you gummy old baggage!" he declared grandly, setting about the knotted knitting that fettered her hands.

The nursemaid's struggles hindered his efforts, so it was many minutes before she was loose. Her hair was another matter. Neither she nor Grimditch could untie it. She clawed at it frantically but it was no use. Finally, she mimed cutting it and pointed to the knife on the table that she had used to shave the barn bogle earlier that day.

A moment later, the blade was scything through her wiry hair and she jumped to her feet.

"A hundred plagues on you!" she raged, lashing out and delivering Grimditch a mighty whack across his face.

"What you do that for?" he howled. "Me rescued you, you wormy old crab apple!"

"That's for taking so long!" she shouted at him as she wiped the webs from her eyes and chased the spiders from what was left of her hair.

The goblin glanced apprehensively at the door. "She will be back soon!" she told him. "You must flee from this place, before it is too late."

"Us both go!" Grimditch nodded as he ran to the door. "But no more smacks!"

Gabbity turned the key in the lock but the door would not open.

"She's spelled it shut!" she cried. "There's no getting out this way!"

Grimditch's bottom lip began to quiver, but she quickly put a stop to that.

"There is another way," she told him. "A secret path. Behind them drapes yonder is a great stone that hinges back as smooth as an oiled gate. 'Tis how She steals outside with no one seeing Her leave this chamber."

The barn bogle darted to the gloomy corner she had pointed at. He tore aside the dark cloth that hung there and revealed the carved stone wall behind. But he could not see any trace of a door. It was far too cunningly concealed. He pushed and shoved but nothing happened.

"Me can't find it!" he grunted in exasperation.

Gabbity was hunting through her bags of herbs and wool, muttering under her breath.

"Me can't find it!" Grimditch repeated.

The nursemaid ignored him. She was too intent on her own search. Presently, she gave a little cry of delight and ran back to the cradle, flourishing something in her hand.

"Missus!" Grimditch grumbled.

Gabbity bent over the infant, lifted him in her arms and placed something around his neck. Wrapping a moss-colored blanket around him, she carried the child to the corner.

"You must take him," she told Grimditch, handing the precious bundle over. "If you love him as I does, then bear the little lordling far from this evil place."

The barn bogle grunted from the sudden weight in his arms. He wasn't that much taller than the infant. His skinny legs almost gave way and his back bowed. Then he stared down at the peaceful, slumbering face crooked in his elbow. For a moment he was speechless and then he straightened his back. He would protect this tiny life with his own.

Then, abruptly, he shook his head in alarm. What was he thinking? He was only a lowly barn bogle. The baby wouldn't be safe with him and he tried to return him to the nursemaid's arms.

"No, no, no, no, no!" he said. "Me can't!"

But Gabbity refused to take the child and she seized hold of the barn bogle's shoulders. Her yellow eyes were burning and fierce. "He must go from here!" she insisted. "You doesn't understand, you stupid beast. You don't know what She intends to do with him."

Grimditch caught the horror in her voice and stared at her fearfully. "What be that?" he murmured.

The goblin took a steadying breath and stroked the infant's hair with a trembling hand. "M'Lady's wanting to celebrate this night," she began. "She's going to come back here and feast. She's going . . . She's going to eat him!"

Grimditch's mouth fell open and his large eyes grew even rounder. He made a strangled choking noise in his throat.

"So you have to take him!" Gabbity implored.

"But . . ." he croaked in anguish. "Him can't never leave here! Your witchy lady has kept him tiny and not growed by Her foul magics. If me carried him off, them snatched years would snap back and crumble him to dust."

Gabbity patted the thing she had placed around the infant's neck. It was a small effigy—carefully knitted in green wool, stuffed with strange-smelling herbs, and with a lock of real hair sewn onto the head. The hair was raven black.

"Aye," she said when she saw the barn bogle guess. "The hair is Hers. I snipped it without Her knowing one day. 'Twas the only way, else the charm would have no power. I made it long ago as a guard against such a plight as this. I never really dreamed it would be needed. I didn't know how wicked She truly is. Thank the serpents for my foresight. I put into this charm what small craft and lore I have. It has the virtue to keep my lordling safe. As long as it stays on him, the mortal years won't gobble him up—so make sure 'tis always there."

Grimditch frowned. "But you is coming as well?" he asked uncertainly.

The nursemaid turned away and pressed a finger into one of the recesses carved into the wall. There was a soft click and a tall section of stone swung backward into a narrow, sharply climbing passage.

"Come!" Grimditch urged. "Me niffs the outside!"

With the child in his arms, he stepped into the tunnel and began hurrying along it, but stopped when he realized she was not following. He peered back at her and saw the nursemaid still in the bedchamber, wiping her nose.

"Quick! Quick!" he called.

"You're such a bluntwitted beast," she answered wretchedly. "Look at that slender tunnel, now look at me. Are you so lacking in brain to notice? Gabbity's got too much comfy padding to squeeze herself through there."

The barn bogle looked at her squat, round shape and let out a groan. She was right.

"But you'll be deaded if you stops here, missus," he said. "She'll come back and pull your giblets out—double fast."

"That don't matter now," she replied. "And I'll have saved my sweet manikin from Her knife. That's enough for Old Gabbity. Now, get you gone."

Grimditch headed back toward her. There had to be some way she could be pulled or pushed or pummeled through.

"You got any goose fat there, missus?" he called. "We could grease you up and try squeezing you out."

Gabbity reached out her hand. "A goblin blessing upon you both," she said sadly, her voice breaking.

Grimditch saw what she was doing. He tried to cry out but it was too late. He heard the soft click and the stone slab silently closed back into place between them. He and the infant were sealed within the tunnel. It was pitch dark in there. Frantically, he ran his fingers over the smooth walls but couldn't find any lever or secret trigger.

"Missus!" he yelled, thumping a fist against the stone.

It was no use. Within the bedchamber, Gabbity closed her ears to his muffled protests. She settled down on her familiar stool and steeled herself for her mistress's return.

Grimditch ceased pounding on the stone. It hurt his fist, and he knew the faster he escaped the Hollow Hill, the better his chances would be.

Wrapping both arms about the infant, he began hurrying up the cramped and dark passage. The cool airs of evening that filtered down from the outside gave him hope and spurred him on. Presently, he saw the night sky peeping through gaps between the branches of a large gorse bush that concealed the tunnel entrance.

Screening the child's face from the spiky leaves, the barn bogle pushed through and emerged on the high slopes of the hillside.

For a long moment he stood there, breathing hard and gazing about him as a strong breeze blew cold and strange upon his shaven face and naked head. The trees that stirred below him were clogged with night shadows: sinister and thick with unknown menace. Where was he to go?

To the west a great fire was blazing in the woodland; black smoke was coiling up in massive pillowing clouds and by wind out over the forest. His old barn lay south, but the High Lady would suspect he would try to return to Moonfire Farm. The Cold Hills lay northward, but it was a desolate region with no shelter for the likes of him. Grimditch turned his attention to the east. From that stretch of the forest, a small bird was racing through the sky. Something silver was glinting in its little feet, but he had no time to wonder what it may be.

Suddenly, the night blared with the strident blast of trumpets. He let out a strangled yelp, believing they were proclaiming his escape. Then, the very ground beneath him began to rumble. He swayed and staggered, backward and forward, slithering down the slope in his woolen socks.

From far below the ground, he heard the thunderous grinding of colossal stones and felt the Hollow Hill shake, as if gripped by an earthquake.

Grimditch had no idea what was happening. He clasped the human child close to him and began leaping down the juddering hillside as fast as he could.

There came the sound of ripping and tearing. As he looked before him, he saw the ground was parting—splitting along the contour of the hill, and across his path, in one huge trench.

Whatever magic was behind this point was far more powerful than anything he had ever heard of. Roots of shrub and wildflowers were torn apart and loose earth went spilling down into the widening gulf. In a panic, the barn bogle rushed toward the gap and jumped across it. Then he hastened, terrified, down to the lower slopes, and only then he paused to glance back.

What he beheld made him suck in a marveling breath.

The summit of the Hollow Hill was rising. Gigantic monoliths were thrusting up from the lower regions of the earth, like vast pillars, supporting the immense grassy crown of the hill's summit. The subterranean halls and mansions of the Hidden Realm were now revealed, and the light from the great silver lanterns spilled out across the forest.

Grimditch did not know that such a momentous event had not happened since before the wars with the troll witches. This was Rhiannon Rigantona's declaration to the world that she, at long last, was free from fear and a divine, invincible force. The time of her true reign had commenced and the tradition of concealment was over.

The silvery green light that fell across Grimditch's face astounded him, but he quickly pulled himself together. Carrying the precious mortal child, he went bounding into the trees, the tails of his frock coat flapping madly and the trumpets of the Unseelie Court sounding a loud and piercing fanfare behind him.

· CHAPTER 13 ·

WARY AND CAUTIOUS

SEVERAL HOURS HAD PASSED since the death of the Tower Lubber. Tollychook Umbelnapper's stomach was growling so loudly that Fly the fox cub started snarling at it. Liffidia put her arms around the animal's neck and calmed him with a whisper in his ear.

"All this waitin'," the boy grumbled. "'Tis worse than the battlin'. I be imaginin' all sorts of 'orrible happenins in store. I almost wishes them Redcaps had stuck a poison dart in each of us and made a quick end of it."

Liffidia threw him an angry look and hissed for him to be quiet. They were in the infirmary, where she had been tending to the sick and injured birds. Peg-tooth Meg was still crouched by the dead Tower Lubber and many of her sluglung subjects were gathered around her, moaning soft, dirgelike sounds.

It was growing dark.

The ominous hammering had only recently ceased and the golden casket was still in Meg's hands. It too had stopped its answering chime and the heart within had fallen into silence.

"My sister is victorious," Meg said at length. "Young Tollychook is correct. It would have been far easier for us all if the Redcaps had succeeded. Now we must wait. She will return to have one final triumphant gloat before she is done with me."

Leaning over the Tower Lubber's face, she kissed his brow with her wide, toadlike lips. Then she arose, her crooked joints creaking.

"I shall await Rhiannon above," she said. "From the battlements, I shall watch her parade from the forest. I will not cower and hide. I am also a daughter of Ragallach; I shall meet her gaze without flinching."

Taking her harp and the casket with her, she ascended the stairs to the roof and her sluglung guards trailed after.

"It won't be too much longer," Liffidia told Tollychook. "Come. Let us go with them and await the end. We might as well all be together. There's nothing more we can do now. All hope is gone."

"I doesn't want to die on an empty stomach," Tollychook complained to the featherless hen matron, who clucked back at him and shooed him on his way.

Finnen Lufkin was still standing upon the battlements, watching the light fail in the sky and keeping an eye on the camp of the Redcaps below. Those vicious creatures had lit several small fires and were sitting around them, singing repulsive songs of brutal slaughter and cackling at hideous jokes. Only the bones of their former wardens remained, and they were well gnawed by now. They were growing impatient and they kept glancing back to the tower, wondering when they should attack again. Would the High Lady be angry if they didn't wait as she had commanded, they wondered?

Observing them, Finnen guessed what they were thinking. He heard Meg and the others gather behind him but he did not turn around.

"That hammering when the key was destroyed scared them," he said. "But they're back to their usual nasty selves and itching to get their knives and arrows wet again."

"They will enjoy my sister's new reign," Peg-tooth Meg said. "Now that she is free from fear, her ambition will be limitless. She will make a world of pain and horror, where suffering will replace love and her cruel whims shall be the only law. Before this day, she was only the blood-soaked tyrant of a small secret kingdom; henceforth her terror will have no bounds."

"How long before she comes back here?" Finnen asked.

"Soon," Meg said. "Very soon."

"Good," he replied. "I don't want to live in her new world."

Finnen stared west across the forest. The sun was taking a long time to set. In fact, it seemed to be growing brighter.

"Fire!" he cried. "The western edge of the wood is burning!"

"That will be her work," Meg told him.

"But that's our home! Our families are in that blaze—my old Nan!"

He whirled around in anguish. Liffidia and Tollychook had pushed to the front and were watching, horrified, at the angry glow in the far distance.

"Me Mam and Dad," Tollychook sniveled.

"Everyone we know . . ." Liffidia murmured.

Finnen's face turned almost as red as the distant flames and he let out a yell of helpless rage that was so loud several Redcaps glanced up at the battlements.

Meg shook her head sorrowfully. "So the immortal tyrant's reign begins," she announced, "with the slaughter of innocents. I am sorry you are stranded here, so far from your families and friends. If any of Tammedor's children were able, I'm sure they would have flown you there so you could try and save your loved ones."

"If I had been the ace wergler I pretended to be," Finnen said, with bitter self-reproach, "I could have changed into a bird myself."

Liffidia turned away. It was too hideous to think about what was happening over there in the land of the werlings.

It was Tollychook who finally said, in a hesitant mumble, "But, Master Lufkin . . . you doesn't need to be good at werglin'—not when there's that fire devil to do it for you."

The other werlings looked at him in astonishment. Then Finnen threw his arms about him.

"Tollychook Umbelnapper!" Finnen cried joyously. "You are the wisest out of the lot of us. Bless you—oh, bless you!"

Peg-tooth Meg gave a great smile and gladly handed over Harkul, the silver talisman.

"Go, all of you," she urged. "Be with those dearest to you at this evil hour."

"But we don't know how to fly," Liffidia told her. "Tollychook and me, we never wergled into birds. There's more to it than just flapping the wings; I know that much. We'd never make it and there isn't time to learn."

"I'd only be a fat bird anyways," Tollychook said morosely. "An' plop right down into one of them there Redcaps' laps."

Finnen looked at his friends and doubt clouded his face. How could he leave them? But Liffidia knew what he was thinking.

"The battle here is over now," she said warmly. "There is nothing anyone can do. But, over there—you could just make a huge difference, Finnen. You're smart and resourceful. You might still save some of them. We've always looked up to you, every single one of us, no matter what you did. Please hurry; please go!"

Tollychook was nodding feverishly in agreement.

"Take this chance, my former sluglung friend," Meg told him. "You have fought so courageously here. If I were queen, I would make you a knight of the Serpentine Order. There is no higher rank in the Unseelie Court. So fly now, Sir Finnen Lufkin and may the old forces of Dunwrach guard you."

At that moment there came the sound of galloping hooves through the forest and everyone turned to see goblin knights and elfin nobles come riding from the trees.

"She is here!" Meg declared. "Go now—hurry!"

Finnen gripped the silver talisman and closed his eyes. He concentrated hard and at once felt cold sparks crackle between his fingers. His back bent and his legs dwindled. A wave of white light washed over him and the fire devil slid through the feathers of his transformed wings.

Meg caught it and stroked the head of the bright-eyed blackbird that had taken the boy's place. It hopped onto her finger and she placed Harkul into one of his little claws.

"You will have need of this to return to your normal self," she said. Finnen cocked his head to one side. Then he spread his sleek wings and leaped from the tower.

Liffidia and Tollychook marveled as he flew straight and fast, high over the besieging enemy who strung their bows immediately and sent volleys of arrows into the air. The blackbird swerved and swooped, skillfully avoiding every one.

"He was always the best of us," Liffidia said softly.

"Tell me Mam I miss her!" Tollychook cried.

The blackbird was already vanishing into the distance—a fluttering fleck almost invisible against the dark smoke that was climbing over the horizon. The silver fire devil glinted briefly in his grasp and then they lost sight of him.

Peg-tooth Meg lowered her eyes and stared down at the troop of mounted knights and nobles who had ridden from the forest. Their bright armor was gleaming and the tips of silver spears flashed, reflecting the flames of the Redcap fires. Lord Limmersent rode at the forefront, his face grim and stern.

"What puzzlement is this?" Meg muttered as she watched them advance. There were not as many as she had expected and her sister was not among them.

Lord Limmersent reined his steed to a halt and stared up at the broken watchtower. Since the secret meeting that afternoon with Lord Fanderyn, he and the other four nobles, together with the two goblin knights and the most trusted members of their households, had searched the forest in vain for clues as to where the High Lady had taken the spriggans and then the Redcaps. Only when they came across an exhausted spriggan deserter and put the fear of water on him did they discover where the battle had been fought that morning, and so they spurred their horses toward the eastern edge of Hagwood. The kluries had remained behind in the hill, to spread the word among their folk, and others, that salvation was finally at hand.

Now Lord Limmersent peered upward, unable to disguise his disdain.

"What manner of creature dwells therein?" he asked himself. "And how am I to parley with it?"

But before he could approach the entrance, the Redcaps leaped from their campfires and ran after the horses, jabbering and snapping at the heels of the riders.

Sir Begwort and Sir Hobflax, the goblin knights, unsheathed their swords and swept the bright blades before the crowding savage faces.

"Keep your distance," they warned. "These are lordly folk. Where are your keepers?"

The Redcaps hesitated, but their eyes were filled with hate and they spat at the horses.

"We ate them!" they boasted, smacking their lips. "By the leave of the Lady Herself. And we'll dine on you and your chargers if you try to enter that there tower."

"What you doing here?" others demanded. "Where is the Lady?"

They surged forward and swarmed around Lord Limmersent and his company, forming a snarling barrier between him and the entrance. "No one is to go in there," they growled.

"Out of my way, gibbet fodder!" Lord Limmersent commanded. "How dare you obstruct me, descendent of a princely house? You are but stomachs on legs whereas the pure blood of the fallen realm beyond the Lonely Mere runs in my veins."

The Redcaps gurgled with insolent delight. "We won't waste a drop of it," they promised greedily.

Lord Limmersent snorted with anger and looked at his fellow nobles. They were just as infuriated as he was. Earl Brennant had drawn two long knives and was pointing them at the throats of the two most vocal and jeering of the Redcaps. The Lady Mauvette was gripping a jeweled dagger and the aged Earl Tobevere had a hand on the hilt of his sword in readiness. The goblin knights were desperate to spur their horses into the mob and go slashing with their steel but there were too many of those bloodthirsty fiends for them to battle.

Lord Limmersent tossed his head in rage. Precious time was slipping away. The Redcaps were obviously expecting the High Lady to return at any moment and then he and the others would be caught in their conspiracy against her. He decided to bluff it out.

"We have been sent by Rhiannon," he lied. "She commands we speak with those in yonder tower. Withdraw, let us pass."

The Redcaps squinted up at him. They had no reason to disbelieve his words but there was something suspicious going on and they shuffled backward reluctantly.

Lord Limmersent regained his composure and led the knights and nobles to the foot of the tower.

He stared up at the battlements again but, in the failing light, could see only dim shapes peering down at him.

"I come to you from the Hollow Hill!" he shouted. "Lord Limmersent am I—noble of the Unseelie Court. We desire a counsel with you."

While he waited for an answer, the Redcaps crowded before the broken entrance. Their own orders were to let no one in or out and they were going to stick to them.

The other nobles grew anxious. They had not imagined they would have to yell their secret rebellion into the sky like this.

Then, from high above, a dry, croaking voice called down, "Hail, Perival Limmersent. Many years have passed since I last beheld your proud face."

Hearing his first name, Lord Limmersent sat bolt upright in the saddle and cursed under his breath. Who was that up there? Who knew him?

"Declare yourself!" he demanded. "Who are you to use my name?"

Peg-tooth Meg gazed down on him, a vague shape in the deepening shadows. "Do the fountains still spout sweet in the courtyard of your halls?" she called. "Long ago, I danced in them."

The noble strained his eyes and searched his memory but could not guess who was atop that tower.

"Let us speak together!" he answered. "It may be our goals are the same."

"Why are you here?" Meg asked. "What do you hope to gain from me?"

Lord Limmersent cast a wary eye over the Redcaps then abandoned caution completely.

"We seek the golden casket made by the Puccas!" he declared. "If you have this powerful thing, what I hope for, what I pray you can grant us, is an end to the Tyrant of the Hollow Hill."

The nobles around him shifted uneasily and glanced over their shoulders at the dark forest. There was no going back now.

On the rooftop, Peg-tooth Meg turned to her sluglungs.

"Shimmil Dunge, my loves," she told them.

On the ground the Redcaps were hissing ferociously. Savage, bestial loyalty to the High Lady flamed in their breasts and their eyes locked on the throats of this treacherous, lying lord and his companions. Their bodies tensed and they prepared to spring.

Then, without warning, a sound so unexpected filled the air, all thought of battle was momentarily forgotten. It was music—a plaintive, sorrowful melody that dripped from above like rain. The Redcaps were confounded and gaped upward while the nobles exclaimed in confusion.

The Lady Mauvette uttered a small cry of recognition and caught her breath. "I know that sound," she said. "I have heard it so many times. But it cannot be . . ."

It was the sound of a harp. Peg-tooth Meg had run her fingers over the strings of the enchanted instrument she had made from the bones of her dead brother. The only tune it would ever play was that of the lullaby their father the High King had sang to his children. Now those soulful notes cascaded down from the battlements and Meg's cracked voice began to sing.

Three young chicks are chirping in the nest:
One a princeling with gold on his crest.
Another the fairest, with love in her breast.
One the darkest, more quiet than the rest.

Little birds, little birds, your father so adores you.
By the joy that you bring, his kingdom is all for you.
With deepest love, the Hollow Hill implores you,
To reign one day—may faerie gold shower o'er you.

"What wonder is this?" breathed the Lady Mauvette. "After so many years."

Every eye was trained upward and so everyone witnessed the same impossible sight at once.

Something was descending. A hunched figure was floating down from the tower. At first it seemed to be sitting on empty air, but then they saw what appeared to be glistening, stretching ropes on either side of it.

The sluglungs had merged together into one great quivering mass and were lowering Meg over the battlements. Sitting in a seat formed from two large clasped hands, she drifted gently down. The gruesome harp was tucked under one of her arms, its strings still thrumming on their own, and the golden casket lay on her lap.

The goblin knights rode their horses to one of the campfires, took up burning brands and galloped back, holding them high over their heads. The crackling light shone across the strange and grotesque figure dangling from the battlements. It had stopped its descent and was now suspended just out of reach. Nobody had seen such a face as Meg's before and they did not hide their revulsion.

Her froglike mouth became even wider as she smiled grimly and her bulging eyes alighted upon each of them.

Even the Redcaps grimaced as the torchlight played over her unlovely features, but they too were eager to see what would happen next.

Finally, Peg-tooth Meg spoke.

"Many years have flowed by since I fled the land of eternal summer beneath the great hill," she said. "Though you do not recognize me, I know your faces well enough."

"Give us your name!" Lord Limmersent demanded.

Meg drew a hand through her lank green hair but, before she could speak, someone else called out, "Princess Clarisant!"

The Lady Mauvette walked her horse forward. Her hands were trembling and a tear rolled down her cheek.

The others stared at her in astonishment. "What crooked jest is this?" Earl Brennant cried. "Why do you address that misshapen toad wife so?"

"Clarisant," Marquess Gurvynn murmured. "That is a name I have not heard in too long a time. The fairest child under the soil, with golden hair and a laugh even more treasured."

"Not that ogress, certainly," snapped Earl Brennant.

The Lady Mauvette made no answer. She gazed up at Meg, ignoring the outward ugliness and recognized the beautiful spirit within her.

Lord Limmersent shook his head, frowning. "As night is to day," he muttered. "Princess Clarisant was as beautiful as you are hideous. And yet . . . I recall well her delight as she danced in my fountains."

The Lady Mauvette slipped from the saddle and sank to the ground in a deep curtsey. "My dearest Lady!" she said humbly.

The nobles could scarcely believe it. But the more they stared at the hump-backed creature suspended from the battlements, the more they became aware she possessed a regal dignity. It was as if the supreme ugliness was but a dense veil concealing a majestic light within, yet glimmers of that radiance were still shining through.

One by one, the nobles climbed from their horses and then knelt with their heads bowed. The Redcaps were murmuring among themselves. Was this really the daughter of the late, beloved King? They looked at one another in confusion. What were they to do?

"Your Highness," Lord Limmersent said. "Forgive our rough manners. These are desperate times and this is the darkest hour. Your return among us is surely a sign of hope."

Peg-tooth Meg motioned for them to rise.

"This is the hope you sought and gambled your lives for," she said, solemnly holding the golden casket up for them to see.

"What lies within?" Lord Limmersent asked. "What is this weapon that can defeat Rhiannon Rigantona?"

Meg held the box against her cheek and stroked it. From inside there came a soul-rending cry.

"Have mercy!" it shrieked. "Have pity! Eternal gulfs of pain and unendurable torment are before me—spare me! I beg you! Release me—release me! Worse crimes are to come—oh, much worse."

The terror and despair of that desolate voice sent a tingle of horror down everyone's spine. Even the horses stamped their hooves and swished their tails and the Redcaps covered their ears.

"What accursed spirit is in there?" The Lady Mauvette asked. "It wails an ocean of sorrow. I cannot bear it!"

"Make it stop!" Earl Brennant implored.

"But it's Her!" Sir Begwort cried. "It speaks with the High Lady's voice, or I have never heard Her speak."

Meg put the casket to her lips and whispered until the voice lapsed into bitter sobbing. Then she looked back at the nobles and said, "Here, inside this lovely treasure, beats all that was good of my sister—it contains her living heart."

"Such a thing cannot be!" Lord Limmersent protested.

"There is no *cannot* where Rhiannon Rigantona is concerned," Meg told him. "Using foul arts learned from Black Howla, she drew it from her breast and placed it within this casket—and then . . ."

She paused, hardly realizing that even the Redcaps were hanging on her words.

"And then she murdered our father."

"The High King?" the nobles cried incredulously.

Meg nodded. "She slew him with our brother's knife, then urged the spriggans and Redcaps to hunt Alisander down. And so he too was killed and thus she gained the throne."

The assembled Redcaps flicked their heads from side to side. They refused to believe it. It was the prince who had murdered King Ragallach—everyone knew that. They had shot him with their poisoned arrows in just revenge.

Stealthily, some of them reached for their bows. They had heard enough of these twisted lies.

Too wrapped up in Meg's revelations, the nobles did not notice that arrows were being drawn from their quivers.

"Locked within this casket," Meg continued, "my sister's heart is safe from hurt and harm and so is she. No power can afflict her now."

"But Fanderyn!" Lord Limmersent interrupted excitedly. "He has the key! This very afternoon we have seen it!"

Meg shook her head. "Did you not hear the clamor before the setting of the sun?" she asked. "That was the end of the key and the destruction of our hopes. You have lost your gamble, my lord. This casket can avail you nothing. Each of us is doomed."

"You sooner than the rest, lying Toadwitch!" a Redcap screeched as he sprang forward and loosed an arrow up at her.

Meg turned her head quickly. There was a rush of air as the dart went zinging past her ear and she felt the flight feathers skim through her hair. But the poisoned tip did not break her skin.

Sir Hobflax spurred his horse into the Redcaps and, in an instant, the archer's head was rolling on the ground.

At once the savage creatures leaped up at the nobles, yammering for blood. Swords flashed and death cries rang out.

"Each of us is doomed!" Peg-tooth Meg repeated as the fighting raged. "Yea, even you, her savage hell hounds. My sister will breed fiends more ferocious still and your worth will be ended."

Not one of them heard her. They were screaming at the nobles. Three of the Redcaps had scrambled onto Earl Tobevere's horse and were tearing at his silver beard. The aged earl hit out at them and reached for his blade but they seized his hand and bit into his wrist. The Lady Mauvette's dagger plunged into two of them. Sir Begwort dragged the third off by his ears and hurled him against the tower wall.

"Bring down the chargers!" the other brutes were shrieking.

A moment later, every little fist held an arrow. Screaming ghastly cries, they lunged at the horses. The beasts whinnied and reared and pounded with their hooves. Marquess Gurvynn was thrown from the saddle and immediately set upon. One of the evil arrows found its mark and was driven into the flank of Lord Limmersent's stallion. The horse bucked and shivered and flung its head back.

The Redcaps jabbered with hellish glee and hurried out of the way as it pranced in a demented circle. With a terrible crash, the animal collapsed on the ground and its rider was pitched headlong into the Redcaps' midst.

There was no time to retrieve the sword that had been ripped from his hand. Groaning on the ground, Lord Limmersent saw a crowd of brutal faces leer over him.

Then, suddenly, there came the blare of trumpets and the earth under their feet began to quake.

The Redcaps yowled and fell back in fear.

Sir Begwort hurried to Lord Limmersent's aid but the noble waved him away.

"Attend to Gurvynn," he ordered.

"The Marquess is dead," the Lady Mauvette replied.

Lord Limmersent rose and retrieved his sword. Then he turned a vengeful face upon the gibbering Redcaps. Another fierce trumpet blast split the night and a silvery radiance spilled out over the forest. From the tower battlements, Liffidia's voice called down, "The hill! The hill is rising!"

Peg-tooth Meg nodded in understanding. "Rhiannon has commanded the Under Magic," she declared. "My sister has proclaimed her supremacy. She is coming for us."

• CHAPTER 14 •

WERLINGS VS. SPRIGGANS

CAPTAIN GRITTLE HAD LED THE SPRIGGANS quickly through the forest. Yelling at the top of his voice, he had berated and ridiculed, threatened and bullied them every step of the way. Even Wumpit and Bogrinkle, who, like him, had not been part of the force that had deserted the Battle of Watch Well early that morning, smarted under his scalding scorn.

Grittle was desperate to prove to the High Lady that they were still the best soldiers under her command. When Chumpwattle, one of the younger lads, stumbled and fell, the captain smacked him about the head and jabbed him with a blade until he scrambled to his feet and trotted along faster than ever. And so the spriggans thundered through the trees and were soon crossing the Hagburn into the land of the werlings.

At the solitary standing stone known as the Hag's Finger, Captain Grittle stomped to a halt and held up a hand for the rest to do the same.

"Alright, you dainty lot," he snapped as he paced down the lines. "Don't forget you're only 'ere because Her Ladyship showed you mercy. Why that is, I doesn't know, but don't you go thinkin' She'll stay in that humor for long—you know what She's like. We have to prove our legion is worth our cheese and worms or we're all fer the chop. Does I make myself clear?"

The others shouted that they understood and saluted as they stamped their feet in unison. Grittle's eyes narrowed.

"That's more like it," he said. "Now, that there yonder wood is where them 'orrible ratlings are. Get yerself some dead branches and lets go storming in with burning torches. Smoking charcoal twigs is what She wants that place to be, come morning, so that's what we'll give Her. Don't you leave out one single tree—set each one ablazin'!"

"And them soapy weasels?" Wumpit piped up.

"Butcher the lot."

The spriggans cheered and hunted for the driest kindling they could find.

It was not long before they were lined up on the grassy track once more, each with a flaming torch in one hand, a knife in the other, and a bundle of wood strapped on his back.

Their captain inspected them. Then with a curl of his lip, he cried, "In the name of Batar! Charge!"

The soldiers rushed into the land of the werlings, cutting the air with their blades and leaving streaks of fire in their wake.

THE WERLINGS HAD NOT BEEN IDLE.

For the past two days, they had been preparing for the inevitable attack. They had incurred the High Lady's fury by destroying her thorn ogres, and expected retribution at any moment. They posted sentries in various wergled forms along their borders and were hard at work improvising as many defenses as they could.

It was Figgle Tumpin, the father of Gamaliel and Kernella, who first spotted the spriggans. Sitting high in a tree, in the shape of a squirrel, Figgle watched them cross the Hagburn. Then he darted back along the branches, leaping from tree to tree, and shouting the ancient alarm.

"'Ware! 'Ware!" he cried. "Wolves! Owls! Witches! 'Ware! 'Ware!" Within moments, every werling was at his or her post and nervously waiting for the signal to begin the defense of their peaceful land.

On the grass below, the spriggans' torches flamed into view. Captain Grittle chose a stately oak and barked at two of his lads to heap their wood around it. Before they could even remove the bundles from their shoulders, they heard a shrill whistle in the night above.

Watching them from a high branch, Diffi Maffin, an old and respected member of the werling council, gave an indignant toss of her head. At the sound of her whistle, two groups feverishly set to work on a pair of thick ropes twined from ivy and honeysuckle, cutting them with their little knives.

"What were that?" one of the spriggans muttered.

"Vermin," Grittle spat.

Suddenly, there was a rush and rustle of leaves overhead. The spriggans craned their necks and saw an immense bough falling toward them.

Yelling, they leaped aside, but two of them were not swift enough and the great branch came smashing down, trapping them beneath it.

"Jibbler's eyes have popped out!" Bogrinkle shouted. "He's a goner!"

"Get Slitchin free!" Captain Grittle ordered. "Them dirty imps are going to pay fer that."

Angrily, he tore the sticks from a soldier's back, piled them against the oak and thrust his torch into them. Within moments greedy flames were licking up the trunk.

"Don't just stand there dithering like rabbits in front of the cat!" he bawled at the others. "Get burning!"

The spriggans hurried to obey but dropped their bundles in astonishment when they heard a small voice call out.

"Hoy—that's my tree you've set light to!"

Figgle Tumpin had marched right up to them. He had wergled back to his usual self but had retained the squirrel tail, as was his habit. With his arms folded crossly, he scowled up at the High Lady's soldiers.

"Put that fire out!" he shouted. "Who do you think you are? Ugly, big-eared villains. Clear off, before any more branches flatten your stupid heads."

Some of the soldiers glanced warily overhead but the others bared their teeth at this bold creature and their knuckles grew white around the hilts of their knives.

"Slice him!" Grittle bellowed.

The spriggans lunged at the werling but Figgle bounded away, his bushy tail flicking impudently in their faces as they rampaged after him.

"Now!" Diffi Maffin called from her vantage point above.

Another rope was cut. Figgle ducked as he ran and a tremendous log came swinging down, whooshing over his head like a deadly pendulum. It was too late for his pursuers to escape and the breath was punched out of them as the log piled into their breastplates. Five of them were swept high off the ground and flung backward.

Captain Grittle watched his soldiers go flying and his temper boiled over. They were being made complete fools by these filthy ratlings.

"Kill them!" he roared.

The spriggans chased after Figgle who, to their fury, was now performing an insulting dance on tiptoe across a stretch of dead leaves and shaking his tail in the most insolent manner.

They raged forward and the leafy ground cracked and splintered beneath them. They were standing on flimsy twigs that snapped under their weight and four soldiers were tipped into a deep pit, the bottom of which was filled with monstrous thistles and freshly cut nettles.

Captain Grittle tore at his hair. Figgle shook with laughter and went scooting up the nearest tree. The spriggan cursed and threw his knife. It glittered through the shadows and embedded itself deep in the bark, just a whisker away from Figgle's head.

The werling grimaced and thanked his luck, then vanished up into the leaves.

"Burn this tree!" Grittle screamed. "And get those clots out of that hole!"

His remaining soldiers hurried forward with their firewood then turned about, quickly.

"That's my elm!" a new voice was shouting. It was Mister Doolan, Bufus's father. He was standing a short distance away and he looked more annoyed than Figgle had been. At his side were thirty other werlings. Captain Grittle regarded them with a snarl but his eye began to twitch as he saw that each of their hands held a large stone.

"That's for Mufus!" Mister Doolan cried, letting one of his missiles fly. It arced through the air and struck Captain Grittle squarely between the eyes. The spriggan yowled and, as his hands flew to protect his face, another stone hit his elbow.

"And that's for Bufus!" Mister Doolan added. "Wherever he may be!"

With that, the other werlings threw their stones and every one found a bare, fleshy target.

The spriggans hopped and flinched away in pain from the horrible hail, but Captain Grittle demanded they stand their ground. Stones were no match for steel and the honor of the legion was at stake. But the frenzied pelting was relentless. A supply of stones had been stowed in little heaps on the ground and the aim of those detestable wer rats was stingingly accurate. The spriggans dropped their torches and were driven toward the edge of the woodland. Then, somewhere above, that infuriatingly haughty female voice called out another order.

At once, four more heavy logs came plummeting down as the leaves under the soldiers' boots flew up, revealing a hidden net. Howling in surprise, the spriggans were scooped up. Before they realized what was happening, they were squashed together like so many plums in a bag and, an instant later, were dangling from a lofty branch.

"I'm gonna puke," one of them burbled.

"Get off my head!" another shouted.

"When I find out whose knives are jabbing my backside, they'll eat my fists!" promised a third.

Other voices gave muffled shouts. Captain Grittle wanted to yell too but the back of someone's knee was across his mouth and a hobnailed toe was kicking his ribs. He himself was upside down and his sword arm was wedged tight in the knot of bodies that crammed this humiliating snare. How could they have been so careless? His face grew redder and redder, from shame and fury.

Wrenching his other arm free, he pulled a dagger from somebody's belt and began hacking at the net that held them.

The ivy and honeysuckle ropes gave way and suddenly the net split open. The captives were disgorged without warning and they tumbled back to earth, shrieking with fright. They slammed onto the ground in a writhing mass. Bones cracked and knives sliced through skin, boots thudded into backs and heads were bumped and bloodied.

Captain Grittle had landed clear of the sorry pile. He was severely jolted and grazed and he could feel a great bruise thumping over his cheekbone. But the more serious injury was to his honor and pride.

He staggered to his feet and whirled around murderously. The infernal ratlings had disappeared.

"Smoke and cinders," he hissed. "That's all there'll be left of this plaguey place. By my blood, I swear it."

The oak that he had set alight was now blazing—a magnificent spectacle to his vengeful eyes. When every tree was aflame there would be nowhere for those loathsome vermin to hide.

Rounding on his lads, he bellowed at them to pick themselves up and carry out their orders. He didn't care if one of them had broken an arm, bitten through his lip, or lost an ear. They had a job to do and, so far, he was disgusted with their unmilitary conduct.

In the treetops, Figgle Tumpin watched them hobble to retrieve their bundles of kindling and pick up their torches once more. All the while they peered around—suspicious and cautious. Gamaliel's father grinned; the next surprise would be even better than the last.

The spriggans piled the sticks against three trees and their captain growled at them to fetch more. Covered in thistle spikes and nettle stings, Chumpwattle finally succeeded in clambering out of the pit and went lolloping off to obey. In a small clearing, he saw a great mound of dry twigs and called his comrades to help collect them.

Six spriggans hurried over and began gathering sticks from this strangely fortuitous heap. As they did so, several werlings, who had wergled into moles, popped their heads up from the soil directly behind them and crept stealthily out of their tunnels. The ends of ivy ropes were lying innocently in the grass. The spriggans were far too intent on their task to notice them, or to even feel their bootlaces being tampered with.

As soon as the werlings dived back into their burrows, the female voice called down, "Now, Mister Goilok!"

Captain Grittle had just plunged his torch into the heart of the kindling at the bottom of the Doolan elm and was watching with satisfaction as the flames encompassed the trunk. When he heard those words, he whirled around and saw what his flustered soldiers had failed to notice. Just beyond the mound of firewood, a row of strong silver birch saplings were bowed out of shape, their leafy tops tethered to the ground by taut, straining ropes.

In a flash, Grittle knew what was about to happen. He hollered at his lads to get away. Some of them whisked their heads around stupidly; two tried to run but tripped over their feet. The first of the silver birches was suddenly released. It sprang back up with quivering force.

Chumpwattle was laughing and pointing at the two spriggans who had fallen over. An instant later, one of them wasn't there. He had been torn along the ground by the rope tied to his bootlaces. He ripped through the mound of sticks and was then catapulted into the night. The rope snapped and he went soaring over the trees.

It happened so fast that the other spriggans simply stood there, dumbfounded. His shrieks had not even faded when realization dawned and they finally stared down at their own boots. A second tree went whipping back and another spriggan was shot into the sky.

Chumpwattle fumbled for one of his knives and stooped to cut the rope that tied him, but the weapon fell from his trembling fingers. Suddenly his legs were wrenched from under him and the ground dropped away. Higher and higher he rocketed. The wind screamed in his big flapping ears and his armor rattled wildly. The cinder track that bordered the wood rolled by far below, then he saw the expanse of the Barren Heath. All too soon the momentum failed and he braced himself for the crash. Then as he toppled out of the sky, he saw where he was headed and screeched in horror.

A moment later, he landed with a mighty splash in the Lonely Mere, rapidly followed by four more.

Captain Grittle had witnessed his hapless soldiers cast into the air and the rage turned cold inside him.

Of the sixteen spriggans who set out with him, only eight remained, and two of those were still rolling on the forest floor, gasping, after the log had swung into them. The rest of his fighting force looked battered and dented and the traps had made them jumpy.

He grunted and ground his teeth and called upon his years of training and command. His eyes flicked from side to side. There was a strategy to all of this. The enemy was deliberately keeping them on the outskirts of the wood. Every trap was designed to prevent them from pressing deeper into the trees, to engage them here at the edge. Grittle almost admired the skill and cunning behind these tactics. It was all very efficient, almost military. But just what were those little tree rats protecting? Not their homes, some of which were already ablaze. What secret lay at the heart of this land?

An unpleasant grin split the captain's face. He was determined to discover what that was.

"You two stop clutching at yer guts and fall in!" he shouted to his soldiers. "The rest, make sure yer torches are burning bright and everyone follow me. Don't let none of them tiddly mites lead you astray—no matter what they does."

He sprang forward and darted southward into the trees with his eight remaining soldiers hurrying after him.

Figgle Tumpin watched in dismay as the invaders rushed off. They had other defenses to keep those brutes busy here at the fringes of the woodland.

Figgle ran along the branches and joined a large group of werlings who were poised with ropes and nets.

"What is happening, Mister Tumpin?" asked the elderly but commanding Diffi Maffin.

"They're making a dash deeper into the wood!" he explained hurriedly. "We need to lure them back here. I'll go pretend I'm hurt and get them chasing me."

"That won't work!" Tidubelle Tumpin cried, pushing to the front and smiling grimly at him. "They've seen you dodge and duck around already and know how quick you are. They won't fall for it again. We need to use our wits. This is wife work. They might just think they stand a chance of catching me."

"And they'd be right!" her husband retorted.

A terse glance from her told him what she thought of that and in a trice she had leaped from the branch onto the one beneath, then scrambled down the trunk.

The spriggans were charging deeper into the wood. They were just running past the old apple tree, beneath which the werling council met, when they heard a frightened scream.

Captain Grittle turned and, by the light of the torches, saw a small stricken werling woman staring at them a little distance away, petrified with terror.

"Help!" she yelled, too afraid to move. "Help!"

Bogrinkle lunged aside to snatch at her but Grittle caught him by the neck and yanked him back.

"Don't trust it!" he growled.

"But I can catch that, easy!" Bogrinkle protested.

"Keep to this path," his captain warned.

Tidubelle pretended to master her fear and tried to run. With great dramatic effect, she let out a howl and artfully tripped over a tree root then nursed her ankle as though she had twisted it. "Ow . . . ow!" Tidubelle yelped as she tried to stand.

The spriggans stared at her. It was too tantalizing. She was practically begging to be caught. Every instinct burned in them to leap at her, but their captain slapped their slavering faces.

"Don't you go buying none of that there mummery!" he berated. "'Tis only more dust in our eyes. This way is where we're bound. Yonder is where those tree lice want to keep us away from, so let's press on. That she-rat would be off up a tree sooner than you could blink and then we'd find ourselves in another pit or snare."

Tidubelle scowled as the spriggans hurried on, ignoring her. Her face looked as vexed as that of her daughter, Kernella, often did, and she kicked the root she had pretended to fall over.

Silently and swiftly, her husband scrambled down the tree to join her and others quickly followed.

"I tried my best," Tidubelle said sadly.

Figgle hugged her. "I know, Belle," he sighed. "We've all done our best, but it wasn't enough."

Mister Doolan held up his hand abruptly. "Listen!" he hissed. "Those devils have found the Silent Grove."

The werlings held their breaths.

"Then we've lost the battle," Figgle murmured.

The spriggans had hastened on and rushed down into a wide, basin-shaped dell where many ancient beech trees grew. This was the heart of the werling land. Grittle and the other soldiers knew it at once.

Even their uncouth and brutal senses could tell that this was a sacred place. The trees were incredibly old and misshapen. Great bulges and bumps disfigured them, yet they were magnificent and somber and commanded attention. Wumpit had the uncomfortable feeling they were alive and aware. It was as if they were watching and waiting. All was hushed and still and the leaves that trembled overhead made no sound. The air itself seemed different. It was thick and sleepy and peaceful and a faint musty sweetness floated beneath the branches like incense. Wumpit didn't like it one little bit. Neither did the others.

Their captain sniffed and stuck out his tongue at the disagreeable scent.

"More tricks?" Bogrinkle asked suspiciously.

"I ain't so sure," Grittle answered. "This is deeper, there's magic in these 'ere beeches, old wild magic, sucked up from way down."

"Does a forest god live here?" Wumpit wondered in a fearful voice.

"There ain't no forest gods!" Grittle snapped back. "Only . . . Her Majesty."

"And Batar," one of the others added.

"Aye," the captain said with a nod. "Her and the bloody Wolf of War. That's all there is."

Wumpit thought of the brass wolf's head back in the spriggan dormitory. "We didn't leave any offering to Him afore we set out," he said unhappily. "And the others didn't leave none this morning neither. 'Tain't no surprise they lost that battle and why we been thrashed so bad by such tiny wer-rats. Batar's angry with us."

The captain struck him fiercely and rounded on the rest. "That's enough of that sort of talk!" he yelled. "We're going to show them vermin we're not to be duped and made fools of. I doesn't care what sort of magic flows through this place—I wants it torched!"

"No!" cried many voices suddenly.

The spriggans turned. Assembled on the surrounding slopes stood every adult werling who dwelled in that land. Defeat was in their faces and they looked anxious and afraid.

"Ho!" Grittle declared. "Come to watch, have you?"

An elderly, silver-haired specimen, with an authoritative bearing and a defiant expression on her lined face, stepped forward. It was Diffi Maffin, and when she spoke, the spriggans recognized her voice as the one that had given the orders to spring the traps.

"You must not set flame to these holy trees!" she said. "They are sacred to us."

Grittle leered at her. "What makes them so special?" he demanded.

"They are our history and heritage," she answered proudly. "Our forebears are interred within them. They are the living tombs of our ancestors. We know every name of every generation placed inside and revere and honor each one. The blessed beeches are our future resting places. We will surrender to you if you do not harm them. There is nothing we prize so highly and we are nothing without them. You have conquered us—we have nothing left to fight for."

The captain's face twitched again, half suspecting some new deceit but one look at those small, ludicrously honest faces confirmed she was speaking the truth. He signaled to six of his lads and, with drawn swords, they approached the werlings.

"Round 'em up," he ordered. "Keep them penned in. If they try anything, start hacking."

The spriggans drove the little people together like miniature cattle and stood in a circle around them. The werlings looked up at their ugly faces and eyed the glittering steel of their blades. There would be no mercy from those villains. Wives and husbands, friends and neighbors hugged one another and were thankful that they had sent the children over to the Barren Heath earlier that day to hide in burrows. At least they would be spared.

Captain Grittle swaggered up the sloping bank and surveyed them with a contemptuous glare.

"Puny low breeds," he growled. "Think you can make donkeys out of Her Highness's finest warriors and then give in when it gets too big for you?"

He raised a hobnail-booted foot and gave Diffi Maffin a kick that sent the elderly councilor sprawling.

"I never was one fer dumping carcasses in holes," he declared with a malicious grin. "Such a dirty, heathen custom. Cremation is so much tidier. I does like to be tidy."

He snapped his fingers and Wumpit and Bogrinkle ran immediately to the nearest beech. To the werlings' horror, they laid their kindling down and within moments a greedy fire was blazing.

"Stop it!" they begged. "Our families! Our loved ones—our glorious lineage!"

Captain Grittle guffawed and shouted to his soldiers to continue.

Presently, every tree within the Silent Grove was burning. The heat and the roar of the flames were unbearable. Bogrinkle and Wumpit came hurrying up the bank with their hair smoldering and their faces blackened with smoke.

The werlings could only stare at the awful spectacle. Some were mouthing the names of their ancestors, but most of them were too aghast to do anything but watch as the enchanted and mysterious trees withered and charred in the destroying flame. Perhaps it was the shimmering haze or the stinging smoke in their eyes, but it seemed to them that the beeches were writhing and twisting in agony.

Captain Grittle threw back his head and laughed, then gave orders to set the rest of the woodland alight.

"And when every tree is burning," he announced, "then me and the lads will get our knives wet."

One by one the oaks and chestnuts, rowans and sycamores were put to the flame. The hazel tree in which children had received their wergling instruction blazed fiercely and the council apple tree was engulfed in rivers of brilliant fire.

Enjoying themselves immensely, the spriggans herded the defeated werlings away from the Silent Grove and through the burning woodland. The air was scorching. It burned their mouths when they breathed and singed the hairs on their heads. The night was filled with choking smoke and sparks. Flakes of drifting ash swirled thickly in the hot draughts, glimmering like clouds of sizzling butterflies. Their whole world was on fire. Everything they knew was gone.

At the western edge of the wood, where the trees grew thin and a verge of grass and wildflowers lay before the cinder trackway, the spriggans halted and looked back at their handiwork.

"Never been a fire like it!" Captain Grittle said proudly. "Proper inferno. She won't have no complaint nor grumble about that. It's enough to blister even the moon's crusty hind parts. Job well done, that is, lads."

He turned to glower at the werlings, pulled a blade from his belt and added with a sickening hiss, "Or, should I say, a job half done?"

The other spriggans held up their swords and knives, admiring the polished steel and how it mirrored the ferocious, raging light.

"We should skewer some of these," Wumpit said, pointing at the defeated werlings with the tip of his knife. "They might make a tasty bite if roasted."

"No more than three each if they do," the captain declared. "I want to hang the rest from poles and take them back to Her so She can count the little corpses and see we've done our duty."

"Let's get jabbing then," Bogrinkle said. "I hopes they dance about a bit and make it lively."

"Just kill 'em," Grittle ordered sternly. "But I bags that uppity old harpy what gave the orders before—and the fat one with the bushy tail."

The werlings closed their eyes as weapons were drawn back and each spriggan selected his first victim.

FINNEN LUFKIN FLEW as fast as his new wings would carry him. The vast sprawl of Hagwood rushed beneath but he saw only the rim of fire that fringed the forest's western edge. He did not notice the desperate figure of Grimditch clutching the little lordling upon the Hollow Hill, nor did he glance back when the trumpets blasted and the ground rumbled.

The angry glare of greedy flames shone red before him. If only he could fly faster, he might arrive in time to help the werlings—unless it was already too late.

He flew into the suffocating smoke and the furious beating of his wings made it surge and eddy in turbulent whirls around him. His bright blackbird eyes were streaming and the baking heats of the fires below were singeing his feathers.

Flying as low as he dared, he tried to see through the leaping flames but there was no sign of the other werlings. Were they being burned alive within the trees or had they escaped? He called out at the top of his voice but his cries were drowned in the raging firestorm.

Hurtling through the burning woodland, he finally beheld the furious, unstoppable fires that squalled throughout the Silent Grove. The horrendous sight was so alarming that he stopped beating his wings in shock. It was a disastrous blunder. Down he dropped. His feathers were burning and he yelled in pain.

The blackbird fell to the steaming ground, a smoking, straggly bundle rolling helplessly down the slope into the grove.

Devouring flames raced in every direction and the intense heat seared his lungs when he gulped for breath. Finnen looked around for the fire devil that had fallen from his grasp. The silver talisman was lying halfway up the bank, gleaming an infernal red, and he leaped upon it desperately. The wings shrank into his arms and the smoldering feathers dissolved. The bright yellow beak melted into his face and Finnen Lufkin swept the hair from his eyes.

"The beeches!" he exclaimed, overthrown by despair. "Everything we are and have been, our history, all gone, all burning."

He tore his eyes away from that dreadful scene and stared into the woodland beyond. The trees there were like mighty pillars of fire upholding a lofty ceiling of smoke and sparks. Then he glimpsed something through the flaming tempest that made his heart thunder in his chest: A gang of spriggans were herding the werlings toward the cinder trackway.

Hope burned in Finnen's veins more fiercely than any of the surrounding fires. There was still a chance. But what could he do on his own against armed soldiers?

He glanced around feverishly. Spriggans feared nothing, except the High Lady and the touch of water. His grandmother had told him many stories about them when he was younger and he ransacked his memory for anything that might help him now.

Was Liffidia wrong to have such faith in him? He knew he was a fraud. His great wergling skill had been a grotesque cheat. He had chewed wood shavings stolen from the Lufkin beech to boost his powers of transformation and the shame of that ghoulish crime would always torment him.

A wild and reckless idea flashed into his mind and Finnen broke into a huge grin. It was a crazy plan that probably wouldn't work but, whatever else he was—cheat, liar, fraud—Finnen knew he wasn't a coward.

With fierce determination, he strode down into the maelstrom of the grove once more. Old fallen beechnuts were exploding on the ground and the seething air was filled with their flying shrapnel. Flames were dripping from above and smoke as thick as mud flowed densely between the blazing trees.

His jaw set, Finnen marched fearlessly into the dark, billowing fumes. The thick black vapor wreathed about him and, in a moment, the boy was lost completely in the churning, blinding smoke.

THE SPRIGGANS' KNIVES WERE POISED to spear their chosen werling victims when a strange sound cut through the roar of the massive fires.

The spriggans jerked their heads back toward the flaming woodland and their blood ran cold.

"What were that?" Wumpit warbled.

Bogrinkle spluttered and began to tremble. "I knowed what that were!" he gibbered. "Was a w . . . w . . . wolf."

The other spriggans gaped fearfully. "No," they burbled. "Can't be."

Captain Grittle scolded them. "You superstitious, thin-blooded ladies!" he jeered. "'Course it weren't that!"

Suddenly, the fearsome noise blasted out again. This time it was louder and nearer and unmistakable. It was the howl of a wolf.

"There ain't no such beasts in Hagwood!" the captain yelled, trying to quell his own rising panic. "Not since the troll witches slew 'em all, long before our time. You lot know that."

The howl ripped through the night once more and four of the spriggans began backing away.

"Batar!" Bogrinkle gibbered. "The God of War has come to punish us!"

"There's more hot air in you than in the whole of that blasted furnace!" Grittle barked back. "'Tis only the fire wind wailing through hollow logs."

Wumpit's face fell and he raised a quaking finger, pointing through the trees. "Well that ain't no wind!" he shrieked. "It's Him! I said He was angry! We didn't leave an offering and now He's here!"

They stared into the burning wood and every spriggan whimpered in fright. A great shape was running under the flaming oaks, racing toward them. Its savage eyes were more hellish than the fires it leaped through and its ravening jaws were snapping and snarling.

"No!" Captain Grittle cried.

It was a massive, monstrous wolf.

The spriggans screeched and fled to the trackway. Only their captain stood his ground, but the knife was quivering in his fist and his knees were buckling.

He had never dreamed such a hideous moment would ever come. Batar was more terrible than he had imagined. The figure was as large as a horse, the coarse wolf fur was streaked with scarlet, and the fangs looked sharper than his best blades.

"Spare me!" Grittle wailed, falling on his knees and cowering. "I'm a brave warrior—I am—I am! It's the others you want—not me!"

With a rush of fur and muscle, Batar leaped at the Captain, snatched him up by the scruff of his neck, and shook him violently.

The spriggan squawked and squealed, pleading for his life. The immense wolf tossed its head and sent him tumbling through the air. He landed with a clatter of armor and weapons on the cinder path and Batar pounced on top of him, pinning him down with powerful paws.

The great jaws came slavering down. Captain Grittle felt the hot breath burn on his exposed throat and waited for the end. But the Wolf of War did not tear into his flesh. Instead, it bit the medals from his breastplate and spat them out, one by one.

There was a final threatening growl and the monster lifted its heavy paws off Grittle's chest and paced backward, letting him run free.

His hobnail boots went crunching over the track and he rapidly caught up with the other spriggans. Too terrified to speak, they charged along the path and left their God of War far behind.

Batar watched them tear into the distance then turned. The wolf's terrible eyes fell upon the werlings who were still huddled on the ground. They were faint from fear. One grisly fate had been replaced by an even more horrendous doom. Now they were going to be devoured by the foul and hideous monster.

Then, to their astonishment, from the creature's gullet, a familiar voice came issuing.

"Is my nan in there?"

The werlings goggled at the gigantic shape. Before their eyes, the fur and sinew blurred. The demonic wolf dwindled and shrank. In its place, chuckling at their monumental surprise, was Finnen Lufkin.

There was a stunned silence and then an almighty cheer. Everyone rushed forward and surrounded him. His frail grandmother threw her arms about his neck and wept proudly. Hundreds of questions were fired as they clapped him on the back and shook his hands vigorously. How did he ever wergle into such a huge creature, they wanted to know. How was it possible? Where had he been? Where did he go with Yoori Mattock and where was the respected elder now? What was happening beyond their borders? Would the High Lady send other soldiers? What were they to do now?

Everyone was shouting at once and Finnen couldn't make himself heard.

Finally, Diffi Maffin called for quiet. "Let the boy speak!" she commanded.

The excited werlings suppressed their relief and bubbling curiosity with difficulty.

"Proceed, Master Lufkin," Diffi Maffin prompted with an encouraging wink.

And so Finnen told them what was happening far across the forest: of the plight of Liffidia and Tollychook, besieged in the tower, and the battles that had already been fought that day. He spoke of his time down in the caves of Peg-tooth Meg and explained who she really was and how she was the rightful ruler of the Hollow Hill.

No one had heard such a grim and terrible tale and they marveled at the ordeals he and the others had endured. Then Figgle, who had been listening with mounting impatience, could contain himself no longer.

"And where are my children now?" he interrupted. "Are they trapped in that tower too?"

A look of intense sorrow passed over Finnen's face. "They were," he answered. "Gamaliel and Kernella were fetching weapons from the cellars, but . . ."

His words faltered but his expression said everything. Tidubelle and Figgle turned pale and held on to each other.

"What happened?" Figgle asked in an empty voice.

Finnen could not bear it. He had struggled all day to push his grief aside and do what had to be done, but now the dreadful loss of his friends threatened to overwhelm him. With a lump swelling rapidly in his throat, he told of the flagstoned floor that had collapsed on top of them. Then, in the crowd, he saw Mister Doolan and his wife.

"Bufus," he began, "was with Gamaliel and Kernella when it happened. He was lost too."

The werlings shook their heads in disbelief and for a while the only sound was the roar of the burning woodland.

"And at this very moment, the forces of the High Lady are attacking the tower," Finnen said. "Nothing can stop Her."

Diffi Maffin pursed her lips in concentration. Such matters were beyond her knowledge and experience. Rhiannon Rigantona was too great an enemy for any of their kind. She turned once more to Finnen.

"You have not yet explained how you managed to wergle into such a gigantic beast as that frightful wolf!" she exclaimed. "How is it possible to change into something so many times bigger than yourself? It has never been done before. It is a breakthrough in werglecraft."

Finnen looked into her curious, wrinkled face then dropped his gaze and stared at the ground.

"I was never the great wergler I pretended to be," he began.

A murmur ran through the crowd.

"So how did you do it?" asked Diffi Maffin.

"The Silent Grove is on fire," the boy answered somberly. "All those blessed beeches, all those entombed Wergle Masters and adepts are burning, burning fast. So what I did, what I had to do, was walk right into the heart of that smoke, as close to the trees as I dared—and breathe in deep."

The faces of the werlings fell. Some of them uttered small whimpers of disbelief. The admiration they felt for the boy disappeared instantly as the realization of what he had done sank in. Diffi Maffin shuddered. Finnen's grandmother squeezed his hand. Her love for him never faltered for a moment.

"Our most hallowed place," Diffi Maffin whispered. "Our most honored ancestors, our cherished family trees have been put to the flame and you defile their sacred memory by doing this! Is there no scrap of respect in you, child?"

Finnen could feel the reproachful glares before he even lifted his eyes to meet them.

"I'd rather you'd let the spriggans kill us!" someone shouted.

At first, the boy had been ashamed, but that feeling was quickly replaced by anger. There wasn't time for this. Tollychook and Liffidia were still in the most terrible danger and he knew that he would gladly inhale the enchanted smoke a thousand times if it could save them.

"I can't believe you ungrateful lot!" he said in a defiant voice. "You really expect me to apologize for rescuing you. Well I won't!"

"What you have done is wicked and profane!" Diffi Maffin answered. "You have desecrated the revered dead, and insulted our traditions and history."

"The grove is finished!" he told her. "That old way of life is finished. There's no sense crying over it! But look at the chance that's been given to us—an amazing, miraculous hope."

He turned to the muttering crowd. His eyes were shining with more than just the reflected firelight and his voice was charged with passion.

"Don't you see what's happened here?" he cried. "It's a blessing— we've been granted a fantastic way to fight. The only way we really understand and are good at. When I breathed in that smoke, I could feel the might and skill of those old masters coursing through me, making me strong. I knew I could become anything I wanted."

The werlings did not want to hear any more of this nauseating and blasphemous talk and began walking away from him. The depraved boy would never understand. How could they trample over their traditions and violate their history?

"Listen to yourselves!" Finnen shouted, incredulously. "You're clinging to something that's already dead—in every sense. Would you really sacrifice your futures for the sake of what's past? Even when Meg was at her maddest, down in the caves, she was saner than the whole lot of you! She knew how important change is. Look where all our hiding has got us—our homes are burning, our old lives are gone forever. We can't live by those rules anymore and the High Lady will see to it that we don't live at all. More of Her warriors will come to kill us."

"Better that than what you're suggesting," a disgusted voice barked back at him. "And when the fires are out, you'll want us to mix the ashes into our porridge as well, no doubt."

"We won't survive long enough to see the fires go out!" Finnen shouted back. "This night sees the end of everything—us included. If we go battle the High Lady's soldiers now, we might just do some good, somehow. It's better than waiting here for them to come slaughter us."

He cast his anxious gaze around the frightened and distressed crowd and caught sight of a plump couple listening intently to his words as they huddled close to each other. They were the parents of Tollychook.

"We must go save your son!" Finnen told them. "Or at least die in the attempt!"

The Umbelnappers looked at one another uncertainly then shook their heads. "Us can't meddle with the big doings of lordly folk," they said humbly. "Us can't help our poor lad."

Finnen glared at them, too angry to respond. This was hopeless; precious moments were being squandered. With a resolute toss of his head, he made his decision.

"No more words then," he announced. "If no one will come with me, then I'm going on my own."

He gave his grandmother a final kiss on her cheek and, with a fierce scowl, pushed his way through the crowd and headed back to the burning woodland.

"Maybe there is one other who will help," he murmured to himself, but he shivered at the very thought. Then, remembering his friends, he stuck out his chin and ran between the flaming trees.

The other werlings shifted uneasily as he disappeared into the horrific blaze and vanished from sight. They glanced at one another guiltily.

"That boy's mad. You should have stopped him," they told Diffi Maffin. "It's to his death, he's gone. That's for sure."

"Yes," she answered mournfully, "I know. . . . Yet he's the bravest of us all."

· CHAPTER 15 ·

THE IMMORTAL GODDESS OF THE WORLD

LIFFIDIA LOOKED OUT FROM THE BATTLEMENTS of the broken tower and saw the glimmering lights of the Unseelie Court winding through the forest. There were so many lanterns it looked like a river of emerald fire had spilled from the open hill. Drums were beating and trumpets were blowing and heralds were proclaiming the approach of Her Great Majesty, Rhiannon Rigantona.

"There be a mighty lot of them," Tollychook observed unhappily.

The girl agreed and drew her fingers through Fly's fur for comfort.

Beside them, the sluglungs had formed a glooping conglomeration that rippled with apprehension. Their floating eyes had crowded together to stare at the Hollow Hill as it emptied, the faerie realm pouring out in a seemingly endless stream; their lipless mouths gibbered forlornly.

At the foot of the tower, Peg-tooth Meg was also gazing at the advancing multitude. Before her, the nobles of the court who had conspired against her sister were waiting with defiance or dread upon their faces. Surrounding them, the Redcaps toyed with their bows and licked their teeth.

The forest resounded with the full might and pageantry of the Unseelie Court.

First came the drummers: stumpy and stout goblins with drums almost larger than themselves slung from their necks. Next came the heralds: long-legged creatures called powries, wearing tunics of silver and crimson. As a thunderous chorus, they called out the many titles of the High Lady.

Striding behind them came the klurie trumpeters. Each of them bore two trumpets: one black and one gold, each fashioned in the shape of a hissing serpent that coiled around its bearer's shoulders and waist and faced outward. Following the trumpeters, ranks of armored goblins marched bearing pike shafts, iron maces, and war banners. Their heavy trudging caused the branches to tremble overhead. Then came a troop of goblin knights upon their coal-black steeds, which stamped and snorted and blew steam from their nostrils.

Upon the battlements, the werling children beheld the momentous force approach in dumbstruck silence. They had never dreamed how great the numbers would be.

Smaller creatures bearing lanterns and incense burners flanked the fearsome knights, filling the forest with hazy, perfumed light and threads of green and purple smoke. Then rode the lords and ladies, upon their gray horses and accompanied by every member of their households. Even the dairymaids were there, looking suitably stern and carrying large wooden butter paddles as weapons.

After them came the klurie pages, bearing pennants showing the badge of the black owl. The matriarchs of the spriggan families were next, looking every bit as fierce as their sons and grandsons and similarly armed to the teeth.

Rhiannon Rigantona, the Tyrant of the Hollow Hill, Supreme Ruler of Hagwood, goddess of the unsuspecting world beyond, followed upon Dewfrost. A cloak of dark-blue velvet trimmed with silver was draped from the High Lady's shoulders and a tall, diamond-studded crown sat upon her flowing black hair. Her pale complexion was as lustrous as the winter moon, her eyes as remote. She stared fixedly ahead, expressionless and still. Perched upon her shoulder was the owl. It too was silent, its head ducking and rising with the motion of the horse, keeping its golden eyes perfectly level.

Countless more goblin knights and foot soldiers followed and the innumerable lesser folk brought up the rear. Even the torturers had been summoned from their dungeons and they wheeled iron barrows filled with cruel implements, just in case their skills were required.

The grassy ridge between the edge of the forest and the tower shone with the glow of countless lamps as the denizens of the Hollow Hill came striding forth.

Liffidia and Tollychook watched the mighty host flood onto the ridge, spilling down the slopes and mustering in formidable ranks. The night sky curdled with clouds and thunder growled menacingly in the distance. Over the Cold Hills in the north, streaks of lightning forked and flashed. A great storm was on the move but the werlings did not notice, their attention wholly captured by the events below.

"I can't bear being up here any longer," Liffidia said suddenly. "I need to go down and be with Meg. The soldiers are going to come up and kill us anyway. I'd sooner be down there so we can die together, wouldn't you?"

Tollychook thought that he would much rather be home in bed with a full stomach and dreaming of pies but, as that was impossible, he nodded glumly.

Liffidia turned to the undulating mass of sluglungs.

"Time to go," she said softly.

Croaks of agreement came from many mouths and their bobbing eyes blinked and winked at her. From that great, glistening heap, three hands came stretching. They wrapped around the werlings and the fox cub. Then, squelching and quivering, the formless sluglung mound went oozing over the battlements and rolled slowly and stickily down the wall.

Held firmly in a gluey hand, Tollychook squeezed his eyes shut. He didn't like this at all. Liffidia pressed her lips together and watched the ground draw gradually closer.

On the ridge, the trumpets and drums ceased, and the heralds held their breaths.

The High Lady came riding from the rear.

The Redcaps that surrounded Lord Limmersent and the rest of the conspirators bowed low. Peg-tooth Meg clutched her harp tightly and waited. Her sluglungs came dripping down beside her and the werlings swallowed nervously.

Running in front of the High Lady's horse were thirty female kluries. They were the owl dancers. Black, feathered masks covered their unlovely faces and their costumes sported wings attached to their arms. Shaking their heads and shrieking in high voices, they came bounding into the space that had been left clear between the opposing forces and spun around wildly in a euphoric, leaping dance before dropping to their knees and raising their wings to welcome the Queen.

Dewfrost walked regally between them, then stamped to a halt. Rhiannon's dark eyes glittered at the broken watchtower.

Peg-tooth Meg stared back at her.

The thunder grumbled louder in the distance and a bolt of lightning smote the raised summit of the Hollow Hill.

Everyone watched and waited. The High Lady's forces wondered about the identity of the grotesque woman clutching the strange harp. They stared in revulsion at the bobbing blobs of goo standing guard around her. And why were Lord Limmersent and the others already here? Had they been sent on ahead? Where were the spriggans? And where were the keepers of the Redcaps? It was all most perplexing and remarkable. But in spite of the questions that fermented and frothed in their minds, no one spoke. They could all sense this was a tremendous, critical moment, heightened by the electric jags that streaked across the sky.

It was Meg who broke the silence.

"You have returned, my sister," she said. "Come to deal me the final blow with your own hand, as you did to our beloved father, the High King."

Hearing her words, the denizens of the Hill uttered gasps of surprise and wonderment. Even the owl dancers lowered their wings and looked at the ugly woman in confusion.

"Yes!" Lord Limmersent called out. "This is indeed our Princess Clarisant. We have been deceived these many years. Rhiannon Rigantona lied to us all. It was She who murdered King Ragallach, not Alisander. Clarisant is our rightful ruler!"

The army looked over at the High Lady for an answer. Her face remained impassive and cold. At her shoulder, the owl puffed out its chest and cleared itss throat.

"Thus speaketh the illustrious Lord Limmersent!" it cried. "Behold the fumbling fool, caught out in his hapless and shipwrecked conspiracy. Know now, faithless worm, that the architect of thy seditious plot, Lord Fanderyn, lies dead and cold within the Hill. Didst thou truly believe thou couldst claim kinship twixt our exulted Majesty and yon deformed toad crone? What fevered madness hath boiled thy wits, my lord?"

"He speaks the truth!" Meg declared. "I am Clarisant, though I do not expect any to believe me. My sister knows; that is enough."

"Rhiannon Rigantona knows nothing of the kind!" the owl repudiated. "Thou, foul-faced ditch hag, are in the employ of My Lady's enemies and will utter aught they hath schooled thee to say."

"Be silent, Master Beak!" Lord Limmersent demanded. "We are all weary of your venomous voice. What does your evil mistress say to this?"

The owl drew itself up to its full height and, in an arrogant tone, said, "The Queen shalt not debase her dignity to even speak of it. She hath commanded me to be her tongue in this. Seize the traitors, bring them before Her."

At once the Redcaps pounced on Lord Limmersent and the rest of the conspirators and dragged them forward.

Peg-tooth Meg looked at her sluglungs. "We must join them," she said grimly. "One last fight, at the very feet of my deathless sister."

The sluglungs gave gargling shouts and braced themselves for battle one more time.

"Take her!" the owl commanded.

There was a roar. The goblins charged and the sluglungs sprang at them. Swords and maces went slicing and swinging harmlessly through the sluglungs' jelly bodies, while their clammy fists went thumping under the visors of astonished warriors who tumbled from their horses and went clanking down the grassy slopes.

"Megboo!" the sluglungs chanted. "Ussum punchum!"

Liffidia and Tollychook shrank against the tower wall. Hooves and armor-clad feet were stomping and crashing everywhere.

The sluglungs snatched weapons from scaly goblin hands and turned them upon their owners. Clamor and uproar filled the air and the sky thundered as if in response. The leaders of the klurie tribes who had been present at the secret meeting had spent the afternoon stirring up resentment against their Queen and gathering support among their folk. They were too afraid to join the fighting straight-away, but when they saw one of the goblins kick Lord Limmersent and another spit at Lady Mauvette as the Redcaps dragged them by, that was too much. Banners were hurled down and knives drawn. They leaped upon the goblins' backs and took them by surprise. The trum-peters blew one sharp blast then cast off their instruments and jumped into the battle to fight alongside their kin.

Seeing this, the spriggan matriarchs rushed forward, brandish-ing as many weapons as they could hold and dived into the fighting, shouting filthy oaths at the rebeling kluries.

The mounted nobles rode their horses among the fighters in a riot of bright, clanging steel. Death cries rang out across the ridge.

With the battle clashing around her, Peg-tooth Meg walked pur-posely toward her sister.

Snarling and snapping, the Redcaps had wrenched Lord Limmersent and the other conspirators before the High Lady's horse and were now itching to go join the battle.

The noble tried to stand but they kicked the back of his knees and he dropped to the ground.

"You have captured us, pitiless Queen," he shouted, tossing his head proudly. "Yet I will not beg for mercy, nor recant. A murderess you are, a slayer of your own kin. May my final words denounce you!"

225

The High Lady's eyes glinted down at him. But still, she did not speak.

"Hold the rebel cur's head!" the owl screeched to the Redcaps. "Grip it firm and tight."

The savages obeyed, their clawed hands grabbing at his long hair and pulling his head backward.

The owl chortled wickedly then spread its wings and flew down to land on the noble's chest.

"Was there ever so profound a fool as thee?" it mocked, waddling a little higher. "None can vie against My Lady. She is untouchable as the stars. Neither violence nor time can depose or destroy Her now. She hath ascended beyond the reach of thy petty ambitions."

The owl clicked its beak then licked it with its little tongue. "What conceit and enmity sizzles in thine eyeballs," it observed as it pressed its flat feathery face closer. "Doth they add zest to the flavor, I wonder?"

Hissing with grisly glee, the Redcaps wrenched the Lord's eyelids wide but, before the owl could tear them out, Meg pushed her way through and smacked the bird away with her large hands.

The owl was sent reeling. It fell to the ground but was back in the air almost immediately.

"Call an end to this bloodshed, sister!" she demanded. "You have me; let the others go free. Stop this wanton killing."

"Bind the frogwitch!" the owl screamed.

The three Redcaps holding Lord Limmersent rushed at Meg but she thrust the golden casket in their faces and they fell back, afraid. That bewitched object was crying, calling out in the High Lady's own voice, begging to be released from the burden of life.

The courtiers who heard it drew their breath and clutched at whatever charms protected them.

"'Tis naught but a trick!" the owl declared. "The hag is adept at throwing her voice."

"What does Her Majesty say on this?" Lord Limmersent demanded, rising from his knees. "Surely She must have words; let Her deny this box contains Her own beating heart."

Sitting rigidly in the saddle, the Lady Rhiannon merely gazed down at them and made no answer.

"Why does she say nothing?" someone in the crowd muttered.

"She has been silent since we left the Hill," remarked another.

"Yes, sister," Meg called out, holding the casket high for everyone to see. "Here is the thing which you have hunted for these many years. The smallest measure of all that was good in you, the residue of your conscience and the sediment of your pity, here they lie. Are you not *heartened* by its return?"

Gradually, the bitter fighting ceased. The goblin knights were filled with doubt and they stared at the glittering box with marveling eyes. The kluries wiped their knives on their tunics and the nobles put up their swords. The spriggan matriarchs paused, mid-thrust, and cast their narrow eyes on that golden casket. All of them murmured in disturbed whispers.

Disappointed that the fighting had ceased, the sluglungs plopped to the ground and went running to join their mistress, cuffing and slapping anyone who stood in their way. The deep voice of thunder rolled overhead and the first spots of rain began to splash. The sluglungs gargled with delight to feel it on their skin but the female spriggans let out horrified shrieks and ran for the trees.

"Enough of this!" the owl screeched impatiently. "Do not listen to this slime harpy; obey thy Queen! Kill the traitors. My Lady's undying favor to he who cuts off this hag's loathsome head!"

The Queen's army stirred and gripped their weapons but were reluctant to recommence the fighting. The High Lady's uncharacteristic silence unnerved them; even the Redcaps were uneasy. Why was she sitting so still upon Dewfrost? Why would she not speak? Why did she not give the command? She had never held back before. As her army waited in silence, that wretched voice was weeping within the golden casket, imploring to be destroyed. Was the Queen of Faerie so fearful of what that box contained that it robbed her of speech and movement?

Suddenly, a commotion broke out at the rear of the army. Voices were raised in anger and outrage. There were scuffling sounds and someone came forcing his way from the forest, pushing the smaller folk aside. The owl returned to Rhiannon's shoulder and peered back.

A large goblin warden was striding through the ranks. He was carrying something in his great fist, something that kicked and squealed and cursed.

"Your scabby ear tastes like a cow's bum!" the something squawked. "But you'll get bit again till you lets go. That's a promise, you sweat-scummed sun dodger! Leave a poor wayfarer be. Hims done nobody no harm. He'll crack your skull for you though, leather brains—that's another promise—oh yes!"

The assembled guards and nobles around the High Lady parted as the goblin warden came pushing through. He was a wide, solid brute with an even more solid-looking head. He was taller than Waggarinzil had been and clad in mail that was too tight. One of his fleshy earlobes was bleeding where a large piece had been bitten off.

Lifting his right arm, he shook the richly clad thing that dangled from his fist to quiet it, then stood to attention beside Rhiannon's horse.

"Sergeant Thripplefoil, Warden of the Second Eastern Gate, Your Majesty!" he announced. "Come to deliver this dandy fish we just caught."

Rhiannon looked down at him and her eyes grew wide when she saw what he held in his fist. There was Grimditch, in his burgundy velvet finery. His shiny, hairless face was a portrait of fury and he swung his arms and legs like windmill sails to strike his burly captor. The goblin gave him one more violent shake then threw him roughly to the ground.

"Smells like a barn bogle," the door warden said with distaste. "But I never saw one so primped and dollied up afore."

"Thou hast done well!" the owl praised him. "Where didst thou net this bright fish?"

The sergeant removed his helmet and bowed. "'Twas back yonder," he said, jabbing a thumb at the forest. "Me and the boys was just falling in at the rear of the call out when we sees this 'ere gaudy gingerbread go flitting from shadow to shadow. 'There's a rogue up to no good business,' says I, so we laid hands on him after a bit of a chase, and when I saw what he'd been thieving, I hauled the fancy knave to the front for Her Majesty's inspection."

Lying crumpled on the ground, Grimditch glared up at the goblin and kicked him in the knee.

The sergeant cursed and struck him harshly.

"Been nowt but snapping teeth, knuckles, and gut kickings since we catched him," he said ruefully. "We would've popped the sly villain straightaways if it'd just been him."

"Who else was there?" the owl demanded.

The goblin looked back down the aisle he had made through the courtiers.

"Doodiggle!" he called. "What's keeping you? Get a haste on. Bring out what this dirty brigand was making away with."

A voice cried out to him and, presently, a smaller figure came jostling through the crowd. It was another goblin warden, shorter in stature but just as ugly and short tempered. In his arms he carried a bundle wrapped in a moss-green blanket.

"The little lordling!" everyone gasped.

"Aye," Sergeant Thripplefoil declared. "This 'ere bogley fiend was snatching him away, carting him from the Hill. 'Napping him, he was, the dirty babe thief."

He spat on the barn bogle's bald scalp, but Grimditch was too intent on staring at the wriggling infant in Doodiggle's arms to notice.

"No, no, no, not hold so tight!" he barked. "And don't wheeze your dungy breath on his sweet face—you hobbly clod."

The onlookers regarded Grimditch with horror. The human child was beloved by everyone. He was the one pure flame in that corrupt kingdom. They reveled in his presence on the rare occasions Rhiannon permitted them to see him.

"Now doth I perceive the dirtiest depths of this foul treason!" the owl called out. "The frogwitch and the rebel lords lured the court hither so they might steal him whom our Queen so loves whilst he lay unguarded in the cradle. Yea, him whom we doth dote on and glory in. What base depravities! What heinous painmongers these felons be, to even consider such a crime!"

"A month with the torturers is too good for them!" one of the pages cried.

"Hand them over!" the torturers called, selecting suitable, serrated tools from their barrow and testing their sharpness with their thumbs.

Rhiannon remained coldly silent and detached. The owl chuckled softly to itself.

"Hold!" Peg-tooth Meg shouted as the hatred swelled around her. "This is untrue. I wish my sister uncrowned, yes—but I am blameless in this. Ask the thief why he did it."

"A thing of slime thou art!" the bird snapped back at her. "Yet thou cannot slide out of this. Thy guilt is as plain as thy face!"

"Grimditch will tell you!" the barn bogle blurted with sudden vehemence. "He'll tell you why he ran with the bonnie babe! To save him from Her, that's why!"

He jumped to his feet and pointed accusingly at the High Lady. "She's mad, madder than you licky lords guess at. Oh, you never dreamed how stinkful bad She be, but Grimditch do—he do, he do! He knows!"

With the rain pattering down on his face, he snarled up at the frozen countenance of the Queen and his voice blistered with condemnation as he shouted, "Going to eat him, She is! Yes, dine on his pretty pink flesh, the butchering beldam."

"Liar!" the owl screeched as the court uttered cries of disbelief and even Peg-tooth Meg looked shocked and revolted at this fresh testament to her sister's evil. "'Tis bogle-ish mendacity. Sergeant Thripplefoil, tear out the thief's tongue! At once!"

The goblin made a grab for Grimditch but he ducked beneath Dewfrost and dodged the many hands that came reaching for him.

A flash of lightning crackled overhead and the thunder roared in their ears. The baby cried out and pushed his hands from the blanket. In the stark flaring light flash, the owl saw for the first time the woolen effigy Gabbity had placed around his neck.

"What is that crude, idolatrous object?" the bird demanded. "Remove it, show it to me!"

Doodiggle clasped his claws about the charm and prepared to rip it free.

"NOOO!" Grimditch bawled leaping out from beneath the horse. "The lordling will die to dust! Don't! Don't!"

Sergeant Thripplefoil lunged at him but the barn bogle jumped aside and sank his teeth into Doodiggle's arm.

The goblin yowled and hurled Grimditch away. The imp went crashing into the gawping Redcaps, only to spring up once more, consumed with dread and panic.

"Must not!" he raged at Doodiggle, who had clutched hold of the knitted effigy once again. "Take your filthy paws off that! 'Tis what keeps him safe! You'll kill him—leave be, leave be!"

Peg-tooth Meg took a fearful breath as she realized what the barn bogle meant.

"You must not remove that!" she urged. "The child's life depends on it!"

"Ignore them!" the owl commanded. "Give the thing to me!"

The goblin began pulling at the thread around the baby's neck. Grimditch wailed in despair. How could he make them listen? He looked wildly from the infant to the goblin and then up to the cold, emotionless face of the High Lady. All he could do was buy precious moments for the baby at the cost of his own life—perhaps if he gave everyone something else to think about . . .

Like one demented, he let out a terrible yell, snatched a poisoned arrow from a Redcap's quiver, leaped up at the High Lady and plunged it deep into her thigh.

"Feel a barn bogle's sting, Wicked One!" he screamed.

The uproar that followed was louder than the thunder. The owl squawked in outrage. The surrounding army bayed for Grimditch's life and Sergeant Thripplefoil caught hold of him by the throat. How dare he raise a hand against the glorious, deathless monarch! The High Lady's royal person was sacred and inviolate.

"Treacherous scab!" he spat, squeezing his claws around the barn bogle's windpipe. "Popping's too good for you but you've breathed yer last gasp!"

Grimditch choked as the goblin strangled him and his desperate struggles grew weak. His eyes bulged in their sockets and his face turned purple. His head lolled to one side and the last sight he saw before darkness rushed in was of the human child. A sad, loving smile spread over his face.

And then something incredible happened.

Rhiannon Rigantona, immortal goddess of the world, slumped forward and fell from the saddle. Her owl let out a shriek and took to the air to save itself as she thudded onto the ground, her blue cloak furling over her.

Sergeant Thripplefoil flung Grimditch down and rushed to the High Lady's aid.

"What ails you, Majesty?" he cried, tearing the velvet cloth from her face. At that moment, a blinding streak of lightning illuminated the ridge. The goblin let out a startled yell at what he saw and jumped backward. The once-ravishing face was now a mask of death. The dark eyes were open and unblinking in the rain and the pearl-white skin was now webbed with ugly black veins.

"She . . . She is dead!" he gulped incredulously. "The Queen is dead! The venom of the arrow has done its work."

He stared down at the feathered shaft, still buried in the High Lady's thigh. Then he took a staggering step backward, unable to comprehend it.

No one who saw that fallen corpse made a sound. The Redcaps gibbered silently and dropped their bows as if they burned. The knights lifted their visors for a better view and swore under their breaths. Even the horses shied away and shook their manes. The nobles of the court murmured in confusion, while the blue-faced pages leaned against one another and bit their lips.

Only one thought reigned. It was beyond impossible. How could the deathless succumb to such a commonplace wound? They could not believe it and for many minutes they could do nothing but look on her. Lord Limmersent tore his dumbfounded gaze away and stared questioningly at Peg-tooth Meg. The green-haired woman was blinking in consternation as a turmoil of emotions broiled inside her. The sluglungs' shapes sagged and they gathered around their Megboo sympathetically, holding hands and merging into one another.

Many of the Unseelie Court could not see what had happened and those at the back or standing on the lower slopes pushed their way to the front, anxious to learn. Then they too shook their heads in stricken amazement and struggled for an explanation.

Liffidia and Tollychook dared to venture closer. All they had seen was the High Lady fall from her horse. With Fly running beside them, they hurried across to Meg and took in the desolate scene.

Among the high-ranking nobles, fearsome warriors, and cunning kluries, only one person was blunt and direct enough to give voice to what everyone was thinking secretly.

"The 'orrible tyrant be dead then," Tollychook remarked flatly. "Good riddance! I be plum glad."

His words were like a pebble dropped in a pond. The ripples ran out around him and soon everyone was echoing that opinion.

"The Queen is dead. Her reign is ended. The days of evil are over!"

At first, the words were uttered in hushed whispers but, as everyone realized there was nothing to fear any longer, the whispers rose to shouts. They could say what they liked without terror. There would be no more pitiless retributions, no capricious executions. The Hollow Hill was finally free. Stunned disbelief turned into joyous celebration. The trumpeters took up their instruments again and blew triumphant blasts whilst the dairymaids began to dance in the rain. Only the torturers were downcast as they wondered what would become of them and their cherished implements.

Peg-tooth Meg strode forward and gazed down on her sister.

"I never sought this, Morthanna," she said. "You were my blood, and I loved you. That is why I gave the key to the Smith to take, those many years ago. I could never have killed you. That is where we differed: I have a heart."

Bowing with sorrow, she placed the golden casket next to Rhiannon's body. The drummers had joined in the revels and the riotous jubilation was now so loud that no one heard the anguished voice still crying out from the box.

Liffidia dug her fingernails into her palms. None of this seemed real. They had endured and suffered so much from the High Lady. It couldn't be over, not this easily and quickly.

"Something's wrong," she murmured and she forced herself to

touch the dead woman's hand. The flesh was already cold. "I don't know what, but it's just wrong; I can feel it. The way she just sat on her horse, staring, not saying anything."

Doodiggle was standing close by with his foolish mouth hanging open. Meg walked over to him and took the baby.

"He will be in my care now," she said.

The goblin relinquished his charge without question but others who were nearby asked, "By what right does she take our lordling?"

When the nobles of the court saw this, they rode their steeds closer and pointed their swords at Meg threateningly.

"The precious infant is not yours, frogwitch!" they exclaimed. "He belongs to the Hollow Hill and shall be returned there."

Lord Limmersent threw up his hands. "Have you learned nothing?" he shouted. "This is Clarisant—her claim to the throne is now undisputed."

"I dispute it!" one of them cried.

"As do I!" called another. "We do not believe this toad-skinned mud horror is the fair Clarisant, who disappeared into the night so many years ago."

"The line of Ragallach is ended!" they declared. "A new ruler must be chosen. Many here are descended from ancient princedoms; the best of us will be the new High King!"

Arguments broke out and, all along that grassy promontory, throughout the High Lady's great army, long-standing quarrels, grudges, and smoldering resentments came to the fore. Now that they were free of Rhiannon's rule, there was nothing to stop them. Already armed for battle, they turned upon one another with fist and blade, mace and spear, axe and sword. Soon all was pandemonium.

Lord Limmersent stared at the riot, aghast. That which he dreaded most was happening as he watched. The diverse, rival factions of the court, which the awe and terror of Rhiannon had long held in check, were igniting to ravaging flame. There would be strife and bloodshed. Civil war would rip the Hill apart.

"You fools," he murmured helplessly. "You ambitious, greedy fools. You will destroy us all for the sake of a golden crown. The one true heir is before you. This is the Princess Clarisant!"

As the celebrations and violent arguments continued, Liffidia splashed through the ever-widening rain puddle in which Grimditch lay.

"Poor thing," she lamented. "Is this Gamaliel's friend? The one who took the key?"

Peg-tooth Meg crouched beside her and rested the baby on her creaking knees.

"This must be he," she said. "Was there ever a king of Elfdom or hero of great renown who performed such a deed as this lowly barn bogle?"

She lifted the blanket from the infant's head so that his blue eyes could see his devoted savior one final time.

"There lies a king among barn bogles," she whispered in his little ear. "And one more fit to rule than any of those who now contest for the throne. My blessing on him and all his impish breed."

Fly the fox cub stepped warily up to Grimditch and licked his cheek.

To Liffidia and Meg's surprise and delight, the barn bogle spluttered and coughed to life.

"Madam!" he moaned in a groggy daze. "Not in front of the neighbors!"

Bewildered, he sat up and rubbed his bruised throat. "Me not deaded!" he said hoarsely. "More lives than a pusskin, that's Grimditch!"

His eyes were rolling independently in their sockets and only when they swiveled to a stop did he see Meg holding the mortal infant. With a jolt, his fears returned.

"Cast your concern aside, Master Grimditch," Meg assured him. "There are none here who will harm you or your ward now. You have done the impossible this night. You have rid the world of Rhiannon Rigantona. You delivered her death blow; all here are grateful, though they do not understand it."

Grimditch waggled his shaven head at her, hardly taking in her words.

"There be some prime ugly women in this lousy forest," he groaned. Then he noticed Liffidia and clapped his hands with recognition. "A skin swapper!" he cried. "Grimditch is their friend. They like Grimditch; he like them!"

He looked around giddily. The rejoicing courtiers were singing and laughing, almost hysterically, while the rest were quarreling and dueling over long-remembered slights for eventual supremacy. It was a peculiar, discordant spectacle and he rubbed his eyes in confusion. Then he saw the High Lady lying on the ground. Some of the subjects who had suffered most under Rhiannon's bloody tyranny were already creeping closer. Their hunger for revenge was hot within them. They wanted to trample her into the mud and cut her body to pieces.

"No," Grimditch burbled. "How can such a thing be? Foul witchy Queen cannot die."

"We do not know," Meg answered. "Yet there She lies, dispatched by your poisoned arrow."

The barn bogle's shaved eyebrows bunched together. "Don't seem possibles," he murmured. "Not at all, no, not no how."

"That's what I thought," Liffidia agreed. "It was far too simple; it doesn't make any sense."

"Well I be happy She's gone," Tollychook put in. "Easy or no, makes no difference in the end: She be nowt but worm food now."

"She weren't made of mortal clay," Grimditch protested, narrowing his eyes and sniffing the air suspiciously.

"Gaze long on Her," a bitter voice interrupted. "Gaze long so that thou shalt remember full well the infamous deed thou hast done!"

Grimditch and the others looked up sharply. Perched upon Dewfrost's saddle was the owl. Amid the wonder and amazement, it had been forgotten.

"If you do not wish to join Her in death, begone!" Meg threatened him. "The sands of your life's hourglass have nearly run out. Many here hate you as much as they feared my sister. You are without protection now, blood-drenched, guilt-sodden bird."

The owl's head revolved slowly as it regarded the disorder and celebrations. "Not one of those vulgar ingrates mourns Her passing," it observed coldly. "Not a single tear hath been shed. No crumb of fealty reveals itself. Now do I perceive the right and wisdom of Her great scheme. Why did I ever doubt it?"

With a flurry of its wings it flew down to land upon its fallen mistress's breast and stooped toward her neck.

"One final kiss?" Meg remarked with disgust. "Woe-begotten, sin-soaked creature."

The owl nipped at a slender chain around the High Lady's neck with its beak, then glared back at Meg.

"Slow-witted, gullible crone!" he hooted with arch contempt. "Thou hath fully earned the oblivion that is due unto thee! Yea—thou and the rest of yon treasonous, faithless mob. It is thy lives which are spent, not mine!"

Gripping the silver fire devil that had hung about Rhiannon's throat, it spread its wings and, with an exultant, crowing laugh, soared into the rumbling sky.

"The new age of Her boundless dominion hath begun!" he proclaimed. "And death rides swift to thee on bristled backs! Long live the Deathless Majesty of Rhiannon Rigantona, Goddess of the World!"

Meg and the others watched the owl disappear over the forest. With fear clutching at their trembling spirits, they stared back at the High Lady's body and, sure enough, her shape was already dissolving. The enchantment of Fikil was dispelled and the true form of the figure lying dead on the ground was revealed. The slender outline shriveled and bulged, the velvet cloak dissolved in the rain, and the raven tresses shrank into a short crop of spiky white hair. The wrists of that dumpy, squat female were tied together with thick rope and a knitted shawl had been bound tightly about her face, gagging the warty mouth. From her expression, it was plain that Gabbity Malatrot had died an agonizing death from the arrow's venom.

Grimditch threw back his head and yowled. His anguished cry cut through the merriment and rioting that surrounded him and every voice fell silent when the Unseelie Court beheld what had happened.

The High Lady was still alive.

Frightened shouts broke out and panic enveloped the crowd.

"Where is She?" they wailed. "What will She do to us? We are lost!"

Beside themselves with fear of the terrible vengeance that she would inflict upon them, the members of the Court did not know what to do. How could they hide from Her? Every creature present quailed at the prospect. They had shown the true extent of their hatred for Her cruel regime; there could be no pardon from that. Hers was a realm devoid of forgiveness.

"We have heated the coals of our own tormenting!" they wept. "Our lives are forfeit."

Still cradling the human infant, Peg-tooth Meg stood forward and Lord Limmersent knelt before her.

"Command us, Highness," he implored. "Your subjects need you."

The misshapen woman stared at the assembled army. They were leaderless and mortally afraid. Even the most courageous soldiers were despairing and the Redcaps were shaking with fright. The lesser folk were alarmed and distraught beyond measure. In their anguish, even the proudest elfin nobles turned to her for guidance and counsel.

Meg's crooked back clicked as she tried to straighten. Blinking the driving rain from her large eyes, she addressed the Unseelie Court with the authority that only the daughter of a king possessed.

"My sister has betrayed you all," she announced. "You are surplus to Her plans and no longer needed. The casket that contains Her heart is now locked forever and so She is finally free of death's clutches that haunted Her throughout Her long reign. She has sent you here this night, not only to slaughter my people and myself, but to empty the Hollow Hill. That once-unassailable fortress is now open and undefended for Her infernal forces to seize."

"Her forces?" Lord Limmersent asked in astonishment. "What other force is Hers to command? The entire Hill is gathered here."

Meg looked into the dark forest. "Her foul lieutenant said this," she told them. "'*Death rides swift to thee on bristled backs!*'"

"What can that mean?"

"That my sister is in league with the unclean brood of the Cold Hills," she said with horror in her voice. "The troll witches are coming, riding on their wild boars—and we are stranded out here."

· CHAPTER 16 ·

THE FINAL BATTLE

THUNDER BELLOWED AND LIGHTNING CRACKED. Every starkly illuminated face was agape with terror.

The troll witches were the most cruel and malevolent scourge ever to have afflicted the realm. The wars against them had lasted many bloody years and were considered the grimmest battles in history. Under Black Howla, the head of that sinister sisterhood, the witches had rampaged throughout the land, destroying the lesser kingdoms to steal the magic of their rulers. Since Black Howla's death, they had retreated to their caverns in the Cold Hills, but they were still the chief creatures of nightmare for the inhabitants of the Hollow Hill. Dread of them dogged every unquiet slumber.

"Return to your halls!" Peg-tooth Meg commanded her frightened subjects. "Only there will you be safe . . . for a time."

"But the Hill is open!" one of the nobles cried. "We shall be defenseless there also."

"The Under Magic will hear Ragallach's daughter!" she replied in
so forceful and definite a voice that no one doubted her. "You cannot
hope to fight the troll witches and win. They will have grown strong in
these dormant ages, sucking power out of the earth. If you are caught
out in the open, a battle will commence unlike any there has ever been.
Make haste; gain the sanctuary of the Hill before Rhiannon."

The whole of the Unseelie Court who, only a short while ago, had
refused to recognize her as Princess Clarisant, now accepted that fact
without exception. She was their only hope.

"Lead us out of this deadly night and we will pledge our swords to
your service!" one of the nobles swore, and soon everyone was salut-
ing her, promising undying allegiance to the disfigured daughter of
King Ragallach.

Meg bowed in gratitude, but she knew there was no time for this.
They had to depart at once and she gave the order to leave. Lord
Limmersent took the reins of Dewfrost and held them out to her.

"Mount your sister's horse," he urged. "Ride at the head of your
people and guide us safely home."

Meg passed the infant to Grimditch, who received him solemnly.
Then she clambered clumsily into the saddle.

"The little shobblers will ride with me," Meg said, and Liffidia and
Tollychook were lifted to sit in front of her.

"What about the injured birds in the infirmary?" the girl implored.
"We can't abandon them—they were the Lubber's children."

Meg looked up at the huge outline of the ruined watchtower that
danced in and out of the lightning.

"We must," she said unhappily. "There is no time to collect them.
We must hasten to the Hill without delay. I pray the spirit of my blind
love will watch over his darlings this night."

She turned the horse toward the forest and rode through the moving masses. Her subjects bowed as she passed but stared curiously at
the sluglungs marching proudly in her wake. Keeping his adoring eyes
upon Liffidia, Fly trotted alongside Dewfrost, carefully avoiding the
clopping hooves.

"Look to the lesser folk!" Meg instructed. "Leave no one behind and give aid to the stragglers. Foot soldiers and knights, join me at the front. I fear the way to the Hill may be barred against us."

The Unseelie Court streamed into the trees, desperate to return home. Precedence and rank were abandoned as all they craved was to be secure within the refuge of the Hollow Hill. As they poured into the forest, Grimditch lingered by the body of the goblin nursemaid.

"Me must get goin', missus," he said forlornly. "Me doesn't want to leave you here in the cold and wetness, but the little lordling needs his bed. You understand. Forgive Grimditch. Him so sorry."

Crouching ungainly in the saddle, Peg-tooth Meg rode to the front of her new army, flanked by Lord Limmersent and his fellow conspirators. The goblin knights and pike-wielding infantry followed.

Holding tight to Dewfrost's mane, the two werlings stared ahead at the midnight forest. The silver-green light that spilled from the raised hill in the distance hardly penetrated the dense tangle of leaves overhead and, with the lamp bearers trailing behind them, the path was invisible in the dark. Only the momentary flashes of lightning illuminated the way.

Tollychook gripped the horse's mane tenaciously. He expected every new flash to reveal a horde of invading troll witches. Liffidia was also afraid. Her childhood had been fueled by stories of troll witches: bestial hags who spent their days drawing strength and power from the earth currents and storing it in stones.

The forest rolled by painfully slowly. If only everyone had been on horseback, then they could gallop to the Hill and be there in hardly any time. This plodding march was excruciating. She could feel her nerves being whittled away and her heart was thumping in her chest. In the jumbled ranks behind, the nervous talk gave way to an anxious silence broken only by thunderclaps as every eye was trained on the raven black shadows beyond the trees.

Rain was pelting the ground and not even the leaf canopy afforded any protection. Meg and her sluglungs were oblivious to the cold and wet, but the rest of the frightened host was soaked to the skin and shivering, growing more and more despondent with each passing moment.

Gradually, they became aware of faint voices mingled with the noise of the storm. At first they were vague and indistinct, but soon everyone could hear the ugly shrieks and harrowing screams amid the thunder.

The Unseelie Court uttered dismal cries and gathered close together.

"They're here," Liffidia whispered fearfully.

"Secure the path!" Meg shouted. "The way to the Hill must be kept open! Every rider follow me! Infantry, remain with the rest, defend them and take them safely home!"

She spurred her horse and charged deeper into the forest. The sluglungs yelled and bounded after her. One of them stretched his arms up to the overhanging branches and began swinging recklessly through the trees, moving at such a speed that the others copied him. Lord Limmersent and the other nobles galloped in pursuit with the goblin knights racing behind.

Dewfrost practically flew along the path. She went at such a pace that the werlings were nearly flung from their seats and Liffidia regretted her earlier wish for haste. The pounding of countless hooves filled her ears, but she could still hear her fox cub barking in the distance—he had been left far behind. Beside her, Tollychook buried his face into the horse's mane and clung on for dear life.

The track curved to the right and the ground began to rise. The Hollow Hill was almost within reach. Flickering beams of silvery-green light were filtering through the trees, illuminating the way. Meg urged Dewfrost on and the sluglungs whooped and hollered as they swung alongside her.

A crackle of lightning came shooting from the shadows and struck the path before them with terrible force. There was a violent explosion of earth and the horse reared. Meg was thrown from the saddle but quick, clammy hands saved her and she was deposited safely onto the ground.

A peal of horrible, raucous laughter issued from the darkness. Dewfrost snorted and stamped and shook her head. Somehow the werling children had managed to hang on and were dangling from the horse's mane. The nobles and the goblin knights drew up alongside the beast and Lord Limmersent calmed her, holding her steady while Meg climbed back into the saddle.

The sluglungs dripped onto the path and stared into the gloom.

A second bolt of lightning blasted from the dark. This time it slammed into one of the sluglungs and the startled creature burst apart. Charred lumps of smoking jelly flew everywhere and his companions hopped up and down, wailing with grief and distress.

More vile laughter ensued. Peeping timidly through Dewfrost's mane, Tollychook glimpsed large shapes moving through the shadowy undergrowth of the surrounding trees. Then, a familiar voice cut through the darkness.

"You look as grotesque squatting upon my horse as you would hunched upon my throne, Clarisant," it purred contemptuously. "Yet you will never reach it. There is no sanctuary in the Hill for you. You fled many years ago and cannot claim its refuge now. The time has come to pay the price for your sordid elopement."

The bracken rustled and a slender figure stepped from the shadow of a wide oak and into the trembling light. The Unseelie Court held its breath.

Rhiannon Rigantona was cloaked in wolf skins. A crown of antlers was upon her head, woven into her braided raven hair. Necklaces of smooth round stones threaded onto leather strips adorned her pale throat where the silver fire devil gleamed once more. In her left hand, she carried a wooden staff, bound about with lodestones, large black pebbles charged with powerful forces. The owl sat upon her shoulder. The grass trembled and twisted as she approached and the drooping twigs of the trees curled up to clear the way. Even the forest itself obeyed her now.

Only Peg-tooth Meg could meet her stabbing stare without shuddering and, unlike the rest of those gathered there, she regarded Rhiannon with a mixture of pity and loathing.

"You are lost, sister," she said. "Deathless and unequaled you may be, but your new realm will be a blighted and barren, joyless world. Who will serve you; who could endure such unrelenting tyranny?"

Rhiannon gave a snarling, repulsive laugh. "Is there ever a lack of craven-hearted worms?" she answered. "Those who save their skins by selling those of their friends, or even their own offspring? Humankind shall serve me. They are so easily persuaded and ever ready to yield to the strongest oppressor. How they yearn for subjugation. Yet that is no concern for you, unhappy, deformed pond spawn."

"You have betrayed your high-born blood!" Meg cried. "You have deceived your own people and allied yourself with our father's greatest enemies."

"I abjure the line of Ragallach!" Rhiannon snapped. "I renounce the blood that ties me to you. I have better sisters now—they claimed me long ago and I am their revered Queen."

She raised her staff and gave a commanding shout: "Come forth, my loathly sisters!"

Lightning spiked down from the heavy clouds above, drawn to the stones bound to the staff. The electric jags snaked and sparked around them and Rhiannon's laughter was joined by other harsh voices.

At last, the darkness beneath the trees was banished as countless forks of blinding white fire came blasting down. In the stark glare of the jumping light, the enemy was finally revealed.

They were hideous: hulking hunched hags with unformed faces like pitted and weathered boulders, set with glaring orange eyes. Pebbles and stones were bound into their wild tangled hair and many more were hung about their short necks, strapped to their foreheads, and wrapped around thick wrists. Their arms were short but their hands were large as spades with fingers like twisted roots. Wrapped in wolf-skin cape, each crone bore a cudgel or stave tipped with lodestones and they whirled them in the air, tearing lightning from the heavens.

There were hundreds of them riding on the backs of monstrous, snorting wild boars. Many of them were accompanied by the thorn ogres: small, brutish creatures created by the High Lady that had been missing from the attack upon the Wandering Smith several days ago. Sitting between the ears of the enormous hogs and crouching on the hags' shoulders, they shrieked in gleeful, croaking voices, anticipating the carnage to come.

Nine of the troll witches sported fresh and gruesome additions to their staves. Jammed on the tops of them were the heads of a sprig-gan gang they had encountered as they came tearing down the cinder trackway. The faces of Captain Grittle and his lads decorated the cudgels, frozen in expressions of shock.

The werlings spluttered with horror at the scene and Dewfrost whinnied shrilly and backed away. Meg clenched her few teeth and the sluglungs gibbered in fretful voices. Lord Limmersent and the other nobles fumbled with their swords, and the goblin knights cursed behind their visors.

Rhiannon threw her arms wide in welcome.

"Now my sisters," she called, "this squalid forest is yours at last. Torment it, destroy it, and kill them all."

Holding their clubs and staves high, so that the lightning played and spat across their lodestones, the troll witches of the Cold Hills screeched with mordant glee as they charged forward. The wild boars ripped up the ground with their curved tusks before stampeding toward the frightened horses. The thorny imps clacked and clicked their woody limbs as they rocked to and fro, their evil faces grinning ever wider.

"Their numbers are too great," the nobles cried.

"Give me a sword!" rang Meg's resolute reply. "My sister is beyond the reach of blade, but these hags have plenty of blood to spill, though it be black and steaming. Beware their staffs—cut off their hands if you can. We are fewer in number but still we fight! For my father the High King, for the Hollow Hill—for Hagwood!"

Inspired by her courage and bold words, the Unseelie Court took up her cry and every weapon was drawn. Sir Hobflax handed Meg his best sword, a glittering, Pucca-forged blade.

"For the glory of the Hollow Hill!" the goblin barked. "And for you, Queen Clarisant!"

Meg swept the sword from side to side, slicing through the rain. "Hold tight, little shobblers," she told the werlings huddled in front of her. "These are the final frantic beatings of our doughty hearts. We will die bravely, as did Prince Tammedor."

Before Liffidia or Tollychook could make any answer, she gave a defiant yell of challenge and Dewfrost galloped forward to meet the enemy head on. Meg's cavalry charged after her and the sluglungs rushed alongside.

The forest was filled with the clamor of combat. The troll witches pulled down lightning from the sky and flung it at the horses. Steeds and riders were hurled high into the air and ravening tusks gored deep into flanks. Breastplates were split asunder and heads were hammered from shoulders. Thorny imps sprang at the horses and clawed at their eyes and wrenched open the goblins' visors to bite their faces. The ghastly, feral shrieks of the troll witches rose above the clash of the swords, echoing under the trees.

Tollychook and Liffidia were utterly helpless. As the hags came charging in, they could see the grains of grit and filth ground into their pocked troll hides and smell their foul, moldy breath. Liffidia was shaking uncontrollably and flinched with every new burst of lightning that ripped through the shadows.

Meg's sword thrust and chopped, but the troll witches were merely playing with her, baiting and screaming with laughter, running their hogs around and around, in and out of the horses' paths and weaving through the trees. They had waited a long time for this night, and would relish every last drop of pain and suffering.

Standing at the edge of the conflict, Rhiannon Rigantona's dark eyes sparkled as she watched. Another horse and rider were blasted over the forest by a blinding spear of lightning. White flames were burning within Sir Hobflax's armor and shooting from the eye slots of his hounskull helmet. He soared through the darkness, leaving a smoking trail in his wake.

Rhiannon laughed cruelly.

"Thus endeth the Unseelie Court," the owl commented in her ear. "And all else who dare oppose thee, My Lady."

The vile bird's mistress smiled as two more knights and their horses were catapulted into the night. Then she licked her lips and said, "Seek a safe vantage point, my loyal lieutenant. I am entering the fray—I must kill Clarisant myself; it is a pleasure I cannot be denied. But first of all, I require a mount."

The bird obeyed her and found a branch that commanded an excellent view while the High Lady strode forward and lifted her staff.

Throughout the long empty years scraping and starving in the Cold Hills, the troll witches had thirsted for such a vicious encounter as this and Rhiannon had promised them many more. The foul wizened faces rushed through the leaping shadows yelling and shrieking with murderous glee.

One of the witches, the Widow Hakkra, was delivering crippling blows with her stone-covered cudgel atop her monstrous hog Ironback. Then she saw Lord Limmersent riding alongside one of her sisters, engaged in a bitter duel. He had become separated from the rest of the riders and was too vulnerable to ignore. Brandishing her cudgel, intent on smashing in his brains, she rode forward feverishly.

Lord Limmersent brought his sword down upon the shoulder of a hag called Mother Shaler. She snarled at him when the blow caused her staff to fall from her hand and she pulled on the ears of her wild boar to bring the animal to a halt. Without hesitation, the noble thrust his blade clean through the great hog's neck and it keeled over, sending the troll witch sprawling. He permitted himself a grim smile and turned his horse about, only to be confronted by the Widow Hakkra.

Her cudgel was already raised and he knew he was doomed.

There was a searing streak of light and, to his wonderment and the witch's short-lived astonishment, Rhiannon's carefully aimed lightning blasted into her.

The Widow Hakkra bellowed as she hurtled through the air. Lord Limmersent watched her spin into the trees then stared back at the High Lady in confusion. Why had she spared him? But her sinister attention was fixed solely upon the wild boar. She wanted Ironback, the fiercest hog in the sounder, and she wasn't going to spend a breath commanding Hakkra to give it up. Her will was the only law now, and every life was hers to end, whenever the impulse drove her.

Extending her hand, she hissed words of summoning and the massive wild boar tossed its ugly head and raced across the battleground to meet her.

Rhiannon Rigantona climbed onto his bristled back and, with murder burning in the depths of her eyes, searched for her sister in that beleaguered knot of death and despair.

"The toad queen is mine!" she called when she saw Meg struggling against three troll witches. "It is I who must blast the life out of her!"

In the thick of the battle, Dewfrost reared and kicked at the troll

witches' fearsome swine. Holding to the reins with one hand and setting her sword to sing with the other, Peg-tooth Meg fought valiantly,
calling the name of her dead love as a battle cry. But she was barely
keeping the enemy at bay, and it was a fight she could not possibly win.

All around Meg the knights and nobles were gradually diminish-
ing in number. A flux of lightning exploded in the chest of Sir Begwort
and his breastplate shattered like glass. A shard slashed Dewfrost's neck
and a white-hot spark scorched her flank. Neighing wildly, the mare
bucked and bolted with terror—dashing through the enemy lines and
leaping over anything in its path. Meg was almost thrown but held on,
and yet no command she gave could stop the horse's mad flight.

Tollychook had tied a hank of the horse's mane around his waist
so, even if he lost his grip, he would not fall. Liffidia had not been so
prudent. As Dewfrost jumped over a hog and rider, the mane slipped
from the girl's fingers. Before Tollychook could catch her, she slithered
down the horse's shoulder and was gone—her terrified cry swamped
by the roaring din as the battle swept over her.

"Mistress Nefyn!" the boy bawled. He whisked his head around
and stared past Meg's streaming green hair to the spot where Liffidia
had fallen. There was no sign of her. Hooves of horses and swine and
the tumult of the fighting obscured all else. What chance of survival
had a small werling girl in the middle of that trampling destruction?

"She'm be crunched into the soil or shredded by tusks by now," he
sobbed.

Still trying desperately to control the fleeing horse and remain in
the saddle, Peg-tooth Meg could do nothing to comfort him.

Heeding no voice but that of her own fear, Dewfrost burst through
the ranks of the enemy and plunged headlong into the forest.

Meanwhile, the remaining army of the Hollow Hill had finally
caught up with the nobles and goblin knights and were storming in
with their pikes and spears. Perched upon klurie helmets, the Redcaps
fired their arrows and many hogs stumbled and crashed as their poison did its work. Milkmaids clouted umpteen heads and even the
shrunken race of oakmen scampered forward to engage the thorny
imps in combat. But there was no defense against the lightning that
the troll witches wielded.

From its vantage point, the owl surveyed the seething spectacle impassively. Its golden eyes watched Dewfrost bolt into the forest, and saw Rhiannon Rigantona set off upon Ironback in pursuit. It swooped from the branch in haste to follow its divine mistress.

With the sea of war raging around him, Lord Limmersent marked the owl flying overhead and urged the Unseelie Court to fight their way through the forest.

"Warriors of the High Queen!" he yelled, rallying the knights and foot soldiers to his upraised sword. "Clarisant rides unguarded and certain death pursues her! Ride! Run! Fight your way through this darksome night and protect her with your lives!"

With renewed vigor, he slashed and kicked the swarming forces of the enemy and drove his horse through. Shouting Clarisant's name, the Unseelie Court battled southward, in the direction of the Witch's Leap.

✦ CHAPTER 17 ✦

TO THE WITCH'S LEAP

WHEN THE HOLLOW HILL HAD OPENED and the earth had shook, Gamaliel and the others had feared the worst and thrown themselves to the ground.

Curled up like hedgehogs, they waited, and waited. But all that happened was that they heard the sound of the trumpeting fanfare in the far distance as the Unseelie Court progressed toward the ruined watchtower.

"Someone's having a shindig," Bufus muttered, rising to his feet. "They must be bonkers."

"What sanity has there been these past days?" Gamaliel asked, picking himself up.

Kernella pouted peevishly. "I'm sure Finnen won't be there," she said. "He'll have far more important things to do than be at some rotten old party."

Master Gibble brushed the grass from his ragged gown and cocked his long ears toward the remote noises.

"That is the pomp and blare of a conqueror," he uttered gravely. "The High Lady is on the move."

"And so are we," Gamaliel told them. "To the Witch's Leap."

His sister huffed and looked at Bufus who only shrugged in return.

"Is it absolutely necessary for us to venture there?" Terser Gibble asked forlornly.

It was Bufus who answered him.

"If Gammy says so, then we're going," he said sternly. "Come on, Wibble—you're not scared, are you?"

"I'm petrified," the wergle master mumbled.

They resumed the march in ponderous silence, stopping at intervals so Kernella could wergle into a squirrel and scurry up the tallest tree she could find and look out over the forest roof. The colossal, dark mass of the Witch's Leap grew steadily closer until finally her scouting expeditions became unnecessary. The ground was rising and the immense, oppressive bulk of the Witch's Leap reared up on their left, like a slumbering leviathan, blotting out the thickly moving clouds that pulsed and flared with the oncoming storm.

Its looming presence was daunting and they wondered what they would find when they reached the top of that dizzy height. The closer they drew to the lower slopes, the more agitated Master Gibble became. He began to babble, chattering about anything and everything and getting on everyone's nerves until Bufus told him to button it.

"But I cannot proceed!" the tutor protested, his head twitching uncontrollably. "Charming and gladmaking as your company has been—and it genuinely has been most pleasant to be among you once more—I really cannot accompany you another step toward that lofty rise. The very marrow in my bones shrivels at the idea. I cannot—and I won't and that's that!"

"What's rattled you so much?" Bufus asked, irritably.

Master Gibble rubbed his bony elbows and shuddered. "That place," he muttered. "It's not called the haunted crag for naught. The leader of the troll witches jumped from that great height to her death hundreds of years ago when she was trapped there by the High King. But her evil lingers still: They say her shrieks can be heard in winter storms. And there are other things that shift in and out of the dark—nameless, shapeless, unquiet horrors. I am too craven to venture closer. How can you even think to trespass on that fearsome spot?"

The children looked at him in mild surprise and then considered one another. Master Gibble was right—a week ago only Bufus would have imagined himself brave enough to venture to such a place, but he would never have actually gone there. They had all changed since then.

"You don't understand," Kernella told the wergle master. "One of us will die before tomorrow; it's been prophesied. Whether we run away and hide in the fields or bite a spriggan on the nose, it'll still happen."

"So we might as well make the most of it," Bufus put in. "If that means paying a call on the ghoulies and ghosties of the Witch's Leap, then so be it. They can't be any worse than what we've already seen."

Master Gibble fidgeted uncomfortably. "That precipice was cursed long before Black Howla dived to her death from it. There's badness in the very boulders."

"Maybe there is," Gamaliel said, "but that's where we're going. If you don't want to come, then go your own way—but we can't waste any more time arguing about it."

"Then you go without me!" Master Gibble retorted miserably. "I can't wergle on the outside or on the inside. I'm just the same as always, puffed up with vanity and pride. The jug of my courage has always been empty. I wish it were not so but there it is. I've as much substance and backbone as thistledown, dithering on the wind. There, it shames me to the marrow but I can't be more than I am. The Great Grand Wergle Master is a vacillating, cowardly wretch!"

Bufus pulled a disgusted face. "I knew you'd flit off at the first whiff of danger," he told the wergle master. "Yellow as a dandelion, that's what you are."

"I told you not to speak to him in the first place," Kernella grumbled as the two of them plodded away.

Gamaliel regarded his former tutor one last time. Terser Gibble was the most pitiful sight and he couldn't help feeling sorry for him.

"I'm glad we met again," the boy said warmly. "In fact, I think it was meant to be. You're the one Nest sent us to meet, not Gwyddion—I'm sure of it."

Master Gibble stared at him, bemused. He did not understand a word about Nest or Gwyddion.

"Do not squander your breath by speaking to me," he answered, averting his eyes. "I am not worth any kindness. Why should anyone send you to meet this apology of a creature? I am a hollow emptiness, a vacuum devoid of pride or worth. Let me crawl away and cower like the insect I am."

Gamaliel stepped forward and pressed the tutor's hand in his own.

"But you have helped me, Master Gibble," he said. "You reminded me who and what we are and, tonight, that's what I needed most. So much has happened, I'd almost forgotten. We are werlings, not warriors or knights, or champions, just the little werglers of Hagwood and I wouldn't change that for anything. So thank you."

The boy smiled then turned to follow his sister and Bufus.

Terser Gibble stood there shaking and suffering. The boy's simple affection had affected him deeply. He had never deserved it. He had always been a braggart and had a mean, needling nature. Now his breaths came sharp and shallow. He despised his own cowardice but feared the path to the haunted crag even more.

Gamaliel's gentle voice called back. "Go far from here. Very soon war is going to sweep over this place. Don't get caught up in that."

Gibble jerked his head in answer but the boy was already lost in the gloom ahead.

"There go some of my youngest pupils," he murmured when he was quite alone, "and each is worth a hundred of me. Terser Gibble, if you had a scrap of self-respect left, the shame of this would destroy you."

He covered his face with his hands and began stumbling away, down the path, as fast as his spindly legs could bear him.

"Even the Lubber's sparrows were braver than that scaredy pimple!" he heard Bufus Doolan's scornful voice cry out.

The rain began spitting from the sky and the werlings pressed on.

"It's just us again, then," Kernella stated.

"Not if what Flatface Gibble said was true," Bufus told her. "Remember the nameless horrors. We'll be bumping into them soon enough."

"I'll give them a few names they won't forget," the girl promised.

They both chuckled. The ground continued to rise and the trees became ever more twisted and gnarled. Gradually, gargantuan thistles and impenetrable thickets of bramble replaced the bracken and snaking roots that protruded from the soil. A deathly stillness lay over this forsaken part of the forest, and although it was spring, the must and decay of an ancient autumn filled their noses.

"Perhaps the seasons don't even visit this place," Kernella remarked.

"I don't blame them," Bufus said, kicking through a heap of soggy, moldering leaves. "Stinky, messy dump!"

The heavens growled overhead.

"Even the thunder sounds muffled here," Gamaliel observed.

"The rain's still wet enough, though," Bufus grumbled, pulling his woolen hat down over his ears.

They trudged on, growing more and more uneasy. At first they thought it was merely the leaping shadows cast by the lightning, but then they caught movements in the corners of their eyes.

"We're not alone," Kernella whispered.

When the werlings whirled around to confront the skulking shapes, they could only see the somber darkness beneath the misshapen trees.

"Just go away!" Kernella shouted. "You don't scare us!" But her voice sounded less confident than she had intended.

"Bog off!" Bufus yelled.

From somewhere behind them came a soft murmuring. The werlings could not catch any words, but it was an unpleasant whispering, made up of snarls and hisses and bristling with hostility. More ugly voices joined in and it spread rapidly, sweeping through the trees and undergrowth until it surrounded them. Then the thistles began to rustle and creak, as though stealthy creatures were moving between them, closing in on the werlings.

"What are those things?" Kernella asked uncertainly.

"I don't know," Gamaliel answered. "I can't see them; just keep catching shadowy blurs in the corner of my eye."

"I think that's what they are," Kernella said. "Dark smudges, without any proper shape."

"I thought you were going to name them. . . ." Bufus muttered.

"Oh, I have," the girl said, swallowing nervously. "They're Scary Whatsits."

"That'll do just fine," he agreed.

"If they're ghosts, they can't hurt us, can they?" she asked.

"I've no idea," her brother said. "But the fear of them might if we give in to panic. Hold hands and follow me. The trees thin out up ahead; we can turn 'round there and face them if they come after us."

The children linked hands. Gamaliel went first, followed by Kernella, while Bufus brought up the rear. With determined yet frightened expressions, they strode between the thistles as the whispering grew ever louder. The hatred behind those muttering voices was unmistakable.

Gamaliel had done many brave deeds over the past days, but leading the others through that murmuring night was one of the most courageous. The undergrowth was thick with repulsive voices and formless patches of darkness rushed between the woody stems ahead.

"We just want to get past," he said aloud, edging to the side. "To reach the cliff. We don't want to harm you."

The hissing, cruel laughter that followed made Kernella's skin crawl. She had the overwhelming and unpleasant feeling they were being herded by the Scary Whatsits. She imagined a pit strewn with gnawed bones, similar to the lair of the candle spright, and gripped her brother's and Bufus's hands even tighter.

The Doolan boy gave an answering pull and then squeezed the cold fingers that had slipped into his other hand.

His eyes almost popped out of his head. "Whose fingers are those?" he cried in horror.

Throwing his hands in the air, he let out a scream and pelted past Kernella and Gamaliel. That was enough for the Tumpins. They too shrieked and raced after him. Terrified, the three of them crashed through the thistles and the shapeless beings swarmed in pursuit. The trees clattered their twigs overhead. Indistinct black shadows spilled from the hollows of diseased oaks and joined the hunt.

The woolen hat was torn from Bufus's head and Kernella's hair was snatched and pulled. Gamaliel almost tripped over some hidden obstacle, and a wintry breath spat at him. A dark cowl fell across his face. He yelled and ducked beneath it, tearing at the shadows that flew before him.

The werlings burst from the trees and onto the open stretch that lay before the seven pines at the cliff edge. The ground had become bare rock, covered in dry, crackling needles, and was littered with fir cones. Wheezing and panting for breath, the youngsters skidded to a halt and spun around, waiting for their pursuers to come rushing from the undergrowth.

The tall thistles rattled and shook and shadows surged thickly around their stalks, but nothing came forward.

Gamaliel puffed and gasped and wiped a sleeve over his forehead.

"They won't come out," he said. "I bet lurking in the forest, frightening travelers is the worst they can do."

"They do it really well though!" Bufus cried, trying not to think of the spectral fingers he had squeezed as he rubbed his hand on his jerkin with a shudder.

"Well they won't be doing that for long!" Gamaliel shouted, as fury replaced his fright. "The final battle is coming to this crag, so they'd better creep back into their crevices! Go on, slink away. A bitter ending is coming for all of us!"

"Just what are you expecting to happen up here?" Bufus asked.

Gamaliel made no answer but walked farther up the crag toward the towering pines. The massive sprawl of Hagwood spread beneath them in every direction. Southward, toward the Devil's Table, the world was cloaked in profound night. Kernella's gaze was fixed upon the east, where the broken watchtower stood alone on the grassy promontory. It was so far away, no more than a splinter of stone jutting into the fulminating sky. A faint, spluttering glimmer of yellow light upon its roof showed that the rain had not yet extinguished the small fire the Tower Lubber had kept burning there. She turned to the others but they were looking in the opposite direction—their stricken, horrified faces were lit by far brighter flames.

Kernella caught her breath and stared across the forest roof, westward, toward their home. The land of the werlings was ablaze.

"'Fire burns the homely sky,'" Bufus breathed. "That's what Nest said."

"He said a lot of things," Gamaliel muttered grimly.

His sister covered her mouth. "She did it," she said desolately. "The High Lady burned them. Our families—everyone."

"Maybe not," Bufus comforted her, trying to sound hopeful. "Your mum and dad might have escaped; they all might have. Even my old man isn't completely useless."

"That's what She'll do to everything," Kernella said. "Burn and destroy, spoil and turn to dust anything She doesn't like or that gets in Her way. Until it happens to your own family, you never really understand what that actually means. Our home is gone."

"We came so close to putting an end to Her," Bufus sighed, running his fingers through his dripping hair. "So close."

Gamaliel waited for one of them to blame him for losing the key, but neither of them did. They were beyond such pettiness now and they had both come to respect him. A grateful smile appeared on his chubby face.

Suddenly, a deafening boom of thunder made all three of them jump and they wrenched their eyes northward. The great round summit of the Hollow Hill looked eerie and majestic in the distance, upraised on huge monoliths. The silvery-green light that shone from the lanterns within flowed out over the treetops, but the werlings had no time to marvel at the vision. In the forest vale between, they could hear echoing shouts and cries of battle. They saw countless streaks of lightning pulled from the clouds to go sizzling down in lethal strikes. The children gaped, speechless.

"*Such power,*" a whispering voice softly rasped.

The werlings nodded. Each of them thought one of the others had said it.

"*Mightier and more terrible than anything before,*" it continued. "*Tearing the very lightning from the sky.*"

"It's horrible," Kernella breathed, her eyes dazzled by the brilliant display of crackling light.

"*How can we stop that?*" the voice asked mournfully.

"Nothing can," said Gamaliel in a flat, beaten tone.

"*Against magic so strong, so unstoppable, there is no hope.*"

"None," agreed Bufus. "None at all."

"*We were fools to even try.*"

Gamaliel's head began to nod. An aching fatigue was creeping over him. His sister and Bufus felt the same leaden heaviness seeping through their bodies.

"*Who are we to resist that power?*"

"We're no one," Gamaliel uttered thickly. "Just silly little werlings."

"*Listen to those cries,*" the bewitching voice whispered. "*Lives are being lost down there.*"

"So many . . ." Kernella murmured. "So many dying."

"*This night tolls with death. Our families are lost in flames and our friends are being slain. We too must die.*"

"I don't mind," Bufus said groggily. "I'm ready. Nest said, one of us . . . one of us by morning."

"*Why one alone when we could go together? The war will kill us anyway. We cannot escape it and there will be nothing left for us.*"

"I was . . ." Gamaliel began slowly. "I was going . . . going to . . . try . . ."

"*Too late for that,*" the compelling voice insisted. "*The battle is already lost. Listen to the shrill agonies. Do we wait to burn like those poor brave heroes yonder? Must we feel the tempest's fire blasting into us?*"

"I don't want to die that way," Kernella said with a fretful frown on her sleepy face.

"*Or be cut down by blades or crushed beneath hooves?*"

Bufus closed his eyes. "Let it be over," he pleaded.

"*Yes, we can decide our own way—a quick, peaceful way. Surrender ourselves into sweet darkness and feel no pain.*"

"I'd like that," Kernella sighed.

"*We have not slept for so very long, and the path has been hard. Let us sleep deep, now and for always.*"

The children's heads slumped onto their chests. They were completely under the spell.

"*Let us join hands once more,*" the lulling voice crooned. "*That's right, now . . . this way. Follow my words. Walk here, come—come to the endless sleep. Such rest we will find there, such delicious relief from all our pains and troubles.*"

Holding hands, the werlings stumbled forward, barely awake. The voice lured them on, enticing them, promising a syrupy oblivion, freedom at long last from the strife and grief that had plagued them.

And so the spirit of Black Howla seduced them ever closer to the cliff edge. The pine needles crunched under the children's feet as they passed beneath the seven pine trees. Exposed upon that staggering height, the cold winds gusted around them.

"*A little farther,*" Black Howla called. "*That's it, my loves—almost there . . . just two steps and we shall be at peace.*"

"With Mufus," Bufus murmured dreamily.

He took another step forward, pulling the others with him. The empty night blew before his closed eyes and the precipice was now only one more step away. The rock dropped sharply into blackness below.

"Will Finnen be there?" Kernella yawned.

"*All our desires are there,*" Black Howla said, her voice floating out into the storm in front.

Kernella prepared to walk off the cliff.

"YOU, GIRL!" a stern voice bawled furiously. "Stand still! Stop daydreaming! Bufus Doolan, wipe that stupid smirk off your face, you nasty child. Gamaliel Tumpin—was there ever such a clumsy, bedwetting wergler?"

The commanding voice was instantly familiar. It cut clean through the cloying words of Black Howla's enchantment and resonated deep within the children's sleeping selves immediately. They did not dare ignore it.

"You're late—all of you!" it cried. "How dare you!"

"I'm sorry!" Gamaliel spluttered, his consciousness struggling to the surface. Was it his first morning of wergling instruction? He must have overslept. Why hadn't anyone woken him?

ROBIN JARVIS •

Kernella grabbed her wergle pouch instinctively. "I did my homework!" she blurted. "Honest I did—weasels are easy!"

"Come here at once! All three of you! See me—right now, no excuses! Don't make me wait or I really will lose my temper!"

The children snapped their eyes open.

Terser Gibble, the one and only Great Grand Wergle Master was standing beneath the last pine, his ragged gown flapping in the storm. But his face was not that of the school's scolding tyrant that he had compelled his voice to be. It was contorted with terror and anguish for his former pupils and his beady eyes were streaming with tears.

The children stared dumbly at him. Then, with a sickening lurch in their stomachs, they realized where they were—one slight nudge away from death. Kernella yelled and flung herself from danger. She ran to the wergle master and threw her arms around him.

Black Howla's frustrated screech blistered through the air above them, circling up into the pine trees.

"Begone, pestilential shade!" Master Gibble shouted fiercely. "I will not let you hurt these children. They are in my care now."

Black Howla shrieked with scorn. *"Your pupils will live only long enough to curse you for saving them! My own pupil is on her way here. She will find fitting ends for you all. Expect no swift death—this night and all hereafter belong to my sisters."*

The spirit's hideous laughter tore higher through the branches until it was lost on the wind.

Kernella looked up at Master Gibble and beamed at him. "You came back," she said. "Even though you were so scared, you came. You saved us."

Master Gibble wiped his eyes as she hugged him. "Your brother was right," he said. "Wergling can happen on the inside."

He glanced over to where Gamaliel and Bufus were still standing close to the cliff edge.

"Come away from there!" he barked sharply.

Bufus and Gamaliel looked at one another. The world plummeted away before them and the ledge was wet and slippery. Gamaliel could read the other boy's face and knew what was running through his mind. He shook his head violently.

260

"No!" he shouted.

"Think about it, Gammy!" Bufus yelled into the rain. "It would be so easy. One of us three has to die. You know that. Why not me? It makes sense. I've done what I promised my brother, I've made it to the end and done my best to make him proud. If I go now, you and Nellie over there might just make it!"

Gamaliel glared at him. "Don't you dare!" he raged. "This isn't over yet."

"Look around you!" the Doolan boy cried in exasperation. "Evil Queen, massive win; good guys, a big fat nil! We lost. The war is done and dusted!"

"Not yet," Gamaliel answered with a defiant grin. "There's still a chance—a mad, stupid, tiny scrap of a chance!"

Bufus blinked at him. "You really are barmy," he said.

"I must be!" Gamaliel laughed. "Because even though you're the biggest pain I ever met, I like you. And what's more—I need you. The world needs you."

Before Bufus could answer, Master Gibble's bony fingers took hold of his ear and he did the same to Gamaliel.

"Get away from the edge!" the tutor repeated.

They were hauled over to where Kernella was waiting and she folded her arms and scowled at Gamaliel.

"What are you up to?" she asked. "It's time you explained why you brought us here."

"You heard Gwyddion," her brother answered. "He said the deciding moment will take place up here. The days will either be forever dark or 'golden evermore.'"

"That bloodthirsty crackpot also said you were the Blessed One!" Bufus scoffed.

Gamaliel shrugged diffidently. "I don't know about that," he said modestly. "But . . . I have been chosen and this is where I am meant to be tonight."

"Stop this!" Kernella told him crossly. There was a determined look in his eyes that alarmed her. "We're just going to wait here and see what happens, aren't we, Master Gibble?"

The wergle master was not listening. His attention was fixed on the valley between the Hollow Hill and the haunted crag. The curtain of lightning was moving closer and the noise of battle was growing louder. The armies were rushing through the forest, toward the lower slopes.

Terser Gibble stepped through the pines and down onto the stretch of bare rock.

"They're coming this way," he breathed fearfully. "Young Tumpin was right again."

The children hurried to join him and their eyes grew round at what they saw. The noise of the battle was louder now and they spotted the owl flying low over the treetops. Thunderous hooves were galloping closer. They caught sight of a great silver-white horse hurtling up the ridge, skidding through the heaps of wet leaves, crashing blindly through the thistles and tearing through the brambles.

"Why is it coming this way?" Kernella asked.

"A madness whips that poor beast along," Master Gibble answered. "What horrors has it seen?"

"Look!" the girl cried, pointing wildly. "There's a rider trying desperately to control it. . . . Oh no."

Her voice choked in her throat as she recognized the figure crouched low in the saddle, her dark green hair streaming in the tempest.

"It's Meg!" her brother gasped.

"She'll plunge right over the edge if she doesn't halt!" Kernella squealed.

"Stop the horse!" Bufus yelled at the top of his voice as he sprang forward. "Stop it! You'll be killed!"

As they watched the insane steed race nearer and heard Meg begging it to halt, they heard a second voice yowling. The children drew anxious breaths.

Master Gibble looked down at them. "That sounds like . . ."

"Tollychook," Gamaliel said. "He's with her!"

Dewfrost thundered on. She was almost clear of the gnarled, rotting oaks; soon her hooves would clatter and spark over the bare rock, fling herself through the pines, then leap off the cliff.

Kernella turned her head away, but what she saw creeping up behind them made her scream even louder.

⁕ CHAPTER 18 ⁕

OVER THE EDGE

WITH BLOOD STREAKING DOWN HER NECK and smoke pouring from her burning flesh, Dewfrost ran like a demon. To flee was the only thought in her frightened mind, to run as fast and as far as she could, without stopping.

With his hands gripping tightly to the horse's mane, Tollychook's arms were almost wrenched from their sockets in the fiercely jarring, bouncing ride through the forest. He felt battered and sick and for once was relieved he had not eaten anything.

Dewfrost bounded over a thicket of briar and the ground began to rise. It was then Meg realized where they were headed.

Nothing would stop the beast, so they would have to jump clear before it threw itself over the cliff edge. It was racing along at a break-neck speed, but it was their only chance.

"We must jump to save ourselves, little shobbler!" she cried to Tollychook.

The boy goggled up at her. "You can't mean that, missus!" he shrieked. "We'll break us necks and split our heads wide open!"

"We must risk it!" she answered forcefully. "Else we will plunge to our deaths. The Witch's Leap awaits us at the end of this road."

Tollychook stared at her a moment longer as the full meaning of that dawned on him. Then he began scrabbling feverishly at the hank of mane tied about his waist.

The high thistles and distorted trees rushed by.

"Hurry!" Meg called. "Hurry!"

Tollychook grunted and strained and tore his fingernails but the knot had tightened.

"I can't get loose!" he yelled in panic. "I be stuck!"

Dread and dismay shone in Meg's eyes as she gazed down at the small plump figure sitting in front of her.

"You must!" she told him. "Try harder! Cut it—bite it through!"

"I doesn't have no knife!" he wailed. "And I can't chew through that—me belly's in the way!"

Meg cast a fearful face forward. The pine trees were already visible in the distance. The wooded stretch was coming to an end and they were on the final furlong. It would be safer to jump here, where the weeds could break her fall—but she could not abandon the young werling to certain death.

"Let me aid you!" she said, reaching for the knot with one hand while clinging to the reins with the other.

Dewfrost burst from the undergrowth and the solid rock echoed beneath her hooves.

Meg's nails clawed at the stubborn knot but it was no use.

"You go, missus!" Tollychook shouted desperately. "Don't fret 'bout me!"

The woman's large, froglike eyes glittered at him and her wide mouth smiled.

"We go together," she said and she clasped her hand about him tenderly.

Dewfrost tore over the barren expanse of rock. The rain and thunder filled their ears but Tollychook thought he heard familiar voices calling his name. The world swept by in a blur. He saw seven towering pines flicker in and out of the lightning. A heartbeat later he felt the horse's powerful muscles judder and tense as it prepared to leap between the trees and off the crag.

Tollychook squeezed his eyes shut and held on to Meg's fingers.

The horse launched herself into the night. She flew into the air and the emptiness of that terrifying height yawned before them.

"Tammedor," Meg whispered.

Dewfrost whinnied and thrashed her forelegs in the storm.

Tollychook felt as though time slowed down. They had cleared the cliff edge and only a black gulf was beneath them.

The horse whinnied again. Then there was a jolt and she was snatched backward in midair.

Dewfrost neighed and screamed but her legs and body were caught firmly in sticky ropes. She tried to toss her head, but that too was held tight. She struggled and twisted but could not break free.

Tollychook dared to open one eye and let out a disbelieving shout as he took in the astounding sight. Meg murmured in wonderment.

They were suspended above the rocky ledge and between the trees. A taut net, bejeweled and beaded with the rain, radiated out from the pines on either side. One of the ropes was close enough for him to reach. He touched it and found that his hand was now glued fast.

"Eurgh!" he exclaimed, trying to pull free. "It's sticky as a . . ." He swallowed his words as the truth flooded over him.

"Oh, 'eck!" he burbled.

They were caught in a colossal spider's web.

Strung across the space between the seven trees was a gargantuan cobweb and Dewfrost was snared within it. All energies spent, her great heart thudding in her chest and with eyes rolling, the silverwhite mare hung there.

"'Tain't possible," Tollychook said, taking a breath. "Unless . . ."

There was only one creature in Hagwood capable of spinning such a web, and he was suddenly gripped by a new terror.

Behind him, Meg was marveling and shaking her head in amazement. Then, from below, voices called up to them.

"Hoy, Chookface—stop wriggling. You'll only make it worse."

"Stay still!" Gamaliel called. "Help is on its way."

Kernella gazed up at the incredible spectacle. It had happened so fast she had scarcely had time to take it in.

The nightmarish Frighty Aggie, a huge part-wasp, part-spider monster, had scaled the cliff face and woven an enormous, enchanted web between the trunks of the trees to catch the leaping horse. When Tollychook looked upward, he glimpsed a sinister, yellow-striped shape withdraw into the shadows of the high branches. Before he could yell out, he saw a familiar figure descending on a single strand, grinning at him.

"Master Lufkin!" he greeted in surprise. "What be . . .?"

Holding the sticky thread with one hand, Finnen saluted him with the other and winked cheekily at Peg-tooth Meg.

"Don't be scared!" he said, drawing level with them. "Agnilla won't hurt you. She's here to help."

"But she be Frighty Aggie!" Tollychook hissed.

"And she was one of us once," Finnen answered sternly. "She brought me here, bless her. Now hold still while I cut your hand free. Aggie's webs are tough as old roots."

He took a small knife from his belt and set to work. Then he cut through the hank of hair that was tied about Tollychook's waist.

"Now grab onto me and we'll join the others," Finnen instructed. He looked to Meg but she assured him she could jump down unaided.

And so Finnen and Tollychook glided to the ground and Meg dropped beside them.

Bufus, Gamaliel, and Kernella dashed forward and bombarded Finnen with questions. He was equally eager to learn how they had survived the collapse of the floor in the watchtower.

"I thought you were killed!" he laughed.

"No such luck!" Bufus snorted. "I've been lumbered with this daft pair of Tumpins all day!"

"To ride on Frighty Aggie's back!" Gamaliel cried. "How in Hagwood did you manage that?"

"She didn't hurt me when I met her the last time," he replied. "I had to gamble on her not doing it again. She was the only help I could bring."

"You spoke to her?" Tollychook cried in astonishment.

"Yes," he answered. "She isn't the terrifying horror we always believed she was. And I've made her a promise."

"Promise?" Bufus asked. "What promise?"

Finnen didn't answer; instead he gazed up at the pine tree where Aggie had concealed herself and shook his head. "The real tragedy is," he said, "there's a tiny corner of her mind that remembers who she was before she wergled into that shape and got stuck. Can you imagine the torment of that?"

"But how did you know to climb up the cliff?" Gamaliel asked.

"I didn't! It's the way she brought me! I had nothing to do with that. I had no idea where she was taking me."

"Oh, Finnen!" Kernella cooed. "You're so brave! You're a miracle!"

Bufus groaned loudly. "There she goes again," he said.

It was a lovely, joyous moment. The war and everything they had gone through in the past two days had been temporarily forgotten. They were just five friends delighting in their reunion. Meg watched them and hung her head forlornly, knowing it would be all too short lived.

"And where's Liffidia?" Finnen asked.

Tollychook lowered his eyes and the happy moment ended.

Gamaliel pulled away and thought about what lay before him. It was time. He stepped across to Peg-tooth Meg and, in a frightened but solemn voice, asked, "The gold casket, can I see it?"

Meg sensed the urgency and dread in his words and she gazed at the boy curiously.

"Why do you wish that?" she asked.

"I just want to see it again," he insisted.

"I do not have it," she said. "I left it in the mud, down by the ruined tower, with Gabbity."

"You don't have it?" Gamaliel repeated, aghast. "But . . . !"

"Do not fret yourself. It was of no use," she assured him. "Rhiannon has won."

Gamaliel stumbled away from her and leaned against one of the pines, reeling with shock. He wouldn't be able to test his crazy plan after all, and in spite of his disappointment, a surge of relief washed over him.

Standing apart from the group, Master Gibble fidgeted and felt awkward. The wergle master had hung back while the others welcomed Finnen. Too much unpleasantness, born from his own jealousy and resentment, lay between them and he felt ashamed and out of place. Seeing his discomfort, Kernella whispered something in the boy's ear and Finnen walked over to him.

"Good to see you again, sir," he said.

Master Gibble's head gave a twitch. Unable to trust his trembling voice or meet the boy's eye, he looked up into the branches of the pine trees and cleared his throat.

The many eyes of Frighty Aggie were shining down at them.

"Poor unhappy, lonely creature," he said. "What a terrible price to pay for a want of wisdom. Mistakes can cost so very dear. We are all misguided in our way, some more than others."

"She's here now," Finnen told him. "That's what matters most and what will be remembered tomorrow. What's in the past is forgotten."

"But I—she has done such detestable things. Can it truly be forgiven?"

"Oh no," said a harsh voice nearby. "Nothing is ever forgotten, or forgiven—and for you, Master No Nose, there will be no tomorrow."

Everyone turned. A great wild boar was prowling up the rocky slope, carrying Rhiannon Rigantona on its back. In the stormy sky above, the owl was circling.

The High Lady's dark eyes surveyed the scene beneath the pine trees and her mocking laugh pierced those gathered there.

"What an elaborate way to stop a horse," she said, regarding the ensnared Dewfrost in the web. "That mare always was highly strung. Why didn't you just cut off her head? Far simpler."

Meg rose. Her bent bones creaked and she glared at her sister.

"You deal out death too readily," she said.

Rhiannon tugged on Ironback's ears and the hog grunted to a halt.

She dismounted and ran her fingers over the staff in her hands as the owl alighted upon her shoulder.

"It's certainly time I dealt with you, toad-face," she replied coldly. "And those vermin that scurry around your ankles. Shall I call down the lightning and explode those tree rats one by one while you watch? Would that pain you as much as the death of blind Prince Tammedor? Probably not."

The clamor of the battle was close now and the foremost riders were already on the lower slopes. Rivers of lightning were streaming from the sky and several diseased trees caught fire or were blown apart.

"Soon there won't be a single one of your new subjects left alive," Rhiannon told her sister, with a snarl. "But what a grand view of the destruction you have up here. I do so adore watching rebels burn."

The rocky ground shuddered as fiery bolts blasted from the sky. The army of the Hollow Hill fought bravely, but by the raucous crowing of the troll witches, Meg could tell they were not winning. She could only watch as knights and nobles, kluries and Redcaps, weary with battle, were flung into the air or ran, burning, into the forest.

Rhiannon's eyes danced over the grueling battle raging its way toward the ridge. Her face was an image of controlled pleasure and excitement. Those many long, fear-filled years had finally come to an end, and she anticipated many more bloody conflicts in the days ahead. The realms beyond Hagwood would fall before her just as easily. The world of humankind would humble itself and build temples in her name.

At the forefront of the battle, Lord Limmersent was being pursued by two screeching hags. He rode his horse hard and with great skill, swerving and dodging the jags of lightning that ripped past him.

He was the first warrior to break through the wooded stretch. Holding his sword before him, he galloped up the ridge, cursing the High Lady's name.

Rhiannon watched him dashing toward her then casually lifted her staff. The dark heavens thundered and a thorny stream of electric flame crackled down, spitting and seething around the stones bound to its top. As Lord Limmersent charged closer, Rhiannon pointed her staff and unleashed the lightning.

Kernella covered her eyes. A horrific explosion of blue and yellow flame engulfed both horse and rider, and they were hurled back into the woodland where their smoking bodies set light to the surrounding thistles.

The owl chuckled ghoulishly.

"The music of suffering is very beautiful to me," Rhiannon purred. "I will fill the land with such a song as has never been heard before. But you do not look as though you relish it quite as much, sister. Have you had enough?"

Crouched on the ground, Meg merely stared at her sister in disgust.

Rhiannon gave a callous laugh. The lightning continued to blaze atop her staff. The smoldering air around it was charged with tingling static that lifted her hair and bristled the owl's feathers. She was the undoubted High Queen of the world.

Finally, she turned her caustic attention to the werlings.

"And so, dear baby sister," she said with finality in her voice, "it is time to dispatch your performing mice. I wonder how well they burn. Let us see, shall we?"

She lowered her staff and was about to strike when Master Gibble leaped in front of the children, causing her to laugh all the more.

"Cowards and traitors blaze just as well as would-be heroes," she told him. "You are no protection."

The wergle master met her vicious glare without a twitch or jerk of his head. But a nudge in the back from Finnen caused him to glance past the High Lady, at the bare expanse of rock behind her. What he saw shocked and exhilarated him and he knew he had to keep Rhiannon's attention, distract her from what was approaching.

"Spare us!" he begged. "Spare *me*—and I will tell you every secret of my people."

Rhiannon snorted. "You squalid wer-rats have no secrets!" she cried. "And your life is not worth buying twice."

"Don't be so sure!" Finnen yelled back, guessing what Master Gibble was up to. He knew they had to keep her distracted just long enough.

"An' you might think you be pretty," Tollychook piped up, "but you be the ugliest hag in the whole of this forest!"

"And far too skinny!" added Kernella honestly.

The High Lady regarded them with contempt. Were they mad to insult her so? In a moment they would be screaming amid sizzling flames, yet Bufus was making obscene gestures at her and Gamaliel wasn't even looking in her direction.

Then, above the din of battle, she heard a curious slapping noise close by.

Rhiannon spun around. Charging toward her, their broad, webbed feet splashing in the rain, were the remaining sluglungs—and at their head, looking more fierce than ever before in her young life, was Liffidia Nefyn, riding upon Fly.

When Liffidia had fallen from Dewfrost, Fly had come tearing to her rescue. Now, catapult in hand, she fired a fir cone at the owl and it struck it smartly on the beak. The bird squawked and its eyes watered with the pain.

The sluglungs came bounding along behind Liffidia, shouting, "Megboo—ussum come, ussum help!"

"Shimmil dunge, boys!" Liffidia cried.

The sluglungs whooped and ran smack into one another, forming one large glob of jelly with many arms that raced forward and, as Rhiannon brought her staff around to blast them into smoking cinders, their strong, clammy hands wrenched it from her grasp and flung it over the edge of the cliff. The staff continued to crackle with lightning as it tumbled into the darkness, illuminating the sharp craggy wall until the lodestones struck the water of the Crone's Maw far below and the fiery bolt was extinguished.

The sluglung mass gurgled with satisfaction and went bouncing over to Peg-tooth Meg, landing between her and her sister, prepared to defend their beloved Megboo.

The werlings rejoiced to see Liffidia alive and well. The girl loosed another fir cone. It hit the owl on the side of its head, and she grinned at her friends. The bird shook itself then flew up to a high branch out of range. Perched there, it lifted its gaze and took comfort in the spectacle of the fighting on the lower slopes. Then its eyes opened wide with surprise and disbelief. Something was moving through the forest.

Down on the ground, Rhiannon was stalking toward the werlings. "You only postpone your deaths," she said. "My sisters will reach us soon. I will take up one of their staves and blast you into the night. No charred fragment of you will ever be found."

As she spoke, new sounds erupted from the approaching battle. The ghastly mirth of the troll witches was changing to shrieks of dismay and the hogs were squealing in fright.

"My Lady!" the owl called overhead, "My Lady! Behold the valley!"

The High Lady looked up quickly and drew a sharp breath.

Through the trees, she could see a mob of horrendous shapes rushing from the forest and onto the wooded slopes. They were unspeakable monstrosities, unlike any creature anyone had ever seen: great fiendish nightmares sporting brutal-looking horns, with enormous fangs in snapping mouths and tails that lashed behind their powerful bodies and cracked the trees. Some ran on four legs and others on two. Some were covered in scales, others in coarse shaggy fur or long spines and bristles. They bellowed in voices deep as the thunder and their ferocious roars caused the swine bearing the troll witches to flee in panic.

The remnants of the Unseelie Court cried out at this new, unexpected foe and their horses neighed in alarm—but the unnatural terrors were not interested in them. The strange, frightful horde swept right past, chasing the troll witches higher up the ridge.

"What are they?" Rhiannon breathed incredulously. "What deep pit has belched them forth?" She rounded on her sister and stared at her with new respect. "So, in your damp caves you bred more than frogspawn. What foul arts did you use to conjure these malignant demons?"

Meg stared at the monsters and shook her head in denial. "I do not know those abominations," she uttered in fearful wonder. "Can there be a power in Hagwood greater even than yours? Even your foul sisterhood is afraid. Hear how they squeal louder than their mounts."

The conglomeration of sluglungs gibbered unhappily at the fearful sight and the werlings held on to one another as the horrors came storming farther up the slope.

The troll witches were yowling in dismay. They had never encountered anything like these harrowing devils before. Never in their darkest dreams during the long exile in the Cold Hills had they envisioned such ferocious, repellent creatures. Where and how had they been hiding? What momentous, sinister force could have created and nourished them? What unearthly powers did they possess?

Their wild hogs would not stop. The same blind impulse to run that had possessed Dewfrost now seized every one of them as they tore up the ridge toward the Witch's Leap. The lightning continued to streak down into the hags' staves and cudgels, but the terrified troll witches were unable to discharge it into the enemy's repulsive fang-filled faces because the panicked swine would not turn about.

The thorny imps that rode with the hags scuttled down the boars' snouts and wrenched on their tusks or tore at their nostrils but nothing would halt them. Neither threat nor violence could compel them to stop.

They ran, swift and reckless, out of the wooded slope and over the rocky expanse.

"No," Rhiannon yelled. "Sisters! Sisters!" She dashed forward and threw out her arms but the demented wild boars stampeded past her. Even Ironback joined them in their terror and the helpless troll witches screeched and swore. A mesh of lightning blazed fiercely in their wake as they were swept to the cliff edge. The great hogs squealed and grunted their last but did not slow and, in their madness, they threw themselves off. The hags toppled with them. Their echoing screams split the night and the lightning chased them down. High above, the voice of Black Howla shrieked but was lost when a tremendous clap of thunder boomed throughout the tortured sky.

Gamaliel shivered. Under his breath he muttered a line from Gwyddion's poem, "*whence swine and witches fly.*"

The lightning ceased abruptly as the last of the troll witches perished on the rocks below. The crag was dark once more—but the battle was not yet over. Those fearsome new creatures were still advancing up the slope. They were terrible to look at, being horrendous fusions of savage and fanciful beasts. The fangs were slavering, the horns were sharp and twisted, the claws were razorlike and barbed. Knots of bulging muscle swelled scaled, spiny or fur-covered shoulders and the limbs were long and strong. They truly were a blood-freezing sight—although one of them appeared to possess an enormous squirrel's tail, which swished and flicked behind it.

With snarling jaws, they prowled before the High Lady, snapping and biting.

Rhiannon Rigantona returned their hostile stares, undaunted. Hate and malice marred her lovely face.

"Whatever you demons may be," she spat and her words echoed across the crag with such force that the stones trembled and leaves shook, "you hold no terror for the Goddess of the World—I am deathless and cannot be harmed."

Such was the force of her voice and the virulent power that burned in her eyes, the unnatural beasts were cowed and they drew back uncertainly.

"You have wrought the destruction of the sisterhood," she continued angrily, "and you will feel the full might of my vengeance. I will rip the earth open and return you to the abyss from whence you came."

The monsters began snuffling and one of them whimpered. Meg and the werlings looked at them in surprise.

"They did it!" Finnen hissed to the others, almost bursting with joy. "Those fabulous, daft old werglers did it! Oh, dab crack—bless each and every one of them!"

The werlings gazed at him in confusion. Even Master Gibble did not comprehend what the boy was babbling about.

But Finnen's rejoicing was short lived. The enchanted smoke of the Silent Grove had done its work and the monstrous forms shimmered and shrank. Scales disappeared and the mighty limbs dwindled. Fangs and claws retreated and savage snouts returned to blobby noses and dimpled chins. The horde of terrifying demons that had sent the troll witches racing off the cliff melted down into their true forms: the little werlings of the western border of Hagwood.

The children gasped and shook their heads in disbelief. Terser Gibble could not believe his eyes; such enormous transformations were not possible.

Still wearing his squirrel tail—but now of squirrel size—Figgle

Tumpin rushed forward to embrace his children, Tidubelle right beside him.

"Mam! Dad!" Tollychook blurted, dashing over to the Umbelnappers to bury his sobbing face in their arms.

Bufus Doolan was soon being squeezed by his own father and, instead of pulling a face and squirming as was usual, Bufus never wanted to be let go.

"Well done, everyone," Diffi Maffin applauded the rest of the werlings. "Most successful—I feel twenty years younger."

Rhiannon Rigantona watched in stunned silence until the sound of gentle laughter made her turn toward Peg-tooth Meg.

"And that, my dear sister," Meg told her, "is why I delight in the company of these vermin that scurry about my ankles. Are they not remarkable? They are so small and insignificant, yet they have bested Black Howla's unclean crew and are braver than any of the old knights in our father's time. The menace of the Cold Hills has been vanquished at last, and all it took were these silly creatures with hearts bigger than the shapes they assume."

The High Lady glowered at her then glanced down the slope. The survivors of the Hollow Hill had regrouped and were hastening toward them.

"The sisterhood may be broken on the rocks below," she snapped. "But I am not beaten. I will fly down the cliff and fetch just one stave from a dead hand. That is all I shall need to destroy everything upon this accursed crag. But you, Clarisant, will die now!"

She reached beneath her wolf-skin cloak and pulled out a long curved knife. Before the sluglungs could stop her, she lunged forward.

Yet the blade never reached Meg. A glistening strand of silk whipped around the weapon and yanked violently. Rhiannon shrieked in rage as the knife was ripped from her hand and she staggered backward.

High above, Frighty Aggie creaked and clicked her jaws in mockery and drummed her legs upon the trunk of the pine tree.

"Oh, Agnilla." Finnen grinned. "You old beauty!"

By now, the knights and nobles of the Unseelie Court had reined their steeds to a stop behind the crowd of werlings, and behind them hurried the foot soldiers, esquires and pages, the kluries and the milk-maids. A band of Redcaps came scooting between the horses and, with vicious yells, sent a flight of arrows into the air. They plunged into the High Lady's breast and lodged deep between her ribs.

Rhiannon glanced down dismissively, no more concerned with the arrows piercing her flesh than if a flying ant had blundered into her. She took hold of the quivering shafts and, with a casual twist of the wrist, ripped them from her skin and tossed the poisoned arrows on the floor. The wounds healed immediately.

"You cannot assail me," she addressed the growing crowd, with a half-smile on her sneering lips. "If I wished, I could walk amongst you, unhindered, and whisper words of death in your ears that would cause you to wither and retch your lives away, or make you slay those dearest to you. But this little war has dawdled overlong already and it is time to make a swift end of it. When I have made this entire forest a desert of ash, I shall depart to be worshipped as the Goddess I am, across the whole of the world."

Her eyes glinted and the malevolence that beat out of her caused each of them to catch his breath. In her face, they saw their deaths and knew they were inescapable.

Reaching for the silver talisman at her throat, Rhiannon ran to the edge of the precipice. Her cloak dripped to the ground, her crown of antlers dissolved, black feathers shot from her fingers and her arms became great dark wings.

Kernella blinked—in place of the High Lady's elegant form was a large black owl.

"Lumme," murmured Tollychook.

Fikil the fire devil glittered around the owl's neck as, with one last glare at the ragged gathering of her enemies, Rhiannon flew into the rainy night.

"She will return—and swiftly, with a troll witch's stave," Meg declared. "This time there will be no respite from her vengeance. Let us take these snatched moments to remember those who have fallen in battle and count ourselves fortunate to have fought alongside them. We must take comfort in the knowledge that we did everything in our power to stem my sister's evil, even for a brief while. Be quick and say your farewells. Kiss your loved ones and hold them tight."

The assembled werlings obeyed and waited for the end. These final, dread-filled moments were worse than everything they had endured so far. Knights removed their helms and the nobles dismounted as the rest of the Unseelie Court knelt before Meg for the first and final time. The mass of sluglungs separated and hugged their Megboo sorrowfully.

Gamaliel's upturned face caught sight of the milk-white barn owl leaving its lofty perch in the pine tree to go spiraling down after its mistress. The boy lowered his gaze. All around him, everyone was preparing for the end. His own kind were huddled in groups, clinging sadly to one another. Liffidia had buried her face into Fly's wet fur and Master Gibble laid his hand upon Finnen's shoulder. The boy's grandmother had remained behind on the Barren Heath with the rest of the elderly and very young and Finnen wished he could hug her one last time.

The Unseelie Court was wrapped in contemplative silence, recalling the friends and rivals who had perished in the battle, and repenting their old quarrels. Some were murmuring the lineage of their fathers, others were praying to half-forgotten forest gods, and the rest simply stared at Peg-tooth Meg's hunched figure and drew strength from the steadfastness of her gaze. They wished she could have ruled over them; what a beautiful place the Hollow Hill would have been.

Meg's arms were around her sluglungs. Only seven of them had survived. They sighed and muttered in doleful voices, their hands fusing together as they looked up at her. And the rain continued to pour.

As Gamaliel's eyes drifted over the dripping assembly, he saw a solitary figure picking its way carefully through the kneeling courtiers. Although the figure was now shorn of hair and clothed in rich apparel, Gamaliel recognized his waddling gait immediately.

"Grimditch!" he shouted. "Grimditch!"

Still carrying the human infant, shielding it from the rain as best he could, the barn bogle had followed the battle in his stocking feet. It had been a grisly road. Trudging through the ruinous desolation of blackened corpses and burning trees, he had been appalled by the death and devastation around him and mourned the loss of so many warriors and hillfolk who had fought bravely.

The sights he saw on that macabre march tempered his mischievous nature and he knew that, if he somehow survived that awful night, they would stay with him for the rest of his life. In a low voice, he sang to the infant in his arms to keep it sleeping, and spare its innocent eyes.

Trumpeters were mangled within their battered instruments. The aged Earl Tobevere lay dead beneath the wild boar that had killed him, which, in turn, had been shot by Redcap arrows. Close by, the Lady Mauvette was facedown on the trampled ground and the klurie that had rushed to her aid was only a smoking husk.

Once he passed a goblin milkmaid dangling upside down from the branch where a thunderbolt had blasted her. Even in death, Squinting Wheyleen's eyes were askew and her two long plaits were still swinging beneath her. With a whispered blessing, Grimditch gently closed her eyelids and pressed on.

And now, finally, he had caught up with the survivors stoically waiting for death to come and claim them. There was nowhere safe in the entire kingdom, or beyond, for him and the baby. Perhaps he too should take his place among the defeated.

Then he heard Gamaliel's familiar voice calling to him.

"My little skin swapper!" he bawled. "You is safe! Grimditch glad— me missed you!"

He crouched down and Gamaliel ran to him.

"You old bogle!" the boy greeted. "I never thought I'd see you again. But what happened to your hair and what have you got there?"

Grimditch lifted a fold of the blanket and Gamaliel saw the baby slumbering within. He uttered a gasp of surprise.

"The human child!" he cried.

"'Tis Farmer's little'un," Grimditch said. "Me won't be parted from him now, not never."

Gamaliel had so many questions to ask but there wasn't time. Instead, he tugged at the barn bogle's velvet sleeve.

"I want you to meet my family!" he said urgently. "Before it's too late. They'll want to see the bogle who saved my life. And my sister's here—the one who caused so much trouble by listening to the candle spright."

Grimditch glanced across at the clumps of werlings and hesitated.

"Wait," he said in a shameful voice. "Me did a bad thing. Me rooted in your furtly bag and pinched your pretty key. Grimditch sorry."

Gamaliel smiled sadly at him. "I know," he said. "But it's too late to cry over that."

"Me was only after a lend and a looksee," the barn bogle promised. "Grimditch would've give it back."

"It doesn't matter now," the boy said, forgiving him. "Come and see Finnen; he's here too."

Grimditch twisted his mouth to the side then reached into the pocket of his frock coat. "If me swaps faerie gold for faerie gold," he mumbled shyly, "we be friends again, yes?"

"We are friends!" Gamaliel assured him. Then his eyes fell on the object the barn bogle took from his pocket, and the blood quickened in his veins.

It was the golden casket.

CHAPTER 19

THE HUB OF ALL DESTRUCTION

WITH HER EBONY WINGS OUTSTRETCHED, Rhiannon Rigantona swooped down the rocky cliff face. Her mind was burning with the lust for revenge. Nothing would survive this night.

Above her, the owl followed fast. Its golden eyes were fixed upon her and it quickly closed the distance between them.

"My Lady!" it called, flying eagerly to her side. "Let me assist thee. Two sets of talons can lift a stave more easily than one. Then what an inferno thou shalt ignite."

Rhiannon turned her flat owl face to her most faithful servant and the bird felt faint when it gazed into her gorgeous dark eyes. Although the badge of the black owl adorned her banners and the shields of her warriors, he had never seen her assume that shape before and the sight of it beguiled him. Had she done it especially to please him?

"We must hurry, my provost," she commanded. "It pains me that they still live."

Paired in flight, they circled downward through the driving rain, the tips of their wings almost touching.

The barn owl was breathless and regarded her covetously. Its worshipful mistress had never appeared more bewitching or desirable in its eyes. As it stared at her, an ache and a thirst blossomed within it. It had always loved her as a dutiful slave should, but now it yearned for her.

Its mind was racing and its inflamed heart convulsed in its chest. It gritted its beak and tried to deny such powerful feelings. What was this madness that itched in its blood and threatened to dispel the cool and calculating reason that had always been in thrall to her every command? These new, disturbing emotions alarmed the owl and it fought against them. But then, even as it struggled, in that fatal instant their feathers brushed and the barn owl's prodigious intelligence was totally overthrown.

"My Lady!" it hooted, flying into her suddenly. "Thou art mine!"

Startled, the High Lady floundered in the air as the barn owl collided with her. Whirling through the rain, they plummeted like stones.

"You dare attack me?" she cried.

"I dare to love thee!" it answered feverishly. "And in this sublime form thou shalt always remain."

The barn owl gripped the silver talisman in its claws and bit through the chain. With a triumphant laugh, it tore the fire devil from her neck, pushed it into its beak, then swallowed it whole.

"Now thou art locked in owl shape forever!" it hooted. "Ours shalt be a perfect union."

Rhiannon shrieked and beat her wings in the traitor's face. They thrashed the air and the plunging fall was arrested. The two owls circled each other—one impassioned and amorous, the other incensed.

She had never expected her loyal provost to betray her and the shock of it disordered her thoughts.

Around and around they flew, looping and wheeling before the sheer cliff face, and her wrathful silence made the barn owl believe its misguided courtship had found favor with her.

"We can journey whither the wind and fancy take us!" it exclaimed, displaying its snow-white feathers proudly. "Such a match hath ne'er been. You know how much I adore thee—wouldst thou ever find so constant a lover as thy true lieutenant? Nay! My love for thee is deeper than the Under Magic and higher than the farthest star."

Rhiannon's eyes glittered and she glided closer. The barn owl clicked its beak and fanned its feathers wide. Too late it beheld the true nature of her stare as, with a mighty screech, she flew at her target. Her talons raked across its chest and she tore out a blizzard of plumage.

The barn owl screamed in surprise and they vied with one another, battling in the air.

"Spare me!" it shrieked. "My Love—spare me! My Lady!"

She drove the owl against the cliff wall, slamming it against the rock. It pushed her away, but she pounced upon it more fiercely than ever. The owl screeched as she shredded its plucked flesh. Again and again it kicked out with its feet and heaved itself against her, but there was no escaping the frenzy of her murderous rage.

Her cruel beak reached for its throat and its white feathers were stained crimson as she tore the silver talisman from its gullet. The owl's golden eyes looked on her one last time before she cast her victim away. It fluttered clumsily away, unable to call her name. Then it tumbled lifeless out of the sky.

Rhiannon flew down past the gushing waters of the Crone's Maw at the foot of the cliff, not pausing to look at the body of her devoted provost. A scattering of bloody feathers floated on the gurgling stream nearby.

The submerged corpses of troll witches, thorny imps, and wild boars filled the waterfall's foaming basin and more lay broken on the surrounding rocks. To anyone other than Rhiannon Rigantona, it would have been a harrowing place, crowded with violent, shattered death, but she surveyed it unmoved.

Alighting upon a boulder, she reached with her talons for one of the stone-tipped staves still gripped in a dead witch's hand and dragged it free. Then she glared upward. The night sky boiled above the towering cliff and the clouds were rent by lightning.

"Now, Clarisant," she hissed as she soared into the air once more. "Feel the full measure of my anger."

HIGH UPON THE WITCH'S LEAP, the suspense was unbearable. Everyone believed the High Lady was tormenting them—it seemed she was keeping them waiting deliberately, dragging out their final despairing moments. Such was the extent of her twisted pleasures.

Finnen left Master Gibble's side. He had seen Gamaliel hurry to the farthest pine accompanied by a bald bogle, and when he joined them, he found his friend sitting against the tree, gingerly opening his wergle pouch.

"What are you doing?" Finnen asked.

Gamaliel Tumpin looked up at him and grinned. "Wish me luck," he said.

"This isn't the time to become a mouse," Finnen told him.

Gamaliel chuckled faintly. "No," he answered. "It isn't." Delving into his pouch, he brought out the untidy tangles of fur and useful odds and ends that he kept there and breathed deeply.

Kernella pulled away from their parents and scurried over.

"What's he doing?" she demanded crossly.

Gamaliel opened one eye. "Don't you remember what Nest said?" he asked. "I'm the chosen one."

"Who's Nest?" Finnen murmured.

"Nothing and nobody!" the girl said resolutely. "Just something we dreamed up when we hit our heads. Only my stupid brother would go on believing it."

"Shut it, Nellie," Bufus Doolan told her as he approached. "Leave Gammy be. I've learned to have faith in your daft brother—you should as well."

Finnen crouched beside Gamaliel. "Why are you the chosen one?" he asked intently. "Who chose you—and for what?"

Gamaliel gazed past him, remembering that fearful night when they had escaped from the lair of Frighty Aggie.

"The Wandering Smith chose me," he replied. "Aggie's poison was in me, remember—the poison of a Grand Adept. The Smith made a poultice and put it on my shoulder. Now, I don't think he was just drawing out the poison; I think he was putting other stuff in."

"What stuff?" Finnen asked.

"Gamaliel's right," Liffidia added as she knelt beside them. "I remember! The Smith didn't just put a poultice on. You were there, Finnen, you know."

Finnen lowered his eyes. "The Smith uttered strange words over Gamaliel," he said. "Then he pushed charms against his skin and dripped blue liquid onto the wound."

"And he sang over it," Liffidia continued. "We couldn't hear what but it . . . it was some sort of incantation."

Gamaliel grunted. "Then he placed the golden key, the magic key he had made, into my wergle pouch. I understand now. He knew he would never reach Meg's caves. The High Lady was hunting him. So he took a great gamble on a clumsy little werling. He chose me—don't you see? I mustn't fail that trust."

He showed them the bundles of fur in his hand. "The key was right there," he said. "I held it; I ran my fingers over it. I remember it exactly and the magic of those who made it is in my blood."

"No!" Finnen shouted. "It's never been attempted—it's too dangerous."

"Not for me," Gamaliel answered brightly. "I am the chosen one! The Smith saw to that. Nest said I was the key to this whole sorry business. He actually said those very words! I am the key!"

Finnen looked around for Master Gibble and discovered he was standing right beside him. By now all the other werlings had gathered around them and were whispering among themselves.

"Tell him!" Finnen cried anxiously to the wergle master. "Tell him!"

Terser Gibble looked at Gamaliel and shook his head. "He knows the risk," he told Finnen. "Now, move back; give the lad space."

Gamaliel closed his eyes again and inhaled. He thought of the intricate golden key flashing and winking on his palm in the sunlight. He recalled the weight and feel of it and pictured the Wandering Smith's gruff, kindly face encouraging him on and called upon whatever magic the last of the Puccas had passed on to him. Then he concentrated hard, harder than he ever had in his whole life.

In the branches above them, the eyes of Frighty Aggie gazed down and her grotesque head swayed from side to side. The sky shook with thunder and the pines shuddered.

WITH THE STAVE SUSPENDED FROM HER TALONS, the black owl rushed higher and higher. The cliff face raced by as barbed tongues of lightning jabbed and flickered toward the lodestones.

Acrid smoke laced the air. The western wood was still burning, though not as fiercely as before. The torrential rain had doused many fires, but not those of Rhiannon's hatred and revenge.

She flew up into the night, high above the pines, and came swooping down. Before she reached the rocky ground, the owl gripped the bloody fire devil in one claw and the stave in the other.

The bird form vanished as she became the terrible Rhiannon Rigantona once more, clothed in a robe of glittering shadow, with a crown of black diamonds flashing upon her brow.

At her silent command, more lightning ripped from the sky and wove a lattice of brilliant white fire around her. She was an incredible vision—a radiant figure wreathed in a pillar of crackling flame. Forks of lightning raked outward from her, shining far across the forest, hitting the upraised Hollow Hill and smiting the ruined tower in the east. The great forest of Hagwood leaped in and out of shadow as the blinding forces streaked from the Witch's Leap. Rhiannon Rigantona stood at the center of the lightning—the hub of all destruction, a bringer of death.

Rhiannon advanced menacingly and the lightning ripped and roared about her, carving rivers of fire into the pines and gouging channels into the rock at her feet. The Unseelie Court beheld her with dread and awe as they nervously awaited the first destroying blasts.

The dazzling spectacle of the High Lady turned a baleful face on Peg-tooth Meg. The hunched woman stood before the crowd of werrats, a peculiar gleam in her froglike eyes.

"Sister!" Meg welcomed boldly. "You're just in time. You must see my performing mice. They have one final trick that you must not miss."

Rhiannon bent her eyes to the ground, and there was Gamaliel. Even as she watched, he raised his right hand. In place of his forefinger, there was now a delicate, gleaming key. Grimditch was holding the golden casket out to him and the voice within, her own pitiful voice, was wailing.

The High Lady saw the danger. She swung her stave around, but it was too late. Gamaliel pushed his wergled finger into the tiny keyhole and turned.

There was an almighty crash of thunder and the ground trembled. The enchanted golden casket clicked softly as the magic of many dark years was undone. The intricate pattern of flowers and ferns that covered its surface began to move. Fronds and petals untwined and unlatched and the ruby set into the top began to glimmer.

Rhiannon screamed as a fine line appeared all the way around the chest and cold air suddenly rushed into the unsealed box. She clutched at her empty breast and stumbled back in anguish, the stave dropping from her hand.

Darkness fell. Everyone stared at the casket. Gamaliel lifted it wide open, then turned away, revolted.

"Destroy me!" the throbbing, glistening heart within pleaded. "End this torment—I beg you! Please—Please!"

Gasping and consumed with terror, her chest racked with searing pain, Rhiannon slumped against one of the pines and shrieked for her life, but no one was listening.

The beating heart was crying out for death. Gamaliel felt dizzy and weak and he fell back against the tree trunk. "Do it!" he implored Finnen.

Breathlessly, Finnen Lufkin took the small knife from his belt and looked around at the sickened, horrified faces of the other werlings. Then he glanced up at Peg-tooth Meg, who nodded gravely.

"It must be done," she said. "And I cannot."

The boy raised the blade over the pulsing heart and prepared to strike.

"Now!" the heart beseeched him. "Slay me now!"

Finnen's hand trembled. One sure blow would bring an end to so much despair and suffering. And yet, hearing that piteous pain-filled voice, he hesitated. It would be murder.

Two firm hands suddenly grasped his. "You always was soft, Lufkin!" Bufus Doolan shouted as he thrust down hard.

Rhiannon screamed. Red flames shot up from the casket and the two werlings were hurled backward. Answering flames burst out from Rhiannon's breast, the fire wrapping around her body.

The whole sprawl of the forest shook and the lanterns of the Hollow Hill burned dim in the distance. The werlings fell to the ground and a tear streaked down Meg's cheek. Then a ferocious gale came tearing from the Cold Hills and ripped across the Witch's Leap. It hammered into the High Lady and tore her off her feet. Still clawing at her chest and shrieking and writhing in the crimson flames, she was sent spinning into the air—out over the cliff edge.

Her dying screeches were drowned in the violent windstorm that smashed her against the towering rock face—all the way down to the Crone's Maw far below.

Beneath the pines, the werlings held on to one another as the tempest raged. Meg's green hair streamed wildly about her and she turned her ugly face into the scouring squall.

"It is over!" she yelled. "The Tyrant of the Hollow Hill is dead. The evil is gone—forever."

She raised her arms and the heavy, curdling storm clouds were ripped asunder and sent racing to the horizon, revealing a clear night ablaze with stars. The wind dropped abruptly and the beautiful silver disc of the moon shone down upon them.

Finnen stared at the smoking golden casket. As the red smoke cleared, he found that the casket was empty.

"We did it," he spluttered in disbelief. "We really did it!"

He sprang to his feet and gave a shout of joy and everyone—werlings, goblins, nobles, Redcaps, oakmen, milkmaids, kluries, sluglungs, and even the horses—threw back their heads and rejoiced. A trumpet blared out, announcing the death of the tyrant and the start of a new age. Drummers began beating a lively rhythm and armor clanked as knights and warriors danced. It was the most incredible, miraculous moment. The years of terror were truly over.

"Gamaliel!" Finnen cried. "You're amazing!"

It was then he noticed that Gamaliel was still and quiet.

Grimditch was stroking his hair. "Little skin swapper not well," he said mournfully. "There is a winter in his blood."

Finnen grabbed Gamaliel's hand. The key was still in place of his finger and his hand felt cold and hard. Horrified, he stared at his friend's face. It had turned a sickly yellow.

"Gamaliel!" Finnen shouted. "Wergle back! You must. You did it, it's over! The High Lady is dead. You saved us—you saved everything! Wergle back!"

Kernella and her parents knelt beside him and Tidubelle carefully lifted her son's head onto her lap.

"Change back!" Kernella ordered him.

"He can't," Terser Gibble said gently. "We are only permitted to wear animal shapes. Insects are forbidden—more so are inert, lifeless objects."

"But he did it!" Kernella cried. "He did it!"

"The wergle is not yet complete," Master Gibble told her. "When it is, there will be nothing living left of the lad to undo the change. He knew that would happen."

"You don't know what you're talking about!" Kernella snapped at him. "He's my brother; he can do anything. He's better than you ever were—and braver!"

Master Gibble knew that was true and he bowed his head in respect.

Kernella looked up at Meg. "Help him, please!" she implored.

"There is nothing I can do," the woman answered regretfully. "There is more to this than your simple shape changing. Gamaliel has invoked the enchantment of the Puccas. He has set the Smith's power in motion. None can contest their skill."

"Wait!" Finnen cried, reaching into his belt. "The Puccas made the silver fire devils—this must be able to do something!" He took out Harkul and pressed it into Gamaliel's left hand.

"Come back," he urged. "Gamaliel Tumpin, come back to us. By the power of Harkul, I order it!"

Gamaliel took a wheezing breath but did not change back.

"It isn't working!" Kernella wept.

"The passwords!" Figgle cried desperately. "The ancient, unlocking passwords. Everyone—sing them!"

The werlings all began to chant.

Amwin par cavirrien sul, olgun forweth, I rakundor.
Skarta nen skila cheen . . .

Gamaliel's eyes flickered open.

"It's no use," he said in a strained whisper. "This was meant to be. I chose Sacrifice. I stood on the altar of the Dooits. I won't live to see the dawn. I'm glad it's me, and not Kernella or Bufus."

"Don't say that!" his sister said.

Gamaliel tried to move his arm but it was rigid and the creeping yellow pallor had now reached his left hand. The fire devil fell from his grasp. A pricking numbness was filling his fingers.

"It's my days that will be golden forevermore," he said faintly. The boy looked up into his mother's face, and through her anguish, she smiled at him—the smile that he so loved. Then his eyes clouded over and his breathing stopped.

Finnen turned on his heel and stumbled away, Bufus dropped to his knees, and Grimditch rocked to and fro, with the mortal infant cradled in his arms. Tollychook and Liffidia held on to each other and sobbed, while the Tumpins grieved.

Silence fell over the lofty crag; the jubilation ended.

THERE WERE NO CELEBRATIONS for many days. Too many had died, and there was far too much to be done. Peg-tooth Meg led the Unseelie Court back into the Hollow Hill and commanded the Under Magic to close it. If any members of the court still doubted her right to the throne, that settled it once and for all.

The fallen were gathered from the battlefield and laid with great reverence in the many halls and courtyards under a preserving enchantment until new tombs could be built. These were constructed down in the expansive torture chambers, which were no longer needed.

The carcasses of the troll witches and their wild boars were flung without ceremony into the glade of the blood moths. The thorny imps were burned on a bonfire at the foot of the Witch's Leap. No trace could be found of Rhiannon Rigantona's body, and it was commonly believed she had been utterly consumed by the red flames as she fell. A popular rumor, however, claimed that the body had really been dragged away by a thorny imp that had survived. But no one really took that seriously.

The coronation of Peg-tooth Meg took place one bright April morning upon the green summit of the Hollow Hill. Blue banners and birdsong filled the sky and the hilltop was garlanded with white and yellow flowers.

Beforehand, Meg spoke to her sluglungs in private. She offered to change them back to their former selves, to return them to who they were before they had drunk the dark waters down in the caves. Without hesitation they voted unanimously to remain as sluglungs and she was glad. She had also decided not to use Harkul to transform back to her previous appearance. Hagwood needed a just and benevolent ruler, not one who was fair of face. The only beauty that counted came from within. Besides, this was how Prince Tammedor had last known her and that was good enough for her.

The coronation was suffused with sadness. Only one trumpeter had survived and his solitary playing proclaimed the new queen with a lonely, somber sound. The roll of the honored dead was read and tears gave way to grateful cheers and tributes. The survivors would not let sorrow burden their hearts completely. A supreme victory had been won, by the bravest of heroes. Those valiant sacrifices had not been in vain. They had delivered Hagwood from the darkness into the light. The years of tyranny were finally at an end and this was a day of celebration. Harmony and goodness would now reign and the Hollow Hill would become a haven for the lost and weary, filled with song, laughter and compassion.

When the coronation feast was over, and even Tollychook was satisfied by the variety and splendor of the dishes, the glorious reign of Queen Clarisant, as she was called thereafter, began. She proved to be the fairest ruler there had ever been and all her people loved her.

Grimditch the barn bogle was made royal protector of the little lordling and lived in the Hill in a sumptuous chamber stuffed with plump velvet cushions. But sometimes he would creep to the stables and sleep upon the straw there, for old times' sake. In the library, Clarisant sought the secret knowledge for a way to peel away the spells that Rhiannon had wrapped around the human infant. She hoped he would grow, and in time, when he was old enough, choose whether to remain with them or seek his own kind in the world outside.

The werlings were given the woods and wild orchards below the broken watchtower for their new home. Liffidia was as good as her word and took charge of the Lubber's infirmary. Fly proved to be an invaluable help. Even the naked hen matron grew to like the gentle, loving fox, and in time her feathers grew back.

The body of the Tower Lubber was interred beneath the tower, once the cellars had been repaired. On certain moonlit nights, it was said that his specter walked the battlements, gazing out toward the Hollow Hill, his sight restored. Only Kernella ever actually witnessed this close at hand, but she was far too sensible to admit it.

Terser Gibble was forgiven by the werlings and resumed his role as tutor to the children, even though he could no longer wergle. But the art of transformation became ever more elusive and difficult to practice for everyone, until it was eventually determined that without the Silent Grove, the werlings would lose their power completely. But some still held out hope, for in the royal chambers, Queen Clarisant discovered a velvet pouch containing seven beechnuts that she gave to the werlings with her blessing.

Bufus found life a little dull after everything he had been through. He would often take off and explore the forest, sometimes disappearing for weeks at a time. He always knew that, somewhere, Mufus was proud of him.

Finnen Lufkin kept his promise to Frighty Aggie. He returned to her lair on the night of the coronation and, with Clarisant's permission, gave her Harkul. The monstrous spider wasp seized the fire devil in her foul jaws and devoured it. A shower of silver sparks blasted instantly from her mouth and she reared up as white flames spurted from her joints and her eight legs burned fiercely. Finnen leaped back as she spun around then collapsed. There was a flash of searing light and, when he opened his eyes, he saw only a frail, wizened werling woman lying on the smoking ground. The boy knelt beside her. In a grateful whisper, the aged werling thanked him before she died, ancient and spent—as Agnilla Hellekin, the greatest wergler of them all . . . except for one.

In the great courtyard behind the main Eastern Gate of the Hollow Hill, there is now a silver fountain. The great doors are always opened to permit the rays of the rising sun to fall upon it and one of Liffidia's former patients flies in every day with a fresh flower to drop into its trickling waters. No one passes that place without bowing and the werlings have been granted their own little entrance to the Hill so they may visit it any time they wish. At the top of that fountain, there is a small golden figure—but it is not a statue. It is the wonderful hero about whom songs are still sung. His courage was never ever forgotten; they owed him everything and his name is always spoken with pride. His selfless act not only brought lasting joy and peace to the realm, it was also an inspiration, for all who lived through those perilous times and the generations that followed. Gamaliel Tumpin—the savior of Hagwood and the world beyond.

• A BIOGRAPHY OF ROBIN JARVIS •

Robin Jarvis (b. 1963) was born three weeks late on a sofa in Liverpool, England. As a child he always had a pencil in his hand, and was always drawing and making up stories for the characters who appeared in his sketchpads.

When Robin was very small, one of his favorite television programs was an animated puppet series called *The Herbs*. This is what Robin would look like if he somehow managed to enter the world of that show:

Robin's school years were spent mostly in art rooms, although he greatly enjoyed the creative writing assignments in English classes, where his sole aim was frightening the teacher. After a degree course in graphic design (during which Robin decided he really preferred making monsters out of latex to anything related to graphic design), he worked in television making models and puppets.

One evening, while doodling, he started to draw lots of mouse characters and had so much fun inventing names and stories for them that he decided to put them in a book. Thus began his writing career. *The Deptford Mice* (1989) quickly established him as a bestselling children's author.

Robin has been shortlisted for numerous awards, and won the Lancashire Libraries Children's Book of the Year Award. One of his trilogies, Tales from the Wyrd Museum, was on a list of books recommended by then–British Prime Minister Tony Blair for dads to read with their sons.

Robin still likes to make models, usually monstrous characters from his own stories. These models are good for his book events at schools or bookshops; when the audience is tired of looking at him, he can whisk a creature out of his bag to distract them. One such monster was extremely effective at scaring away the forty-three cats owned by Robin's next-door neighbor.

Robin gets his inspiration for stories from all sorts of sources. Once, on a hike through the forest, he heard a racket up in the trees and saw two squirrels chasing each other. The thought suddenly occurred to him that perhaps only one of them was a real squirrel and the other only looked like one. And so the werling creatures were born, and by the end of that hike Robin had *Thorn Ogres of Hagwood* drafted in his head.

Robin usually includes one small, portly character in most of his books. This character is not the hero, but instead a friend or brother of the protagonist—someone a bit clumsy and a bit too fond of supper. The character is, in fact, Robin. In the Hagwood books, Robin decided to include himself as one of the principal characters for a change. And so, Gamaliel Tumpin is based on Robin when he was young, when his older sister would boss him about and make him tidy his room during the school holidays.

Robin lives in Greenwich, London, and has an old, deaf West Highland White Terrier named Sally. He has recently discovered that making monsters on the computer is much faster than using clay, plaster, glue, armature wire, fur, dental acrylic, resin, and latex, and it doesn't make such a mess on the kitchen table.

Robin Jarvis at the age of two or three, complete with scab on his knee.
Very Gamaliel Tumpin.

Robin, age two and a half, on a caravan holiday. He was always told that the light above his head in this picture was his guardian angel. Imagine the disappointment when he realized it was the camera flash! But Robin is always ready to believe anything.

A photo of Robin from the early 1990s, holding some mole figures he made for a German commercial. The figures were used for advertising sausages. He doesn't think the sausages were actually made from moles, but maybe . . .

Gamaliel under glass, to keep him safe from marauding thorn ogres and other predators.

Robin at home, thinking up some new gruesomeness.

THE HAGWOOD TRILOGY

FROM OPEN ROAD MEDIA

OPEN  ROAD

INTEGRATED MEDIA

INTEGRATED MEDIA

Find a full list of our authors and
titles at www.openroadmedia.com

FOLLOW US
@OpenRoadMedia